BENEATH THE FLOODLIGHTS

BENEATH THE FLOODLIGHTS

MARTIN TRACEY

AuthorHouse™
1663 Liberty Drive
Bloomington, IN 47403
www.authorhouse.com
Phone: 1-800-839-8640

First published by AuthorHouse 07/11/2011

ISBN: 978-1-4567-8183-5 (sc)
ISBN: 978-1-4567-8184-2 (ebk)

Printed in the United States of America

This book is printed on acid-free paper.

For Maggie my rock
And my two pebbles Paige and Heather

Also for Dean Richards, 1974-2011

Martin Tracey has always enjoyed a deep interest in the supernatural and he likes to specialise in this type of fiction, yet he aims for his novels to remain believable so that the reader can be gripped by the horror that unfolds. He is also the songwriter and co-performer of *Raging Bull* which can be found on *Old Gold Anthems—the songs of Wolverhampton Wanderers*, and his life-long passion for music and football is apparent in his tales of chilling suspense. In *Beneath the Floodlights* Martin typically puts his own original stamp on the vampire tale to give it a deliciously new perspective as the world of vampires meets the world of football. Martin is a native of Birmingham, England and is married with two daughters.

Acknowledgements

My thanks go to my immediate family for encouraging me to write this book and for allowing me the need to compromise our quality time occasionally. Your understanding is simply invaluable. I love you all.

Thanks to Mom and Dad for the unbelievable encouragement and support you have altruistically given me since the day I was born.

Thanks to the two Mark's for the fun we shared when we were kids kicking a ball about on the grass of Burford Road Playing Fields. It is with you guys that my passion for football began, you two playing for Villa and me playing for Wolves! All three of us played for England! Happy days!

Thanks to anyone and everyone who has engaged in banter with me over the years regarding our respective football teams which includes friends, Brothers-in-law and work colleagues (this list is not exhaustive). We live in a unique culture in Britain where football is such a way of life that it continues to stimulate the conversations of almost every social gathering one can think of. Our passion for *the beautiful game* is so integrated within our being that the flip of a football result has the ability to influence how the remainder of our day unfolds. We should continue to celebrate and embrace such a culture.

Thanks also to Mr Stoker, Mr Tarantino, Mr King, Mr Laymon, Mr Boam, Mr Jeremias, Ms Fischer and Ms Rice for your fantastic vampire creations and interpretations. Without the foundations that you have laid I could not have written this novel.

Prologue

Royal Sutton Coldfield, England, 31 October 1529

The moon was full.

Perfect.

With eyes of evil Josiah Connor looked at his wife across the heat of the burning log fire.

She returned a seductive smile to him that radiated a unique strand of equal measured wickedness.

The smile could in fact have been described as more lustful than seductive, naturally but intentionally executed to signify one of the acknowledged seven deadly sins.

And before long the couple would be stripped naked to indulge in a variety of lustful sexual activity and fireside debauchery in every way imaginable. If witnessed their athleticism would belie their usual slothful demeanour, though their perversion would not surprise anyone who knew of them.

For it was well known to the local community of Royal Sutton Coldfield that Josiah and Alison Connor did not contribute anything constructive to society whatsoever and a wise man knew to keep his wife, his children and even his animals away from the very strange couple who lived on the hill.

To carry out any kind of a sin came natural to the Connors, in fact they thrived on living by such wicked behaviours and more, but their forthcoming intricate display of the documented seven held significant purpose and meaning tonight.

They wanted to mock, seize and even prostitute the number seven, agitated by the acceptance of the number being so often connected to something good or sacred. God supposedly created the world in seven days, Jesus Christ spoke seven times on the cross, there are seven virtues for the foolish to abide by and it is regarded that there are also Seven Wonders of the World. It seemed that the list was endless regarding the influence of goodness held by the number seven.

But the Connors understood only too well that the power of evil can so often run in parallel to the power of good, hence the very existence of the seven deadly sins.

Josiah and Alison Connor would ensure that at some point tonight all of the recognised seven deadly sins would be represented as their forthcoming intentions unfolded.

But first they would drink to their imminent achievements of evil.

Josiah handed his wife a glass of the red nectar that he had just poured and he lustfully watched as she gulped the red liquid down at a ferocious speed.

The blood of the goat and the old man trickled down the sides of her mouth demonstrating the speed in which she had devoured the drink.

To Josiah, Alison had never looked more beautiful.

He poured her another glass and watched her repeat the display of greed. The sight of his evil lover drinking the blood so passionately aroused him considerably.

He too began to drink the blood of the goat and the old man.

To accompany their bloody cocktail of evil, Josiah and Alison ate a meal of rotten fruit and undercooked meat. The old man and goat would never be found, and probably never be missed. Josiah had chosen his victims carefully to avoid repercussions.

The couple continued to eat and drink even when their wicked bellies became full symbolising the sin of gluttony.

Anger and envy were never far away from the Connors' emotional outlets as they intensely disliked the pathetic community they lived among, envious and angry at how their preferred worship of Satan never seemed to have the equivalent acceptance in society as those who followed the word of the Lord Jesus Christ. These followers of Christianity were said to be decent and holy people, promoting peace and living in a pacifistic state, only wishing to bring good to the world, yet these same people had usurped the days of the Pagan calendar and claimed them as holy days of their own. Though not Pagans themselves the hypocrisy of the Christians in the eyes of Josiah and Alison Connor angered them intensely.

It was understood that the seven deadly sins appeared in the Holy Bible, a piece of literature that amused Josiah and Alison Connor when they looked around them at the acts of evil unwittingly carried out by the Christians of Catholicism and the Church of England, never stopping to think that all their battles, loss of life and evil methods of torture actually symbolised a practice better suited to Satanists than those said to follow Christianity. After all were they not actually at war over the same God?

At least worshippers of Satan were united in their quest.

King Henry VIII, who was no stranger to Royal Sutton Coldfield, had indeed paved the way to this internal Christian destruction with his imminent dissolution of the monasteries and desire to divorce from the Roman Catholic Church, and Josiah and Alison had often surmised that the tyrannical King of England was secretly a Satanist himself. It seemed that the king was as blood thirsty as they were with his ordering of beheadings, soon to include his wives no less, and Alison had actually spotted the royal huntsman out on the local grassland one day following his slaying of a deer. Concealed by bushes Alison had became excited when she witnessed the king bend down to the dying beast and mop some blood from the fresh wound of the animal with his bare hand only to then proceed to place the bright red fluid upon his lips and tongue. This unexpected spectacle of the king's actions had helped inspire tonight's sadistic ritual for Alison and Josiah.

As much as the Bible agitated the Connors they realised that such a piece of literature needed to be laid down in honour of their own master, so that future generations would always have a point of reference when living their life by the desires of Satan. They believed that the Holy Bible would always need a rival when it came to documented evidence that bore influence over ones chosen path.

This is why they had penned the *Live Tome*, the authoritative book that Satanists could always follow in order to serve Satan. *Live* to depict and celebrate the fact that wickedness was indeed *alive* as told through this book. The word *live* also cleverly chosen as when spelt backwards, a mechanism that so often represented callings to Satan, such as the reciting of *The Lord's Prayer* backwards or the inversion of a cross to depict the Antichrist, it would reveal the word *Evil*. "Tome" meaning a work of writing but the Connors also liked the way it resembled the word *Tomb*.

A comprehensive volume of evil writing, the rituals of tonight and the subsequent catastrophic impact these rituals would ultimately have on the world would belong to just one Gospel of the *Live Tome*. The many collective Gospels of *Live Tome* would ultimately go on to serve all strains of the evil underworld from the likes of demons to werewolves.

The Connors were perceived as futile members of society who idly wasted their days away, little did the community realise the dedicated work that had gone into their written satanic offering.

Their work had made them proud.

And tonight they would be rewarded for their work by Satan himself.

For when they copulate in the forthcoming hours they will conceive a child, but not just any child. Satan will bless the sperm of Josiah as it penetrates the life vessel of Alison to form a child that will begin a reign of terror for centuries to come.

A child that will grow to challenge everything that is perceived as being good in the world.

The child shall be born on the seventh day of the seventh month, to highlight the seven deadly sins and yet to mock the pathetic number seven that is so widely referred to in the world of good.

If days of the calendar can be usurped and abused then so too can numbers.

Josiah and Alison know this for they have written the spell to accompany their ritualistic fornication. The spell is detailed in the chosen gospel of the *Live Tome* so that other worshippers of Satan can perform the same ritual for centuries to come to ensure the world is infested with servers of Satan.

And these new servers of Satan will roam the Earth and will catalyse the meaning of the seven deadly sins.

They will show pride in their achievements, they will show greed, lust and gluttony as they indulge in simultaneous acts of sexual desire and the drinking of human blood. They will naturally show anger at the world that isolates them and who fails to understand them.

The twisted law of the land will enable them to show envy at the way mere mortals are allowed to go about their day to day business without fear of being a target of hatred.

They too will be envied by humans as they will be given the gift of immortality for as long as they continue the practice of drinking human blood. For only an entity of evil could ever crave the taste for human blood yet their reward would indeed be immortality. The struggle of conscience for those who do not serve Satan will considerably amuse those who do.

Such immortality will only be halted by the challenge of something holy such as a crucifix or splash of holy water, for the immortality is secured only by the very essence of evil.

They will be perceived as slothful by those who do not understand their existence as they spend much of the day hidden away from daylight preferring to show their capabilities in the hours of the night.

And these new servers of Satan will have a name.

They will be known as *The Vampire.*

Chapter 1

Beacon Park Football Stadium, Birmingham, England. Present day.

It was the final day of the season and Kingsbarr United were staring relegation in the face. It was not a position that they were accustomed too, they had consecutively served in the top flight of English football for the past fifty years, but the reality was that they needed to take all three points from today's match in order to guarantee their survival from the dreaded drop.

The tension was crushing. The loyal Kingsbarr fans could feel it as they loyally flocked to their home ground by the thousands, team captain Johnny Knox could feel it as he tied the laces to his colour co-ordinated gold boots, millionaire chairman Peter Cogshaw could feel it as he nervously puffed on yet another cigar, but the man who could feel the pressure more than anyone else was Kingsbarr United team manager Daryl Weir. He knew that if he was to be the first post-war manager to lead the Midlands based club into certain relegation; he would also most likely be out of a job before the morning papers had even had time to speculate on his departure from the club.

Daryl quietly closed the home team's changing room door shut in an attempt to secure some privacy for himself and his players. The thought warmed him despite his angst.

Yes they were his players. They were his team, and in spite of their current league position and loss of form he loved every single one of *his* boys.

For now at least they belonged to him.

He addressed the team with genuine emotion that cut through his soft Scottish accent, daring not to believe that it could be for the last time.

"Okay boys, you know what you have to do. It's in your own hands now. A win today and you will have done it; you will have remained in the English Premier League, the finest football league in the whole of the world. Just think about what that means for a second. I believe that you will win today and I believe that you deserve to be in the top flight of English football. This is a massive club with enviable tradition and success and that is why I chose each and every one of you to represent it because I know that you are the best bunch of lads there is. Now you go out there and hold your heads high. The Kingsbarr crowd will be right behind you, you know they love you but they will become impatient if we don't get a goal early in the game, so you need to rise above any anxiety that is displayed or voiced from the stands. It's been a long hard season but today this is your cup final, a one-off game, if you win that's it, job done.

Go out there and enjoy it.

Go out there and win it."

Chapter 2

Bucharest, Romania. Present day.

The young girl known as Afina was now regretting the argument that she had earlier encountered with her boyfriend. Not because of the content, she felt perfectly justified in slapping him across the face and storming out of the bar as he pathetically tried to squirm his way out of explaining why he had been sleeping with her best friend, but this altercation had resulted in her having to walk the dark and deserted Bucharest streets alone and it was not proving to be a pleasant experience.

As the sound of her clicking heels sang out into the freezing cold air they eerily reinforced the notion that she was very much alone. But as irony would have it, Afina's insecurity at realising that she was totally by herself also allowed her mind to naturally suspect that she must actually be sharing the dark, cold night with somebody. Or something?

There must be someone else nearby.

There must be someone lurking in the darkness of the shadows.

There must be someone following close behind.

Afina began to quicken her pace.

For some unexplained reason she hadn't been able to spot a taxi driver on her homeward journey, but she realised that she didn't have the means to pay anyway as she had left her address earlier without her purse expecting that bastard Alexander to pay for the evenings delights. That was before the barmaid had informed her of his exploits with Diona, her supposedly best friend, in the very same bar only the night before.

Afina was certain that she could feel a presence behind her as she walked, but every time she turned around she saw nothing. The feeling of uneasiness was overwhelmingly strong but she was convinced that it was not her imagination leading her astray from reality. She could easily be forgiven if her mind was playing tricks on her for the unsettling environment could not possibly instil any feeling of security.

Suddenly she heard a noise, not from behind as she was expecting but from ahead.

She froze to the spot.

She contemplated turning around and running back into the direction that she had come from, but she realised that she was now only about another ten minutes away from the safety of her flat.

I could make it in six minutes if I ran. She thought.

Unfortunately Afina realised that in order to reach her destination she needed to continue in the direction of where the noise had been.

"Alex, is that you?" she instantly regretted her question as it echoed clumsily into the night. Afina knew that it was extremely unlikely that Alex would be there, as he hadn't passed her on the way home, but she clung to the thought that perhaps he knew of a shortcut to get ahead of her.

She heard the noise again, rustling followed by the banging of metal.

Petrified, Afina failed to think of her next move.

"Who is there?" she cried out nervously.

"Meow!" the reply instantly traded Afina's fear for relief as a scrawny looking cat appeared from a hoard of rubbish bags crudely positioned at the end of the nearby alley.

But then Afina began to feel uneasy once again. *There could still be someone hiding down that alley,* she thought. *Waiting to pounce!*

In spite of her fears she concluded that her only option was to walk straight ahead. The quicker she was home the better. Then Afina began to feel drops of water fall onto the fair skin of her pretty features.

Great! Now it's raining! Symbolic of my night so far!

She plodded onwards and cautiously eyed the opening to the alley as she neared it. She couldn't see anyone near the street pavement, but the alley was so dimly lit it was near impossible to tell if someone could be lurking in the shadows or one of the doorways further into the passage.

Her heart raced as she passed the entire width of the passageway. She glared into the darkness of the alley, squinting and fighting with her eyes to make some sense of the thwarted shapes on offer. To her relief it proved to be an uneventful experience.

As her chewed heels now made tiny splashes on the wet surface caused by the introduction of the rain into the eerie night Afina was still convinced that she could feel a presence around her. She expected to hear footsteps at any moment from behind, it was still possible that someone had been hiding in the alleyway or had even been tailing her since she had left the bar.

But when she did finally realise that something else was to contribute to the sounds of the night after all, she was not prepared for the locality in which its presence would finally appear. Instead of whoever, or whatever, it was that had been stalking her choosing to pounce from behind or appearing in advance on the trail home, it came from a most unexpected location indeed. Unpredictably it appeared from above her.

Afina squirmed as she heard the flapping sound above her head. It sounded close and it sounded like it could only come from a bird of astounding proportion, but when she looked up into the dark sky all she could see was the stars and the moon. The moon, however, heightened her fearful state. It was a full moon.

Afina quickened her pace even further as she headed for home, her destination getting desperately closer by the second.

The flapping noise continued overhead.

Afina began to break into a jog, too scared to even look up now, as the flapping noise seemed to become accompanied by a clicking sound.

Birds chirp, they don't click!

Afina removed her shoes and began to run. Her heels had been hindering her pace and she was determined to reach home as quickly as possible.

The flapping and the clicking continued. The clicking noise now seemed to be fused with the sound of a type of disturbing shriek.

As Afina ran she was amazed that the clicking noise reminded her of a dolphin.

Don't be stupid dolphins can't fly!

Then her heart sank in a troubled realisation of what it could be flying above her.

A bat.

The creature above her must be a bat. But Afina was unnerved at the giant size that this bat appeared to be. She remembered learning at school in her last term only four years earlier that often a human would not even know that a bat could be in the near vicinity to them, as they were capable of gliding through the air with admirable swiftness, camouflaged by the darkness of the sky with their black bodies.

But this bat could be heard.

She turned the corner and she could see the block of flats that included her accommodation in sight. By now Afina's heart was beating profusely and she was fighting for her breath. She had never been the sporty type and the anxiety wasn't helping her breathing either. Her raven coloured hair flew into her face often restricting her view as it became wetter by the second with the ice-cold rain. Her plump breasts ached as they pounded degradingly with every stride.

The noises above her continued matching whatever speed she increased too. Afina nearly suffered a heart attack there and then when the clicking and shrieking noises were replaced with the disturbing sound of human laughter!

People cannot fly!

The laughter continued, mocking Afina in her desperate attempt to reach the salvation of her home.

Then suddenly the laughter and all the other noises stopped. But Afina was convinced that she had witnessed something enter the gateway to her building at a lightning speed.

Whatever that creature is it is waiting for me. It is waiting until I turn the corner into the gateway and then it will get me.

No it won't!

Afina kept her eyes firmly fixed on the gateway as she ran down the passageway at the side of the shops that sat just before her block of apartments. She had quickly decided that she was going to enter the building at the rear entrance. She was convinced that the creature or whatever it was had not seen her latest route home as it hadn't yet appeared from the darkness by the time that she had ran along the passageway.

She reached the back entrance in record time and fumbled with her keys. She found the correct one and entered it into the lock. She was not accustomed to using this entrance but to her relief the door opened easily and she entered the building.

So far, so good!

Afina gave another huge sigh of relief as she closed the door behind her and leant on it using her back in order to catch a much needed breath for a brief moment.

Afina lived on the thirteenth floor and she walked over to the lift and pressed the button that displayed an arrow signalling upwards. She was amazed how for once she appreciated the stale smell of urine in the building and felt strangely reassured at the familiar sight of used syringes and discarded condoms.

She felt that her luck for tonight had miraculously changed for the better when the bell rang uncharacteristically quickly to signal the arrival of the lift. The lift arrived with its familiar shake and the scratched metal doors slowly opened apart.

Afina was a little taken aback when the lift revealed a man to be inside. She couldn't help but notice how attractive he was in spite of his pasty complexion. His hair was strikingly jet black in stark contrast to his unusually pale skin and he had a tall elegant frame.

"Salut." (Hello).

"Salut," replied Afina nervously. Okay he was good looking but Afina had expected him to have got out of the lift by now. He seemed to be lingering for no apparent reason as he stared intensely into Afina's eyes.

The stranger began to grin slowly and as he gradually revealed his teeth, Afina could see that they were even whiter than his skin. As the grin became broader a rush of terror raced through Afina, for at either end of his mouth appeared a set of fangs pointing out over his lower lip.

Then he laughed and Afina instantly recognised it as the same laugh that she had heard circling above her on her race home. The impossible realisation ravaged her brain.

A vampire has followed me home!

But in Romania it wasn't an altogether unexpected experience. In Romania the people take their legends very seriously.

Before she could do anything Afina was dragged into the lift with great strength from a single arm of the vampire reaching out into the corridor. With one swift movement he pulled her closer to him and pressed the button to shut the doors of the lift.

Afina hadn't even had time to scream but as the vampire sank his teeth into the left side of her neck her fear was quickly replaced by a strange and overpowering state of arousal. With every drop of blood that was sucked from her veins the state of arousal increased and she soon lost the notion to fight against the vampires clutches. As she grew weaker the vampire quenched his thirst for human blood and he gently allowed Afina to drop to the floor in a state of bliss unconsciousness.

As the vampire looked up he noticed the lift doors open once more to reveal a figure as ghostly white as him in appearance. His hair was distinguishing grey in colour and styled to masculine perfection. He purred with the aura of power and charisma.

"Well done Andrei, I have taught you well I see."

The vampire grinned revealing his fangs once more only this time, like the rest of his mouth, they were coloured by the red of Afina's blood.

"Thank you Master. I am glad that I please you."

Chapter 3

The first half had not gone to plan for Daryl Weir and Kingsbarr United. As strikers Giuseppe Rossi and Leon Davis kicked-off for the second half Kingsbarr were unbelievably 2-0 down on their own ground. They were literally forty-five minutes away from relegation.

Ironically, the Kingsbarr team had played quite well. Rossi had hit the post and his silky skills had proved a handful for the City defence, but Davis was struggling to make an impact after being thrown into this game straight from the youth team squad on account of the ever-increasing injury list of Kingsbarr United.

Leon Davis had also been given his chance because Kingsbarr's top striker Gerry Spalding was currently spending a stretch at Her Majesty's Pleasure following a Grievous Bodily Harm charge against a burglar who had had the audacity of pressing charges after breaking into Gerry's home. As Gerry had got up to go to the bathroom needing a pee, he had inadvertently caught the intruder on his landing in the middle of the night. Naturally feeling a duty to protect his wife and daughter who were sleeping nearby Gerry felt that his only option was to beat the scumbag within an inch of his life. Various polls in the media on television and in newspapers had fully supported Gerry's actions, as was the opinion of the club who had vowed to stand by Gerry all the way, but unfortunately the judge had decided that he wanted to make an example of a Premiership footballer by issuing a custodial sentence commenting on how "No-one was above the law and nobody had the right to take matters into their own hands no matter how justified they felt their actions were." Giuseppe Rossi for one sorely missed Gerry's absence from the team.

Rossi was a nimble Italian striker with silky touches and two good feet, but he was also "lightweight" and relied on the power of Spalding's huge presence up front to take the knocks and set up chances for him to score. Since Gerry's time in prison Giuseppe's chances of scoring goals had noticeably dried up.

City had scored both their goals totally against the run of play in the final three minutes of the first half. The first coming from a dubious penalty decision after Jody Roper had wrongly been adjudged of handling the ball in the penalty area. Jamaican international goalkeeper Alvin Braxton had got a hand to the penalty turning it onto the post but unfortunately the ball cruelly trickled over the goal line to put City one goal to the good. It was a valiant attempt by Braxton who was a more than impressive shot stopper, but ten years earlier the 38 year old goalkeeper may have just dived that split second earlier and his huge gloved hand might have proved strong enough to have totally saved the penalty. The Kingsbarr defence were so shell-shocked from that initial goal that they lost their concentration and totally messed up an attempted offside line to allow the city striker time to run at goal unchallenged and neatly put City into an undeserved 2-0 lead. Braxton had stood no chance.

As the game reached the hour mark Kingsbarr had still not pulled a single goal back in spite of peppering the City goalmouth with wayward shots and below-par attempts at goal. It was extremely frustrating for Johnny Knox. He was the type of player with the never say die attitude and he loved Kingsbarr United—his club. As a youngster he had dreamed of playing for Kingsbarr United as he watched his heroes light up the world of football from the terraces of Beacon Park, the Kingsbarr home ground. And now here he was playing in his sixteenth season for them as a first team player, but this was the first time that he had ever faced relegation with them.

It was hard for Johnny, and many others to comprehend that Kingsbarr United could be in this unlikely position.

Then he heard the familiar inspirational call from the terraces by the Kingsbarr United supporters. It made him proud to hear them chant his name, just as he had cheered for his Kingsbarr heroes all those years ago.

"Knox, Knox get in the box," came the recognizable chant from the Kingsbarr fans. It was a request that they would always affectionately cry out to urge Johnny to run from deep in his midfield role in order to get into a dangerous scoring position inside the opposition's goalmouth. His magnificent timed runs were legendary in the game. Johnny had an extremely impressive scoring rate for a midfield player, averaging a goal every three games throughout his career, and his eighteen goals this season, ensuring his status as top scorer above any of the clubs strikers, had enabled the Kingsbarr United relegation battle to stretch until the very last game of the season.

"Knox, Knox get in the box," chanted the Kingsbarr fans again, but Johnny's footballing experience enabled him to realise that they were being a little impatient with their request even if it was understandable given the score line and urgency of the occasion. Johnny knew that the time was not quite right to bomb forward just yet as it would leave a gap in midfield that could be easily exploited by the City players. Instead he waved to the fans in acknowledgement of their affection at chanting his name and the Kingsbarr faithful clapped and cheered at his affinity with them. In spite of the intense pressure of Kingsbarr needing to achieve something from this game, the fans momentarily left their anxiety behind and were soon light-heartedly swapping their chant to "Johnny, Johnny give us a wave." However, their faith in Johnny was soon to be rewarded.

Johnny witnessed Jody Roper make a fantastic tackle on the City player and as he emerged with the ball cleanly he had the vision to spread it out beautifully to the Kingsbarr number seven and Chinese international winger "Charlie" Cheng who was positioned on the right flank. Cheng controlled Roper's pass fantastically well and after showboating past two city players he was off on one of his exciting runs as he headed for the City by-line. Once Charlie was on such a determined run equipped with his lightning pace Johnny knew that the City players would never be able to catch him. It was now time for "Knox to get in the box."

Johnny sprinted up the field to reach the City penalty area and without even looking up Cheng sent in a lovely cross that fell out of reach and in between the two central defenders of City. As Johnny's head connected with the ball perfectly accompanied by the momentum of his run forward the City keeper stood no chance and watched helplessly as the ball nestled into the top right hand corner of the net.

2-1! Game on!

Johnny ran to the Kingsbarr fans that were sat behind the goal that he had just scored in, punched his fist in the air and kissed the badge on his gold and blue striped shirt, which depicted the three crowns of Kingsbarr United. The fans responded with cheers and a large amount of elation. They began to praise the name of their team captain in song once more. "There's only one Johnny Knox," they sang.

Johnny's celebration of running to the crowd had earned him a yellow card as well as his nineteenth goal of the season, but he philosophically concluded that some things were worth getting booked for. He was still punching the air as the players finally regained their respective positions ready for the restart.

The City strikers kicked-off to restart the game and felt intimidated as the home supporters sang their hearts out above the travelling fans. The tension was electrifying as the Kingsbarr supporters urged and cheered at every kick their team made. Kingsbarr began to play even better than they had done all match, Johnny's goal had seemed to settle their nerves but had compromised the nerves of the City players and they began to make mistakes. Kingsbarr were enjoying a vast amount of possession of the ball and played in a style that belied their league position.

With five minutes of normal time remaining suddenly the youngster Leon Davis picked up the ball on the edge of the area and surprised everyone when he dribbled past three defenders leaving only the goalkeeper to beat. As the City custodian dived at his feet Davis intelligently chipped the ball over the descending green-jersey-clad torso of the keeper and everyone watched in anticipation as the ball seemed to move in slow motion on its journey towards the City goal. As it dipped the ball hit the crossbar and rebounded back into play. Both sets of players seemed to be spellbound offering no reaction as they hypnotically watched the spinning ball in flight. Everyone that was except Johnny Knox and he desperately threw his body forward to head his and Kingsbarr's second goal of the night. The crowd went wild once again and Daryl Weir ran along the touchline like an excited school kid belying his 54 years of age. At 2-2 Kingsbarr still had a chance. Whereas a win guaranteed them survival a draw would be good enough if Rovers failed to win in their respective game. They were sitting one place below Kingsbarr United in eighteenth position, with one point less and with a far inferior goal difference. Some of the Kingsbarr supporters had smuggled transistor radios and mobile phones into the stadium and there were rumbles soon filtering through the crowd that the Rovers game was currently a 0-0 score line. Everyone who was in allegiance with Kingsbarr United were suddenly feeling an amazing wave of optimism for even if Kingsbarr were to lose to City they would still have survived relegation by their superior goal difference. Surely a draw would now be more than enough as the final whistle edged ever nearer.

The last few moments of the game proved tense beyond belief as both sides pushed for the winner but finally the referee put the whistle to his lips to signal the end of the game with the score ultimately remaining at 2-2. The Kingsbarr

United crowd went wild, as did the Kingsbarr players along with their manager Daryl Weir.

They had done it. They had finished one point above Rovers in seventeenth position. They had survived relegation.

As Johnny Knox, Charlie Cheng, Jody Roper and Alvin Braxton jumped gleefully around the centre-circle in a huddle, Johnny noticed the mood of the crowd begin to change. He then glanced over to Daryl Weir and the team coaches and noticed that they were no longer smiling. Johnny broke away from the huddle and ran over to Daryl Weir.

"Boss what's wrong we made it didn't we?"

Weir put a hand on Johnny's shoulder. "We celebrated too soon Johnny. Rovers scored a winner in injury time. They won their game 1-0 and so they finish one point above us. Just one lousy fucking point. Next season Johnny you'll be playing football in the Championship, and I think I'll be out of a job."

Chapter 4

To say that Johnny Knox was gutted when Kingsbarr United became relegated from the English Premier League would be a major understatement. But today, sitting on the beautiful soft sanded beach in Mangalia he was much more philosophical about the situation. As he leaned back into his sun lounge he looked out to the shoreline through the darkened lens of his designer sunglasses to affectionately observe his wife and daughter playfully splashing and enjoying the warm ocean of the Black Sea coast. He realised that he truly had a lot to be thankful for. Okay he loved football, he loved Kingsbarr United but he loved his family more.

He began to consider that playing in the Championship was simply a new challenge that he should rise to and even relish. A fight for promotion would be a new experience for him following his previous years of success in the top flight and European competitions, and he believed that Kingsbarr should at least return to regularly winning matches again by competing in this lower division. It hadn't been much fun uncharacteristically losing game after game in the Premiership last season that's for sure.

Johnny had had the choice to remain playing in the Premiership if he had so desired. Daryl Weir, who had actually hung on to his job as team manager, had received plenty of offers for Johnny during the closed season. He didn't want to sell Johnny but had promised not to stand in his way if Johnny wished to remain a Premiership player. Daryl realised that Johnny's place in the England national side had been compromised due to Kingsbarr's fall from grace, even though

Johnny's form had remained consistently high throughout the previous season. If Johnny was to play in the Championship Daryl knew that the politics of the game would virtually ensure that Johnny would totally fall out of favour with the England manager. To Johnny's credit he wanted to remain at Kingsbarr United and help win them promotion back into the Premiership. He had signed for Kingsbarr at 15 years old as a schoolboy and had broken into the first team at the tender age of 17 earning himself a reputation as the perfect all-round midfield player. He was a hard but fair tackler with a natural competitive character, but Johnny also possessed natural pace and the ability to distribute the ball intelligently, attributes not usually associated with the ball winner of the team.

Unfortunately four members of the first team squad had not thought like Johnny and had been tempted to play again in the Premiership by signing for other clubs. Their attitude disappointed Johnny; he felt that they should shoulder the responsibility of relegation and stay at the club to make amends. At least Charlie Cheng had remained at the club. He had been approached by a couple of Spanish clubs from La Liga as well as the Premiership teams, but like Johnny loyalty was a major characteristic of his make up. Johnny looked forward to the Chinese international's phenomenal touchline runs torturing the defences of the Championship teams.

Johnny stared admirably at his wife in her black bikini. Sheena Knox's long hair was almost as black as her swimwear but as naturally dark as it was it had still become pleasantly affected by the sun-kissed climate. The suntan that she had attracted onto her shapely figure made him boom with pride. He had noticed the other men of the beach gaze at her, but this didn't worry Johnny, he knew never to be jealous secure in the knowledge that their relationship was solid and built on unshakable foundations. Unlike many footballers' wives Sheena was not a trophy wife, although she was of stunning natural beauty. She and Johnny had met at the tender age of 14. Actually they had met at the age of 11 when they became enrolled in the same class at secondary school, but it was not until the penultimate year of leaving Perry Vale Comprehensive School that they began to ultimately fall for one another.

Seeing his wife from an unusually distant viewpoint enabled Johnny to study her beauty in a whole new light. He was amazed at how flat her stomach had remained all these years together, especially when they regularly gave in to their mutual vices of take away Indian and Chinese food. He stared at Sheena's stomach and affectionately remembered when at the age of 18 it harboured their only children to date, Callum and Saffron, twins, one boy and one girl. By the time Johnny had reached his nineteenth year he was married, a father of twins and a full England international. Now at the age of 33 looking out at his wife and daughter, with his health intact and his ability to play football still consistently high he reminded himself again how lucky he was. On the grand scale of things what did it really matter if he was to be playing football in a lower division next season?

But in spite of all of this Johnny still had a massive void in his life. A void that he hoped would one day be resolved. It was the reason why the family's pre-season holiday had once again been in Romania, as it had been consistently for the past eight years. Each year the trip to Romania wasn't just a holiday for Johnny, it was more of a quest. Johnny would never give up hope of finding Callum.

When Saffron and Callum were six years old the Knox family had come to the Black Sea Coast of Romania for the very first time and instantly fell in love with the place. Johnny had promised his nagging son that he would take him for a drive in the hired 4x4 jeep so that they could take a look at the impressive Fagaras Mountains, also known as the Transylvanian Alps, while the female members of the family relaxed at the pool or wandered along the golden beach. Sheena had been worried about the boys' adventure from the beginning, but she armed them with a more than sufficient packed lunch and kissed them goodbye as they headed off. She was never to see her son again.

It was a long drive to the mountain range along some very challenging and winding roads. On one blind corner a mountain animal appeared from nowhere running into the path of the jeep causing Johnny to instinctively brake and swerve in an attempt to avoid the beast. This resulted in the vehicle leaving the road and violently descending down a steep embankment and ultimately crashing into a mound of rocks. The position that the jeep had landed at meant that it could not be easily seen from the road and foliage also camouflaged its existence from any traffic that may be passing by. Johnny was immediately knocked unconscious from the accident, but fortunately, and somewhat miraculously he avoided any serious injury. As he awoke into his groggy state his primary instinct was to attend to his six-year-old son, but to his horror as he turned to the passenger seat he could see that Callum was not sitting there. Ignoring his own injuries Johnny limped out of the vehicle and searched the immediate vicinity for what seemed like hours expecting to find his son lying nearby, possibly thrown from the open-topped jeep during the crash, but Callum was nowhere to be seen.

Eventually Johnny flagged down a passing car on the winding road ahead and fortunately the two farmers could speak acceptable English. They helped Johnny search for Callum with meticulous effort, but they too could not locate the missing boy. In the end they persuaded Johnny to leave the site and talk to the Romanian authorities. They kindly escorted Johnny to the nearest village where he was able to inform the police. They returned with Johnny to the site of the crash and they too painstakingly searched for Callum, but they also could not locate the missing child. It was if he had disappeared off the face of the Earth. In the weeks that followed the Romanian television and newspapers appealed to the Romanian public to look out for a six-year-old English boy with dark brown hair and eyes who answers to the name of Callum, but their pleas were in vain. Initially some suspicion had fell on Johnny as to the disappearance of his child, but after careful interviewing the police were satisfied that Johnny had not been responsible for anything sinister towards the boy. Johnny's distressed state at the disappearance of his only son could not be ignored. The police feared that Callum had been abducted from the scene of the crash and possibly murdered, but without a body or even a suspect they were reluctant to make Callum's disappearance a murder investigation. Instead Callum remains registered as a missing person enquiry, his disappearance remaining a total mystery. But every year Johnny returns to Romania to canvass individuals and keep the search alive by appearing on Romanian television appeals, hoping that one day Callum will be found. Johnny obviously hoped to find his son alive, but even if his dead body were to be found at least he and Sheena would have some closure on the tragic situation. With the uncertainty surrounding Callum's existence they weren't even able to go through the natural process of grieving. The uncertainty was an ongoing tormenting experience.

Incidentally Sheena had been brilliant about the heartbreak despite her own anguish. Unlike Johnny himself she never once blamed him for their son's disappearance and it broke her heart to see Johnny beat himself up over the tragedy time and time again. It was a miracle that Johnny was able to play football with the torment that he felt inside, but he had an incredible will and ability to focus on matters at hand. Johnny possessed the power to do everything with conviction. When playing football nothing else mattered or even entered his head other than what materialises on that pitch for the next ninety minutes. When he was with his family nothing else mattered but caring for them. When he was searching for Callum nothing else mattered but the quest to find his missing son.

Looking out to shore again he counted his blessings for still having Saffron, his beautiful daughter who bore a remarkable resemblance to her mother. Saffron was convinced that Callum was still alive drawing inspiration from that "sixth sense" that twins so often possess.

"Its okay, Dad," she would often say in her sweet reassuring way. "I know Callum is safe and being looked after. I can feel it inside of me all the time."

Johnny would return her words with a hug and a smile, thankful that his daughter was so optimistic about her brother's well-being. Although he himself never gave up hope, Johnny still feared the worst on occasions, and one of the hardest aspects to have to face concerning Callum's disappearance was never having any closure on the existence of his son.

Johnny's eyes broke away from Sheena and Saffron as they happily paddled and splashed in the ocean and he looked down at the newspaper that he had purchased a few hours earlier. As he always did when he revisited Romania he would buy the English newspapers that had been exported to the country but he also purchased the Romanian newspapers in a hope that a mention of Callum would be in them. He had managed to teach himself some basic Romanian but he often needed to ask for the assistance of a Romanian resident to interpret newspaper clippings that he thought might offer some hope. Usually they never did.

Scanning the newspaper, not being able to understand much of the writing Johnny stumbled upon the photograph of a very pretty face. He wondered what the story about her could be about. He glanced up from the paper to check on Saffron and Sheena, something he did frequently obsessed with the need to protect them following the tragedy surrounding Callum and he noticed something very unusual.

Walking along the tide was a stunningly attractive girl, but what was strange was the fact that unlike the other swimsuit clad females of the beach, this girl was wearing a full set of clothes exposing only her face and hands. The clothes were also jet black in colour, another peculiarity considering that the temperature was touching eighty degrees. At least she was wearing sunglasses but they too were jet black in colour. As she moved closer, the girl turned her head in Johnny's direction. He noticed how her skin was ghostly white in colour and she also lacked colour in her lips. He failed to understand how this could be considering the recent sunny climate. For someone to have totally avoided the colouring of the sun seemed impossible unless they had simply locked themselves away for a very long time.

Johnny sensed that their eyes met, regardless of their respective sunglasses shielding their irises. He felt a powerful aura massage his soul as his eyes became locked on her snow-white splendour. Then Johnny, mesmerised by the peculiar beauty of this girl suddenly felt a sense of familiarity about her face. It puzzled him as she eventually turned her head away from Johnny and passed on by down the beach.

Spellbound by the sight of the girl that had just passed by Johnny once again returned to the newspaper and then he realised why the girl had looked so familiar to him. The picture of the pretty face that he had only moments earlier stumbled upon in the newspaper was that of the same girl that had just walked along the beach.

Startled by the coincidence Johnny felt compelled to investigate who the girl could be. He called out to a fat man who was lying near by. "Scuzat'ima. Excuse me, could you help me please?"

The fat man rose from his indentation in the sand and came the short distance to Johnny.

"You are English, no?"

"Yes, yes I am English. I wonder if you could help me please?"

"Yes, I can try."

"Good. Thank you very much. Could you tell me what this story in the newspaper is saying please? The one associated with the picture of this girl."

"She is very pretty."

"Yes, what does it say?"

The fat man took a while to indulge the contents of the story, before returning to talk to Johnny again.

"It is unfortunately a tragic story sir. This girl is missing. Her body is missing."

Immediately the word *missing* connected with Johnny's torment and sadness surrounding his own son's disappearance more than eight years ago. But then he realised that this girl could be found. It seemed that her fate could be more successful than Callum's."

"This girl is missing you say. Well I have just seen her walk along the beach didn't you see her too?"

"I was dozing sir, until you called me over that is. But I think you must be mistaken, you couldn't have seen this girl."

"I did, I swear to you. She stared right at me."

"But Sir this girl pictured in the newspaper is dead."

"Dead, what do you mean dead? You said she was missing."

"I said that her *body* was missing. This girl was found dead in a block of apartments in Bucharest. She had two puncture wounds on her neck and had lost an awful amount of blood. While she was in the autopsy room waiting to be butchered all over again her body mysteriously disappeared. She seemed to just vanish into thin air."

"My god that's terrible. What was her name?"

"The article says that her name was *Afina*."

Chapter 5

Fosturnea School of Football Excellence. A secret location somewhere near the Fagaras Mountains, Romania.

"Faster, faster," ordered Cezar Prodanescu to the trainees as they practiced their shuttle runs. "If any of you are to make the grade in the English Premier League then good fitness is a key issue to your success. The elite personnel of English football consider levels of fitness to be extremely important. As a trainee of the Fosturnea School of Football Excellence you must aspire to be the very best. To play football in the English League, the original home of football is the pinnacle of any footballer's career. It is without doubt the greatest football league in the world and I want each and every one of you to have the chance to play in it. If you are patient and respond positively to my training methods then you shall all live our dream."

"But Master, we are thirsty and hungry. It is very late. You know that quenching our thirst is the key to our fitness."

"Andrei," came the stern reply from the master, also known as Cezar Prodanescu. "The night is still young, there is plenty of time for you to work hard and earn your reward to feast later. Remember that you shall be acutely disadvantaged when playing football on Saturday afternoons so your general fitness levels must not rouse any suspicion. The fitness levels that you portray from dusk till dawn will never be brought into question, but during the hours of daylight you must all rise to the challenge. Now enough talk, I want twenty more shuttle runs from all of you at twice the pace. Afterwards we will wind down with some shooting practice."

"And what shall we do then Master?" asked another Fosturnea trainee, smiling as he deliberately shot the loaded question.

"And then my boys, we will go out into the night and literally paint the town red . . . *blood red*."

Chapter 6

Chairman's office. Kingsbarr United Football Club

"What do you mean there isn't enough money to strengthen the squad. We have just made almost eight million pounds from selling four of our best players."

"Daryl, you are in no position to come into my office making demands. You are lucky that you kept your job at all after leading the team to relegation."

"Don't try and treat me like a fool. I still have three years of my contract left Peter, so I suspect that a princely compensation pay-off wasn't such an attractive proposition for the club."

"It is true that money is tight Daryl, we lost millions of pounds in television rights and various other deals by exiting the Premier League, hence the lack of funds available to make any additions to the squad. But let me tell you this, I strongly resent your allegation as to your position Daryl, the board and myself felt that we owed you some loyalty, after all you have won this Club each and every one of the domestic competitions at one time or another in recent years, and we can not forget the two European Champions League victories either. Being European champions is not something that can be dismissed lightly. We believed that a manager of your experience and calibre will easily lead this team back into the Premier League."

"Peter, it won't be as easy as you think. The Championship is a very competitive league. You really have to work hard and roll your sleeves up and frankly if we don't replace the four lads that have left us we could really struggle to gain promotion.

Apart from Johnny Knox and Charlie Cheng we haven't got enough depth in quality, some of the lads still with us from those Champions league victories are starting to slow down now, as they grow older. You know that I love them all but they are not the players they once were, and this season we are going to have to ask them to play more games in this division than they ever did in a premiership season. I am going to need a deep enough squad to be able to rest them from time to time."

Peter Cogshaw puffed on his big cigar before answering. "Then Daryl you will have to replace them with free transfers. Anyway throw the kids in; some young blood should just do the trick."

"Peter, the Kingsbarr United youth team finished bottom of their league, they performed even more abysmally than we did. The kids at this club simply aren't good enough to step in. I've gambled on young Leon Davis since we lost Gerry to prison, and although I can not question his hunger and commitment to the cause he simply doesn't quite make the grade for Kingsbarr United."

"Daryl I'm sorry. You will have to make do. There simply isn't enough money to support any large financial signings. Kingsbarr United performed the unthinkable last season by getting relegated; now it is up to those individuals to perform and get this club back where it belongs. In the Premiership. Who knows maybe a good cup run will generate some money for new signings."

Daryl sank back into his chair shaking his head, reluctantly resigned to the facts concerning the financial situation of the club. "Okay I can see that my motivational skills are going to have to be at their best in order to succeed this season. I'll do my best. You know I love this club Peter."

Peter Cogshaw flicked the ash from the end of his cigar and leaned his stout frame forward towards his despondent team manager as an attempt to show his sincerity. "Daryl, as I have always done since that distant day that I first appointed you manager of this football club, I have every faith in you."

Chapter 7

Johnny was sure that the girl that he had seen on the beach was the very same girl that had been reported dead in the Romanian newspaper. He finally convinced himself that he hadn't seen a ghost, although she had definitely appeared white enough in colour to be mistaken for belonging to the spirit world. He realised that everyone had someone who looked like him or her in life. Even Kingsbarr United had run a competition in the match day programme recently searching for look-alikes of the squad of players. He didn't think that the fork lift truck driver who won the best "Johnny Knox" look-alike was anything like him though and he remembered how the whole of the squad had fell about laughing at the "Alvin Braxton" winner.

It was the last night of this year's holiday to Romania and Johnny had once again disappointedly drawn a blank as to the whereabouts of his missing son. Downhearted, Sheena had encouraged him to take a walk around the resort whilst she and Saffron packed the suitcases.

As dusk was closing in Johnny could still feel the warm air about him as he paced about the resort. He headed down to the harbour for one last look at the sea. Tomorrow he would be back in Birmingham in the West Midlands, the furthest point in England from any ocean waves. As he approached the harbour Johnny felt his sleeveless arms surprisingly flinch a little as a slight breeze blew in across the open sea. With the warm climate he had naturally opted not to wear a jumper over his yellow sports vest. With his arms exposed he was able to glance down at one of the several, but in the main tasteful tattoos that decorated his body. The one that poignantly caught his eye was the symbolic English rose with the names of his two children etched around the red petals. He used his index finger to affectionately stroke the letters of the name of his daughter Saffron and then he felt a tear well in his eye as he went on to stroke the imbedded blue ink of the second name Callum. He forced his eyes away from the tattoo and instead looked towards the ocean in an attempt to ease his pain.

He rested on some white railings for a few minutes as he looked out at the mysterious blue water and his imagination wondered as to the secrets that it might hold beneath its silky surface. He became annoyed at himself for allowing his thoughts to picture people going to their watery graves instead of admiring the sheer beauty of the coastline, but his mood was low and his heart was heavy following yet another trip to Romania devoid of success of unearthing any news about his missing son. He moved his eyes up to the sky to see the shape of the moon dimly breaking through the clouds. He recalled how whilst on trips abroad playing in European competitions with Kingsbarr or on international duty for England, he would tell Callum to look up at the moon because the moon could be seen all over the world no matter where you were. He would tell his son that although his daddy may be far away he was still somewhere under the moon and if he looked up at it before Mommy put him to sleep his daddy would be looking up at it too. He even told Callum that if they both blew a goodnight kiss into the air the moon could pass it on to them. He had omitted to explain to Callum that some countries could have differing time differences. As Johnny glanced up at the moon tonight he wondered, and hoped, that Callum was somewhere looking up at it too, thinking of his dad.

Johnny checked his watch. Nearly ten minutes to eight. The taxi was coming to the hotel at eight-thirty and they were due to be in the air before ten. He turned away from the sea and moved away from the harbour to head back to the hotel.

He crossed the street with out a single vehicle approaching and moved along the row of tavernas that faced the sea front.

"Mr Knox. We'll see you and your family again next year I hope." The voice came from a jovial looking individual with a bushy moustache and flowery shirt.

"Yes Felix, I should think we'll be back again next year."

"It's my Romanian stew and fine beer that calls you across the skies isn't it Mr Knox?" Felix owned and managed one of the tavernas in the prime location of the harbour front and he was currently serving up his self proclaimed legendary stew to a good looking Norwegian couple who were sitting at a candlelit table.

"Yeah, that's right Felix." Johnny didn't wish to correct his good-natured friend on the real reason why the Knox family returned each year to Romania. "I'll see you next year."

"Give my warmest wishes to your beautiful wife and daughter. Have a safe journey my English friend."

"Thanks Felix. Best wishes to your family too."

Behind the bar of his establishment Felix proudly kept a signed photograph of himself standing with Johnny along with a Kingsbarr United football jersey, which had also been signed by the midfield star.

As Johnny turned the corner onto the cobbled street to begin his return to the hotel he was startled to see a young boy descending towards him with four angry looking men chasing behind. Johnny was further concerned to see that one of the men was holding a pitchfork. The frightened child ran desperately towards Johnny, and Johnny instantly positioned himself like a shield between the boy and his assailants protecting him from their assault. The four men halted a few metres away.

"What is wrong with you?" enquired an astounded Johnny. "Leave this boy alone he is just a child."

The man with the pitchfork spoke first.

"This has no concern for you Englishman. There is no need to become involved."

"Well that's too bad because now I am involved. If you want to get to this boy you will have to go through me first."

In spite of his brave words Johnny half expected the man with the pitchfork to lunge at him at any second. Instead the four men simply looked at one another as if to plan their next move telepathically.

A second man spoke. He appeared less intimidating than the pitchfork chap. "Please, we don't want any trouble. Just let us speak with the boy."

"I'm worried that your intentions are not just to talk to him. Say what you want to say and then go, but I'm staying."

"This is no concern of yours." Pitchfork.

"Yeah, so you said. Look what can he have done that is so terrible? The poor kid's terrified to death."

"*To death,*" Pitchfork again. "An ironic choice of words."

The less intimidating man spoke again. "Look. There are things about this boy that you do not understand. Things that you would not want to understand. It is in your best interests to continue walking up the hill and to leave us to deal with the boy. Just pretend that this meeting has never occurred." Although presented amicably Johnny sensed a chilling factor in the words of the man.

"I'm sorry, I can't let that happen," replied Johnny. He knew that he was hopelessly outnumbered, and may have to possibly contend with a pitchfork being thrust at him but there was no way he was going to hand the boy over without a fight, it would be like sending a lamb to the slaughter.

"English pig! I'm losing my patience with you now move out of our way." Pitchfork was becoming agitated at Johnny's defiant stance.

"You know, you really should seek out some anger management classes."

The man holding the pitchfork took a step towards Johnny but one of his friends put an arm across him to prevent his attack.

A third man now spoke. "Okay Englishman have it your way for now. Don't say that you haven't been warned. Let's see how much you care for the kid by morning time."

"What the hell are you talking about? He is just a little boy."

"That little boy killed my sheep." Pitchfork

"That's not all he'll kill." The fourth man now spoke, his greasy ponytail swinging as he shook his head.

"How much was your sheep worth? I'll pay you for it and then you can just leave the boy alone."

"10 million Lei"

"About £200. Okay if that's what it takes. By the way, it's Euros these days you know for you guys. Where have you been hiding or is change something you find difficult to embrace?"

Johnny pulled out his wallet and begrudgingly handed the pitchfork wielding man three hundred and fifty euros cash.

"There, that more than covers your loss now fuck off and leave the kid alone."

"Your words may not be so brave in a few hours friend." Ponytail again.

"What planet are you guys on, he is just a little boy. What real damage can he possibly do?"

The least intimidating of the four men spoke again. "We will leave you and the boy for now then Mr. Knox." Johnny's eyes moved sharply. "Yes of course I recognise you. I am a big football fan. But I must warn you; if my friends see the lad again I cannot guarantee his safety. This boy is not what he seems."

Johnny didn't answer, confused by all these warnings about a seemingly innocent child.

The four men turned and walked away leaving the boy clinging with fright to the back of Johnny's legs.

"Please be careful Mr. Knox, "called the less intimidating man as they moved further away. "I mean it most sincerely."

What puzzled Johnny most was that he knew the man meant it.

Chapter 8

Once the four men were out of sight Johnny turned to the boy and gently held him by the shoulders.

"Do you understand English?"

The boy nodded.

"What is your name?"

"Radu."

"Well Radu, why did you kill that man's sheep?"

The boy shrugged. "I was hungry."

"Fair enough, I guess."

"Where do you live? I'll take you home."

"I live where I can?"

"What do you mean?"

"I have no home."

"Where are your parents?"

"They are both dead. I am an orphan."

"Is there not an orphanage that I can take you to?"

"I ran away from there. It was horrible. I was teased and attacked all the time."

"Do you like it in Romania, Radu?"

The boy shrugged again. "Its okay I guess, but I have no friends here and people don't usually like me. Where are you from?"

"I'm from a place called Birmingham in England. There are many buildings and no sea or beach, but people are happy there most of the time."

"Are there children with mamas and tatas?"

"Yeah, lots I guess."

"It sounds nice."

Johnny took a sharp intake of breath and looked to the sky whilst he ran his fingers through his hair. His mind was racing as he thought on impulse.

"Radu, is your life in danger from those men if you stay around here?"

"Yes."

"I'm not always going to be here to protect you."

"But I like you."

Johnny looked up to the sky again as he contemplated what to do. The poor boy was in a desperate state and worse still his life was in danger. He ran his fingers through his hair once more, a life long habit whenever he was deep in thought. His hand then moved to the back pocket of his jeans where he felt the slight bulge protruding through the denim.

It was a crazy plan but surely it was worth it. It was worth it to save this little boy from a life of misery or even death. Johnny then pulled his mobile phone from his other back pocket and dialled the familiar number.

The tune of one of George Michael's upbeat melodies rang out in the hotel room from Sheena's phone.

"Hi babes, where are you?"

"Sheena I can't explain now but just trust me. I'll meet you at the airport; don't wait for me at the hotel. You and Saffron go straight to the airport okay."

"Why? What for Johnny? What's going on?"

"I can't explain now there isn't much time. There is just something that I've got to do. I'll see you and Saffron at the airport."

"But Johnny—"

"Bye Honey"

Sheena heard the line go dead.

Chapter 9

"Felix, Felix I need your help quickly," called Johnny running into the taverna.

"Johnny, calm down. Haven't you got a flight to catch? And who is the kid?"

"I need to talk to you in private."

Felix sensed that his English friend required some urgent assistance and he called out to his teenage daughter to take over the running of the taverna while he took Johnny and Radu through to his living quarters that were positioned to the rear of the establishment.

"Okay, what's going on Mr. Knox?"

"What I'm about to tell you may sound crazy Felix but just go with me. I'm taking this boy back to England with me."

"You are correct, it does sound crazy."

"His life is in danger if he stays here Felix; I've just had to rescue him from some very unpleasant locals who were intent on harming the boy. I can't let them have a second chance at hurting him."

Felix stroked his moustache as he digested what his English friend had just told him.

"Why don't we just go to the police Mr. Knox?"

"I don't trust those guys Felix and the police are not going to give this boy 24 hour protection now are they? It's simply not worth the risk. Besides from what the boy tells me he has very little reason to stay in Romania. He tells me that he is an orphan and that he lives on the streets."

"So how are you going to get him out of the country successfully my English friend? Have you really thought this through? If you are caught trying to smuggle a boy illegally out of Romania it will be you who the police will be most interested in."

Johnny fumbled into his back pocket and pulled out a wine coloured booklet.

"This passport belonged, err, belongs to my son Callum. I always carry it with me when I return to Romania on the hope that I will be returning to England with him. Well it looks as though Callum is not going to require its use on returning from this holiday either."

Felix rested a hand on his English friends shoulder. "Johnny, are you sure that you are not taking this boy as a substitute for your missing son?"

"No, Felix. I just want to help the child. But I guess, this poor kid could easily have been Callum"

"So how can I help you my friend?"

"Well it's silly really, for although I always bring this passport with me, the photograph of Callum was taken just after his sixth birthday. He would be fifteen by now, so not only would he look different to the enclosed photograph the passport is hopelessly out of date. Do you know anyone who could help me make a few alterations on the passport, to give the impression that it hasn't expired?"

"May I?" asked Felix as he took the passport from Johnny's grasp. He looked at the photo and then glanced at Radu who had obediently listened quietly as the two men had discussed his destiny.

"This boy does share some similarity to the photograph of your son. An unsuspecting passport controller would not ask questions I'm sure. You should see my own passport photograph; you would swear it wasn't me. Altering the dates however, could be a much more difficult prospect altogether."

"Can you suggest anything, Felix?" pleaded Johnny.

Felix turned to Radu. "Tell me boy. Do you really wish to accompany Mr. Knox to England, to live amongst the fiercest rainfall and freezing temperatures?"

Radu smiled and nodded his head eagerly.

"Strange boy. Okay I think I know someone who can help us. We must go now as we don't have much time."

"Where are we going Felix? Who will help us?"

"I know the very man, he often does a bit of how do you say it . . . dodgy business."

"Who?"

"Dr. Lazar."

"The village doctor! I would never have believed it!"

"Believe it Johnny. Come on, follow me."

Chapter 10

Johnny had only ever met Dr. Lazar on one previous occasion, some three years earlier. A local fish dish had not agreed with him and Dr. Lazar had been able to prescribe some medication to restrict the number of increasing trips to the toilet!

As the village doctor opened his door Johnny was still able to find the humour within to marvel at his bizarre appearance. Dr. Lazar's extremely bushy facial hair eclipsed Felix's moustache into pure insignificance, which was no major feat by itself and Johnny remembered how the doctor's left eye always seemed to be squinting beneath its hideous eyebrow giving the impression that his right eye was continuously magnified through a monocular spy glass of some kind.

"Felix, what can I do for you?" (Spoken in Romanian) "You know my surgery is now closed."

Although Johnny could not understand what Dr. Lazar had said, the disgruntled tone in his voice could not be escaped and Johnny sensed that the doctor was not best pleased at being disturbed.

Felix continued the conversation in Romanian and was appearing to have success by all accounts in explaining the need for Dr. Lazar's help.

Dr. Lazar turned to Johnny and spoke in English.

"Felix tells me that you need my help, and only because he has explained your predicament to me am I prepared to help you. A friend of Felix's is a friend of mine, but I have some conditions that I need satisfying in my own mind."

"Okay, what are they?" replied Johnny.

"Are you sure you want to help this boy. There are things in Romania that you do not understand Mr. Knox and it could be that the men who were chasing this boy had very good reason."

"I am sure Doctor. I fail to see what reason would be good enough to justify the hatred in their eyes towards one so young."

"Very well, it's your funeral as you English say." Johnny was bemused yet impressed at the doctor's knowledge of the English saying.

"Secondly, the cost will be cheap for my services as a favour to Felix. 100 euros, but it must be cash only. There can be no record of any transaction between us."

"I have that money right here Dr. Lazar."

"Very good Mr. Knox. You must understand that what you are attempting to do, getting this boy safely to England is a very dangerous proposition. Even if you succeed in your quest you will still have to stay on your toes for the rest of your lives in order to keep your little secret secure. I must have your word that if things do not go to plan for one reason or another that neither myself, nor Felix for that matter, will ever be implicated in the smuggling of the boy."

"Dr. Lazar you have my word."

"Very well, then come in and let me assist you."

Dr. Lazar led them up some creaking stairs to a room that sat above his surgery. For him his home and surgery conveniently belonged to the same premises. He offered three wooden chairs of very basic design to his unexpected visitors and then sat down himself into a dusty, worn looking cloth covered chair that did however serve the purpose of supporting his larger than average frame. He then switched on a table lamp to give the only contrived light to the room.

"May I have your passport Mr. Knox?"

Johnny took Callum's passport from his back pocket and passed it to the doctor.

For the first time Dr. Lazar spoke to the boy. "What is your name child?"

"Radu, Sir."

"WRONG!" The doctor's loud reply startled Felix and Johnny as well as the boy. "Until you reach England your name is Callum Knox, for that is the name on the passport. Do you understand?"

Radu nodded nervously.

The doctor reached over to a chest of drawers and pulled out a scalpel from the top drawer. He grinned at Johnny and spoke, "a scalpel has more than one use Mr. Knox, but of course there are no questions asked as to why a doctor of medicine has one in his possession."

With that the doctor turned to the rear pages of the passport and with admirable precision began to slice the plastic covering along the tip of the page used for identity purposes. Within five minutes he was able to peel back the plastic covering to expose the page in its raw state. Next he placed the passport onto a computer scanner and his captivated audience of three watched Callum Knox's photograph and identity details flash onto the monitor screen via some impressive software. He then began to hit the keyboard and was able to alter the date of birth, the passport issue date and the date of expiry accordingly. Then he printed off the transformed details looking every millimetre the genuine article, miraculously even including watermarks and securing the all-important microchip. When he carefully cut this to size the new details could be placed over the original details enabling them to blend with amazing accuracy. The original plastic covering was then replaced over the restructured identity page and stuck down with skilled precision. The end result was a passport that was as good as new except the dates had been altered, but to the naked eye it was near impossible to spot the doctor's tampering. It truly was a remarkable job well done and Johnny was convinced that it was 100 Euros well spent.

"I could have altered the photograph and the name Mr. Knox but I believe in a minimalist approach. The less tampering the less likely the alterations are to be noticed. Only the most vigilant passport controller who has bags of time and indeed motivation and reason would be able to notice the changes."

"You have done a wonderful job Dr. Lazar. Thank you." Although impressed with the doctor's unlawful work Johnny could not help reflecting on the passport with a heavy heart, for his beloved sons date of birth had been removed from the passport forever. He sighed a deep breath and told himself that the passport could now be used for the good of saving Radu. In a way Johnny took comfort that by using Callum's passport, it meant that his son was also helping with the orphan's plight as well.

"Before you go Mr. Knox shall I examine the boy as my medical duty dictates?"

"Okay, I guess so."

Dr. Lazar leant over to the boy and instructed him to open his mouth and stick out his tongue.

"Your throat seems okay but I can't help noticing how pale you look."

"Well as the boy has been living on what scraps he can find in the streets I guess that he hasn't been receiving his correct balance of nutrients," offered Johnny.

"Yes, I suppose that would explain things," replied the doctor. "I'll just feel his glands."

Dr. Lazar felt under the glands of Radu's neck and gently pulled at the boys clothing to gain access to the required area.

"What caused these two marks on your neck then boy?" enquired the doctor.

Felix shot a look of concern at Johnny, but Johnny was puzzled how the doctor's words didn't have any element of surprise in them, as if he was fully expecting to discover the marks on Radu's neck."

"I think I once suffered chicken pox or another type of rash. The spots on my neck were very itchy and I scratched them. I made them bleed and I have always kept the marks since."

"I don't mean to be rude Dr. Lazar, but the boy and I must leave now. We have a plane to catch."

"Indeed you have Mr. Knox. Good luck and have a safe journey."

The three men shook hands and quickly said their goodbyes. Felix led the way out, followed by Radu and finally Johnny.

Just before Johnny left the house Dr. Lazar rested a hand on his shoulder.

"It is still not too late to change your mind Mr. Knox."

"We'll be fine Dr. Lazar and thanks once again for your services."

"Please. I must give you a small gift before you leave. A token of friendship from one countryman to another."

Johnny felt Dr. Lazar slip something small, hard and metal-like into his hand.

"This gift is designed to offer protection Mr. Knox. Please never underestimate the power that it holds."

"Thank you Doctor. You are very kind."

"Good luck once more Mr. Knox." And with that Dr. Lazar closed the door behind them.

Johnny looked down at his hand to see what mysterious gift the doctor had given him. He was puzzled but believed that he should remain grateful as he looked at the object that sat in the palm of his hand.

Dr. Lazar had given him a small silver crucifix.

Chapter 11

As she sat anxiously in the uncomfortable blue coloured seat of the aeroplane, Sheena Knox was beginning to regret her decision for herself and her daughter to check in and board the plane destined for Birmingham International Airport. She wished that they had simply waited for Johnny in the Baneasa Airport lobby, but she had sensed Saffron's anxiety at her father's absence and wanted things to appear as normal as possible to the teenager. Inside her gut Sheena was as concerned as her daughter and now that Johnny had not showed so close to the time of departure her fears were growing as to what could have happened to him.

Johnny's cryptic phone call had offered no security, simply instructing Sheena and Saffron to go to the airport directly with out him.

But why?

Was he in some sort of danger and the instruction to go without him was simply so that his wife and daughter wouldn't also be in danger?

Should she have read more into his message?

Did he actually need her help?

Sheena stared out of the small window hoping to see some sign of her husband heading towards the plane, but he was nowhere to be seen and her concern for his safety was rapidly increasing.

"Perhaps he has found out some news about Callum, Mom?" offered Saffron.

Sheena squeezed her daughter's hand and smiled. "Let's hope so honey. I'm sure your father will be here any minute."

But Sheena was becoming less optimistic by the second.

"Here keep the change," instructed Johnny as he threw a wad of Romanian money at the taxi driver and led Radu by the hand at record speed into the airport lobby.

"Mult'umesc" replied the startled but appreciative driver.

Johnny raced to the check-in desk allocated for the flight to Birmingham.

"Buna ziua. My son and I need to board the flight to Birmingham please."

The stony faced receptionist asked to see their passports.

Johnny handed them over and prayed that Callum's would not raise suspicion now that it was designed to get Radu out of Romania. He fought desperately against his anxiety as the receptionist seemed to take an eternity studying the passport and then intermittently shifting her eyes towards Radu's direction. Johnny was convinced that she suspected something was amiss, but finally she handed the passports back to Johnny who was at this moment in time sweating more than he ever had done on the training ground.

"The passports are fine Mr. Knox, but only you are scheduled for the flight to Birmingham. I have no data regarding your son. Do you have a ticket for him?"

Johnny fumbled into his wallet and produced a single airline ticket. "Here, I have mine but unfortunately I can not locate my son's ticket. That is why we have checked in so late; I have been searching everywhere to find it. I am very sorry."

"I am sure you are Mr. Knox, but as I said your son is not even scheduled for the flight and without a ticket for him I don't see what I can do."

"Well there must be some mistake; I wouldn't book a flight for myself without including my son now would I?" Johnny prayed that his bluffing would hold up.

"I had a discussion with your wife earlier and she kindly alerted me to the fact that you were going to arrive late, I find it difficult to understand why she didn't mention that her son was also delayed, don't you Mr. Knox?"

"Well, err; I guess she just assumed that as she had our daughter with her you would understand that I naturally had our son with me."

The receptionist didn't speak but highlighted her annoyance by raising her eyebrows.

"Look", began Johnny. "I know the plane is due to leave soon and I know that I have been a bit naughty arriving late and losing my son's ticket, so to save any more difficulties let me purchase a new ticket for my son."

"I am afraid that the flight is fully booked Mr. Knox."

"Well I will still pay a full ticket price and my son can sit on my lap for the journey."

"I am sorry Mr. Knox, but that is strictly against airline regulations." The receptionist was beginning to mellow slightly at the desperation that Johnny was openly displaying, but she was also keen not to let her "jobsworth" crown fully slip.

"Look, Mr. Knox. There are two seats sitting vacant on that plane at the moment. You have one reserved for yourself and another gentleman has the other seat reserved but he too has also failed to check-in as yet. I am prepared to wait for a further five minutes to see if he arrives and if he does not then I will allow you to have his seat for your son."

"Mult'umesc. Thank you, Thank you" said Johnny.

Just then a distinguished looking character slid up to the desk. "Buna seara. Please accept my apologies for checking-in so late, but I have been snowed under with some private business. I also felt a bit peckish and decided to have a *bite* to eat. I never much care for processed airline food I'm afraid. My name is Professor Cezar Prodanescu and I have a seat booked on the flight to Birmingham International Airport in England."

Johnny's heart sank instantly.

The receptionist checked the gentleman's flight ticket and passport and stated the words of condemnation of Johnny's dilemma. "Thank-you, Professor Prodanescu. Please go to gate three and you may board your plane." The receptionist looked towards Johnny and appeared to have genuine sorrow in her eyes. "I am sorry Mr. Knox"

The professor sensed something was amiss. "Is something wrong?" enquired the professor.

"I was hoping to board that flight with my son, but there has been a bit of a mix up with his ticket. If you hadn't have checked in just then he was going to have your seat."

"Well that's awful. I'm in no great rush to get to Birmingham, I'm sure that the young lad can still have my seat and I am sure that this young lady can find me a seat on a later flight." The professor shot a persuasive look towards the receptionist that made her blood run cold and she obediently punched in some numbers on the computer.

"The next available seat is on a flight scheduled for tomorrow morning at 8.20 a.m. take off. You can have that one if you wish Professor."

"Well that sounds fine to me. I will check into the airport hotel for the night and indulge in the delights of my home country for one more evening."

"Professor Prodanescu, that is most generous of you. Please let me pay for your ticket and I will also pay the bill at your hotel and any additional expenses that you may occur," offered a relieved and grateful Johnny.

"Nonsense, I don't need you to pay for me, I'm just pleased that I have been able to assist you in your quest to fly with your son. He is your son isn't he?"

"I have already said that to you Professor."

"Of course you did, I forget things so easily these days."

Johnny looked at the professor and in spite of the generosity that he had displayed to him Johnny witnessed an unnerving sense of darkness in his eyes.

"He doesn't look like you though does he Mr. Knox? But then my children don't look like me either."

Johnny was beginning to wonder if the professor was on to his little scam of sneaking Radu out of the country under the guise of Callum Knox.

"What is your name?" asked the professor to Radu. The boy appeared terrified in the presence of the professor and Johnny answered the question for him.

"His name is Callum."

"Callum, I see. The boy does have a familiar face. Correct me if I am wrong but you are Johnny Knox the famous English footballer aren't you?"

"Yes I am." Johnny was convinced that as the professor had recognised him he probably also knew of Callum's disappearance. He also sensed that he had seen Radu before too.

"Well thanks again for your generosity Professor, but my son and I really do need to board the plane now."

"Oh, but I can't let you do that now can I Johnny?" The professor stopped Johnny from walking away by placing an icy cold palm on his chest.

No one spoke for a short while before the professor continued. "The least you can do for me Mr Knox is to give me your autograph before you board the plane."

"Oh, right. But of course."

The professor handed Johnny a piece of paper and Johnny signed it with his name.

"Thankyou Johnny. I hope you and your family have a safe journey."

"The same to you Professor."

Johnny and Radu hurried away from the scene and the enigmatic Professor Prodanescu towards gate three. Fortunately the tight timescale meant that Passport Control were less vigilant in their passport scrutiny than usual and before long Johnny's plan had finally been realised as they boarded Flight BIR7666 to Birmingham.

Sheena couldn't believe her eyes when she saw her husband come up the aisle followed by the head of a small boy bobbing up and down behind him. The infantile dark brown hair looked very familiar as it moved with the youngster's movements. The boy had his head down and as yet she hadn't been able to see his facial features. A volcano of excitement erupted inside her.

He's done it. Johnny's finally done it. He has found Callum.

But then Sheena's excitement quickly turned to heart wrenching disappointment and bewilderment as she realised that her only son would now be the same age as the daughter sitting beside her.

Sheena's attention quickly turned to just who was this boy accompanying her husband?

Johnny finally made his way to his seat and as luck would have it the seat that had been destined for Professor Prodanescu was amazingly next to Johnny's. He gently sat Radu down and looked towards his puzzled wife.

"What's going on Johnny?"

"Just trust me for now Sheena; I'll explain when I can. But for now all you need to do is act like this is your son."

Sheena shot a look at her husband that suggested to him that although he had survived the daunting risk of smuggling a boy out of his native country and dealing with an unnerving and intimidating professor, his biggest challenge of all was still ahead of him when he would have to explain to his wife exactly what he was playing at.

Chapter 12

Knox Residence, Toppmost Avenue, Private Estate near Lichfield

"You do understand why I did it don't you babe?"

"Johnny all I can think of right now is the welfare of this child, what on Earth is wrong with him?"

"It's probably just travel sickness from the flight," offered Johnny in desperation.

"Yes it could be, but yet again we don't know anything about the boy's medical history, it could be anything. I could kill you Johnny, I really could. You must be out of your mind to kidnap a boy like this. Because that's what it is when you strip away all your good intentions. You have kidnapped him. Shit, I'm involved now too aren't I? And even Saffron could be implicated. How could you be so stupid?"

"Sheena, how could I have kidnapped him? He doesn't belong to anyone for me to kidnap him from! The poor little mite is an orphan, used to living on the streets. He came with me of his own free will. His life was in danger for Christ's sake?"

"There are procedures to follow, Johnny. Legalities! And by the look of him his life could be in danger right now. I've never seen a child look so ill."

Radu had unexpectedly taken ill on the flight back to England. He had developed a raging fever and his conduct had seemed to adopt a pattern of disturbing incoherence. He had repeatedly claimed to be thirsty but all the fluids that he had been given on the plane, and since, had failed to quench his thirst. It had been an almighty effort by Sheena and Johnny to keep Radu calm and prevent him from drawing attention to himself and them. At times his behaviour was near hysterical. But at least they had now managed to get him inside their home without hopefully raising too much suspicion on the way.

"Sange, Sange!" cried Radu.

"There he goes again Johnny. What on Earth does he mean? He is beginning to frighten me."

"I don't know what he wants. Let's get him up to bed."

"I'm giving him one hour Johnny; if he doesn't show any signs of improvement then I'm calling the doctor."

"You can't do that can you, what will the authorities say? Let alone the press. We can't alert anyone to his existence just yet."

"Johnny, if something terrible happens to him the authorities will have a lot more to talk to you about than smuggling him out of Romania. Come on, you'll have to carry him upstairs."

Johnny reached down and picked Radu up who had quietened from his manic impulses of frantically shouting out the word "sange," but he still appeared gravely ill.

"Shall I put him in Callum's bed?" enquired Johnny as he ascended the stairs with the boy's head resting on his shoulder. His frenetic behaviour had seemed to exhaust the child.

"No, he can go in one of the guest rooms. Johnny, I know you miss Callum, I miss him too, but this little boy is not your son. He is not a substitute like in your football matches. This is real life Johnny, not a game."

Johnny kicked the door open to the bedroom and laid Radu on the bed. Radu seemed to drift off into near unconsciousness but quietly still mumbled the word "sange" as he drifted.

Sheena soon followed into the room regretting her harsh words to Johnny. Together they looked down at the boy who now seemed to have the most angelic face. It was hard to comprehend that only a few hours earlier they hadn't even known of his existence, but now here he was sleeping under their roof.

"He is cute isn't he?" said Sheena putting an arm around her husband.

"Yeah."

"Perhaps it was travel sickness after all, he seems fine now. I guess it's been quite a day for him. It was bound to be a little confusing for Radu to say the least. Let him sleep and we will see how he is in the morning."

"Perhaps he reacted badly to flying. I guess it's the first time he has been on an aeroplane, it probably just freaked him out."

"Johnny, you need to go and see Art Eddowes tomorrow. He needs to try and make this mess legal somehow."

"You mean we are going to keep Radu?"

"I guess we will have to. The poor little guy needs a proper home."

"You know he will never replace Callum, Sheena. That was never my intention. And I will never stop trying to find out what happened to Callum either."

"I know babe." Sheena reached forward and kissed her husband.

"And don't worry about the legalities. For the right price Art Eddowes can work miracles. He is the most efficient solicitor there is, and thankfully possibly the most bent too. There is no point in us having all this money if we can't put it to good use once in a while, and Radu needs us."

Just then Radu was joined on the bed by the family cat.

"Well it looks like Keegan is fond of the new addition to our family anyway. I wonder what Saffron will say though, this is her home too."

"Don't worry Mom," said Saffron as she also entered the room. "It will be fun to have a little brother about the place.

What Johnny and Sheena had failed to realise though was that Radu hadn't simply calmed down because he was naturally tired and in a secure environment.

Instead he was growing weaker by the second.

Chapter 13

Sheena calling read the display on Johnny's mobile phone as it rang out the tune of "Nessun Dorma." Johnny checked the rear view mirror of his convertible sports car and safely pulled over hitting the hazard lights so that he could take the call.

"Hi babes, it's as good as done. Art says the paperwork can easily be done and he can pull a few strings to make Radu's adoption legal. He even suggested running it in the press with himself overseeing it, he reckons we'll be hailed as heroes for adopting a Romanian orphan, but I told him to hold back on that idea, as we just wanted to give Radu a happy and stable upbringing. I made it clear that we weren't adopting him as any kind of publicity stunt. How is the little fellow, has he woke yet?"

"Oh *he's* fine. It's Keegan who isn't."

"What do you mean?"

"I mean he has killed the fucking cat."

"What!"

"Radu has killed Keegan! I don't quite know how but I went into the bedroom this morning and Radu was sitting up in bed without a glimmer of the illness he was portraying last night, but Keegan was lying next to him in a small pool of blood."

"Did you ask Radu for an explanation?"

"Too right I did, but he said he couldn't remember anything about last night."

"Well perhaps Radu didn't do it, perhaps Keegan got caught up in some kind of freak accident."

"Johnny, he was lying right next to Radu on the bed. That kid may be cute but he is also fucking weird. Look he has made me curse twice already in this conversation and you know that I never usually swear, Johnny."

"Okay, I'm on my way home. I'll talk to Radu and see if I can make any sense of this." Johnny began to recall the warnings given to him by the four men who had chased Radu on that last night in Romania. One of them had specifically stated that things could be different come morning time. Now the warnings were beginning to ring true.

"But you have to meet up with the squad for the pre-season fixtures."

"I'll phone Daryl and tell him I'll drive to Scotland myself later and skip travelling on the team coach. Luckily the pre-season tour isn't overseas this year."

"Hold on Johnny, it's okay . . . I don't believe it?"

Johnny sensed the anxiety in Sheena's voice.

"What is it Sheena?"

"It's Keegan. He . . . he is alive! He has just walked through the back kitchen door. But he was dead. I'm sure of it!"

"Well obviously he isn't Sheena!"

"Whatsmore he has got a bird in his mouth. A huge wood pigeon almost the size of him with its head missing!"

"But Keegan's crap at hunting!"

"Not anymore he isn't"

"Is everything okay now honey?"

"Yeah, I'm sorry Johnny. I'll sort Keegan and this dead bird out and you carry on to meet up with the boys. I'll ring you later. Have fun in Scotland."

"Okay babe. Call me if you need me."

"Bye, love you."

"Love you too. Everything's going to be okay, Sheena. I promise."

Chapter 14

Broad Street in the heart of Birmingham's city centre is the gateway to many of the city's prize assets. The National Indoor Arena sits at the very southern tip of Broad Street and is a major venue for various high profile rock and comedy concerts. Based near to that are the city's resident theatre company and their playhouse and opposite that is the registry office for marriages, births and deaths. The adjacent Conference Centre is even able to boast the hosting of the G8 Summit in 1998 when the world leaders met to discuss key issues. The then USA President Bill Clinton enjoyed a pint of Real English Ale whilst sitting in the glorious sunshine on the balcony of *The Malt House,* a canal side pub, generously waving to the city folk of Birmingham as they walked by. Birmingham's famous canal network is actually best accessed from Broad Street, and it is often not realised by many that Birmingham in reality holds more waterways than Italy's Venice. But Broad Street is also a haven of quality nightlife to rival any city in Europe, or even the world over, comprising of an impressive cocktail of hotels, restaurants, bars and clubs.

Professor Cezar Prodanescu had earlier checked into one such hotel and was now sitting in one of the bars leisurely sipping a *Bloody Mary.* This was after all his favourite tipple. He had chosen to sit near the front window that looked out directly onto the street in a bid to keep himself entertained by the unsuspecting population that presented themselves to him as they hurried to their own particular destination.

Groups of lads with their testosterone raging passed by wearing immaculately ironed shirts, belying their usual claims that it was women's work to iron as they could simply do it better than they could. It didn't matter that in just a few hours time the inevitable result would be that those same expensive shirts would be hanging untidily out of their trousers complete with a decoration of beer stains.

The professor noticed that there were definitely more people going out in groups than as couples, including mixed sex groups, and their ages could span from anything between late teens to early forties.

In contrast to the groups of males with their smart shirts and designer jeans or trousers, the female night owls appeared to prefer wearing as little clothing as possible, with extremely short skirts and skimpy tops. The professor momentarily turned away from the window to gaze across the inside of the building and noticed many of these groups intermingling giving the impression that the bar was more like some sort of human cattle market where individuals could offer themselves up for some late night entertainment with a complete stranger, or even strangers. It was reassuringly clear however that some groups were simply out to have a good time collectively by staying close and loyal to their friends.

Professor Prodanescu then noticed something very unexpected. A young lady sitting on her own, seemingly without any company at all. This was not a usual sight in the bars of Broad Street. The professor got up from his chair and moved in the direction of the woman assuming that she may be glad of some company. Before he had reached her however, his passage was rudely halted by a shaven-headed yob clumsily banging in to him spilling some of the contents of the professor's Bloody Mary.

"Oi Dad. Watch where you are going."

The yobs insolence seemed to amuse his two equally unappealing friends.

"I think you will find that you banged into me," replied the professor calmly. "You are very lucky that my drink only spilled on to the floor and not on my shirt. You see my shirt is white and I would not have liked a red stain on it."

The yob was surprised that the older stranger with a foreign accent had dared to stand his ground and he turned to confront the professor.

"Listen pops, I'm not quite sure where you are from but luckily for you the night is young and I don't feel like smashing someone's face in just yet, so be a good little foreigner and get out of my fucking face before I change my mind."

"I am afraid I must correct you again, for it is you who is in my face."

One of the yob's side-kicks decided to speak up. "Come on Smithy. Leave the old boy alone; we have got a lot of serious drinking to do."

"If I see you later foreigner, you will be sorry."

Still unshaken by the yobs menacing presence Professor Prodanescu moved his face in closer, never once breaking his stare. He appeared to gently grab the yobs upper arm but he began to squeeze it with an unnatural and enormous pressure.

"You had better hope that I don't see you later Smithy, or it will be you that is sorry. I may yet make you responsible for subjecting a red stain upon my shirt. The red of your blood."

Smithy became uncharacteristically unnerved by the professor's intensity and wisely retreated from the situation, pretending to laugh away the incident in a pathetic attempt not to lose face in the presence of his cronies.

Satisfied for now that the confrontation was over, the professor began once again to move towards the lone woman.

"Hello, I hope you don't mind but I am new in town and I noticed that like myself you seem to be drinking alone. Would you mind if I joined you?"

The young lady brushed a strand of her blonde hair behind her ear as she looked at the professor and contemplated his proposal. Okay, he was older than she was but to her that gave the stranger an essence of trust. Besides he was extremely good looking and charismatic, and appeared to make a welcome change to the single-minded morons that usually propositioned her on a night out. His accent also possessed a curious appeal.

"Sure, take a seat. My name is Lily."

"Lily, such a beautiful name and such a beautiful flower. It is appropriate for someone as pretty as you."

"Flattery will get you everywhere. It was my grandmother's name."

"And I am sure that your grandmother was just as beautiful as you. In fact perhaps I have met her?"

"I doubt it, she has been dead for over 10 years and I know that you are not that old."

"Lily, I may have been around a lot longer than you think."

"You may have some distinguishing grey hairs showing, but you can only be in your late forties at the most . . ."

Cezar raised his eyebrows as if to say, "guess again."

"Fifties? No way I don't believe you."

"My dear Lily. A gentleman never asks a lady her age and he certainly never discloses his own."

"You are a gentleman aren't you? Forgive me I did not mean to be nosey."

"Nosey?" enquired the professor.

"Oh, it's an English expression for prying. Can I be nosey again and ask this particular gentleman his name?"

"Of course. If I was a true gentleman I would have introduced myself at the outset."

"You seem a safer bet than the jokers that usually come in here. So what is your name?"

"Professor Cezar Prodanescu."

"Blimey, a professor no less. Very impressive. I noticed your accent, but couldn't quite place it until now on hearing your name. Am I correct in thinking that a name ending in *escu* is Romanian?"

"Very good, I am impressed. Now, it is my turn to be . . . how do you say . . . nosey."

"I'll allow it," smiled Lily.

"Why on Earth is a beautiful young lady like you sitting on her own?"

"Well believe it or not I think I've been stood up."

"Stood up? Another English expression?"

"Yeah, it means my date has not shown."

"The man must be a fool."

"No Cezar, I'm the fool. I was engaged to be married for three years. We had the wedding booked and everything arranged and then I discover that Lucas, the guy I was going to marry, has cheated on me not once, not twice, but so many times he can't remember by his own admission. He is a serial cheater. And I was still prepared to give him another chance. We had arranged to meet tonight and discuss our future. He was meant to show over an hour ago. He hasn't phoned or texted to tell me if he is still coming or running late at all."

"You shouldn't have to Lily, but why don't you phone him. You never know he may have been injured in an accident."

"Cezar, don't make excuses for him. I should have known that you would see his side of things. All men are the same. I thought that you might be different."

"Lily, I apologise. I did not mean to offend you and I am certainly not taking the side of this Lucas. I simply wish to know if he is definitely not coming because if that is the situation then I would like to take you out of here for a *bite* to eat, or even to the theatre. I have noticed that one of my favourite musicals is showing, *Blood Brothers*. It would be my treat naturally."

Lily reached over to Cezar and stroked his cheek. Although tender she was surprised at how cold it felt.

"You know what Cezar that sounds a lovely idea. You really are very sweet. I would love to accompany you on this evening. And do you know what we are going to celebrate. We are going to celebrate my finally getting rid of that loser

Lucas. It is definitely over between us from this very moment on. Why on Earth was I giving him another chance anyway? To be honest with you Cezar I stopped loving him weeks ago. He killed every bit of love that I had in him and I was still willing to meet him tonight. Why?"

"Because I have been around long enough to conclude that you are a lovely and considerate young lady. You are a selfless individual who puts other people's happiness before your own. Well tonight Lily you are going to be the centre of attention and I am going to give you a night that you will never forget. We are going to go out on the streets of Birmingham and literally paint the town *red*."

"Oh Cezar, I can't wait."

As Lily reached for her handbag, Cezar turned to see Smithy, the ill-mannered yob from earlier making his way up the staircase towards the toilets.

"Sit tight, Lily," he instructed. "I just need to pop to the Gents for a moment before we leave."

"Okay. Don't be too long."

"Don't worry, Lily. I won't be any time at all."

Chapter 15

Daryl Weir had deliberately chosen his native Scotland as the venue for the team's pre-season tour so that he could once again soak up the delights of his beloved homeland in addition to enabling the player's to participate in some valuable preparation matches for the season ahead.

The choice to avoid travelling overseas for a costly pre-season tour was also a major relief for chairman Peter Cogshaw. Furthermore the decision to travel from Birmingham to Scotland by road, quite a considerable and lengthy distance, was a deliberate cost cutting exercise by Cogshaw, who was still smarting about being relegated to the Championship. The squad had requested to be flown by plane to Glasgow and then they could transfer to a travel coach from the airport, but Cogshaw felt this was an unnecessary expense. For once Daryl Weir didn't put up much of a fight on behalf of his players as he wanted to scrape as much money together from whatever means possible to improve his squad after losing some key players, and in truth he relished the thought of admiring the countryside of his beloved Scotland through the relaxing view of a coach window. Besides he was terrified of flying, no matter how swift the time of the flight could be.

Of course travelling by coach meant that the squad finally reached their hotel fairly late in the day. It was in a beautiful setting overlooking Loch Lomond, a sight that made Daryl Weir boom with pride.

It was Daryl who got off the coach first, and waited at the steps until each member of his squad were safely off the coach, giving the impression that he was a teacher minding a group of school kids on a school outing. The protectiveness of *his* squad simply came second nature to Daryl.

It was anticipated that some 200 or so loyal Kingsbarr United supporters would also be making the trip up to Scotland to support their team on the pre-season tour. About twenty-five of these hardcore fans had even managed to check into the same hotel as the squad of Kingsbarr players and they had been waiting eagerly in the car park for the coach to arrive.

The players collected their luggage and headed for the entrance of the hotel where the Kingsbarr fans greeted them.

"Hi Johnny, will you sign this for me?"

"Gene Macgoree, you must have my autograph more than a hundred times already."

"I know Johnny, but this is now adding your signature to the official Kingsbarr pre-season tour magazine."

"You are certainly a true fan, Gene. I hope we make this tour worth your while." Johnny took the magazine from the fan's grasp and duly signed his autograph.

"Macgoree. Are you in your homeland too?" intercepted Daryl Weir keen to share his passion for his homeland with whoever would listen.

"My father was Scottish. He came down to Birmingham to be with my mother. He was a musician in a band from Scotland. They were fairly successful and toured the UK having a regular spot in the Birmingham pub where my mother worked as a barmaid. They fell in love; the rest is history as they say."

Gene Macgoree was a simple yet complex character. Many thought him to be a bit odd but a harmless enough person. His full title was actually Gene Macgoree Dip.para.psychol MOC MSFTR, in recognition of his Diploma that he had achieved in Parapsychology. He was by his own admission a fairly asexual person never possessing a great craving for the sexual pleasure from either men or women. Instead, his passion was investigating the paranormal and following Kingsbarr United, and as long as he was able to actively participate in those two things he was *as happy as Larry.*

In his late thirties Gene Macgoree was below the average height of a British male standing little over 5 feet 5 inches tall. He was not particularly fussed about his appearance choosing to spend his money on ghost-hunting equipment, books for research and Kingsbarr United memorabilia instead of the latest designer fashions. Of course he always purchased a season ticket for Beacon Park each season as well. Gene's neglect of designer clothes was not due to any shortage of money either; he made a decent enough living appearing on satellite TV shows answering questions about the paranormal and had even penned a handful of successful books on the subject.

Macgoree had always worn a beard ever since he was able to grow one and his severe short-sightedness was compensated by round metal framed spectacles, not unlike the ones made famous by John Lennon, although Macgoree needed to have the lens so thick that his eyes appeared to be something like three times their natural size.

In spite of his lack of height and unthreatening appearance, Gene Macgoree also had an amazing lack of fear. He had single-handedly maintained ghost hunts, often sleeping alone in a cemetery or a suspected haunted house, and was also a self-proclaimed expert in vampirism, yet at present there was no Diploma or Degree available to recognise his fascinating and admirable knowledge on the subject. Gene did however believe that this was probably for the best at present, as he didn't believe that society was ready to accept the concept that vampires *do* really exist other than in Hollywood movies and comic books. Gene also realised that some misguided individuals had claimed to be vampires when they simply belonged to a warped cult where they drank each other's blood, but possessed no supernatural tendencies or powers whatsoever. He was keen not to be associated with such people. He was happy instead for those who did know of his curiosity in vampires to see it purely as a bit of fun and not anything unhealthy at all, as presented in his love of Black Sabbath music and vampire DVD collection.

How horrified they would be to know that he had in fact carried out many genuine vampire slayings.

Johnny handed the autographed magazine back to Gene.

"Thanks, Johnny. I'll add that to my collection."

"I reckon that your collection would fetch a tidy sum on an internet auction site."

"Johnny. How dare you suggest such a thing? You know I could never part with any of my Kingsbarr memorabilia."

"I know Gene, I'm only joking. You must have a big room put aside for it all."

"Oh, yeah. I've err . . . got the space alright." Gene felt uncomfortable with Johnny's question knowing that the "big room" was a secret locked vault under his Victorian home, which also safely guarded his equipment used for his paranormal investigations and his vampire slaying paraphernalia too. "Oh, Johnny by the way, congratulations on the adoption of your son."

"Oh thanks. The young lad needed a home so we were happy to give him one."

"This sick world needs more people like you and your wife in it Johnny."

"Thanks, Gene. That is a nice thing to say."

"The boy is Romanian I believe."

"Yes that is correct. Do you know Romania at all?"

"Yes, I know it very well Johnny. My line of work can sometimes dictate my presence there. In particular the Transylvanian area of the country."

"How interesting, we must chat more sometime. I must get into the hotel now though Gene. You take care."

"You take care too Johnny. I want you to know that I am always available should you or any of your family need me. Including Radu."

"Okay, Gene," replied Johnny, thinking that Gene's allegiance was a little strong. "That's very reassuring to know." He knew that Gene was a massive fan of Kingsbarr, but he had always respected the privacy of the players and was always keen not to appear intrusive.

Daryl Weir crudely interrupted Johnny's trail of thought "Come on Knox, shift your arse!"

"I'm on my way boss."

Chapter 16

As always on away games Johnny was sharing his hotel room with his midfield partner Vincent "Bruiser" Bradshaw. Fortunately Vincent was in the shower when Johnny phoned home to Sheena.

"Hi babe. How are things?"

"I don't know Johnny, Radu's acting real weird again."

"How?"

"Well he was getting a bit wild and feverish again and started shouting out s*ange* like before."

"What does that mean? *Sange*? Why does he keep acting like this?"

"I'm beginning to think he may be hallucinating when he gets hungry, the kid could be suffering a low blood sugar deficiency or something. I think we need him to be checked out medically. Now we have him legally adopted it shouldn't be a problem."

"Well is he okay now?"

"I've locked him in his room."

"What? You can't do that."

"I had no choice. You weren't here and he was going so wild I was frightened for Saffron. I know he is only a small child but he was displaying the rage of a wild animal. I'm not sure if we should even get him checked over by a child psychiatrist."

"What on Earth could be wrong with that boy? How is Keegan? Has Radu hurt him again?"

"That's another weird thing. Radu and Keegan have been inseparable all day, as if they have been the best of companions all of their lives. When I was trying to discipline Radu, Keegan started hissing at me as if he were trying to protect him. I have managed to lock him in the room with Radu as well although I don't know how I managed to do it. Keegan has always been such a loving and docile cat. It's as if Radu has brought something out in him."

"Sheena, you sound crazy!"

"Well how crazy is this. I started to cook Radu a joint of steak, as I was concerned that it was his hunger driving him wild, and it had hardly been in the frying pan when Keegan ran up and dragged it out and brought it to Radu in its uncooked state. And do you know what they did?"

"No."

"Our new son and the family cat began to eat it! They were like savages; especially Radu, and they ate the whole fucking thing . . . See I'm fucking swearing again now . . . Then they looked up at me with the blood from the steak still dripping down their manic faces. Radu stated to demand more and kept shouting that fucking word *sange, sange* so that was when I got them up to the room under false pretences promising Radu that there would be more raw meat if he waited in the bedroom whilst I popped out to the butchers, which I never did of course."

"Do you need me to come home Sheena?"

"No. I can cope, but I'm not unlocking that door until morning. Radu seems perfectly genteel in the daytime, but as soon as night starts drawing in he goes wild. He is craving raw meat for Christ's sake, and whatsmore he has eaten it! If he is not ill now he certainly soon will be."

"This sounds like pure madness Sheena. I don't like the thought of you putting up with this by yourself. Are you sure that you will be okay?"

"Yeah, anyway Radu seems to have calmed down now. He has stopped trying to bang the door down for the last 5 minutes or so. I'll be okay."

"Is that the *fucking slag* on the phone, Johnny?" Vincent Bradshaw had finished his shower and had ventured unnoticed into the room.

"Yeah, Vinnie. It's Sheena."

"Hi Vinnie."

"Sheena says Hi Vinnie."

"Hi Sheena and *Fuck off* . . . Sorry."

Johnny terminated the conversation, "I'll be home in a few days. See you soon."

"Okay Johnny, good luck with the football matches. Goodbye."

Johnny heard the phone line go dead and he hung up.

"Fucking hell Vinnie, can't you put a towel around you; you'll put me off my cocoa."

"Jealousy will get you nowhere, Johnny. When God cursed me with Tourette's Syndrome he knew that he had to even things up by blessing me with such a magnificent cock between my legs. The girls don't need to rely on me to whisper sweet nothings in their ear when I can fuck their brains out with the 'Beast of Bradshaw.'" Vinnie then took his manhood proudly in his hands. "They have all they need right here."

"Whatever."

"By the way, blood."

"What?"

"Blood."

"What are you on about Vinnie, or are you displaying a tick my friend?"

"I heard you on the phone to *the fucking slag* Sheena. You said you didn't know what sange meant."

"Go on."

"It is Romanian for the word blood."

Chapter 17

"Hello Smithy!"

Smithy let the cigarette fall from the corner of his mouth as it fell open. He hardly had time to zip up the opening to his jeans after relieving himself at the urinal before Cezar Prodanescu was lunging at him with unnatural force. Cezar slammed Smithy against the wall and even allowed the pathetic yob to take a swing at him, which Cezar easily dodged to his obvious pleasure as detailed by his mocking laughter.

"You'll have to do better than that Smithy," mocked the professor, but Smithy never got a second chance to defend himself against his much stronger opponent.

Cezar punched Smithy in the stomach completely knocking the breath out of him and as the yob doubled over, Cezar caught hold of him and flung him crashing through the door of one of the cubicles resulting in Smithy badly smashing his head on the ceramic base of the toilet as it halted his flight.

Cezar followed his victim into the cubicle and stood astride the blubbering yob as he lifted his barely conscious body by his clothing.

"Now listen to me you piece of insolent scum, and listen well. Can you hear me?"

Smithy managed a slight nod of acknowledgement as he drifted in and out of consciousness.

"There is no place for you on this Earth, you are nothing more than a waste of space infecting the air that good people breathe, and for that I am not going to grant you the pleasure of eternal life. As much as I will despise the taste of your shitty blood, I am going to drain every last drop from your pathetic body and I will spare you no mercy at all."

By this time Smithy was virtually paralysed by the weakness from his injuries and an overwhelming sense of fear and confusion, but Cezar was still able to take a tremendous amount of satisfaction from the unmistaken terror that Smithy was unable to conceal in his eyes.

For a few seconds those eyes of Smithy's widened, speaking silent volumes inspired by complete shock and pain as Cezar penetrated the yobs neck with his vampire fangs.

When the professor had finally completed the killing, Smithy's eyes remained open but were now lifeless and glazed—a snapshot of the vicious and merciless slaughter by the master vampire known as Professor Cezar Prodanescu.

Cezar casually glanced down at his shirt and smiled at the irony of a small bloodstain as he recalled the earlier confrontation that he had shared with Smithy.

Content with his slaying, Cezar turned from Smithy's blood-drained corpse to face an uncalculated problem.

A witness.

The toilet attendant was staring nervously straight at the professor. Sweat was ferociously running down his head like a waterfall of trepidation.

"What did you see boy?"

"Nothing Sir, honest." The words were barely audible as they quivered in their African accent.

Cezar realised that the toilet attendant was lying and had ultimately seen too much.

"Sorry son. I'm not usually greedy. I've had more than enough for one night, but I'm afraid this is a classic case of you being in the wrong place at the wrong time."

"Please don't hurt me," stammered the attendant, but Cezar began to protrude his vampire fangs once more and promptly sank them into the neck of the youth. Although Cezar felt that this unfortunate person didn't deserve the exact same fate as Smithy, to save complications the attendant was also denied eternal life as an incarnate vampire.

Cezar went across to the sink area and picked up various bottles of aftershave, usually the tools of the trade for the African toilet attendant, and quickly emptied them all over the bodies of his two victims. He then searched around in Smithy's pockets and found a cigarette lighter which he promptly used to set fire to the corpses. Fire was one of the few ways that would definitely ensure that neither of these two would be coming back to life as a vampire. More importantly, for tonight's purposes it would conceal any traces of vampire activity and should hopefully reveal the deaths as nothing more than a tragic fire accident.

Cezar came out of the toilets amazingly and fortunately unnoticed, and he remained incognito as he smashed the protective glass to the fire alarm that was placed on the wall near by.

Panic quickly rippled through the occupants of the club as the fire alarm rang out through the pandemonium. Cezar managed to return to where a bemused Lily was waiting and grabbed her hand to lead her out of the bar.

"Come on, let's get out of here," said the professor.

"What's going on? Cezar, you have blood on your shirt."

"I was on my way back to you Lily, when someone suddenly shouted 'FIRE'. God knows exactly where in the pub it is, but I suggest we don't wait to find out."

"But the blood on your shirt, Cezar. How did it get there?"

"When someone shouted 'FIRE', a chap nearby smashed the glass on the fire alarm and I think he cut his hand in the process. His blood must have spurted on to me. Never mind, a splash of blood on my shirt is a small price to pay to get out of here alive, we owe a lot to that quick thinking individual."

As Cezar got out of the door into the cool air on Broad Street Lily turned to speak. "Well Professor Prodanescu. I have hardly been in your company and already you are showing me a *hot* time."

Cezar smiled. "Believe me my dear Lily, the night is still young."

Cezar and Lily walked off down Broad Street away from the pub and its chaos just as the Fire Brigade arrived.

Radu's thirst was raging and his hunger for blood was increasing at an alarming rate. He walked over to the window which had been propped open earlier by Sheena to let in some fresh air and before long he had ventured out into the darkness with his new friend Keegan following close behind. They each scoured the streets around them for any likely and unfortunate prey.

Keegan spotted the snooty ginger cat that belonged to the lawyer at the house opposite. The two felines had never seen eye to eye, with the ginger cat usually edging the outcome of the squabbles. With Keegan's new persona and desire for blood, this time there could only be one victor. And Ginger knew it; displaying the extraordinary sixth sense that animals do when faced with the supernatural he could see a significant change in his old sparring partner. He turned on a sixpence and headed for home as fast as his little ginger legs could carry him, but it was a futile escape as Keegan reached his old enemy in lightning and unnatural speed and pinned Ginger down with the strength unbecoming of a cat.

Keegan's claws dug deep into his enemy's back as he could see the pathetic terror staring from the ginger cat's eyes pleading Keegan to spare its life. There was no chance that Keegan was going to let the cat live and he sunk his fangs into Ginger's neck. With each sucking of blood down his gullet, Keegan became more and more satisfied knowing it was the last time that his enemy with the unimaginative name would ever be picking a fight with him. Keegan realised that he was now top *dog* around here.

Suddenly Keegan's pleasure was interrupted as Radu grabbed the barely lifeless cat from Keegan's clutches.

"Hey, Keegan give me some."

Keegan didn't resist Radu snatching his prey, obeying his newfound master just as the "hounds of hell" would obey the Devil himself.

Radu sucked what little blood was left of poor Ginger and then tossed him aside far from satisfied.

"Come on Keegan, we need to find more sange."

The two comrades ventured further into the night and thanks to Keegan's hunting skills were able to feast upon a total of five rats, two wood pigeons, a nest of collared-doves and a magpie between them. It was enough blood to keep them satisfied for another 24 hours.

They returned to the house and back through the open window undetected. Later Sheena checked in on them and was relieved to find them curled up together sleeping like babies totally unaware of the night of blood sucking that they had enjoyed.

Tonight it had been a feast of pets and urban animals. It wouldn't be long before their appetites would demand a much bigger catch.

Chapter 18

In the hotel bar the majority of the Kingsbarr United squad and a hardcore of twelve or so Kingsbarr supporters were enjoying a few late night beers. With the first game of the pre-season tour of Scotland not for another two days Daryl had allowed this to happen as long as they didn't go overboard with their frivolity. Daryl Weir could be a strict disciplinarian when it came to managing his squad of players, but even he believed that the ethos of all work and no play was an unhealthy one.

Giuseppe Rossi, the squad's Italian striker was as silky with his feet on the dance floor as he was on the football pitch and he was disappointed at the lack of opportunity that was available in rural Scotland for his idea of nightlife. He prided himself on his conquests of the opposite sex and was unrivalled as the team's recognised playboy. Although this frivolous side to Rossi far from pleased the disciplined Daryl Weir, the Scottish manager also had the intellect to understand the marketing commodity of his good-looking Italian striker.

His lifestyle possibly hindered Rossi from being a truly exceptional footballer; he could show patches of pure brilliance but was an inconsistent player and he was particularly suffering in the team without the support of the influential Gerry Spalding along side him. Weir realised though that if Giuseppe had been in consistent mood last season then his Italian striker would more than likely have been another player to have left the club. The Kingsbarr United manager was confident that even a below-par Giuseppe Rossi should be capable of causing the defences of the Championship sides a lot of problems.

"I don't mean to cause offence boys but I am so bored. Is there nowhere around here with a bit of life?"

"Is our eloquent company not good enough for you Giuseppe?" joked Johnny.

"As much as I love your company Skipper, you are incapable of satisfying my needs as a man if you know what I mean."

"Fuck me," intercepted Vinnie. "The Italian Stallion's on heat again."

"I can not help it if I like to give pleasure to the opposite sex. I believe God put me upon this Earth to bring happiness and joy to as many women as possible." Giuseppe crossed himself as he spoke.

"St. Giuseppe, the patron saint of services to women. The problem with that my friend is I do not believe that you are meant to break their hearts afterwards by never striking up a serious relationship with any of them."

"Johnny, variety is the spice of life. Besides it would be inhumane of me to only give my services to one woman. Think of all the ladies who would be deprived of a chance of a piece of Giuseppe."

"Well there is a tasty looking female sitting over there all on her lonesome, and she has been looking this way all night. Don't you want to bless her with your mission on Earth Giuseppe?" said Jody Roper, the Kingsbarr United centre-half.

"Jody, I have already noticed the lady in question and I realise why she is alone. She is not worthy of a piece of Giuseppe with a face like that. She is so pale and haggard looking that she obviously can not attract a male companion to be with."

"Well I think she is a bit of alright," retorted Jody.

"Well in that case my friend, I suggest that you go over and chat her up yourself. As there is nothing on offer for me I think that I am going to get into the manager's good books and have an early night. There is hopefully a good adult channel in the hotel room to keep me entertained."

"Have you forgotten that you are sharing with Cheng on this trip Giuseppe?" said Johnny. "He won't allow you to watch porn in his room."

"Yeah, he is more clean-living than Mother Teresa," laughed Vinnie.

"And I wouldn't argue with him if I was you, he is a black belt in Kung Fu," said Jody.

"Oh well it would be too frustrating watching a good porn film without a woman beside me anyway. I bet it wouldn't be hardcore enough either in this boring place. I know what Jody, you go and pull that girl you fancy and you and her can put on a little show for us."

Everyone laughed.

"Bollocks to that. I think I will go and make her acquaintance though. I can take her back to the room safe in the knowledge that Alvin will be sat at that bar for a good while yet enjoying his rum and cokes and cigars."

"Good luck Jody, I think you'll need it," mocked Giuseppe.

Everyone laughed again.

Jody Roper stood at 6 feet five inches and like Vinnie "Bruiser" Bradshaw and Gerry Spalding he was as hard as nails. Although Daryl Weir didn't believe in dirty tactics on the football field he felt it a necessary ingredient for his well-organised team to possess a certain amount of players who could stand their ground and roll their sleeves up when the going got tough. In Johnny Knox he was unusually blessed with a player who could not only take a game by the scruff of the neck, but was able to portray dazzling flair and skill too.

Jody was a lover of eighties music and even style, sometimes making him the playful target of his team-mates jokes, but they all benefited from the pre-match ritual in the dressing room of Jody's eighties music booming out inspirationally as they prepared for the game ahead. The likes of Wham!, Duran Duran and Spandau Ballet had speared the United team to many a victory over the years, and although the eighties magic had not seemed to help the team last season it was now accepted that the music was always going to be played before a match, possibly even when Jody eventually leaves the club.

Jody's rugged features did not make him an obvious hit with the ladies, and his long curly black hair did little to aid his looks, but he had an unusually angelic singing voice, which totally belied his appearance. He loved getting up and singing his heart out at Karaoke nights, obviously always choosing songs from the eighties decade and was even booked to do a guest appearance at Gerry Spalding's wedding!

He approached the girl who was sitting on her own as the others looked on to measure his success. When he sat down next to her and gave a secret thumbs up behind his back, they knew that his mission to pull her had been successful. However, his teammates were surprised at the speed of his success.

Before long Jody's team-mates were able to witness the newly acquainted couple leave their seats and head out of the bar area.

"Mama Mia," said Giuseppe. "Even I don't usually work that quickly."

"Relax, Stallion," piped up Vinnie. "She's probably a hooker. A girl . . . *fucking slag* . . . on her own in a hotel bar, it doesn't take Einstein . . . *clever cunt* . . . to work that one out." The excitement was causing Vinnie's Tourette's symptoms to escalate.

"Jody wouldn't pay for it," said Johnny. "Who knows perhaps he has finally found the love of his life."

Chapter 19

Cezar and Lily fell into the professor's hotel room amidst a mutual clinch of electric passion. Cezar somehow managed to close the door behind him and turn a light on whilst Lily's hands roamed the well—sculptured torso beneath his shirt, and her mouth and tongue ironically worked frantically at his neck.

If only she was aware of the amount of sinister neck action that Professor Cezar Prodanescu's mouth had indulged in during his slayings as a vampire. Not to mention the blood-sucking that had occurred only hours earlier as the thug Smithy and the African toilet attendant had both fell victims to the master vampire!

If only Lily was aware of the fate that was planned for her own sweet and pretty neckline too.

Before long they had found their way to the inviting double bed and were writhing in pleasure as they kissed and fondled each other upon the silk sheets. By now Lily had skilfully removed Cezar's shirt belying her innocent demeanour, but she was so swept away with her passion for the older man she was surprising herself just how liberating she was becoming in his presence. They had shared such a wonderful evening together that Lily simply forgot to view Cezar for what he really was to her, virtually a stranger.

A noise of pleasure escaped from Lily as she momentarily lost her breath when Cezar's hand found its way up her skirt and gently rubbed at her panties. She was slightly embarrassed knowing that Cezar must have felt the wetness of the black cotton and her obvious vulnerability.

"May I?" enquired Cezar as his index finger ran along the top of Lily's knicker line just catching the top of her pubic hair.

"Even now you find time to be a gentleman. You are so sweet. I will allow you to go further Cezar but I don't want you to think that I would be like this with anyone. It's just that . . . well I really like you Cezar . . . I feel really comfortable with you." The dim light prevented Cezar from seeing her blush.

They engaged in a kiss once more and Cezar gently undressed the younger girl to her obvious delight. He too felt an unusual rush of ecstasy run through him as Lily unzipped his trousers and guided his manhood into her moist opening. She gave a little moan of pleasure as he entered her. Lily benefited from Cezar's wealth of sexual experience as he masterfully thrust into her, first slowly and then to a performance at a much wilder pace that was playing Lily's emotions of passion like a violin. She couldn't help but compare the often ineffectual and selfish performance that Lucas would conjure up for her in the guise of so-called lovemaking. Unknown to her now firmly ex-boyfriend was that she would often pretend to go to the bathroom to "clean-up" when really it was to finish herself off with a spot of D-I-Y. Lucas could never satisfy her and pathetically never really tried, totally ignorant to a woman's needs, but here she was close to orgasm from pure penetration with a man that she had never had sex with before! Intermittently Cezar was able to show her in between his playful thrusts that he knew his way around the important parts of a woman's body.

Funnily enough Cezar was surprising himself just how unmechanical his sexual approach was to this girl that he had only met tonight. His plans for the night had been the usual scenario of picking up a girl, enjoying a bit of casual sex and then drinking her blood by penetrating her neck with his vampire fangs! He was however enjoying this sexual liaison with the young Lily and was in no rush to finish it.

What was more unusual was that he liked her. He really liked her.

Suddenly Cezar became ashamed of his weakness.

Just kill her. He thought to himself.

His thrusting into Lily became more violent and he attempted to detach himself from the situation. He quickly moved his head to her neck and his vampire fangs began to protrude from his gums. Thankfully Lily was so caught up in the moment she did not notice the change in Cezar.

He went to sink his teeth into Lily's inviting neck, but instead he stopped short and found himself kissing it instead. He stopped for a moment and looked at the soft skin of Lily's neckline that presented itself as a beacon of temptation.

He licked the neck with a single movement of his tongue.

He raised his head once more with the determined intention to sink his fangs into her jugular artery and drain the life source from her veins, knowing that the actual crucial moment brings an almighty sexual ecstasy for the victim as well as the vampire that can never be matched in mortal sexual practice. He could make her immortal like himself. She too could be a vampire and they could live together forever.

His open mouth went down to her neck but he simply licked it again.

This was unlike him. He was confused at his feelings for a "living girl". He was a master vampire and he should be above giving mercy. He sent this message out often enough to his understudies in life. *Never show mercy, as mercy could be your downfall.* If the boys at the Fosturnea School of Football Excellence could see him now he would feel so ashamed.

But he thought about the night that he had shared with Lily. An eventful and pleasurable night with a girl who respected him for who he could be, not for what he really was. Cezar had enjoyed the initial meeting in the pub, followed by dinner and a flow of excellent conversation. They had skipped on the theatre trip knowing that it would have compromised the connection between them. Cezar realised at that moment that somehow they had made a real connection. He was ashamed but he had to admit that he liked the feeling of the connection with Lily. Yes, he could make her a vampire and they could be together for eternity but that would only satisfy his own selfish need.

But I am a master vampire. He shrieked at himself in his head.

Cezar raised his head again with the firm intention to kill Lily. Her head was cocked away from him. Her eyes were shut and it could never be more perfect for him to take her now. But he spotted the innocence in her face as she lay there and he simply couldn't bring himself to do it. Besides he had indulged in plenty of blood as a means of survival by emptying the veins of his two ill-fated victims in the Broad Street pub earlier in the night. And that is primarily why vampires drink the blood of living creatures, purely as a means of survival, to take Lily's blood now would simply be greedy.

She will keep for another day. He told himself.

Cezar put the thoughts of being a vampire out of his head and continued to make passionate and genuine love to the girl who had enchanted his evening.

Eventually they fell asleep in one another's arms.

In the Scottish hotel room of Jody Roper and Alvin Braxton another liaison was taking place between another couple of the opposite sex that had only met that evening.

"Would you care for a drink from the mini-bar?" offered the eighties loving centre-half.

"Aye, perhaps a small scotch," replied the girl.

"Judging by your accent I notice that you are a local girl," stated Jody as he handed a glass of single malt to his latest acquaintance.

"Aye, but I am well travelled mind. Scotland will always be my home though."

Jody sat next to the girl and looked into her dark eyes as she teasingly sipped at her glass of whisky. He noticed that they had a magnetic, hypnotic quality about them.

"Would you like to kiss me Jody?" she asked seductively.

Jody gulped with the excitement of the girl's informality. He realised that his conversation often appeared clumsy in the presence of a female and was grateful for the girl's directness. "Yes, very much. Please."

The girl took another swig of whisky and leant over to Jody to kiss him allowing the whisky to pass between their mouths.

"Did you like that big boy?" asked the girl as she squeezed his genitalia through his trousers.

Jody simply nodded, but the girl could recognise his satisfaction by the stiffness of his erection.

She leant back a little and removed her blouse to reveal her small pointed breasts protruding from her slim frame. She did not wear a bra, and in fairness her breasts were firm enough not to warrant one. The redness of her erect nipples complimented her ghostly white skin and the outline of her ribs could be seen easily. Jody thought she was beautiful.

She took the glass of whisky and poured the remains of the single malt over her exposed breasts. She then reached behind Jody's head and pulled at his long curly hair to guide his mouth to her torso.

Jody couldn't believe his luck as he frantically licked the bitter taste of alcohol from her breasts.

Suddenly she pulled hard at Jody's long hair and took him by surprise as she flung him down onto the bed.

She stood up and allowed her skirt to drop to the floor revealing a black g-string, which again contrasted effectively against her white skin.

Jody was mesmerised.

"Do you like what you see Jody?"

"Yes, of course."

"I want you to look into my eyes."

"That is very difficult under the circumstances."

"Believe me do as I tell you and you shall get your reward."

Jody was comfortable with the girl's ability to totally control the situation and obeyed her request by looking into her eyes, managing to somehow avoid peeking at the more obvious parts of her body.

The girl slowly walked towards the bed and Jody could hear the seductiveness of her clicking footsteps as he pictured her g-string clad body and her high-heeled shoes. Initially, not being allowed to look was torture but as he gazed into her eyes Jody noticed the magnetic quality of them once again and they became just as appealing as her breasts and slim figure. As she slowly became closer Jody found himself falling further and further under her spell.

"Would you like to live forever Jody?" asked the girl in seductive soft Scottish tones.

"I guess so," answered Jody, not quite understanding the nature of the question in the light of things. It struck him that he may have already died and gone to heaven.

"Good. I'm going to make you live forever Jody."

Jody took the girls words to mean that she was going to show him an unrivalled sequence of sexual activity that would stay with him forever. He could hardly wait.

By now she had reached the bed and she sat astride the captivated Jody as he lay on his back. Still looking into her eyes Jody was feeling more and more turned on, but at the same time more and more relaxed. He was practically paralysed under the controlling spell of this mysterious girl.

He felt her hand reach under her own crotch in order to reach at his and she began to undo his zip.

He smiled as she reached inside his fly opening to grab at his manhood. She smiled back but her grin unnerved him. He noticed her teeth seemed larger than before and that she seemed to have fangs strikingly pointing over her lips. It didn't matter. The spellbound Jody was so taken in a state of arousal with this girl that he was helplessly committed to indulge in whatever activities of passion she had in store for him.

Just then a sound could be heard from the far corner of the room.

"Alvin is that you mate? Have a heart can't you see I'm busy. Go back to the bar."

There was no reply.

"Don't worry love I bet it's Giuseppe coming for his live show. Fuck off Rossi, get your kicks somewhere else."

There was still no reply.

Then the girl spoke.

"If anyone is in here I will kill you, make no mistake about that."

"Here that's a bit strong isn't it love?" said Jody.

"Silence," was the unexpected reply as the girl smacked Jody hard across the face. Jody was stunned at her response but wondered if this was just another ingredient of her lovemaking ritual. Were they now to enter into an act of sado-masochism while this femme fatale enjoyed a dominatrix role?

The girl sat upright and arched her back forcing her fangs to stick out with venomous forthright from her mouth, like a wild animal waiting to pounce on its prey.

Fuck me, thought Jody as he quickly realised her intent. *She's going to fucking bite me.*

Just then a whooshing sound could be heard through the air, only lasting a second.

The girl froze in her arched back position and a trickle of blood slowly appeared at the corner of her mouth.

Jody couldn't understand where the blood could have come from as she had failed to deliver the bite into him.

Then he noticed that the seductiveness nature of her hypnotising eyes had now become cold and lifeless instead, glazed over like dark chips of marbled stone.

Then he noticed what seemed to be the head of an arrow sticking out through the girls left breast. That same left breast that had only moments earlier been responsible for such moments of ecstasy. He realised that she had been speared from behind and the arrow had pierced her back passing straight through her heart as it finally rested out the front of her body.

Jody realised that she was dead.

The girl's lifeless body seemed to take an eternity to finally fall to the side of Jody, the whiteness of her skin creating the appearance of a tragic Greek statue. He had the unsettling necessity of lifting her lifeless leg from pinning him to the bed and he was shocked by the already coldness of its touch. Once free he jumped up from the bed forgetting that his flies were still undone but fortunately his manhood had not been taken out of its clothing.

Jody saw before him a small figure of a man move into the light clutching a crossbow. The intruder pushed his spectacles more securely onto his nose as he spoke.

"Are you okay Jody?"

"What, are you nuts? You have just murdered a girl in front of me! I am far from fucking okay!"

"She is not a girl, Jody. Well not in the strict sense of the word anyway. She was a vampire and you my friend were about to become her latest victim. Have you been bitten?"

"No. She was about to bite me, then you killed her."

"Thank God for that."

"Look mate, there are no such things as fucking vampires. You need help; we were just going to get into in a bit of rough playing that's all. I'm calling the police." Uncharacteristically shaking, Jody picked up the receiver to the phone that was situated near the bed.

"I wouldn't do that Jody, think of the unwanted press it would attract for you. Picture the headline—KINGSBARR DEFENDER IN HOTEL ROOM DEATH SCANDAL." Jody reluctantly put down the telephone receiver, not really sure what his next move should be. He considered attacking his intruder but wondered how quickly the little man could reload his crossbow. "Besides the police wouldn't believe that she is a vampire either, except certain divisions of MI5 perhaps."

"That's because vampires don't exist you warped prick."

"Look Jody, I know this is all very difficult to take in but a bit of gratitude wouldn't go amiss here. I have just saved your life you know. What do you think she meant when she said that you could live forever?"

Jody just shrugged.

"She meant that she was going to make you into a vampire too and give you eternal life, but that life would have entailed you to be forever on the hunt for human blood as a means of survival. You have had a lucky escape my friend."

"There are no such things as vampires!" said Jody again but as he said the words on this occasion he surprised himself at the doubt in his voice.

"Ask yourself these questions Jody. Was she ghostly pale in her complexion? Did she have fangs? Was she going to bite you?"

Jody nodded.

"Right, and did her fangs look normal to you?"

Jody shook his head like a pathetic schoolboy.

"Right believe me she was a vampire. Her name was Cynthia Mcnulty."

"How do you know that?"

"You didn't even know her name and she was about to have sex with you? Worst still she was about to kill you."

Jody looked ashamed.

"My name is Gene Macgoree."

"Hey, I know you. You are one of our biggest fans aren't you? I hope you are not one of these obsessive nutters who feels you need to protect your heroes."

"Jody, as much as I admire your skills at defending the Kingsbarr United goal I am not about to kill someone for it. I am however a secret vampire slayer and I killed Cynthia Mcnulty because she was a vampire. She belonged to the Scottish clan, or I should say nest of the master Scottish vampire Hugh Stirling. Have a look at Cheryl now if you require further convincing."

Jody looked at the *girl* whom he had earlier indulged in a moment of passion and noticed that she was quickly decomposing at an alarming rate. Her skin and organs was disappearing by the second, leaving only her bones as evidence of her existence.

Jody appeared shell-shocked. "I guess the body of a human being wouldn't have disappeared that quickly."

"That is correct Jody. You see in a sense I have not really killed Cynthia, not the real Cynthia. I've just destroyed the evil metamorphosis that she became. The true Cynthia Mcnulty was killed in 1943, when her real life was taken when she fell victim to the clutches of Hugh Stirling. He killed her and yet he gave her eternal life as a vampire. Now she can finally rest in peace. One day I hope to track down Stirling himself but the master vampires are more dangerous and less accessible than their tragic victims."

"She was killed in 1943?"

"That's right, she was a hard one to track down and believe me there are many vampires out there who are so far undetected, walking anonymously amongst us every day. Fortunately for Cynthia, and as it turns out for you Jody, I managed to discover her existence as a vampire."

"What makes the vampire decompose so quickly once they are killed?" Jody couldn't believe that he found himself asking such questions.

"When a vampire is killed they in effect become human again, at least they take on the human form at the moment they departed from the conventional life that we all lead." Jody looked confused. "Let me explain further, in Cynthia Mcnulty's case her *true* life, that is her human life, was taken from her in 1943. That is why after just ending her vampire life her body that you see before you has been reclaimed as nature intended. Her body now appears as a skeleton because it has decomposed to its original state when she died in 1943, not at the rate of only a few minutes which is what you would expect."

Jody began to quickly summarise everything in his head that he had seen and what Gene had told him. He had knowledge of vampire movies and stories and began to rationalise what had happened tonight. The girl had been pierced through the heart the perfect way to kill a vampire. Her eyes had a hypnotic presence, her skin was ghostly white and she had un-human like fangs. Her body had amazingly decomposed to a state of it being dead over fifty years ago within a matter of minutes of being killed. She had spoke of giving him eternal life and she was about to bite him with those enormous fangs. There was only one conclusion. She was a vampire.

Jody turned to face the little man who was probably the biggest Kingsbarr United fan in football history and spoke to him with immeasurable gratitude.

"Gene thanks for saving my life."

Chapter 20

Professor Cezar Prodanescu woke at a fairly early hour considering the contentment he felt in sharing his bed with Lily and the effectiveness of the hotel curtains that blocked out the morning sunlight. But then again, as with all vampires, his energy levels were at their most fruitful when shrouded in darkness. Being a master vampire however did bless, or curse, Cezar with certain human type qualities that were usually void to the average vampire, and his contented state of sleep should have kept him snuggled up to Lily for a good while longer. Although his mind was in a happy state, it was also somewhat troubled as his human emotions for Lily were surfacing way above the level that he considered natural for a master vampire. He even gently raised her arm from his chest so that he considerately did not wake her as he vacated the bed. Naked and confused he made his way to the bathroom.

Cezar leaned on the sink and stared at his own face looking back at him from the mirror, consciously analysing that this was something that only a master vampire was able to do. Usually of course vampires were unable to cast a reflection. However, Cezar was indeed a master vampire, this being due to the fact that he was born as such a creature and was not simply a victim of the un-dead that prowled the Earth destined to die and then ironically return in the same form as their killer.

His parents were of course master vampires; they had to be for him to continue the *perfect* dynasty. This made him, and very few other vampires belong to an elite top rank of status in the vampire world. Often offspring could be born to a couple who became bloodsuckers by means of falling victim themselves which could earn the descendants undoubted respect within the vampire community, but it was only a pure bloodline of master vampires that really counted as top dog in the ranking of their race. It was master vampires like Cezar, and his father before him who largely controlled the vampire underworld, ensuring that the breeding of the creatures continued by becoming the leader of their particular *nest.* A nest was like an unofficial family that could grow like ripples in water, with Cezar being the *Father* and the initial stone that was thrown to cause the ripples. Every victim that he took ultimately belonged to him. Every victim who his victims took ultimately belonged to him and so on.

A vampire can only be killed by receiving a stake through the heart, being burnt to death (though this takes a considerably long time), being shot by a silver bullet, by being exposed to high amounts of holy water or suffering decapitation. All of these things would also kill a master vampire, but the irony is that if a master vampire suffers a death each one of his or her *living* victims would return to their normal human state with no recollection of ever being a bloodsucker. Killing a master vampire is their only hope.

A major difference between a master vampire and a *normal* vampire is that the master vampire ages, albeit at an amazingly slow rate. It takes hundreds of years to grow from a child to an adult and a master vampire is still immortal unless it is killed by one of the only methods possible. The vampire that is created by becoming a victim is frozen in time at the moment they were denied human life but granted eternal life by their fanged killer.

Although showing clear psychopathic tendencies, the master vampire is usually greatly advanced with intelligence and possesses a full range of human emotions. This enables them to manipulate and blend in easily with society as they build their nest, very often never ever becoming detected through the long passage of time, even centuries. Professor

Cezar Prodanescu had himself lived for centuries, taking on many guises and maximising his vampire empire, but last night something seemed to change in him as his human emotions surfaced higher than ever before in all those hundreds of years. For the only time in his existence he spared a life. What concerned him was how good he felt about sparing Lily's life. By the unwritten rules of the vampire world he should have killed her, but instead he made love to her. Sure he could have enjoyed casual sex with her before taking her life, sexual exploits play a huge part in the ritual of vampirism, but this was different. He didn't want to hurt Lily; he wanted to care for her. He wanted to protect her.

He broke his gaze from the mirror and bowed his head. He began to run the cold water from the tap and made a cup with his hands before splashing it into his face as if to try and awaken some meaning of sense from his confusion. His trail of thought was broken when he felt a hand reach under his groin and gently squeeze at his testicles.

"Good morning stud," whispered Lily as she squeezed.

Cezar returned his face to the mirror and used it to smile at Lily.

Lily moved her hand away from his scrotum, which disappointed Cezar but his satisfaction was restored when he realised that she was urging him to take a shower with her. She started the spray and stepped into the cubicle letting the water run over her hair and down her body. Cezar admired the way the water ran from her gorgeous breasts before he moved forward to join her.

"Cezar, I never asked you what sort of a professor you are?" said Lily as she unscrewed the top from the complimentary shower gel.

"Well I am a professor in two fields actually."

"Well I never. You impress me more and more by the minute. What are they?"

"I am a professor of genetics. I am a geneticist. I analyse DNA for example."

"Well that makes sense; you certainly seem to be a master of the human body from what I can tell." Lily spoke fittingly as Cezar took the shower gel from her and began to rub it into her breasts. "What is the other thing that demands your knowledge as a professor?"

"Well, it is something entirely different. It involves big strong men running around on grass and kissing and hugging each other."

"Cezar, I would never have guessed that you like to practice gay sex with men as well, especially the way that you are now rubbing between my legs."

Cezar laughed. "I don't like men, not in that way anyway. I'm a professor of football believe it or not."

"I never knew that you could be a professor in such a thing. Which line of your work has brought you to England then, genetics or football?"

"Both actually, but that's enough talk my darling, we have better things to do than chat."

As Cezar and Lily kissed each other passionately and fondled at each other's naked wet bodies, Cezar wondered how this girl that had so enchantingly entered his life would react if she knew exactly why he had come to England in relation to both his professions. Furthermore how would she react knowing that she was kissing a master vampire!

He finally decided that he had to make a quick decision in order to save his own sanity. He could kill Lily right now and turn her into a vampire, just another one of his long list of victims. The advantages of this would include the fact that she could share eternal life with him. He could have Lily at his beckoned call for all eternity and they could indulge in feasts of human blood and orgies of vampirism.

But he liked her as she was.

He liked her as the unassuming girl that he had met last night. He liked her sweetness and innocence, although in the current climate she was working hard to belie that persona.

To make her a vampire would be purely selfish on his part. *Selfishness*, this was another new emotion.

Cezar decided that he would not kill her. He decided there and then that he would never kill her and that was his final decision on the matter.

I can be selfish after all, he thought. *Why should only mortals have the luxury of sharing just a normal relationship with a normal girl? But then again Lily isn't normal. She is very, very special. She has made me feel alive without the need to kill. I enjoyed our evening together last night without the necessity of indulging in an episode of bloodlust. And she shall never know what I truly am. To her I am her lover; I am simply Professor Cezar Prodanescu.*

Johnny often weighed up the pros and cons of travelling to away games. He hated being apart from Sheena and Saffron, and now he had the added heartache of missing his newly adopted son Radu. What he did love about travelling away was the banter with the boys and the fabulous buffet breakfasts that were served up in the hotels. The breakfast in the Scottish hotel was of a particular high standard adding the traditional dishes of porridge, kippers and smoked salmon.

Johnny didn't necessarily tailor his diet specifically to what a footballer should, he simply loved his food and ate lots of it, never really analysing the correct protein and vitamin content. He was genetically fortunate not to ever suffer with weight problems and the energy that he burnt up on the pitch and training ground more than compensated for his indulgence anyway.

He loaded up his first helping of both scrambled and fried eggs, accompanied by the kippers and smoked salmon in addition to three sausages, a portion of mushrooms, toast, fried bread, hash browns and a generous helping of beans. He would help himself to croissants, yoghurt, fruit and cereals after finishing that lot.

Johnny spotted that Jody's plate was hardly filled which was most unusual, as he would usually indulge in a similar sized helping of food as himself. The Kingsbarr United players would often contemplate running a book to see who could eat the most out of the two of them, although Vincent "Bruiser" Bradshaw was also capable of giving them a run for their money. The odds were pretty even when it came to downing pints of ale too. Johnny made his way over to the table to join his teammate.

"Hey, Jody are you not hungry? Did that bird you pull last night use up all your strength or has she just put you off your food in the cold light of day?"

"Yeah, she was a bit of a minger mate," joked Giuseppe.

"That's what I like about footballers, the politically correct language that they use," stated Charlie Cheng. "A woman's existence is to be appreciated. You need to look beneath the skin to see the true beauty of a woman. You need to see what she is like inside."

"You would need x-ray specs to look that deep," said Giuseppe continuing his teasing and thoroughly amusing himself.

"Fuck me you'll be burning your bra next Charlie," mocked Vincent "Bruiser" Bradshaw joining in the banter. "So Jody what was she like? *The fucking whore . . .* Sorry!"

"Lets just say she was a bit of a beast," answered Jody.

"So much of a beast that she had pissed off before I got back to the room," said Alvin Braxton in his deep Jamaican accent.

"Well I took a leaf out of Rossi's book. I loved her and then left her."

"Very wise Jody," said Giuseppe pleased at the recognition of his reputation.

"It sounds like she left you," laughed Johnny.

"No way skipper. I had my wicked way with her and then asked her to leave."

"Perfect course of action my friend," said Giuseppe as Charlie Cheng shook his head in disapproval.

"So that's it, there's nothing more to say really. There is no need to talk about it any further." Jody thought back to how the professionalism of Gene Macgoree had mastered the situation by collecting the remains of the vampire girl and then leaving Jody in the hotel room as "he promised to dispose of them as he had done thousands of times before". Jody had decided not to let his friends into the secret that he and Gene shared knowing that they would never have believed him anyway. He had concluded that he simply wanted to forget that the whole sorry episode had ever happened.

Just then Daryl Weir joined them at the table with a bowl of porridge. "Scotch porridge, a fine dish of the world," he declared.

"If you say so Daryl, it's right up there with coq au vin and caviar right?"

The Kingsbarr players fell about laughing at Johnny's teasing.

"Right then Knox, for your cheek you can do an extra five laps of the track and fifty extra press-ups."

"You know I always rise to a challenge boss."

"Make that sixty press ups."

Chapter 21

First it had been Wham! then Duran Duran, followed by The Human League and now the sounds of Spandau Ballet were blasting out into the home team's dressing room at Beacon Park, courtesy of Jody Roper's collection of eighties music. It was the first game of the new season with Kingsbarr entertaining County for their first ever game in what is now known as the Championship.

Although Kingsbarr United had lost some key players once they became relegated last season, expectation was still high amongst the home fans and they fully expected that the ex-premiership outfit would be able to win easily this afternoon.

The Scottish pre-season tour had shown inconsistencies in the team's performance against relatively weaker opposition. Of the seven games played they had won three, lost two and drawn two, scoring a total of seven goals (four of them belonging to Johnny) and conceding five in total to the opposition. Daryl Weir had been able to blood a few of the youngsters in the games and try out a couple of low budget signings, but he realised that his squad was depleted and he was experienced enough to know that being in a lower division did not necessarily mean it would be an easier season than the last. He believed in his players, as he always had done, but he did not share the supporter's optimism at getting off to an instant flying start with today's game. He had briefed his players that they needed to be patient as the game progressed. County would defend deep, hoping to hit Kingsbarr on the counter attack. They would be difficult to break down and an early goal for United would be difficult to achieve. There would be a strong chance that the longer the game went on that the home fans would become impatient as they waited for Kingsbarr to score. County, like every other team in the Championship would be viewing their respective fixture with Kingsbarr United as their own personal cup final. Daryl warned his players that every week the opposition would raise their game considerably to try and take the scalp of a previously known Premiership giant. His overriding advice to the team was if they succeeded in keeping possession of the ball and keeping their heads, then he was convinced that success would come to his players not only for today but for the rest of the season as well.

Standing in the players tunnel ready to lead the team out Johnny stood bare chested as proud as the day he first played for his beloved Kingsbarr United. His pride and passion for playing football had never diminished even though he was no longer playing in England's top flight. To captain the side was still a great and privileged honour, though few would question Johnny's credentials or commitment anyway.

"Come on boys," he shouted encouragingly as he finally pulled his gold and blue striped football jersey on. Like many footballers Johnny held a superstition before playing a game, his being never to pull on his shirt until the very last moment when leaving the players tunnel. Vincent Bradshaw needed to tie his boots up for a total of three times, Charlie Cheng needed to do a session of pre-match tai-chi and Jody Roper always needed to wear an eighties slogan t-shirt under his kit, no matter how warm the weather could be. Today it read "Choose Life."

As Johnny entered the field of play the almighty roar from the Kingsbarr United fans almost deafened him. He was delighted to see that like him, their passion for the club had also remained. He acknowledged their support by waving to all four sides of the stadium, which encouraged the home fans to clap and cheer even more enthusiastically. Johnny took a deep breath through his nostrils and soaked up the electric atmosphere. This was the first day of the new season. It didn't matter to Johnny that it was in the Championship this time around. He just loved playing football, and he especially loved playing for Kingsbarr United. He couldn't wait for the game to kick-off, which was now only moments away.

Chapter 22

Within ten minutes of kick-off Cezar Prodanescu's enjoyment at watching the Kingsbarr United game was interrupted when he felt the vibration of his mobile phone stir in his pocket. He reluctantly left his seat and headed down the steps to the area behind the stand where the toilets and refreshment booths were situated, in order to take the call in the best environment of privacy and quietness he was likely to get.

"Hello, Cezar speaking."

"Master, I'm afraid I have some bad news."

"Andrei, what is it? What's wrong?" Cezar could detect the uncharacteristic distress in the voice of the younger vampire.

"We were attacked in the early hours of this morning."

"Attacked? What do you mean?"

"Here at the Fosturnea School of Football Excellence. We were taken by surprise as we slept. I'm afraid there have been some casualties."

"Who has been killed?" It was an ironic question by the professor considering all of the students at the Fosturnea School of Football Excellence were already *dead*!

"Constantin, Cornel, Dragos, Ioan and Wadim. They each got a stake through the heart as they slept. This was a professional hit Master, it was very well organised. We never saw it coming."

Cezar erupted with anger. "What do you mean you never saw it coming? Have all my efforts at teaching you boys the ways of our world been totally wasted?"

Andrei was shaken by his master's words of anger down the phone, even though there was some considerable distance between them geographically, with the professor being in Birmingham, England and Andrei being in the countryside of Romania.

Cezar quickly realised that he had to keep a lid on his wrath so not to draw attention to himself. Some stewards and refreshment attendants had noticed his raised voice accompanied by some animated body language.

"Andrei, do you know who is responsible for this ambush at all? They were five good cadets those boys. I had high hopes for all of them. At least you have survived, Andrei. Who ever is responsible for this shall pay dearly."

"They seemed to be gypsies, possibly come down from the mountains. They seemed to be led by two extremes of slayer, a young man and an old man. Their approach was very methodical and they were both as strong as an ox, although we did manage to hurt the old man and they fled before they managed to set fire to the premises."

"You say the old man got hurt?"

"Yes, Ringa managed to bite him on the shoulder before the younger man knocked him down to the floor and tipped holy water on him. Don't worry Ringa is okay though; most of the water went on his long boots so his skin was largely protected. We killed about three of their men but the battle was so vicious they won't become vampires; we had to kill them properly with decapitation. This was a new breed of slayer Master; they were extremely calculated and effective. However, apart from the five casualties we still stand in pretty good shape."

"When the old man turns into a vampire perhaps he will come out and lead us to these dogs. From what you tell me though perhaps the others, particularly the young slayer, will never allow that to happen. They will drive a stake straight through his heart at the first sign of him turning."

"It was a good thing that you were in England, Master."

"Well soon the Fosturnea School will be set up in England anyway. This younger slayer will have a long way to travel to find us then. What I have planned will ensure that there are enough vampires prowling this Earth to totally outnumber these pathetic slayers. Vampires will rule the world once and for all, and England will be the catalyst for my grand plan."

"I still think he will try Master to be honest with you. As they fled he made a point of telling me to relay a message to you and I don't think it was an idle threat."

"What did the insolent dog say?"

"He said that soon you would be suffering the same fate as your dirty mother and father. He aimed his threat directly at you Master. He said tell Prodanescu that his days are numbered and he can't wait to see your face as he personally drives a stake through your heart."

"It is he whose days are numbered. Now excuse me Andrei, I have a football match to watch."

Chapter 23

"How is your shoulder Bogdan?"

The elderly gypsy vampire slayer was having his wound bathed with a blend of natural antiseptic elements taken from the Romanian mountains by his younger student.

"It is not good. As you can see blood was drawn so I have to fear the worst."

"I will get that bastard who bit you Bogdan if it's the last thing I do."

"Don't fret my boy. That little vampire was just another one of Prodanescu's puppies. It is Cezar who you must track down and destroy, that way his nest will fold as he perishes; yet all the victims that he callously recruited into becoming servants of the night shall return to their natural human form. However, I am extremely worried for your safety in our quest. You have learnt your craft well to be an extremely efficient slayer, but you are still so young, and Cezar is no easy master vampire to tame. He is one of the deadliest and craftiest that there has ever been."

"It is a good job that I have your experience fighting alongside me, Bogdan."

The old mans eyes sunk with the words of the younger slayer. "Listen my boy, have I not taught you well on the nature of vampirism?"

"Of course you have Bogdan. You have been like a father to me."

"Then you know full well that as I have been bitten by a vampire it is only a matter of time before I too become one."

The younger slayer desperately fought against the realisation of the situation and searched his mind helplessly for a positive solution. Of course there was none.

"Listen to me my boy, and listen well. My heart and soul are still in human form at this moment in time and I want to be able to leave this life as a human. You know what you must do."

Tears filled the youngster's eyes. "Bogdan, I can't do it. I love you too much."

The old man's wound was bleeding heavily and he was growing increasingly weaker, yet he was able to find the strength to reach up and cradle the boy's head with his better hand as he spoke to him again. "God knows that my heart is heavy at the moment but nevertheless my boy, you must drive a stake right through it before it belongs to the world of Vampirism."

"Bogdan, I can't."

The old man raised his voice to depict his authority. "Don't anger me in my final minutes now my boy. I've taught you with all my power and knowledge on the ways of how to kill vampires, especially as I realised that this day could easily fall upon me, and now that it finally has, now that I have become bitten I will soon be joining the very darkest force that we fight to eradicate from this Earth. Now please don't make me ask again. Go and get a stake and drive it through my heart before I turn into one of those godforsaken bloodsuckers."

All the youngster could do was sob uncontrollably.

The old man's failing heart grew even heavier.

"Compose yourself my boy. I'm sorry for shouting at you, but you must be strong. I understand that you don't wish to kill me but you must also understand that you would be freeing me from a life of living hell."

"I know Bogdan. But I can't bring myself to do it."

"Very well then. Pass me my gun and I will do it myself. As always I have it loaded with a silver bullet."

Reluctantly the youngster obeyed the old man's instructions.

"Before I do this final act I urge you to travel to England. I am truly worried for your safety but your time has come. Prodanescu is in England and if you really wish to avenge my killing then that is the vampire above any other that you must slay. He has centuries of blood on his hands and he must be stopped."

"But what about my home here with you and the gypsy community? You have been so good to me."

"My boy, I am about to put a silver bullet through my brain so I will not be in this community for much longer myself. The other men are well equipped to deal with the Transylvanian vampires, but you have all the credentials to travel to England and hunt Prodanescu down. You are the special one. You were the one God himself sent to us that day all those years ago. When I found you alone, such a small and helpless child, I could only conclude that you were heaven sent to be by my side and to bring such joyous light to my life and community. Vampires had taken my wife and my two natural sons from me so you appeared for me like a ray of hope. But I knew and understood that as you appeared so instantaneously it could only be natural that you possessed the authority to leave us when the time was necessary. I never knew when that time would be until now. For it is only now that I realise that the time is right. I am a great believer in fate and I see my passing now as a sign for you to leave the community and to go to England."

"Okay. I'll go to England and I will hunt down Professor Cezar Prodanescu and I will destroy his vampire arse once and for all."

"You have made a dying man very happy my boy." Suddenly the old man looked up to the sky as if he had spotted something "What's that up in the sky darting amongst the clouds. Is it those damn vampire bats flying about?"

The youngster turned around to look. "I can't see anyth—"

The sound of the shotgun rang through the Transylvanian mountains and the youngster closed his eyes with the realisation of what had happened.

He slowly turned his head and opened his eyes, not really wanting to witness the inevitable image that was to appear before him. His tears blurred his vision slightly as he surreally looked down to see the lifeless figure of the man who had been such an inspiration to him lying dead in a pool of blood.

A smoking shotgun was hanging from his lifeless hand.

"Rest in peace Bogdan."

The youngster removed the gun from the old man's fingers and perched it into his belt before reaching one arm beneath the old man's legs and the other underneath his motionless torso in order to lift him up. He fought back the tears as the old man's damaged head dropped with the power of gravity behind his right bicep. The youngster wasn't concerned about the old man's blood staining his clothes and skin; preferring to view the mess as an honour to have his mentor's blood upon his person.

The young slayer was strong, a mixture of genetics from his natural father and the unconventional method of "working-out mountain style", trading weights and fancy running machines with boulders and dirt tracks across stunning landscapes. The old man's literal dead weight posed no problem as he lifted him and returned back to the village undecided just how to inform the remainder of the community of recent developments.

In the main he knew what he had to do.

His actions would be clear even if his words could not be.

He would arrange the great mans burial, insisting on digging the grave himself. That honour must surely fall to him alone.

And then he would bid an emotional but necessary farewell to his adopted community in the Romanian mountains, and head off to England in search of Professor Cezar Prodanescu.

But the master vampire was not going to be the only thing that the young scholar of Bogdan would discover on his return to English soil.

Chapter 24

Daryl Weir's prediction of a tough game had been correct. County had set out there stall to defend deep and had frustrated Kingsbarr with their dogged display. It was true that Kingsbarr had enjoyed the majority of possession in the game, but where County lacked in flair and technical ability they made up for in high fitness levels and tough tackling.

Early on in the game Kingsbarr striker Giuseppe Rossi had had a decent shot hit the bar, but he was getting little change out of the County centre-half who was giving Giuseppe his own personal welcome to life in the Championship by marking him as tightly as he possibly could, with the odd obscenity being whispered in the Italian's ear. The lanky County defender wasn't giving Giuseppe a moment to breathe, let alone allowing him to keep possession of the ball, and his raw strategy of how to defend in the game of football was not always being dished out in a fair manner either. Giuseppe was amazed that he wasn't receiving the same amount of protection from the referee as he was used to in the Premiership, but this was indeed a tougher league to play in and having a physical game was something that Giuseppe Rossi was going to have to quickly get used to.

To Giuseppe's credit he never allowed the County defender to completely intimidate him out of the game and in the final minutes he received the ball from a perfectly weighted pass from Johnny and turned on a sixpence to break away from the lumbering County centre-half. It was a fantastic piece of skill and all the brutish defender could do to salvage the situation was to pull at Giuseppe's gold and blue striped shirt as he headed towards goal, sending the skilful Italian crashing to the ground.

Not before time the County defender was finally shown the yellow card, as even this clumsy challenge on Giuseppe was impossible for the referee not to notice. There had been a second County player making his way towards Giuseppe at the time of the foul, so fortunately for the County centre-half who had committed the illegality and who had acted like Giuseppe's shadow throughout the game, he had been relieved of receiving the dreaded red card which would have resulted in him permanently leaving the field of play.

Nevertheless, Kingsbarr United had now been awarded a free-kick in a prime position of only about three metres outside of the County penalty area. As Johnny retrieved the ball and placed it down at the spot where the foul was committed he glanced across at the referee and smiled as he saw the official holding his arm out and pointing his hand straight at the Kingsbarr United captain to indicate that the free-kick was to be direct.

Johnny's Kingsbarr United team-mates didn't bother to confer with their Captain, as they knew exactly what his intention was going to be. He was going to shoot straight at goal and hopefully score directly from the free-kick. They had seen Johnny do this many times before for both club and country, but it could never be regarded as a guaranteed means of scoring, it took great skill and talent for an individual to score a goal from such a dead ball situation.

The free-kick was about two metres to the left of centre from the County goal, so the front post was to be protected by a wall of four County players whilst the County goalkeeper would need to protect the back post by standing close to it. However he was fully aware that he may need to move across his goal line towards the front post if Johnny opted to lift the ball into that near side of the goal. It was a daunting task for the County goalkeeper who was fully aware of Johnny's reputation at scoring some amazing goals from free-kick situations.

The Kingsbarr United supporters who had been openly critical of their team for about the last twenty-five minutes due to the frustration of having nothing to show from this first game of the season, were now suddenly in an extremely positive mood as they chanted Johnny's name in anticipation that the deadlock could possibly now be broken. They knew full well that if anyone was capable of scoring a goal for their beloved Kingsbarr United, then Johnny Knox certainly could be the man to do it.

Johnny quickly assessed the situation before finally stepping up to execute the ball towards goal. He could see that the County wall of defenders was doing its job well of shielding the nearside area of the goal, but he felt confident that he could still lift it over them and strike the ball on target.

For a split second Johnny considered hitting the ball to where the goalkeeper was standing, knowing full well that this would be most unexpected. Perhaps the flight of the ball could deceive the goalkeeper as he headed across goal towards the near post and instead it would finish up in the far corner as the goalkeeper would be left stranded out of position. But Johnny decided that this was still too risky. If the goalkeeper stood up straight for long enough it would be a simple save for him and Johnny would be left to look foolish as his attempt to score from the free-kick would simply verge on an embarrassing display.

The only viable option for Johnny was to lift the ball over the wall and into the near side of the goal, but he still managed to conjure up an element of surprise to the free-kick. The goalkeeper would expect Johnny to aim the ball into the top corner, as this would be the simplest way to execute the kick with accuracy. It would then be a race against time between the keeper moving across to protect the top corner of the goal and the speed of the shot. Johnny had recognised that the County keeper's display this afternoon had proved that he was a more than capable shot-stopper and he was tall in height as well, so he decided to attempt a more difficult shot of lifting the ball over the wall of players but with enough dip to head towards the bottom corner of the nearside goal. This was a very difficult shot to execute as the ball needed to lift sufficiently to beat the wall but then needed to dip almost immediately after clearing the heads of the County players for it to descend towards the bottom corner. Even if the accuracy were to be mastered it would be difficult to marry it with a decent pace of the ball.

But Johnny was a master of free-kicks.

He knew as soon as the ball had left his boot that he had hit it as sweetly and as accurately as he had envisaged.

The goalkeeper headed towards the nearside of the goal as expected, but he hadn't anticipated the ball to move towards his bottom right hand corner and he helplessly scrambled across the goal-line to try and claim the ball. The goalkeeper's huge size, usually one of his biggest assets, worked against him on this occasion and he found it impossible to get down in time to make the save. The ball was in the back of the net before he had even hit the floor.

The deadlock had been broken.

Kingsbarr United were one goal up thanks to the ingenious free-kick delivery of their captain Johnny Knox.

As the Kingsbarr players surrounded Johnny to congratulate their team-mate on his excellent goal he heard the voice of Jody Roper speak, "that was fucking magic Skipper. If the Brazilians had scored that it would be played on TV replays for the next twenty years."

Johnny also caught the sight of Daryl Weir on the touchline punching the air fuelled by a mixture of pure elation and sheer relief. He could also hear the chants of the Kingsbarr fans roaring with delight at his goal.

What he didn't notice amongst the sea of blue and gold coloured scarves and clothing was the distinguished looking gentleman whom he had met at the airport in Romania the day he returned to England with Radu. Professor Cezar Prodanescu had blended into the crowd quite inconspicuously considering he was not wearing any Kingsbarr United coloured attire. He stood up from his seat in unified admiration with the crowd as they applauded Johnny's exquisite goal. Professor Cezar Prodanescu was impressed by the skill of Johnny Knox and reacted appropriately. The professor was a big fan of football and was delighted to witness such wonderful ability.

In stark contrast however, the professor wasn't subsequently impressed regarding the remaining few minutes of the game as Kingsbarr failed to capitalise further on their lead. To County's credit they "moved up a gear" and actually began to attack the Kingsbarr goal now that they realised they too needed to score if they were to get something out of the game. Their initial hopes of securing a draw with their dogged and deep field defending was now in serious jeopardy.

But it was too little too late for County, and Kingsbarr United hung on to their one goal lead to achieve their first three points in the English Championship on the opening day of the season, thanks mainly to Johnny's wonder goal.

Although today they had won the battle, the players realised that it would be no easy feat to gain promotion back to the Premiership. County had given them a wake up call with their physical approach to the game.

Daryl Weir knew only to well that success and failure lay squarely with him, and as a former Premiership manager at a former Premiership club he realised that his every move at Kingsbarr United was well and truly under the spotlight.

What he and the rest of the players didn't realise was that they were being particularly scrutinised by a professor of football from Romania.

Who just happened to be a master vampire too!

Chapter 25

"Lucas, I've asked you nicely now please will you leave my flat?"

"Oh, your flat is it?"

"You know that it has always been my flat. It's my name on the mortgage, it was mine before I met you and it is mine now we are not together. You have no claim on it whatsoever. I asked you to move in with me a million times, only God knows why now, but you just used this place to come and crash after a night out getting bladdered with your mates. I'm sure now that all the other nights that you told me you were staying at your dad's place you were out sleeping with other women. More fool them too."

"I can't help being irresistible to the opposite sex, Lily." Sadly, Lucas's conceitedness and flippancy in light of the situation did not surprise Lily.

"You wish. You're just some egotistical loser who is only capable of loving himself. The irony is I now realise that the way you behave is due to your low self-esteem, yet you also tried your best to lower my self-esteem. You thought you could forever manipulate and control me, well not anymore Lucas. You are out of my life for good."

"I say when I'm out of your life. I say when we are over and I'm fucking telling you Lily that we are most definitely not over." Lucas's words were now laced with venom and his unpredictable personality switch to one of a menacing disposition didn't surprise Lily again.

"Look Lucas, I don't want a fight. Please just leave the flat. I don't want to be with you any more. We had some good times, but it just hasn't worked out. I'm afraid we are over."

Lucas punched the wall in fury. Lily had become accustomed to several similar outbursts and knew that he wasn't averse to showing violence towards her. "The fuck we are over. Now I'm telling you very nicely Lily, I deserve another chance."

"I'm sorry Lucas," Lily hated herself for apologising to him when she knew there was definitely no reason but she thought by showing some pleasantries he may just leave the flat sooner than later. "I just think we have grown apart that's all. We are different people now. I simply don't love you anymore."

Lucas moved towards Lily and grabbed at her face hard. She could feel his thumb and index finger paining either cheek, but he was squeezing so hard she couldn't move her mouth to speak. Lucas enjoyed seeing the terror in her eyes.

"Do you know what I think Lily?"

Lily shook her head to acknowledge the question.

"I think you've met someone else. You dirty slag you've been shagging someone else." If she were not so frightened Lily would have found the hypocrisy in Lucas's words laughable.

Suddenly her phone rang alerting Lucas to loosen his grip. "I bet that's lover boy now isn't it you dirty whore?"

Lily did not answer him or the phone.

"Well go on slag, answer it. We don't want to keep him waiting."

Lily nervously answered the phone. "H . . . hello."

Cezar immediately sensed the unease in his girlfriend's voice. "Lily is something wrong?"

"No, I'm fine."

"Are you sure?"

"Yes, can I phone you later Cezar?"

Cezar could hear the sound of laughter in the background.

"Cezar, what sort of a fucking name is Cezar?"

"Lucy, who is there with you?"

"It's Lucas, I'm having a bit of trouble asking him to lea—" before Lily had time to finish the sentence an enraged

Lucas smacked the back of his hand across her face causing her to fall to the floor and drop the receiver.

"Lily are you there?"

A few seconds later Cezar heard an unfamiliar voice speak on the other end of the line. "Hi, Cezar is it? So you think that you can steal my fucking bird do ya?"

"I didn't steal her you prick. You lost her all by yourself, you didn't need my help."

"Quite the Prince Charming aren't we. Well don't hang up; I wouldn't want you to miss out on the little show that I've got planned."

"Lucas, I'm warning you. Don't you dare harm Lily."

"Shut the fuck up Mr. Funny accent. I'm going to rape her, did you hear me? I'm going to rape her and you can listen to every sordid little squeal and pathetic cry for help. You won't want to touch her after that will you? After I've dirtied her. After I've soiled sweet little Lily. Mind you I have had her before you anyway haven't I? Though not quite so unwillingly. I think I might enjoy it better this way actually. But even so, when I'm done with the slag I'm going to track you down and hurt you really bad. In fact I'm going to teach both of you a lesson neither of you will ever forget. No one fucking crosses me. Did you hear me you foreign fucker?"

Lucas smiled as he heard the phone line go dead. Turning to his intended victim who was still on the floor clutching at her throbbing face he jeered at her "Looks like lover boy isn't going to tune into our little show Lily. Now be a good girl and get those fucking knickers off or I'll have to remove them myself."

Chapter 26

A and E Dept, Good Hope Hospital, Sutton Coldfield.

"What have we got Donny?" said Dr Charnwood to the attending paramedic. Dr. Charnwood was a tall gentleman with tufts of wispy grey hair, which failed miserably to hide the parts of his head that were bald. Perched upon the bridge of his pointed nose was a pair of ill-fitting, steel-rimmed glasses, which made his eyes appear slightly larger than they actually were.

"This is Radu Knox, son of Johnny Knox and Sheena Knox."

Dr. Charnwood, himself a huge Kingsbarr United fan was aware of the name of the footballer and it registered with him instantly, but a professional at all times he would not allow himself to stray from the urgency that was demanded by the boy's obvious serious condition.

"The boy is suffering from a severely faint pulse rate, extremely low blood pressure, in a state of near comatose and fairly non-responsive," continued Donny the efficient but concerned paramedic. "Although when strength permits he seems to call out words and phrases of a nonsensical nature, most likely caused by some sort of hallucinations that he might be experiencing."

Like all good mothers Sheena had travelled with Radu in the ambulance. After becoming increasingly concerned with Radu's state of health she had decided to contact the emergency services. He had been drifting in and out of consciousness coupled with a severe burning fever and she was at her wits end not knowing how best to care for her newly adopted son.

"Has anything like this ever happened in the family before Mrs Knox?" enquired Dr. Charnwood keen to establish the illness as quickly as possible.

"Err . . . no. Radu is adopted." Sheena was concerned that an authority figure such as Dr. Charnwood would be able to figure out the less than legal adoption of Radu, it was something that played on her mind constantly and when she would hear the phone ring or a knock at the door she half expected social services or the police to be the source of contact ready to cart her and Johnny away for the glorified kidnapping of their Romanian son.

In spite of her fears she felt that welcoming Radu into her family had been the right thing to do. She realised that Radu was better off with herself and Johnny, who had explained to her that the boys life was in danger if he were to be left in Romania, and besides Radu had been happy to come home with them and become part of the family. *For Christ's sake* it had even been the young boy's own suggestion.

And Johnny had pointed out to her many times in his own sweet black and white way that he so often saw the world in, of the sort of privileged life they would be able to give Radu compared to what he would have endured in Romania. One thing football in the twenty-first century guaranteed was money, and Johnny had explained how Radu could be given many things in life that he could only have ever dreamed of. Indeed he had spent hours playing on the playstation up until today before he had fell seriously ill, although Sheena had become concerned at his thirst for the more violent games that were available.

In analysing Radu's life with them, Sheena had realised that he would be able to attend a school that conducted a private education, something he could never have benefited from in Romania. They could give him a chance to become a doctor or a lawyer, something that they sadly could no longer provide for their missing, presumed dead son Callum. With Radu they seemed to have been given a second chance. Johnny had pointed out how it was a win-win situation all round. But no matter how it was dressed up she felt like a criminal and even though the skill and bribery conducted by the solicitor Art Eddowes had successfully secured the adoption to appear legally watertight, Sheena couldn't help but be paranoid about the adoption of their new son when in the presence of somebody like Dr. Charnwood, even though he never suspected a thing. Why should he?

"Adopted, oh I see. Do you know of any hereditary diseases that can be associated with Radu's natural birth parents?"

The question fuelled Sheena's paranoia. "Err, it's complicated."

"How do you mean?" enquired Dr. Charnwood, pushing his spectacles further onto his nose.

"We adopted Radu from a Romanian orphanage, quite legally of course."

"Of course."

"And those places are not run too well, the administration is very poor and corruption is rife." (Sheena felt like a hypocrite using the word corruption.) "Unfortunately there was no record to be found of Radu's birth parents. Our solicitor tried everything in his power to establish some sort of clue to Radu's natural parentage, but like I say we simply do not know."

Dr. Charnwood swallowed every word.

"Okay so we are starting with a blank canvas. Try not to worry Mrs. Knox, your son is in good hands."

Suddenly Dr. Charnwood's concentration was broken when he saw the figure of Johnny Knox burst through the doors to his department. Johnny's entrance had not gone unnoticed by other members of the public who were in the waiting area as they recognised the famous footballer. Johnny had broken several traffic and speeding violations in his mission to tail the ambulance in his Audi. He was now breaking a parking violation.

"Mr. Knox. How nice to see y—"

"Hi Doc. What is wrong with my boy?"

"Well we don't know yet. We will run some tests and place him in the Intensive Care Unit."

"Intensive care? Shit, it must be serious."

"Try not to alarm yourself Mr. Knox," said Dr. Charnwood as he pulled down Radu's lower lid of his right eye and shone a torch to inspect it.

"Well for starters your son appears to be anaemic. Tell me has he suffered any considerable loss of blood lately do you know?"

"No, not that we know of," panicked Sheena. "What is it? Could he be a haemophiliac or . . . god no . . . be suffering from leukaemia?"

"Please, Mrs. Knox. I really can't be sure of anything just yet. I really need to get your son into ICU as quickly as possible and run some tests."

Johnny was fearful for Radu. He had never become used to losing his son Callum, and now this was happening. "With all due respect I would appreciate it if you didn't bullshit me Doctor. What are his chances?"

Dr. Charnwood sighed as he once again pushed the steel-framed spectacles further onto his nose. In all his years of experience as a medic it had never become any easier to break bad news to relatives of the sick and injured. "I'm afraid Radu does appear to be gravely ill Mr. Knox. It appears that he may need a blood transfusion. However, I really don't wish to speculate or worry you unnecessarily without running some tests and establishing exactly what is wrong with your son."

Then Dr. Charnwood looked down at his young patient and noticed something unusual on his neck that he wasn't sure at this moment in time if they would prove significant or not.

They appeared to be something like two puncture wounds in close proximity to one another.

"Mr and Mrs. Knox, do you know how your son obtained these two markings on his neck at all?"

Johnny and Sheena Knox looked at one another blankly.

Chapter 27

Lily had fought bravely in her attempt to keep Lucas at bay in his quest to rape her, but she had suffered a bloody nose and bruised eye for her efforts. Lucas had not altogether escaped unscathed himself though as he felt the pain of two deep and bloody scratch marks down his left cheek, courtesy of Lily's sharp nails as she clawed at her attacker in a bid to defend herself.

Inevitably as the struggle persisted, Lucas had managed to overpower Lily and was currently pinning her exhausted body down by the weight of his own body and obvious greater physical strength. The brute punched her full force in the face causing her to be dazed before callously putting his hand between her legs to rip of her knickers. She winced as his fingers crudely entered her and a tear rolled down her cheek as he callously whispered into her ear how inconsiderate she was that she wasn't wet and ready for action.

Lily desperately squirmed inside as she felt Lucas fumble at his belt, knowing all too well that the next intended instalment to this nightmare was to have his vile penis viciously rammed into her.

Fortunately things weren't allowed to go that far.

Lily's valiant efforts at defending herself had managed to buy enough time for her not to be on the receiving end of Lucas's degrading intentions. She felt a sudden rush of hope run through her as she heard the door to her flat coming away at the hinges.

Lucas, with penis still firmly tucked inside his jeans, turned around to see an ambiguous looking older man standing in the doorway, dressed in black and with a stare that looked capable of breaking down walls.

"Get the fuck out here. This is none of your business."

"On the contrary you little piece of shit. This is most definitely my business as you have made the major mistake of your soon to be over pathetic little life, by hurting the girl who I love."

"You're Cezar? Fuck me you got here quick."

"You would be amazed how quick I can move when I need to."

Lucas got up from the relieved Lily and made his way over towards Cezar.

"Okay old man. So you want to be a fucking hero? Well come on then."

Lucas threw a punch at Cezar, which the professor stopped with ease as he simply caught the scumbag's arm in mid air. Lucas was unnervingly amazed at the strength of the older man and merely froze as Cezar calmly instructed Lily to go into the other room, as what was to follow was not going to be a spectacle for a lady to witness.

When Lily was safely out of the way Cezar finally spoke to Lucas with the chill of the entire Antarctic in his voice, "Shall we continue?"

As Lucas looked into the professor's eyes he was disturbed at the presence of peril that stared back at him.

"You're welcome to her mate. No hard feelings aye, just let go of my arm and I'll be on my way. It's just a bit of a misunderstanding that's all. I won't bother you again I promise."

As Cezar looked into the beady eyes that were soon to become glazed and lifeless, he was bemused at what Lily could have ever seen in this unattractive specimen that now whimpered before him.

"Oh I know you won't bother us again Lucas. I'll make certain of that." Suddenly Cezar's mouth began to protrude an extra set of fangs and he hissed at the frightened Lucas like an alley cat about to attack. Lucas felt a warm trickle run down his leg, too scared to recognise the irony of his now own indignity.

Cezar sank his teeth into Lucas's neck and within seconds he was dead. Just like he had done with Smithy in the pub toilets on Broad Street, the professor had taken his victim to the point of no return. He would not rise again into eternal life as a vampire; instead Lucas's fate was sealed.

For a split second Cezar had toyed with the idea of keeping him alive (alive in vampire terms that is) and then use him like a pawn simply for his amusement. It could be fun to make Lucas squirm forever more in eternal life, to act as a personal slave to the Fosturnea School of Football Excellence. He could be allocated tasks such as cleaning the piss and shit out of the toilets, and be forced only to live off the blood of sewer rats instead of rich human blood.

But no.

Cezar decided he never wanted to see his miserable little face again, and being a vampire ironically concluded that the streets of Birmingham would be safer with out the likes of Lucas parading them, spreading his vileness and contributing absolutely nothing constructive towards society whatsoever.

Cezar ensured that Lucas would never be allowed to attempt to rape anybody again, especially Lily. The snivelling little runt had made a big mistake messing with her.

My Sweet and precious Lily.

There was simply no alternative for Lucas but to pay the ultimate price.

With his life.

Cezar allowed Lucas's lifeless body to fall to the floor and wiped the blood from his mouth as he spoke to his own ears. "I hate the taste of bad blood."

His mouth now clean and presentable, not showing any traces of his vampire savagery only moments earlier, the professor casually popped his head around Lily's bedroom door, the room where she had headed for refuge.

"Don't come out just yet darling. Things have been sorted out man to man, a lady's presence is not yet appropriate."

"Cezar, you haven't done anything silly have you? I wouldn't want you to get into trouble or anything."

"My dear Lily, always putting other people's feelings before your own. A trait I so much love about you. Don't worry I haven't done anything silly. All you need to know is that Lucas won't be bothering you anymore. We have come to, shall we say, an understanding. There is nothing for you to worry about. I'll be back to see you in a moment. Unfortunately I will need to purchase a new rug for you though. I'm afraid it has become a little damaged."

Lily wondered what could possibly have happened between Cezar and Lucas to ruin her rug.

She thought it best not to ask.

Cezar had a very powerful way of speaking with her; his wise tone was always reassuring. He had said not to worry, so she simply would not worry. She didn't view it as an order that Cezar expected her to obey, but simply as trusted advice. Although she hadn't known him long, Cezar's presence and very being had totally mesmerized her. She was hopelessly hooked on him and completely spellbound by his charisma and charm. Above all he had completely won her trust.

"Okay, thanks Cezar. You have this wonderful way of making everything sound right. You seem so wise at every occasion. I'll look forward to seeing you in a short while then."

"Of course. Goodbye for now. I won't be long."

Cezar closed the door and walked over to Lucas's pathetic lifeless body. He picked the corpse up, wrapped it in Lily's fireside rug, which was fortunately large enough to completely cover the dead body, and casually placed it over his shoulder after securing the middle and either end with some heavy-duty tape that he found on the mantel piece nearby. Lily used it for securing her parcels that she often sold on internet auction sites.

Cezar carried the rug that was disguising Lucas's dead body with ease in spite of the dead-weight, and nonchalantly headed down the two flights of stairs and outside to the rear of the apartment block to where the domestic waste was stored until the city council's dustbin men came to relieve the skips and bins of its unwanted contents.

"How appropriate Lucas for you to be put with the rubbish," laughed Cezar as he jauntily spoke to the corpse.

Fortunately no one had noticed Cezar leave the premises and continue with the placement of the rug-clad corpse at the bottom of the large communal bin at the rear of Lily's block of apartments. There was no CCTV in operation either.

Still chuckling to himself Cezar covered the rug with a selection of black bags that had been left full of household rubbish. Before long neither the rug nor more importantly Lucas's corpse could be seen from the naked eye.

Cezar realised that he had until Wednesday to permanently rid the world of Lucas's body, as it was then that the unsuspecting city council workers would make the refuge collection and could possibly discover Lucas's remains. Cezar was not concerned for himself, he would certainly not be losing any sleep over the death of Lucas Casey, and he knew that even if Lucas's dead body was discovered a vampire killing is never a murder that is easily, if ever solved.

He worried for Lily though and he understood that if Lucas's remains were to be discovered then inevitably Lily would be heavily questioned by the authorities and he felt it a simpler process all round if Lucas's body was simply put somewhere where it could never be found.

In the Birmingham inner city suburb of Nechells, Cezar knew of two unlikely vampire allies in the shape of Harry and Keith Ferguson, known to the majority of unsuspecting Brummie citizens as "Ferguson Brother's Scrap Dealers and Car Dismantler's Ltd." What the ordinary human race failed to realise was that vampires intertwined with them on a daily basis and could be found in the most mundane of occupations, however, the world of vampires, most unlike the world of the human race was very intricate in itself. It was much more an extended community who were there to assist and look out for one another.

Within the hour Cezar would have contacted Harry and Keith and they will have turned up in their pickup truck, retrieved Lucas's carpet-clad body from the communal refuge bin, discreetly returned to their yard and placed Lucas in the boot of a Vauxhall Vectra or the like and proceeded to have the vehicle, including Lucas's remains, crushed into a small and unrecognisable metallic cube.

Cezar was confident that Lucas would never be seen again.

He chuckled even louder when he thought of the pathetic stiff that was once Lily's former boyfriend being mangled to unrecognisable pieces in the blades and mechanics of the car-crusher.

His only regret was that Lucas would not be alive to realise his fear while his body became mangled and intertwined with the metal of the old rusty car.

Chapter 28

It was the fifth game of the season and the Kingsbarr United supporters needed a boost. Only a few months earlier they had been watching their beloved team perform in the Premier League, England's finest footballing division and one envied throughout the world, but now after only four games into their debut Championship season, they were embarrassed to see them languishing near the foot of the table.

After the hard fought opening game when Kingsbarr had beaten County 1-0 with a wonderful free-kick from Johnny Knox late on, the season had taken an alarmingly turn for the worse for the Midlands side. Their second game ended ungraciously at 0-0 in a scrappy affair on a rainy night in the north-east of England, and their next two games ended in defeat, including one staged at Beacon Park which resulted in boos from the home supporters and rumblings of shouts such as "WE WANT WEIR OUT."

Daryl Weir realised that it was only a small minority calling for his dismissal—for now at least. He understood that football fans have very short memories and the fact that he had guided Kingsbarr United on several successful European winning campaigns, not to mention the winning of countless domestic trophies, would stand for nothing if the run of poor results were to continue for much longer.

But despite the unrest with the supporters, there was a far more optimistic air about Beacon Park on this particular Saturday afternoon. A welcome boost came in the shape of Gerry Spalding on his return to the squad from his controversial, and largely felt unjust, stretch in prison following his assault on an intruder in his home. National newspapers had ran supportive campaigns of "Free Gerry," claiming that he was a national hero to have protected his family so compellingly, but the judge had stated that unreasonable force had been used and so that was that.

Although Gerry had maintained his fitness levels whilst he had been inside prison by disciplining himself to undertaking strict fitness regimes such as press-ups and running exercises, Daryl felt that he may be lacking some match fitness and had opted to put Gerry on the bench for the start of the game. Instead the youngster Leon Davis would partner Giuseppe Rossi up front, although he hadn't yet shown the promise that Daryl had hoped for this season, particularly as the team were now playing at a supposedly lower level of competitive opposition.

In an attempt to enhance his squad, Daryl had made a relatively shrewd move of bringing in 37 year-old Matt Floyd on a free transfer from French club Marseille. Birmingham born Matt was a lifelong fan of Kingsbarr United and in this being his final season; Daryl had suggested that he join the club, as it would be a nice end to his flourishing and impressive career. Although now undeniably past his best ability, Matt was still a fine and clever player who had played in some of the best teams in Europe including in La Liga and Serie A, and Daryl realised that he was more than capable of making a sound contribution to the Kingsbarr team. Daryl also realised that like Johnny, with Matt being an actual fan of Kingsbarr United, he would always be willing to try that extra ten percent to serve the club that they both loved so dearly.

Unfortunately the paperwork with Marseille had not been completed in time for the opening game of the season, but Matt had featured in the last three games scoring Kingsbarr's only goal in their home defeat. He had looked a good acquisition to the club in spite of the team's poor results. But in Kingsbarr's last game Matt was unluckily stretchered off the field of play with a badly torn hamstring. He would be out of action for at least three months.

So now Leon Davis had another chance to make his mark, but Daryl hadn't been happy with the lad's temperament and attitude lately. He had not adjusted well to the team's relegation from the Premier League and thought that he was already clearly a better footballer than he really was. Yes he definitely had potential, in time and with good coaching and guidance he could be a very good player, but at present Davis was showing the side of the modern footballer that Daryl Weir did not like. In his, and many others opinion, young players were earning more wages than they knew what to do with. They gain celebrity status and it goes to their heads whilst they lose their respect for the game and those responsible for helping to put them where they are now. The lad had worked quite hard when Kingsbarr were in the Premiership and had occasionally shown flashes of brilliance, but he was inconsistent and was still learning his trade, something that he found difficult to comprehend and the arrival of Matt Floyd had done little to massage his over inflated ego. Being honest with himself Daryl wished that he didn't have to play him today.

The game could hardly have started any worse for Kingsbarr United or for Daryl Weir. Straight from the kick-off the visiting team had controlled possession of the ball and within two minutes had taken the lead.

Nobody was any more disappointed than Jody Roper who had been convinced that the inclusion of Wham!'s "Wake Me Up Before You Go-Go" in the pre match dressing room ritual of playing eighties music was destined to get the boys going today.

"What the fuck is wrong with you lads, you look like you are still asleep. Wake me up before you go-go? Wake up and get your fucking act together! Come on!"

Daryl's harsh words did have an effect on his players. He was a manager who was highly respected and had never usually had problems motivating his players. They began to retain possession of the ball but due to being relegated last season, followed by the recent run of poor results and now the worst possible start to today's game they were clearly playing without a great deal of confidence. Most of the play was in the middle of the park and as the game progressed they were not creating any clear-cut goal scoring opportunities and would occasionally lose possession sloppily resulting in them having to work unnecessarily hard to win the ball back.

Then disaster struck.

Vincent "Bruiser" Bradshaw had cheaply given the ball away and in his attempts to make amends he dived in rashly at the Town player making crunching contact with him but not making any contact with the ball. The Town player went down in a heap and Vincent, who was also still on the floor after his sliding challenge, looked up at the referee as he reached into his pocket.

Everyone connected with Kingsbarr United feared the worst.

They were not reprieved of their feelings as the referee produced a red card from his pocket and showed it to the Kingsbarr hard-man.

Vinnie stood to his feet and challenged the referee's decision. "It's me first fucking offence you blind cunt. Show me a yellow card, I accept a yellow but not a fucking red you daft twat."

The Football Association and its referees had been briefed about Vincent Bradshaw's suffering of Tourette's Syndrome and FIFA had instructed that allowances had to be made for Vinnie's sometimes uncontrollable swearing and insults. Although at times like this it was hard to tell if it was the Tourette's controlling his swearing or simply Vinnie himself.

Club captain Johnny also attempted to defend his team-mate, though a little more diplomatically than Vinnie.

"Come on ref, give him another chance. It was clearly unintentional."

"The challenge warranted a straight red card. It was far to rash to be forgiven on my field of play, and unless you want to join Mr. Bradshaw for an early bath Mr. Knox I suggest you keep quiet too."

"Wanker," said Vinnie to the referee as he trotted off the field of play. Johnny wished he could get away with calling the same expletive to the referee but realised that he didn't have any medical evidence to support any such verbal attack on the man in black. He hated the way some of the referees became *little Hitlers* and did not seem to be interested in the spirit of a football match; their sole purpose for 90 minutes was to strut their authority all over the place.

Although a little shaken, the Town player was fortunately not badly injured and was soon on his feet after some attention from the physiotherapist.

From the resulting free-kick Town went 2-0 up.

As the game developed Kingsbarr went to pieces and when the half-time whistle came 10-man Kingsbarr United were astonishingly losing at home by 3 goals to nil.

Boos and chants of "WE WANT WEIR OUT" painfully followed the players into the tunnel.

"Okay boys, Vinnie's sending off was obviously the turning point but I still feel that the 3-0 score line flatters them. We have had far more possession than they have but we just need to turn it into an end product. If they can score three goals in a half I don't see why we can't."

"It will be harder with ten men though, boss."

"If you can't stand the heat Rossi then get out of the kitchen. Do you want to be substituted?"

"Sorry boss," replied the Italian feeling two inches small. "Don't worry I'll work even harder this half. Come on boys we can do it right."

"Of course we can," said Johnny feeling the need to flex his motivation from a team captain's sense of duty.

"That's the spirit boys; you know that you are better than they are. Get stuck in, although I suggest a damn sight less rashly than Vincent did." The Scottish manager cast a disapproving eye towards his Tourette's Syndrome suffering midfielder who by now had showered and changed into his day clothes of a brown suit, cream shirt and club tie. "You can let them know that you are there. Just don't go diving in. Get the ball forward early, we are chasing the game now but try and make all passes count; don't just hoof it aimlessly towards nobody in particular. That's why I'm bringing Gerry on this half. He can play well as a target man and also drop deep to link the play intelligently to Rossi. I hope that prison food was decent enough Gerry because you are going to have to help out the midfield as well as the frontline."

"No worries boss. I won't let you down."

"And I suppose it is me who is coming off?" said a surly Leon Davis who was slouching on the dressing room seat, displaying all the body language that suggested the result or the team didn't matter; only he did.

"I was just coming to that Leon," replied the manager trying to be as diplomatic as possible in the situation. "We are down to ten men and I need to make a change, I possibly should have made it as soon as Bradshaw was dismissed but I wanted to see how things progressed. You are more of a luxury player Leon, Spalding can use all of his experience to try and get something out of the game for us. You are not the type of player to link the play and to be used as a target. You played as well as could be expected lad, but I want you to have a rest this half."

Daryl's sensitive words had little effect on the sulking youngster.

"Experience? What experience would that be then? He's just a fucking jailbird. What's he going to do, go out and beat seven shades of shit out of one of their players? Before long we'll be down to nine men."

"You cheeky little fucker. How's about I beat seven shades of shit out of you instead."

"Anytime Spalding."

Johnny had the good sense to put an arm across Gerry as he made his way towards the insolent youngster. It was enough for Gerry to realise that he shouldn't pursue his anger to teach Leon a lesson he wouldn't forget, even though he probably deserved it. Johnny then turned to Leon.

"Leave it out Leon. I won't stop him a second time."

"Yeah, Leon," said Jody Roper getting involved. "Put your toys back in your pram and chill out."

"Come on Leon, the man's right," said Alvin Braxton in his deep toned Jamaican voice. "Chill out and just accept that you've been substituted man. Worse things happen in life ya know."

"Just everyone calm down and concentrate on the matter at hand. I'm the fucking manager Leon and if I say that you are coming off then you are coming off. I explained my reasons and that should be good enough for you to understand. There is no room for any prima-donnas on my team; you would do well to remember that."

Leon grabbed his clothes in a hissy fit and stormed out of the dressing room with out even bothering to get changed.

"That's two weeks wages you're fined Davis," shouted Daryl as Leon stormed out, then he turned his attention to the rest of his team. "Okay, boys forget about Leon, I'll deal with him on Monday morning. Now you know what you've got to do, get out there and do it."

When Leon Davis had arrived outside the entrance to Beacon Park he had enough presence of mind to have got dressed on the way out, although he had put his trousers over his gold shorts and was still wearing the blue socks of the Kingsbarr United home kit. He noticed that his designer shoes were a tighter fit when worn over the chunky football socks; he had his football boots in one hand and his Kingsbarr gold and blue striped jersey in the other. In all the commotion he had completely left his kit bag behind in the dressing room. He looked down at the three crowns of the Kingsbarr United badge and began to regret his rash action of storming out. *Fuck me* he thought. *Weir will never pick me now.* In that split second he decided that first thing on Monday morning he would go to see Daryl Weir, tell him exactly what he thought of him and hand in a written transfer request, even if it meant going on loan until the reopening of the transfer window in January next year. Of course the conceited Leon Davis fully expected that he could be loaned out to a Premiership club.

"That is very interesting attire, may I say," spoke a voice that seemed to come out of nowhere.

Leon liked the tone of the female voice and didn't instantly recognise the accent. As he looked up to see who had spoken to him he realised how foolish he must have looked. His shirt was on but completely undone showing off his six pack and smooth chest muscles, and the blue football socks could easily be seen between the hem of his dark trousers and his slip on designer shoes.

"I was . . . err . . . in a bit of a hurry."

"So I see," giggled the girl, her raven hair cut into a style that seemed to cup her beautiful pale skinned face. Leon was mesmerised by her. Perhaps storming out of the ground at this moment in time had been a wise decision after all.

Leon was brought crashing back down to planet Earth as he heard the crowd roar as they welcomed the teams back onto the pitch for the second half.

"Look, I really don't want to be here at the moment, and I could really do with some friendly company. Perhaps you could come for a drink with me or something. I need to go home first and shower though. There is a bar in Birmingham's city centre called *Le Persuasion*. I could meet you there in about an hour and a half?" Leon was keen not to divulge the fact that he still lived at home with his parents fearing it would make him appear foolish and uncool, hence his suggestion to meet up with the girl later and not take her *back to his place.*

"No, I don't think so," replied the girl.

"Oh, that's a shame." Leon couldn't believe the extent of his rejection today.

"What I mean is I don't want to be apart from you for the next couple of hours. I suggest that we book into a hotel room in the city centre. You can get showered, I can fuck you, you can get showered again and this time I will join you, then we can go out for a meal and a drink, get absolutely pissed, crawl back to our hotel room and fuck again all night long. How does that sound?"

Leon couldn't believe his dramatic change in good fortune. His jaw was dropping but his penis was certainly rising at the words being caressed towards him by that strange beautiful accent right here in the street outside Beacon Park.

"Th . . . that sounds wonderful." He could hardly speak with the shock of the beautiful girl's informality and the anticipation of what today was now going to behold for him.

"Come on then big boy", said the girl in her sweet seductive voice as she squeezed his erection through his trousers, shorts and underpants.

"Wait I don't even know your name. And what is that accent? It makes me so fucking horny."

"My name is Afina, and I originate from Romania, but I am also from a world that you do not yet understand."

"My name is Leon, and I'm in fucking heaven."

Gerry Spalding made an instant impact to the game. Within five minutes of the restart he had headed the ball against the bar and had fed some decent balls through to Giuseppe Rossi who had forced the Town goalkeeper to make two exceptional saves. His presence on the field seemed to have lifted the spirits of the whole Kingsbarr team and their supporters and the dreadful score line seemed to have momentarily slipped everyone's mind. Town had rarely been out of their own half and the ten men of Kingsbarr United seemed to be playing as if they had at least twelve players on the pitch. They were winning every ball, getting on the end of every pass and more importantly turning their dominant possession into goal scoring opportunities.

Gerry was soon rewarded for his efforts and he pulled a goal back for Kingsbarr United shortly before the hour mark.

Johnny had taken off on one of his famous solo runs from midfield and gained considerable ground towards the Town goalmouth. He had beaten four players before he took a shot at goal that rattled the crossbar and the power of the shot catapulted the ball back into play. Gerry had read the situation perfectly and had allowed the ball to bounce once as he then controlled the ball on his chest and rifled it into the roof of the net.

The Kingsbarr supporters went crazy and the little Hitler of a referee attempted to spoil the party as he booked Gerry for an "over zealous" celebration, but Gerry didn't care. He was back from his nightmare in prison, back with the security and love of his family and he was scoring goals again in the first team for Kingsbarr United. A single yellow card could not deter from the sweet way that he felt right at this moment.

With their tails up Kingsbarr United continued to dominate the play and twice Johnny, who was now in electric form, had felt that he had won a penalty-kick as he was tripped inside the penalty area following some decent dribbling, only for the little Hitler to award nothing. The ten men of Kingsbarr were beginning to feel like they were playing against twelve men, that being eleven town players and the referee.

The Chinese international right-winger Charlie Cheng was also having an inspiring game, and he received a pass from Gerry who had intelligently switched the play from the left hand side. Charlie found himself in acres of space and made it easily to the by-line riding two tackles on the way and crossed the ball out of reach of the Town keeper and towards the far post.

The cross eluded everyone but Gerry had continued his run from when he first fed the ball to Charlie and he arrived unmarked at the far post to head his and Kingsbarr's second goal of the game.

The Kingsbarr supporters went berserk as they could now sense that a comeback was now certainly a possibility. At 3-2 it was most definitely game on.

This time Gerry gave a controlled wave to the supporters, not wanting to suffer for his celebration and gave a sarcastic wink towards the referee.

The ten men of Kingsbarr United, battled and fought and played with a style that at last was expected of such a big club who had only months earlier been in the top flight of English football. Town were being run ragged and could hardly cope with the onslaught of the ferocious football that Kingsbarr were delivering. Fortunately for them their goalkeeper was playing out of his skin, going on to defy shots from Knox, Cheng, Rossi and Spalding who was now sniffing for his hat-trick. Even central-defender Jody Roper had been denied by the heroics of the Town keeper, as following a Charlie Cheng corner-kick, his headed attempt on goal had been superbly tipped over the bar by the Town custodian. In sharp contrast Alvin Braxton in the Kingsbarr United goal was the only Kingsbarr player not to have seen much of the ball this half of the game.

As the clock ticked by, the Kingsbarr United supporters were biting their nails, anxious for their team to achieve a remarkable comeback and draw level in a game that once looked dead and buried. The Town supporters were biting their nails hoping that their team could hang on to their now only slender lead. At half-time, with Kingsbarr United down to ten men it looked like the game was already won as Town led 3-0 and smelled the sweet taste of success knowing that beating Kingsbarr United on their home ground was indeed a worthy scalp to accomplish. Now the Town team were hanging on by the skin of their teeth as waves of Kingsbarr United attacks kept endlessly flooding in on their goal.

Then the fourth official held up the electronic board to indicate that there would only be three minutes stoppage time added on at the end of the normal ninety minutes. If Kingsbarr United were going to equalize in this game they had to do it pretty damn quick.

As always, brilliant under pressure, Johnny picked up the ball just in from the half-way line and the Town players stood around him trying to guess what he was going to do. He looked to his right to see if he could pick out Charlie Cheng, but the Chinese winger seemed to be pretty well covered by the Town left-back. His glance up was enough to unnerve the Town midfielder standing to Johnny's right though, and he wrongly assumed that Johnny was indeed going to pass the ball to Charlie. Instead Johnny headed straight for the gap that had opened up and went on yet another powerful run towards goal. The Town players were chasing him but Johnny's speed and determination was simply too much for them, but then he noticed a Town defender coming towards him from his right hand side. By this time Johnny was just outside the penalty area and in a good shooting position, but he knew that if he squared up for a shot he might just allow enough time for the oncoming Town defender to block his attempt at goal. Worse still Johnny believed that the way the player was thundering towards him he could easily mistime his tackle and end up doing Johnny some serious damage. Johnny also recognised what fine shot-stopping form the Town keeper was in.

So in a split second Johnny engineered a moment of sheer footballing wizardry. As the Town defender came diving in at him, Johnny put his foot on the ball and dragged it brilliantly behind him causing the red faced Town defender to slide along the ground making contact with absolutely nothing! Within the same motion of dragging back the ball with his right foot, Johnny squared it to Gerry Spalding with the inside of the same golden-coloured boot. Johnny's moment of genius totally out-foxed the Town players and even wrong footed their outstanding goalkeeper and Gerry was at last able to bring the scores level as he connected his left foot perfectly with the ball and drilled it sweetly into the roof of the net.

Yet again the Kingsbarr United supporters went crazy as their beloved team drew level, and there was no way on Earth that Gerry Spalding could contain his delight and not indulge in a massive celebration. He kissed the three crowns of the badge on his gold and blue striped shirt before removing it and swinging it above his head as he ran bare skinned around the whole perimeter of the pitch to revel in the celebrations with the United supporters. He was absolutely ecstatic, as was everybody connected with Kingsbarr, and quite probably pretty much the whole of the nation who happened to be tuned in to various radio and television reports showing that on his first game after an unjustifiable stretch in prison, Gerry Spalding had returned to score a hat-trick and had helped engineer one of the all time greatest come backs in the history of football, both on a personal level and in the game itself.

Unfortunately, the *little Hitler* failed to understand the significance of the celebrations and duly sent Gerry Spalding off the field of play for two bookable offences, both earned for celebrating a goal! Gerry didn't care; he was still waving and cheering with the Kingsbarr fans as he left the pitch. Daryl Weir, who was also ecstatic at the contribution Gerry had made to the game, and the fact that Kingsbarr should now at least get a point from the match, decided that he would appeal against Gerry's sending off first thing Monday morning, before he had dealt with the insolent Leon Davis. *How the two players differed in attitude*, he thought. Then he helplessly realised that he may have to reluctantly play the teenager in the next couple of games if Spalding's red card was not rescinded. He knew the rules of football as much as the next person in the game but he could never understand why certain referees failed to apply the simple law of common sense.

With only seconds remaining it was unlikely that Kingsbarr would lose this game even though they now only had nine players on the pitch.

Johnny was adamant that he wasn't going to give Town the chance to spoil the party and straight from their kick-off he tackled their obviously tired centre-forward and chipped the ball over a couple of heads to find Giuseppe Rossi, who controlled the ball with his chest, beat two players and drilled the ball into the bottom right hand corner of the net, giving the Town keeper no chance.

This was amazing!

Against all the odds, nine man Kingsbarr United had come back from 3-0 down to clinching the game and all three points with an incredible 4-3 victory. The other eight players of Kingsbarr, including goalkeeper Alvin Braxton who had run the length of the pitch, were surrounding the Italian striker in a shower of mass hysteria and even the Kingsbarr substitutes, coaching staff and physiotherapists were on the pitch to celebrate.

But suddenly the roars of cheering and joy from the Kingsbarr United supporters, suddenly turned to expletives and cries of "No way" and "you must be fucking joking ref."

To be fair on this occasion it was the referee's assistant who had been responsible for the decision. He had flagged for the referee's attention and informed the *little Hitler* that he believed that Rossi had actually controlled the football with his arm and not his chest.

Subsequently the fourth goal was disallowed.

Both Giuseppe Rossi and Johnny Knox each received a yellow card for their protests and Daryl Weir was reprimanded for uncharacteristically allowing himself to get caught up in the atmosphere as he told all four officials that they were nothing more than cheats and the sooner video evidence was introduced to the game the better so that there "countless fucking mistakes" could be overruled and put right once and for all. He also pointed out to them "how bad decisions like yours can cost managers like me our fucking jobs."

After the crowd and players had finally settled down the referee blew the whistle to indicate that Town could take the free-kick for Rossi's wrongly accused hand-ball, and then immediately blew the final whistle to indicate the end of the game.

The Kingsbarr United supporters gave their team a standing ovation as they left the pitch, and although it had been an incredible come back the 3-3 result was now bittersweet in view of the wrongly disallowed fourth goal.

Also giving the team a standing ovation and expressing his admiration at United's second half display was Professor Cezar Prodanescu who had become accustomed to spending his Saturday afternoon's watching Kingsbarr United play football. Being a professor in football, he had used his clever brain to analyse the Kingsbarr United team and he had his own opinions on how they could be improved.

In contrast Daryl Weir was in a troubled state of mind. He was pleased that his team had made a fantastic comeback to secure a point, and he was pleased in the manner that they played. He realised that the television pundits would constantly replay the Giuseppe Rossi hand-balling incident and had no doubt that they would conclude that Kingsbarr were nothing short than robbed of their deserved victory. But the bare facts remained that ex-premiership outfit Kingsbarr United were languishing near the bottom of the Championship with just five points out of as many games and only one win all season. He may have temporarily halted the calls for his head from the supporters but if results did not improve then they would soon be calling for his resignation. And how much time was Peter Cogshaw going to allow him to try and turn things around anyway? He entered the dressing room with a heavy heart.

"Well done boys. I couldn't have asked any more from you?"

Leon Davis and the girl he had not long met known as Afina booked into a budget Birmingham hotel as Mr and Mrs Barry King. Leon's mind was far away from his disappointment at the Kingsbarr United match less than two hours earlier, and he was yet to learn of his club's incredible result.

Afina's sensuality and ability between the sheets was totally mesmerising him, he had never met a girl like this before in his short-lived sexual life. True he hadn't had many sexual relationships, but he had had enough to be able to know what was a good sexual encounter as opposed to a bad one. Afina was proving to be one fabulous and amazing fuck.

She was currently performing the most amazing oral sex on him and every now and then he would steal a glimpse down at her to see her look back at him while her beautiful raven coloured hair seductively dropped in front of her face and his throbbing manhood.

As he laid his head back he would compliment her on her performance with phrases such as "oh that's so good baby" in between his grunts and groans.

Suddenly he felt a new sensation. It was painful but weirdly enjoyable at the same time. In fact it was pure ecstasy.

Afina, herself in a state of sheer eroticism, had revealed one of her vampire fangs and stuck it into the shaft of Leon's penis. She sucked wildly at the blood as it spurted out, becoming more and more aroused as the metallic, sweet taste trickled down her throat.

Leon was now in a state of arousal he had never experienced before. The sensations raged through his body as he fought for his breath in a state of incredible satisfaction beyond his wildest dreams.

Just as Andrei Botezatu had erotically introduced Afina into the world of vampirism one rainy night in Bucharest, she had now in turn captured another recruit into this exciting incestuous and erotic world of the undead.

Afina looked up at Leon who was in a state of exhausted bliss. Blood dripping delicately from the sides of her mouth she smiled sweetly and spoke softly.

"Welcome to my world," she said.

Chapter 29

"This house is so lovely Cezar, but it is also very big."

"I need it to be extremely spacious Lily my dear. I need enough room to accommodate a laboratory so that I can enjoy the luxury of working from home."

The setting of the house, and its extensive grounds, that Cezar and Lily were viewing, was just north of the midpoint between the Staffordshire towns of Lichfield and Cannock. Set back from a little used B road at the end of a long gravelled drive, the house was even older than it's soon to be Romanian proprietor. Fortunately it was in amazingly good shape. The timber beams were free of any dry rot and woodworm, and the walls and ceilings of its twenty-one rooms were sound and secure. The house had been empty for some years now whilst various heritage charities had considered purchasing it, but although it was a listed building and of significant historical substance it was felt that it lacked enough of a dramatic link to justify the funding for it. In contrast, and not too far away from Cezar's soon to be dwelling, were houses that could boast of accommodating King Charles II when he hid from the New Model Army of Cromwell following the defeat of the Royalist forces at the Battle of Worcester, a history that Cezar's soon to be new home couldn't live up to. However, as far as Cezar was concerned, the charities loss was definitely his gain.

"So you do plan to remain in England then?"

"But of course. The work that I have in mind dictates that I need to live not only in England but also right here in the Midlands. Anyway I can't live in a hotel for ever."

"So it is only work that merits you to settle here?" Lily looked to the floor as she spoke mimicking the behaviour of an insecure child.

"Initially yes it was my work, but you know full well Lily that I now have another good reason to settle down here." Cezar was keen to reassure his English Rose.

Lily moved her gaze from the floor so that her eyes fell gently onto Cezar's face. She was smiling. Cezar was still confused at how her smile could melt his heart so effectively and fill his soul with such contentment. A soul that was habitually so cold and void of any affectionate emotion. His mind wondered momentarily at how the fictitious vampires portrayed in movies and books could feel love, in particular the fatal love that Count Dracula had felt for Mina, and found himself tolerating the artisans of such stories as maybe not being so far away from the truth after all. For he was sure that he was in love with Lily.

Lily moved towards Cezar and hugged him. With their arms still around one another they simultaneously looked out across the pleasant greenery of the South Staffordshire moorland, and the day was so clear that they were also able to see the more tiered landscape of Shropshire with its hills and valleys. The setting of the house wasn't perhaps as impressive as the Lake or Peak District, but it was still in a beautiful location with stunning panoramic views.

In the distance a gentle hum could be heard of traffic moving along the old A5, the M54 and the M6 Toll Road, a reminder that traffic links in the Midlands were never too far away despite the often underestimated beauty that its counties could undoubtedly offer. Entwined with the noise of the traffic were the pleasant sounds of birds singing and the drilling of a nearby woodpecker.

At this moment in time, secure in the arms of her lover Professor Cezar Prodanescu, Lily felt that there was simply no other place that she would rather be.

"I would love to live here," she blurted out.

Lily and Cezar had never spoken about living together, their relationship had certainly been a whirlwind romance albeit cemented with an incredible element of mutual respect and security, but it had simply not had the conventional time span to develop enough to discuss the sharing of living arrangements.

But now she had said it, never intending to, but being swept away in this moment of serenity Lily had become excited inside her soul at the prospect of living in this charming house with the man she undoubtedly loved.

But when she turned to look into Cezar's eyes to see his reaction to her clumsy announcement, her heart sank as she could read that the thought of them living together was clearly not on Cezar's agenda.

"I'm sorry Cezar. I didn't mean to say that. I've just been caught up in a beautiful moment. My mouth has started speaking of its own accord."

"Don't apologise Lily," replied Cezar genuinely desperate not to hurt his sweet lover's feelings. "We have all the time in the world yet. Let's not rush things; I'm sure we could live together one day. For now though I need this to be the base for my Fosturnea School of Football Excellence as well as for my genetic work. I plan to bring the school over from Romania and set it up here. That is why I need so many rooms and all this wonderful land."

Lily knew that Cezar's words made some sense to her, yet they didn't do a great deal to ease her disappointment, and for all his years of wisdom the professor realised that perhaps his explanation could have been a little less direct.

"So you don't want to live with me but you want to live with a bunch of young men in this wonderful house in the countryside, while I struggle to make ends meet in my tiny flat. I'm afraid I find that a bit difficult to comprehend Cezar." If only Lily had been aware of what sinister plans lay ahead for this house, she would certainly never have contemplated living in it.

"Lily, please understand. I am like a father to the boys of Fosturnea. Many of them are orphans and I have given them a path in life."

"And what about your life Cezar? Are you not allowed to have one or is your life simply work, work, work? Well I believe that life is for living. Do you expect me to just wait around for you? It is admirable what you have done for these boys but do you actually have to live with them! My god it's like Elvis and Priscilla all over again."

"Lily, you do not understand."

"You are right Cezar. I don't. Why did you even bring me here today?"

"Because I value your opinion more than anybody else's in the world."

"Well Cezar I will give you my opinion. This house would have been perfect for us to move this relationship to its next stage, but I guess it is equally perfect to convert into a School of Football Excellence for a bunch of young men to live rent free and kick a sack of leather about while a mad professor cons himself into thinking that his only role in life is to be a patron saint to young footballers."

Lily realised that her disappointment with the situation was fuelling her words to uncharacteristically appear spiteful and potentially hurtful, and she was instantly regretting the venom she was unleashing towards Cezar. She shivered as she saw a mist come over Cezar's eyes and sensed a darkness from him that unnerved her. This was a side of Cezar she had never seen before. She had clearly angered him.

"Believe me Lily, the last thing I am is a saint. You are acting like a spoilt little girl and I demand that you stop it. The last time anybody ever dared to speak to me that way never had the opportunity to do it again."

"Cezar, you're scaring me. I'm sorry. It's just that I love you, forgive me. Please. I'm just being silly; I guess I just want you all to myself."

Cezar realised that he had shown a side to Lily that he hoped she would never have to see. It frightened him as much as it had frightened her. He quickly snapped himself out of the anger that he had shown towards her, but remained angry with himself for losing his self-control.

And then a dark realisation began to creep into his mind. For the first time in a few weeks now it dawned on him that perhaps he was being ridiculous to believe that he, a master vampire, could have a meaningful relationship with a mere mortal.

Just how long could he keep his secret from her?

Although Lily's opinion of his soon to be living arrangements had irritated him, Cezar's anger and venom towards her had been fuelled in the main out of his pure frustration at the unusual situation that he now found himself to be in. His sneaking out at night to claim his victims and drink their blood without Lily suspecting a thing was becoming more and more like an act of survival rather than an act of pleasure. His heart fell heavy when he dared to think about how Lily would react if she knew just what he really was. The irony was he felt compelled to protect her; there had been countless opportunities when he could have taken Lily's life and turned her into a vampire also. He knew that if he did this, then they could live together forever, but he felt that if this ever was to be, it could be only by her own choice.

But just how the hell was he ever going to be able to approach the subject with her?

For the first time in his entire existence he was beginning to hate what he was and on occasions even found himself wishing he were *normal*.

But then he would think about his important work that lay ahead and realised his destiny of being a master vampire could only have been a gift from a higher source, though it would be difficult to rationalise his existence as being a god-given gift!

His mind was becoming increasingly tortured.

For now he realised that he must live his life as a double-entity. On one hand he must remain a loyal lover and protector to a girl who was so special to him that he awoke each day with the unusual feeling of contentment and bliss in his belly. On the other he must lead by example to the vampire way of life and proactively claim victims and recruit and multiply his race further with each savage killing.

But following this episode of the collision of the two different worlds of the undead and the living in the guise of a lovers quarrel, something else nagged away unpleasantly at his psyche.

Something that frightened him.

Just how close was I to hurting the one person in my life that I love?

Chapter 30

Kingsbarr United press conference, Beacon Park Stadium.

Peter Cogshaw looked like the fat cat that had got the cream as he puffed at his cigar whilst addressing the gathering of paparazzi and reporters. It was incredible how he had managed to avoid certain rooms in *his* stadium, such as the press conference room, being deemed a public place. These rooms of convenience didn't have fire-sprinklers installed. In order for Peter Cogshaw to enjoy a cigar he seldom cared about compromising health and safety regulations.

"Ladies and Gentlemen, thank you very much for coming today. I have some wonderful news to announce regarding Kingsbarr United Football Club."

"Is it some news about the disappearance of Daryl Weir, Mr. Cogshaw?" asked a fresh faced journalist from the local Kingsbarr District newspaper that was distributed free through the letterboxes of the surrounding area, surviving mainly on the income from private advertising from both domestic placements surrounding the selling of unwanted household items and the half-page spreads financed by local businesses.

Some of the other, more experienced journalists scowled at the young "wannabee", believing that his presence wasn't even merited at such a press conference and they were certainly not appreciative of his early line of questioning.

Peter Cogshaw was also a little put out by the youngster's early claim to grabbing a piece of the action. Not really wanting to deal with the question at this moment in time the chairman answered it as adequately as he could.

"If this press conference was about the disappearance, or indeed what I believe to be the subsequent appearance of Daryl Weir, then I would be accompanied by the police for this press conference. Unfortunately I have no fresh news on Mr. Weir's whereabouts, but the police have advised me that I am not really at liberty to discuss that situation in great detail as it could inadvertently damage their investigation."

The young journalist's cheeks turned scarlet in colour as he realised that his enthusiasm for a quality scoop may have clouded his decision as to when the appropriate timing of his question should have been.

In truth the press conference had been hurriedly called with an element of surprise; nobody really knew what Peter Cogshaw was about to announce that seemed to be so important. It was obvious that things would become clearer following his initial statement, the green journalist with the scarlet cheeks now realised that the law of the press conference dictated that the announcement would come first and that questions were *invited* later.

Peter Cogshaw continued to address the gathering of the press and media personnel with his original intentions.

"Now as you can see Ladies and Gentlemen, to my left there are four seats currently unoccupied, but it now gives me great pleasure to introduce to you a gentleman who is not only going to occupy the seat to my immediate left but who is also going to occupy the current manager's position here at Kingsbarr United. Ladies and Gentlemen, please welcome Professor Cezar Prodanescu."

The room of journalists were stunned as the undoubtedly suave and charismatic individual entered the room, for although he looked every inch a man of distinction and knowledge with his designer suit and well-trimmed hair, nobody had ever heard of him and were confused that Peter Cogshaw would make such an appointment of a completely unknown manager in light of the only recent disappearance of his long serving and loyal comrade Daryl Weir.

"Good morning everybody," spoke the new Kingsbarr United manager in a distinguished Romanian accent. "My name is Professor Cezar Prodanescu. I am of Romanian nationality and I am the new manager of Kingsbarr United. First of all I wish to thank Mr. Cogshaw for believing in me and the methods that I plan to put into practice, which will undoubtedly make this very special football club a team to be feared once again. I know this must be a surprise to all of you so I welcome any questions that you may have."

"Bernadette Grainger, *Satellite Sports Channel.* You are obviously very confident that you can succeed at Kingsbarr United Professor Prodanescu, tell me what credentials do you believe to have that can justify this confidence?"

"Well, Miss Grainger please do not confuse my confidence with arrogance. I am a recognised professor in football, amongst other things, which I hope indicates to you my intelligence, which can be applied using expert tactics to what we all know as *the beautiful game.*"

"I don't for a minute doubt your intelligence professor, but it takes more than academic qualifications, no matter how impressive they may be, to run an English football team, particularly one that appears to be so low in confidence and drive. I am sure that you would agree that for such a job in football, perhaps learning your craft from the University of Life would put you in a better position to manage a team such as Kingsbarr United. Just what experience have you had in the game?"

Cezar appeared completely unphased. "It is a very valid line of questioning Miss. Grainger and one that warrants an appropriate answer. I am actually very experienced and have been around a lot longer than you may think, albeit not necessarily always in the public eye. I have had connections with the Romanian club Steaua Bucharest, although I admit that this was some time ago. But I do not pretend to share the limelight all by myself. I have donated a lot of my time in building the Fosturnea School of Football Excellence in Romania, and it is the players that have graduated from this school that will help me to accomplish the success that this club deserves. In fact the Fosturnea School of Football Excellence will be the key to my success."

"Donald Stroud, *Midlands News*. Could you please elaborate for us Professor Prodanescu? What exactly is the Fosturnea School of Football Excellence?"

"Certainly Mr. Stroud. I am sure that you have heard many stories about the orphanages in my country; unfortunately it is a sad fact that there are many unwanted children in Romania for one reason or another that I do not really wish to debate at this press conference today. However, the Fosturnea School of Football Excellence has acted as a safe haven for teenage boys who have perhaps lost there way in life following unsuccessful experiences growing up in children's homes. I have taken them under my wing and cultured them into having a purpose in life that they can be proud of. Where they once felt like an outcast in society, now with the guidance of the Fosturnea School of Football Excellence they now believe, quite rightly so, that they are a valued member of civilization. I teach them respect and discipline amongst other things, and of course as the name of the school suggests I tutor them into becoming very talented footballers."

"Solomon Morris, *Everyday Newspaper*. I commend you on the time and devotion that you have spent in helping these young men Professor Prodanescu, but are you not perhaps being a tad naïve to believe that they can simply walk into an English football team and be able to play to the standard required. Surely they are unproven and both yourself and Mr. Cogshaw are taking a huge gamble in attempting to rebuild Kingsbarr United this way?"

"On the contrary Mr. Morris. These boys are extremely professional. They train for many hours a day with a dedication usually not found in your average footballer. As you will soon find out their ability is immense and I am confident that they will not only set the Championship alight, they will also go on to prove their worth in the Premiership and indeed European competition. This is a new and exciting era for Kingsbarr United and I am delighted that Mr. Cogshaw has put his trust in me to lead this club into the big time once again where it undoubtedly belongs."

"Ralph Groves, *Birmingham Daily Chronicle*. Mr. Cogshaw may I please turn the questioning towards you Sir? Those cynics amongst us may suggest that you have simply adopted Professor Prodanescu with his belt and braces Football Academy, as simply a cheap option to introduce new players. But as Mr. Morris highlighted earlier could it not backfire on you as being a dangerous gamble even if it is a cheap option?"

Cogshaw puffed once more on his cigar before answering. "It is true that there is limited money available for investment in players since Kingsbarr's unfortunate relegation from the Premiership, and after speaking with Professor Prodanescu it was indeed an attractive proposition to strengthen the squad by introducing young talent and not having to rely on spending large pots of money. But let me tell you this, why should we pay lots of cash to a club that has groomed a player so that they can then make a tidy profit? Surely we can produce quality players from scratch and then we can generate some cash by selling them onto other clubs for big money."

The professor wasn't pleased with the chairman's proposals and his lack of understanding of the essence of his footballing prodigies, portraying his discontentment by glaring at Mr. Cogshaw unnerving him considerably, which didn't go unnoticed by the crowd of journalists.

"No players produced from the Fosturnea School of Football Excellence will ever be for sale."

Cogshaw gulped and an uncomfortable silence filled the room until Donald Stroud, a journalist with the reputation of being a dispassionate vulture spoke again.

"Mr. Cogshaw I know that you have stated that you do not wish to be drawn into the whereabouts of Daryl Weir, but nevertheless some loose ends at least needs tying up. How can you appoint Professor Prodanescu if Mr. Weir has not handed in his resignation or are you also announcing to us today that he is sacked?"

In light of Cezar's menacing aura from the previous statement Cogshaw now welcomed the diversion to talk about Daryl no matter how uncomfortable it could be, leaving *young scarlet cheeks* from the district newspaper kicking himself at another missed opportunity on a personal level.

"Make no mistake; I hope that Daryl is well wherever he is. As you know I have always considered myself to have an excellent working relationship with him, but the fact remains that he is in breach of his contract by not showing his face at this football club for a number of weeks now. I have had no choice but to inject some stability to the team who go into the next game on the back of five straight defeats, including a shock exit from the League Cup by lower league opposition, they are obviously affected by the absence of a manager. I can only assume that the poor run of results up until Daryl's disappearance was simply too much for him, with the unusual events of the Town game being the final nail in his psychological coffin." (Many less viper-like journalists in the room hoped that that wasn't a misplaced pun). "You must remember that Daryl Weir has been a manager who has become accustomed to success throughout his career. I believe that he has decided to simply walk away from the job."

Stroud pressed further. "That doesn't sound like the gritty Scot that we all know as Daryl Weir. For all we know he could be lying dead in a ditch somewhere. Shouldn't you have waited until you know what has happened to him for sure, if for nothing else at least as a means of respect for such a loyal servant to the club?" Stroud could never win any prizes for his tactfulness.

And it was his lack of relevance, as Cezar saw it, in his procession of probing that now signalled Stroud's turn to feel the burning stare of the professor, and even he was uncharacteristically unnerved by the Romanian's intimidating glare. Cezar was clearly unimpressed for anyone to even suggest that this press conference could be about the ex-Kingsbarr manager.

"The police are keeping an open mind; I suggest you do the same Mr. Stroud. Life goes on you know. Time can not stay still." The words were enough to halt the line of questioning about Daryl Weir as the professor spoke in his Romanian accent in a calm but assertive tone, which gave no alternative to the recipient but to portray respect. The magnetic way he spoke and the way he carried himself intrigued and attracted Bernadette Grainger and the other female journalist in the room. It was she who spoke next.

"Kerry Fox, *Daily Universe.* When will we see some of this new *talent* that you have to offer Professor?"

Kerry's innuendo-loaded question lightened Cezar's mood. "Well let's not keep you in suspense any longer Miss. Fox. These other three seats will now be filled by three of my greatest prodigies, who will all be in the team on Saturday. May I introduce to you Andrei Botezatu, Tracaldo and Ringa."

Three tall, well-groomed young men entered from the wings in single file at Cezar's command and sat down in the remaining seats.

Bernadette and Kerry were suitably impressed.

"Andrei is a fellow countryman of mine, but as you have probably guessed from their names Ringa and Tracaldo are both Brazilian. I found these two boys tragically living in the sewers of Rio, but during the day they would kick oranges for hours on the beach. I have now helped develop them into two of the most exciting wing-backs you will ever see. Ringa plays on the right and Tracaldo plays on the left. Their years of acquaintance together have enabled them to develop an uncanny telepathic connection on the football pitch."

"And what *position* best suits Mr. Botezatu?"

Everyone laughed at yet another of Kerry's cheeky questions. Cogshaw and Stroud were particularly relieved at the change in mood.

"I think that I had better let Andrei answer that for himself," smiled Cezar, happy to join in with the teasing with the young tabloid journalist.

Andrei answered in the same accent as Cezar, "I am a centre-forward Miss. Fox with lightning pace. I am extremely single minded, and when I have my sights on goal I always score."

"I'm sure you do, Mr. Botezatu. I'm sure you do."

Johnny Knox entered his front door following a visit to see Radu at the hospital. Sheena had chosen to remain there, never wanting to leave the side of her newly adopted son. Johnny, like Sheena, loved Radu with an unconditional bonding that only parents could ever understand, but he needed the time away from the hospital every now and again, they weren't his favourite places and he needed a break from its captivity in order to massage his sanity. Besides, he believed that his duties as a footballer for Kingsbarr United simply needed to continue no matter how distraught he was regarding the mysterious illness surrounding his son. He realised that as club captain he carried a great deal of responsibility on behalf of the team.

With Radu responding well to another blood transfusion, but still mystifying any known logic of the medical profession, Johnny felt justified at the present moment in time to come home and catch up with the latest news on the Satellite Sports Channel. As he hit the remote control while he lazed back into his leather armchair, he got a shock to see the red headline band at the foot of the screen with the large permanent caption of *Kingsbarr appoint new manager.*

"What the fuck! I'm club captain and I need to find out that we have a new manager by switching on the fucking TV." He cursed Peter Cogshaw as he saw his fat face fill the television screen. Then the picture opened up to reveal a foreign looking gentleman sitting to the left of Cogshaw and three younger men sitting to the left of him. He had guessed that the older man was the new manager, but then on closer look he was gob-smacked to realise that he had actually met him before."

"The professor," he blurted out loud to no one in the room. "It's the professor from the airport. He didn't tell me that he had his sights on Kingsbarr. The crafty bastard."

Johnny instantly cranked the sound up with the remote control to hear a journalist mention his name amidst a question . . . "With the new players you plan to introduce to the squad Professor Prodanescu, will there still be room for the established players at Kingsbarr, for example the likes of Johnny Knox."

"Without doubt I will need to ring the changes at Kingsbarr United, as I stated earlier this is the beginning of a new and exciting era for the football club, but Johnny Knox will remain an integral part of this football club and I can confirm that he will remain as my team captain."

"Thank fuck for that!" said Johnny to himself.

Also watching the press conference live on TV was Kingsbarr United's number one fan and vampire slayer Gene Macgoree.

With Kingsbarr languishing near the foot of the Championship he, like many other fans, wasn't exactly against the idea of a new manager taking over at United. He was grateful to Daryl Weir for the fantastic achievements and loyalty he had shown Kingsbarr over the years, but the harsh reality of football was that quite often you were only as good as your last game. And unfortunately, Daryl Weir hadn't steered a successful Kingsbarr United ship for some time now.

But Gene had immediate reservations about this new Romanian manager and his side-kicks from the Fosturnea School of Football Excellence. He knew that Romania included the region of Transylvania where vampirism was rife, but he was annoyed at himself to allow this to prejudice his thinking towards Professor Prodanescu and Andrei Botezatu.

But could they be vampires?

Macgoree knew only too well that it was possible.

And the name Fosturnea? What the hell did that mean?

Gene was sure that it wasn't a Romanian word, or even Latin.

Eventually the TV cameras cut away from the press conference and returned to the studio where the presenters began to discuss and debate Kingsbarr United's unexpected appointment of Professor Prodanescu. Macgoree took this as a cue to boot up his laptop and access the internet.

In the search engine he entered "Fosturnea."

The search came up with zero hits. He was a little confused that it hadn't even connected to some sort of website for Professor Prodanescu's Football Academy.

It must be an anagram he thought, and with that he abandoned the technological wonder of his computer and opted for the more traditional method of research by using a pen and paper.

He scribbled down the word Fosturnea and began to play with the letters, trying to make some sense of the word.

Something was nagging at his psyche.

There was something he did not like about this word.

Somehow it looked familiar to him.

Playing with the letters he came up with Sofnarteu.

He returned to the search engine and entered the alien word. He wasn't surprised to discover it was another zero hit.

Gene returned to his paper again and began to realign the letters in various sequences. Then he stopped dead in his tracks when he finally stumbled upon the true word from the anagram.

He did not need to use his search engine to explain it.

Nosferatu.

Shit. Nosferatu.

Oh my god it can't be?

Nosferatu.

Gene knew that the word literally meant vampire or vampyr, depending on the origin of the spelling.

He also knew that it meant even more than simply that.

For the Nosferatu were the most powerful ruling class of vampires of Eastern Europe.

Chapter 31

"So playing music before each game is a necessary custom for you boys is it?" enquired Cezar as he stood in the centre of the Kingsbarr United changing room.

"Err, yes boss," answered Jody Roper a little nervously. It was Jody who was largely responsible for the ritual. "I hope you don't mind?"

"On the contrary Mr. Roper. If it helps to motivate you boys into putting on a good display then I am happy to allow it. However, your taste in eighties music leaves a lot to be desired."

"What sort of music are you in to then gaffer?" enquired Johnny tying the laces on his colour co-ordinated football boots.

"I like a variety of music actually Johnny, that would span the centuries of time. For example I like the fine compositions of Mozart and other fine classical composers."

"We want to play football not fucking fall asleep boss," stated Vinnie.

"Don't show your ignorance so freely Bradshaw. Anyway I also like heavy metal music as well, for example Black Sabbath, although I do not actually recognise Ozzy Osborne as being the Prince of Darkness myself."

"I've got some Bon Jovi on here boss. Will that do?"

"For now Jody, anyway turn the sound down I need you all to listen to what I have to say about the game."

Jody duly obliged with the request of his new manager.

"Now then, I've explained and made you all aware that I won't make changes at Kingsbarr United for the sake of it.

Jody is welcome to continue to inspire you all with some music before every game, but the bottom-line is as a football team you are not performing and the league table never lies. This is why some traditions do need to change and I'm starting with this game. We are going to play a 3-5-2 formation, with Ringa and Tracaldo playing as wide wing-backs."

"But boss we always play 4-4-2."

"Yes, Johnny and Kingsbarr are also near the bottom of the table."

"But everyone knows that a 3-5-2 always ends up being a 5-3-2 as the full-backs often get sucked in, and then you're defending with five at the back all game and not creating any chances. No disrespect gaffer but this is the English league and to succeed you have to play 4-4-2. Hell, even our national side have never been able to master any other formation."

"I admire your spirit Johnny and can see that one day you too will make a fine coach and that is why I am happy to keep you as team captain. However, I am the manager of Kingsbarr United at the present time and I wish to play 3-5-2. Ringa and Tracaldo both have lightning pace and have been trained the Fosturnea way. They know that the best form of defence, no the only form of defence is to attack. So do not worry Johnny, the shape will remain 3-5-2 throughout the game without Tracaldo and Ringa being sucked in to a back-five."

"If you are playing with two attacking full-backs, *Brazilian botty boys,* with only three in midfield my guess is you must be dropping Charlie Cheng."

"Yes, Bradshaw that is correct," acknowledged Cezar who had been briefed about the effects of Vinnie's Tourette's Syndrome by the club doctor. "There is no place for a traditional winger in the formation that I plan to play in today's game."

"That's scandalous," said Johnny not holding back. "Over 75% of our goals come from Charlie's supply of the ball. With respect I think you are making a big mistake boss."

Johnny sensed the annoyance in his manager's eyes and a look that uncovered a seriously disturbing dark side somewhere hidden in the pits of the Romanian. In that split second Johnny realised that he and his team-mates barely knew anything about their new manager and what sinister history may come with him. Uncharacteristically Johnny became unnerved by the look in Cezar's eyes, which spoke silent volumes, and the sudden belief that his manager could be capable of terrible things.

Chapter 32

The Romanian moved closer to Johnny so that their faces were almost touching as the dressing room watched in a wary silence. Jody's CD had reached its last track and fell silent as if on cue.

"Don't overstep the mark Johnny." Cezar spoke calmly and collectively but his tone was now unmistakably menacing. "Don't cross me. People who cross me always end up regretting it. Now listen to me and listen well for I will say this only once more. I am the manager and what I say is final. I have made you captain of my team and that I am sure is a wise choice, but know your place Mr. Knox. I expect some loyalty and support. Do I make myself clear?"

"Crystal, gaffer. It won't happen again."

Cezar moved from the invasion of Johnny's personal space and addressed the rest of the squad. "Now has anyone else got something to say about my methods of management?"

Submissive replies of "no boss" hummed around the dressing room.

"Do you understand my decision Charlie? I want you on the bench today and I don't mean just to keep it warm. You are still a valued member of the squad.

"Everything's okay Mr. Prodanescu. I understand.

"Good. I can see that we are all going to be just fine here at Kingsbarr United. We are entering a successful era; I can feel it in my *blood.* Now come on Jody get some happy music on my boy. We are about to play a football match we are not waiting for a funeral."

"Okay boss, I'll just change the CD."

"Oh and by the way Spalding, you'll be keeping Cheng company on the bench too. Andrei will lead the line with Rossi sitting just behind him. Do you have a problem with that?"

Gerry could feel the eyes of his team-mates burning into him as they waited in anticipation for his answer. Johnny could more than handle himself, but they had seen there captain surrender to the persuasion of the new manager, now what about Gerry? He was genuinely as hard as nails and known to be uncompromising at the best of times. Whatsmore his form had been impressive since returning to the team after his spell in prison, including his impressive hat-trick in his first game since his return, and he would have been ideal to link the play for either Andrei or Giuseppe.

There was a long silence as Gerry thought about what to do. He, like everyone else, had noticed the sinister aura coming from the new manager, but nothing could ever scare Gerry Spalding.

Could it?

Cezar had definitely shown enough of his persona to at least influence the big ex-con into being cautious.

At least for now anyway.

Caution and respect would indeed do for now, Cezar hoped that he would never have to conjure up emotions of terror for his players. He genuinely had a passion for Kingsbarr United to succeed without resorting to the depths of horribleness that he was truly capable of.

In a steely tone Gerry finally spoke. "No boss. I don't have a problem with that."

Chapter 33

The Kingsbarr United supporters greeted the players onto the pitch of Beacon Park, feeling a sense of optimism that had been growing for days with the changes at the club, but at the same time a little nervousness accompanied their anticipation. Before his shock appointment to their beloved United, the supporters had never heard of their new manager or any of the three new players that he was fielding today, and when they realised that both Gerry Spalding and Charlie Cheng had been dropped to the bench bemusement began to compromise the feel good factor.

Giuseppe Rossi and the new striker Andrei Botezatu, a prodigy of the Fosturnea School of Football Excellence whom Professor Cezar Prodanescu had promised could deliver so much, kicked-off for the home side.

Andrei passed the ball back to Johnny who looked for options to play the ball forward. An Albion player was quickly onto Johnny to close down the space, but Johnny managed to thread the ball back to Andrei who immediately spread the ball wide to another new recruit, the mysterious young Brazilian known as Ringa.

Andrei had played the ball with some considerable pace but against the odds Ringa was able to control the ball superbly well, knocking it past the Albion left back with ease and somehow getting onto his own pass. Ringa had got to the by-line with lightning speed and he crossed the ball towards the Albion goalmouth.

"What a shame Brian," spoke an elderly life time Kingsbarr fan. "After that amazing acceleration to get to the by-line he has gone and over hit it."

"He moved that quickly Reggie, there was nobody waiting in the box if he had delivered it into the mixer anyway," answered Brian.

Ringa had nobody near him when the ball left his foot and it appeared as though he had completed wasted the opportunity after his initial impressive good footballing accomplishment. The ball bounced at the far side of the "D" of the goal area, but then something amazing happened that none of the Kingsbarr supporters could have predicted.

Portraying the same lightning speed as his Brazilian team-mate, Tracaldo appeared from nowhere to meet the ball and strike it sweetly with his left foot. The Albion keeper never even moved as the ball flew into the top corner.

Although the crowd was stunned, they cheered and clapped in sheer delight. Kingsbarr United were 1-0 up inside the first minute and it was thanks to the ability and startling contribution of the three new players from the Fosturnea School of Football Excellence.

This was amazing stuff.

The Albion players kicked-off to restart the game but they were obviously still shell-shocked from the lightning-paced start from the Kingsbarr United team and they quickly lost possession again as Andrei Botezatu came towards the Albion striker like an express train to dispossess him and head straight for goal.

Two players headed towards the debutant striker and it looked as though if they were not going to succeed in retrieving the ball from his possession, then they would certainly find another, possibly more sinister way, to stop him heading towards their goal.

Cheekily Andrei read their pedestrian attempts to thwart him and he cleverly stopped still and dragged the ball back as the two Albion players collided and landed in a heap on the floor. With the Kingsbarr United supporters clearly enjoying that little piece of unexpected showmanship they began to cheer their new signing as he effortlessly rounded the disgruntled heap on the floor.

Then with the same lighting pace as portrayed by the two young Brazilians he bombed forward whilst not an Albion player in sight could get near him as he dodged and weaved passed them with tremendous ability and speed.

All that remained was the task of beating the Albion goalkeeper who gulped as he witnessed the big Romanian charge towards him not quite knowing what to do in order to defend his goal. Usually he was a brave custodian who would gladly dive at the feet of an oncoming striker, but something told him not to dive at the feet of this player, as he might not be able to get up again!

Instead he opted to stay put and use his body frame to narrow down the angle of the inevitable shot that was to follow from Botezatu. But the Albion goalkeeper's efforts were to be in vain as Andrei hit the ball with such terrific pace that all the goalkeeper could deliver by way of a reaction was to put his right hand up to save the goal, but only after the ball had whizzed past him and ended up in the back of the net to make it 2-0 to Kingsbarr within the first five minutes of the game.

The Kingsbarr supporters were ecstatic as their new Romanian striker strutted towards them cockily and then simply stood in front of them like a Roman gladiator who had defeated a whole army single-handedly while he lapped up the applause and cheering from his enthusiastic audience in the arena.

In addition to their amazement at their new Romanian striker, the Kingsbarr United supporters couldn't believe the start their team had made to the game under the guidance of this little known and mysterious team manager named Professor Cezar Prodanescu. Before long they were chanting his name as the Daryl Weir era appeared to be eclipsed in a most dramatic fashion. "Cezar, Cezar," came the repeated chant.

The chants and applause grew louder at half-time as the Kingsbarr United team received a standing ovation amidst a wave of euphoria.

Before today's game it would have been considered miraculous for Kingsbarr to be three goals ahead at this stage of the game, however, at this moment in time it was miraculous that Kingsbarr were leaving the field at the interval *only* three goals to the good considering the superb way that they had been playing. The irrepressible Andrei Botezatu had helped himself to another goal five minutes before the break, but this was only after he had hit the woodwork on no less than five occasions and the Albion keeper had also got lucky and pulled off a couple of impressive saves in the first half.

Somehow, in spite of Kingsbarr United's dominance of the game, Albion had achieved to gather some kind of foothold on the match and had managed to weather the storm created by the three players from the Fosturnea School of Football Excellence. This was largely by adopting a negative style of football though by putting as many Albion bodies behind the ball as possible. However, it was a necessary reactive style of play if they were going to attempt to stifle the incredible abilities of Botezatu, Ringa and Tracaldo in any way.

What they, or the rest of the occupants of Beacon Park did not yet realise was that there would be even more to come in the second half from these three impressive debutants. For the second half was destined to progress past four o clock, and with the inevitable autumn evening drawing in with its fast dimming light and cloak of darkness spreading across the North Birmingham sky, the vampire's energy levels would inevitably rise and they would produce a display that would be literally out of this world.

As the players approached the tunnel for their half-time regrouping and pep talk (not that they needed one it seemed), Jody Roper approached his new Romanian team-mate.

"Fuck me Andrei, you were magnificent out there, well done mate. You were truly awesome. How do you manage to play like that?"

"Its all because of you Jody."

Jody looked puzzled.

"Me? How can that be?"

"You played "Gold" by Spandau Ballet before the game. I love that song and it inspired me to play well. That song always brings out the best in me."

Chapter 34

Ted Baird was an uncompromising team manager and at the moment he was incredibly disappointed and angry with his Albion team. His was the only voice that could be heard shouting from the Albion dressing room as his players silently hung their heads in shame like naughty schoolboys as Ted laid into them with a tirade of verbal abuse. It was not unusual for his rotund face to appear red in colour, he hadn't looked after his health too well since retiring from his playing days twenty-three years earlier, and his ruddy complexion was now caused by his overweight frame and liking of scotch whisky and ale. At this particular moment in time however, his team's poor first half performance was causing his face to appear even redder than it had done for a long time. He visibly looked as if he could explode at any moment vented by the anger he was clearly feeling.

"What is wrong with you?" he shouted. "You have let them run rings around you as if you are not even on the same football pitch as them. Where is your passion to win this football match for fucks sake? You are allowed to tackle for the ball you know, you're all like a bunch of fucking queer boy statues out there." Political correctness had never been one of Ted's stronger points.

"You're a fucking embarrassment, I have never led a team in at half-time three-nil down before, I want to see some goals from us in the next half of the game. If they can score three goals in a half we can go out and score fucking four. Do you understand?"

"Yes boss," came a subdued reply from a handful of Albion players.

"I can't hear you. I SAID DO YOU FUCKING UNDERSTAND." Saliva sprayed from Ted's mouth like a fountain of venom as his anger reached record breaking levels.

"Yes boss," the reply was significantly louder and more collective this time.

Ted Baird began to calm slightly as he attempted to deliver a more logical analysis of the game.

"Listen boys, there is no way that they can maintain that pace for another forty-five minutes or so. If we keep possession of the ball they will tire and we can pick them off as the game goes on. We just need to keep our nerve and our heads. Stop them feeding the ball to the two Brazilian lady boys on the flanks and that ugly Romanian bastard up front and we can still get back into this game. If we get an early goal second half they will be shitting themselves."

At least Ted Baird had finally acknowledged that his side were losing the game by three goals to nil mainly because of the brilliance of the Kingsbarr team and not necessarily because of his own team's failings, in particular the outstanding displays of Botezatu, Tracaldo and Ringa.

The atmosphere in the Kingsbarr United dressing room at half-time couldn't have been more contrasting. Disbelief was one emotion being felt by the players, but the sequence of high-fives and back patting reflected the elation that was buzzing in the dressing room. The once cynical minds of the seasoned Kingsbarr players had in many ways had all their nagging questions answered. Whatever they had thought previously of the appointment of Professor Cezar Prodanescu as team manager and his unknown products of the Fosturnea School of Football Excellence, they could not deny now that Kingsbarr United were indeed a better team for their inclusion at the football club. This was undeniably evident after only forty-five minutes of football!

The new manager spoke, now armed with the unquestionable respect of his players.

"I am very pleased with the way the game has gone so far, and I do not refer to only Andrei, Tracaldo and Ringa, although now I am sure you can all see the value that they add to the team. You are all playing well and putting in the effort for Kingsbarr United. This is what I expect of my players and I am pleased to say that none of you have disappointed me. But the game is not won yet. We must maintain a positive attitude for the second half with no room for complacency. Johnny and Vinnie, you are clearly winning the midfield battle out there. When you win the ball play it out to the flanks for the two Brazilian boys to run to the by-line. Their full-backs can not contain my Brazilian boys."

"Yes boss," said Johnny, pleased that his contribution to the game hadn't totally been eclipsed by his brilliant new team-mates.

"Sure thing boss, *great fucking praise from the top man.*" Replied Vinnie, his Tourette's Syndrome ticks visibly adopting an element of euphoria.

"I believe that the best form of defence is attack. Just because we are three-nil up I do not expect us to sit back and invite pressure from the opposition. This is a new era at Kingsbarr United Football Club and we will do everything in our power to play *the beautiful game* as it was always intended to be played. From the heart and with plenty of goals. Now go out there my wonderful team and finish the job."

Chapter 35

As both sets of players re-entered the field of play the noise was electrifying from the Kingsbarr United supporters, clearly delighted with their teams first half display and in particular the performances of the three new players.

Andrei applauded the spectators of his *gladiator arena* and even for him, a cold and usually emotionally void vampire; the adoration suitably massaged his ego as they chanted his name.

Inspite of Ted Baird's strong words of encouragement, if Beacon Park were to be likened to a Roman gladiator arena, the Albion players couldn't help but feel like the countless unfortunate victims of the Roman Coliseum of yesteryear, who were pitched to fight the most horrifically uneven encounter against a much stronger force, until their inevitable loss of battle unfolded.

As the referee placed the ball on the centre-circle Andrei glanced up to the sky and grinned as he noticed the grey curtain fall over the stadium as the evening's darkness began to draw in. He also noticed that the floodlights were beginning to dimly glow, realising that the English weather at this time of year dictated that it would soon be quite dark, and he and his fellow vampire team-mates from Brazil would soon be displaying even greater ability as the darkness recharged their vampire bodies like a nuclear power station.

For it was darkness that best suited the make up of the vampire being.

Andrei, Tracaldo and Ringa didn't need to speak to one another to discuss their gratitude at the English elements. As the darkness unfolded their telepathic connection also grew stronger. It was another benefit of being a vampire, the ability to communicate by a telepathic thought process. Andrei grinned again as Ringa communicated to him that the Albion centre-forward had an annoyingly long neck that was simply begging to be torn open.

"*No you don't. Not here, not now. Concentrate on your football. Your time at Kingsbarr United Football club is only for the purpose of football. I have told you that before. There will be plenty of other opportunities to feed from the blood of humans away from the beautiful game.*" The telepathic communication this time came from the authoritative voice of Professor Cezar Prodanescu. The commanding emperor of his Beacon Park Coliseum who undeniably held the power to give his *thumbs up* or *thumbs down* gesture to decide the fate of any victims of his Fosturnea gladiators.

"*Sorry Master,*" came the telepathic reply from the two vampiric footballers like two naughty schoolboys caught smoking behind the bike sheds, totally unknowingly to the other thousands of occupants of Beacon Park, except Tracaldo of course.

It was not long before Andrei had channelled his vampire energy into the game of football at hand and not into the slaughter of human life in the literal sense. Though it was highly probable that more than one match report in tomorrow's sports pages would refer to the Albion players as being "Lambs to the Slaughter."

Johnny had followed Cezar's instructions to perfection and brilliantly won the ball in the middle of the park and spread it inch perfect to Ringa on the right flank. Like Andrei, Ringa was also becoming increasingly charged by vampire energy as the darkness drew into Beacon Park and he easily accelerated past two defenders showing an impressive burst of lightning pace in doing so. So quickly in fact that an attempted foul by the Albion player only resulted in him missing the

Brazilian vampire completely and instead crashing red-faced and sore-kneed into the advertising board.

Ringa crossed the ball towards Andrei who had beaten the offside trap, but the Brazilian had played the ball behind his team-mate who had arrived at the opposing goalmouth quicker than even Ringa had anticipated.

The chance was not over though. The onlookers fell open-jawed as they witnessed Andrei swivel on a sixpence to face the ball but put his back to goal, only for the Romanian striker to then catch the ball beautifully with a bicycle-kick of the highest quality to send the ball into the top corner of the net, and to secure his hat-trick on his Kingsbarr United debut. It was a truly fantastic goal.

4-0 the score currently stood at as Ted Baird knew only too well as he put his head in his hands and felt the bitter taste of what was going to be inevitable defeat. His main concern now was not how Albion could get back into the game, but how could they possibly stop Kingsbarr United, and in particular Andrei Botezatu scoring any more goals. In all honesty he was out of ideas to combat the onslaught.

Andrei approached the home supporters like a proud peacock arrogantly strutting along the touchline with his chest proudly pushed out absorbing the applause of his new worshippers. He continued his triumphant journey along the touchline and inevitably met with the team benches of the two sides. He gave a mocking smile towards the Albion bench and something in his eyes deterred the opposing players from reacting to him. When his eyes met Cezar's he simply nodded towards his team manager, (and vampire leader, unknown to the thousands of unsuspecting adoring fans of course). Via their unique ability to communicate telepathically, Cezar informed his star striker of how pleased he was with the excellent contribution he had made to today's game. The emperor was silently signalling his approval for his champion gladiator.

The game grew ten minutes older and the darkness fell like a curtain across Beacon Park fuelling the energy levels of the three vampire footballers, as the mere mortals simply grew tired. The floodlights cast their shadows across the pitch, but artificial light had no negative bearing upon the vampires in the same way that daylight could. Gone were the days however when daylight was enough to harm or even kill a vampire, as with all creatures since time began the vampire had evolved to cope easily with daylight as the generations progressed over the centuries, but indeed it was still darkness that suited their genetics best. By enlarge a vampire is indeed a nocturnal creature, and its strength is at its prime during nightfall, but just like any other nocturnal animal such as the owl or the fox, being exposed to daylight simply does not cause them any actual harm at all.

Before long with the darkness falling and the strength, and hunger, of the vampires growing the score inevitably became 5-0. Ironically though it was a human being of mere mortal status that scored the fifth goal, albeit set up beautifully by the skill of Andrei Botezatu who showed how he could play the role of provider as well as goal-poacher.

Andrei had magically teased two Albion defenders who stood around him flat-footed like two crumbling statues while he shielded the ball from them, neither of them capable of timing a well-executed tackle against such nimble trickery displayed by the irrepressible striker. He eventually spotted Johnny creating good space for himself with an intelligent run behind the remainder of the Albion defence as they were sucked into attempting to cope with the Romanian.

Johnny was pleased to hear the familiar chant of "Knox, Knox get in the box" realising that his new mysterious team-mates hadn't quite eclipsed his legendary status at the club completely, and he was even more delighted to hear his loyal supporters cheer as he met Andrei's perfectly weighted pass to drill the ball into the bottom corner of the Albion goal to make it 5-0.

Johnny then went on to clinch his second and Kingsbarr's sixth goal of the game minutes later with one of his trademark free-kicks to cement his own consistent contribution to the teams performance, although the dead-ball situation had arose from Andrei being fouled at the edge of the area as he displayed even more football trickery leaving the Albion defender no option but to attempt a clumsy tackle which inevitably resulted in a free-kick being awarded to Kingsbarr United.

It was the Romanian vampire who in due course had the last word of the game though as he scored the final goal in the dying seconds of the match to take his own personal tally to an impressive four on his debut, and Kingsbarr United amazingly eventual 7-0 winners.

The reign at Kingsbarr United of Professor Cezar Prodanescu had begun in electrifying style and his products of the Fosturnea School of Football Excellence had shown their worth in abundance.

The euphoric Kingsbarr United supporters deservingly gave their team a standing ovation as they left the field, impressed with the new regime at their beloved club and with a new and welcome feeling of optimism in their bellies. It had been a long time since their team had conjured up such feelings of excitement, and with the evidence of the new beginnings only being showcased so far at a grand total of ninety minutes football plus minimal injury time, the sheer impact of the new additions to the club in both management and players alike was so great that belief and certainty was already deep rooted and truly cemented.

Sadly, following years of loyalty to the club coupled with some unrivalled and impressive success, there was hardly anybody sparing a thought for the mysteriously missing entity of Daryl Weir. Even Gene Macgoree stood with his Kingsbarr United comrades applauding the new regime at the football club, obviously recognising the improvements in his beloved side, and trying very hard to ignore that *Fosturnea* could have its letters rearranged to instead spell the word *Nosferatu*.

In addition to Gene Macgoree standing amidst the Kingsbarr United supporters was a young man who also couldn't dismiss the impressive display that he had just witnessed from the produce of the Fosturnea School of Football Excellence; however, this was the first football game that he had attended in many years, since he was a small child in fact. His reasons for being at Beacon Park today were nothing to do with football; he had been keeping an eye on the movements of Professor Prodanescu and *his boys* for a few days now.

For once somebody else's vampire slaying mind was one step ahead of Gene Macgoree's, but then again he had the lethal ingredient of vengeance to drive him on and no romanticism to cloud his judgement.

Indeed the young man had the death of his mentor Bogdan to avenge.

But he needed to be patient.

He was acting alone and without the guidance of Bogdan now.

He needed to time the moment to strike to perfection and for now he was happy to allow them to enjoy the game of football.

After all while they were playing football they were not killing innocent people.

Inevitably and perhaps ironically, Andrei Botezatu had picked up the man of the match award and was given the obligatory bottle of champagne, although it was not alcohol that he had in mind as a celebration drink later that night.

He planned instead to indulge in his favourite tipple and longed for the smooth, sweet taste of human blood to be trickling down his throat as he celebrated his outstanding home debut.

Chapter 36

"So this is where it all began, Master. Sutton Park," said Andrei as he brought his metallic black coloured Mercedes Benz to a halt. The sound of gravel crunching under the tyres was the only audible noise in the immediate vicinity. Just before Andrei killed the headlights of the car, the terrified eyes of a fox shone at them before quickly scurrying away, testament to the animal kingdom and their uncanny ability to sense an evil presence.

"It didn't quite begin here, but it was certainly where *they* believed they could end it, Andrei."

"So he is buried somewhere here? It is hard to believe. It seems so surreal now we are finally here."

"Well yes, according to the lost gospel of *Live Tome,* Sutton Park is indeed the final resting place of Adrien Connor, the very first known vampire."

"It's amazing. So many people assume that it is our country of Romania where vampirism began, but it was actually here in Birmingham, England that it all started."

"It certainly was Andrei, and did you know that Sutton Park, the final resting place of our messiah and the place where he spent the final remaining years of his life as an outcast from the then neighbouring village of Royal Sutton Coldfield is the largest park in Birmingham, covering some 2400 acres of woodlands, heathlands and wetlands. Many generations of mortals have used this site for their own personal recreation purposes—families come to feed the ducks, cyclists and joggers exercise around the land, the possibilities are endless, yet all are ignorant to the silenced history concerning its vampire connections and the fact that Adrien Connor rests here."

"And now of course it incorporates the new training ground facilities for Kingsbarr United."

"Indeed it does. The contemporary local residents tried to oppose the development, claiming it would compromise the beauty of the place and harm its wildlife occupants. It seems the natives of Royal Sutton Coldfield have always had a passion for protest; several centuries ago it was against the Connor family, daring to burn alive Adrien's parents at the stake no less before casting him out to the elements of this parkland and finally driving a stake through his heart.

To be fair the residents of the twenty-first century have a more valid point of argument, as Sutton Park after all is a haven of countryside, even though it is amazingly only six miles from the heart of the city centre. But good old Peter Cogshaw made the council an offer they couldn't refuse and so here it is. State of the art training facilities, but only just big enough to incorporate what is needed for the players. It has a gymnasium, a press room for interviews, physiotherapy rooms incorporating healing hydrotherapy water pools, a single consultancy room, kitchens, a mess room and of course a training pitch sheltered by a retractable roof, something often needed with the rainy English weather. The size of the development was at least sensitive to the resident's pleas. This is why Cogshaw was pleased when I explained to him how the Fosturnea School of Football Excellence would be set up off site. An academy of football was impossible to run sufficiently from such a small development, although Beacon Park can still be used to compliment Fosturnea."

"A lot of my team-mates live nearby don't they?"

"Oh yes, Andrei. Four Oaks is a high-class development of houses to the west of the park, many directly overlooking the woodland. As well as footballers, most other Four Oaks residents tend to be surgeons or lawyers. Johnny Knox chooses to live just a little further a field nearer to the medieval town of Lichfield, and of course we are not much further on from him at the Fosturnea School of Football Excellence. Sadly, I doubt whether the inhabitants of Four Oaks and other surrounding areas of the park fully appreciate its history. Its origins go back as far as 1528 when King Henry VIII used it for hunting deer. It also has an original Roman road running through it with other clues to Roman settlements scattered about in the form of various ruins and abandoned water wells. Yes, Andrei as our fellow Kingsbarr personnel look out across the woodlands, I wonder how many of them realise that many of the hills in the park are actually burial mounds, final resting places for the corpses who fell victim to the squabbles of Roman and Anglo-Saxon battle. Fortunately for us Andrei, they don't seem to realise that one special body is also buried here in the form of Adrien Connor. And thankfully by keeping the scale of the development down it prevented them from disturbing his grave. That is instead something that we must do Andrei, with the utmost respect of course."

With his impeccable night vision Andrei was able to notice his mentor produce a largish leather wallet from inside his jacket pocket. Cezar then opened the wallet to reveal a type of wooden paddle, badly damaged around the edges and with the handle broken, which actually helped it fit into a twenty-first century leather wallet. Andrei could also see that the paddle held a sheet of paper in place with a strange style of writing on it.

"What is that, Master?" enquired the younger vampire.

"This is what was known as a hornbook, Andrei."

"A hornbook! That is indeed a most curious description. I can see wood but no horn? Was the handle perhaps once shaped as a horn before it was damaged? Is that how it got its name? I can tell that it is quite antique in origin."

Always pleased with his understudy's inquisitive mind and aptitude to learn Cezar proceeded to explain things further to Andrei. "A hornbook derives from the sixteenth century, so called because the paper was protected by a thin layer of animal horn. This single sheet of paper is the lost gospel of the *Live Tome*, penned by Bourne Connor, only son to Adrien Connor the very first vampire, and it tells us, and only us Andrei, as we have the privileged possession of the document, where exactly Adrien Connor is buried."

Cezar then began to laugh slightly, before contrasting his emotion to reflect annoyance.

"What is it Master?"

"The ironic thing is Andrei, these hornbooks traditionally had the *Lords Prayer* scribed upon them for the unfortunate teachings of sixteenth century children, and Bourne was lucky enough to have a blank one with him when he fled to Romania, chased out of England by the same barbarians who killed his father and grandparents. You know Andrei the poor children who used these hornbooks as their method of learning, looking day in and day out at the *Lords Prayer* were subjected to horrific cruelty and beatings from the teachers. Often they were humiliated by having their naked bodies whipped by birches to the point of extreme and needless injury. Now how noble was that of the fools preaching their religion at those poor children? And it is said that we vampires are the barbaric ones?"

"How did you receive the lost gospel Master?"

"It has only been entrusted to a few vampires since Bourne Connor wrote upon it with his goose feathered quill all those years ago, but I actually came about it by rescuing it from a prolific Romanian vampire slayer named Popescu who had managed to obtain its possession. It was also rumoured that Bourne Connor was slain at the hands of this Popescu. I was able to successfully exterminate him and stop him tracking down the grave of Adrien Connor for whatever sordid reason he had chosen to. I forgot to ask him what his intentions were as I witnessed his head roll away down the hillside after I had decapitated him. But the vampire world, and more importantly the mortal world have since questioned its existence. They do not know that I have it and I believe that it is best to keep it that way to prevent any other threats to its survival. When the time is right Andrei, I will pass it to you for your safekeeping."

"That would indeed be a great honour for me, Master."

"Andrei, you are continually proving to me that it is an honour that you shall one day deserve."

"I swear to serve you Professor and the memory of Adrien and Bourne Connor for the remainder of my vampire life."

"Well my plan is that Adrien will not be a memory any longer."

"You are a true genius Professor Prodanescu. You truly believe that there will be enough DNA in the bones of the grave to bring the very first vampire Adrien Connor back from the dead?"

"Stranger things have happened Andrei. But first we have to find him, and we can only do that by reading the testament from his son Bourne on this hornbook. It is so amusing that the mortals are so familiar with the theory of Count Dracula coming from our country Romania and then crashing into the rocks at Whitby to eventually settle in England, when the truth is the original vampire dynasty actually began here in England and only later did Bourne Connor settle in Romania to teach our country the ways of the vampire."

"Luckily for us he did though Master. We have so many vampires in Romania today, especially in the Transylvanian region."

"Indeed this is true Andrei. We must see England's loss as indeed our gain, but with our football academy and my expertise in genetics maybe I can redress the balance once again for the English. Now let's concentrate on the document Andrei."

With that Cezar began to read aloud the 16th century words of Bourne Connor from the hornbook known as the lost gospel of the *Live Tome.*

" . . . *thus the true dark one of such power borne of such supreme privileges lies unashamedly in the earth of Sutton Coldfield.*

The true prince of darkness . . . How often have we heard that cliché misused on unfitting beings since the writing of this gospel, Andrei?"

Andrei smiled as he thought of heavy metal rock stars and other celebrities who had ridiculously been given that label.

"The true prince of darkness lieth in a grave unmarked. But those martyrs of foolishness do not know that mine father only sleepeth, destined to rise again.

I think that's where we come in Andrei."

Andrei smiled again, this time with an acknowledging nod of the head.

"The grave thus of no marking that protecteth his bones, will always have a marketh of identity, their efforts to silence him will ultimately be in vein."

"Does that make sense Master?" enquired Andrei. "How can an unmarked grave have a mark of identity?"

For once Andrei's inquisitive mind was less appealing to Cezar as he continued to read the passage, which if Andrei were to look in to at a deep enough level he would be able to find all of his answers.

"He lieth with his head facing north, never needing to face the sun when it is darkness that embraces him.

The road so straight runs neath his feet by a distance so short.

He hath no hounds of protection though respect is shown, but the antlers of two deers of the land now protecteth above him.

The acorn so small can yet groweth so tall as can his legacy begin in Sutton Coldfield of England. His wrath borne of the wrong doing of his slaying shall be a seed and a catalyst for the growth of Vampyrsm. We shall never be defeated.

One more marketh of identity can be said of his resting place of the hunting land for us and for them. Land was given to them to hunt but he shall rise again to hunt them. For he curseth the earth that holds him. Whilst he sleepeth so shall the land above him.

He will hold the land barren even that will be too afraid to react.

Even that will respect him.

Until he riseth again."

"Wow," said Andrei, almost disbelieving that he had just heard first hand the lost gospel of the *Live Tome*. "So you think you know exactly where he is buried Master?"

"Indeed I do, Andrei. I came here the other day and followed the clues written down in the lost gospel. It took me a long time but I believe that I have found our messiah's resting place. Follow me."

The two vampires stepped out of the car and the professor led the way as the lights flashed around the black Mercedes as Andrei applied the central locking system from his key fob.

Cezar's trail led him beside the new Kingsbarr United training facilities, fortunately not much light was radiated from the development other than the illuminated crest of the three crowns, another showing of sensitivity took on board for the benefit of the nearby residents.

Within two minutes at the north western point to the rear of the development Cezar brought the two vampires to a halt.

Again, although now once again encompassed in total darkness the vampire's ability to see at night ensured that they could be familiar with their surroundings.

"Look at the soul of your shoe Andrei?"

"Pardon?" said the younger vampire not really sure of the reason for the professor's request.

"Have a look at the soul of your shoe. Is there anything on it?"

Andrei raised the sole of his right Italian leather shoe. There was nothing there.

He then raised the sole of his left shoe.

"Oh shit!"

"Literally!" smiled Cezar. "Do you remember the line from the passage *He hath no hounds of protection though respect is shown?*"

"Yes, I do."

"Well modern day Sutton Park has a massive problem with dog fouling, as you have just discovered to your cost

Andrei. However, when I came here the other day and walked within roughly a half-mile radius of where we are now, I could not find a single piece of dog excrement. Thus enabling me to conclude that this is the area where *respect is shown.*"

"Okay, that makes sense Master," said Andrei wiping his soiled shoe on the grass and a fortunately placed puddle of rainwater.

"Now Andrei, if we walk just a little further west we start to join a very flat piece of land, with rubble and other substances of the earth breaking through the grass every now and again. You will notice that the flat land doesn't meander, it is in a perfectly straight line."

"*The road so straight runs neath his feet so short.*"

"Well observed Andrei. This is indeed a Roman road that stretches through this area of the park so we must walk along it until we find *the antlers of the two deers of the land* protecting the grave."

"But there are no deers in Sutton Park in today's time Master. Surely Bourne was referring to when it was used as hunting land for the villagers?"

"That was my thoughts exactly Andrei. This too had me puzzled for some time but then I looked at the next line—*the acorn so small can yet groweth so tall.* If we stop again just about now and look forward what can you see?"

"I don't believe it! Two oak trees, standing together in perfect symmetry as if they were identical twins."

"Indeed Andrei, and perhaps they would be identical twin deers, because the branches remarkably resemble deer's antlers."

Andrei was gob-smacked as he realised the analogy.

"And now look at the patch of ground beneath it, Andrei."

Andrei looked down to see a patch of ground that if you were not especially looking for you could easily walk past and ignore, but on closer examination it actually had quite a startling contrast to its lush green surrounding environment of grass and vegetation. The piece of land was about eight feet in length by five feet in width and was completely barren. Nothing was growing from it at all. No bushes, no grass, not even any wild flowers or weeds.

"For he curseth the earth that holds him. Whilst he sleepeth so shall the land above him.

He will hold the land barren even that will be too afraid to react.

Even that will respect him.

Until he riseth again."

"Very good, Andrei. Very good indeed. Now start digging."

About an hour later, the athleticism of Andrei Botezatu had enabled him to dig into the ground at a very impressive rate, though it amused the professor to try and understand why his understudy had chosen to wear a pair of classy Italian shoes for digging a grave!

As he felt the shovel begin to hit a different sort of substance Andrei was amazed to witness his master jump into the trench with him and begin to help digging at the earth using nothing but the power of his own bare hands.

The professor suddenly seemed possessed as an inane grin spread across his face while he burrowed away wide-eyed and frantically. Andrei had never before seen his usually so cool mentor so unguarded or animated.

Eventually their efforts enabled a dark wooden box to be discovered. It was most probably a coffin but it bore no name plaque to give a clue to the identity of who lay inside.

The powerful Andrei forced the lid open to reveal two eye sockets coldly staring out at him. As he broke away some more of the lid the two vampires were able to see further evidence of the skeleton.

What presented itself to the professor and his vampire understudy inside the coffin were bones, that's all there was to see, just bones.

Except that was for a wooden stake protruding out of the skeleton's rib cage.

"Adrien Connor," spoke Professor Cezar Prodanescu. "We salute you and we serve you."

Chapter 37

31 October, Halloween.

"Black Sabbath, excellent choice of music for tonight Jody, but could I ask you to turn the volume down for the moment so that I can address you all with the necessary instructions for the game ahead."

"Sure boss, it was Andrei who wanted this on anyway, I must say I don't find it as uplifting as my eighties hits."

"Okay, enough about the music and more about the football. There are to be some changes for tonight's game. Rossi I am dropping you to the bench for tonight, not because you are playing badly but young Leon Davis has been working really hard in training and has impressed in the reserves so I feel he deserves his chance to partner Andrei tonight. We can always bring you on later as a fresh pair of legs if things are unexpectedly not going to plan."

"Okay Professor," Giuseppe couldn't hide the disappointment in his voice but took the news like a true professional, and he hated to admit it but that little wind-up merchant Davis had been playing really well lately, the whole squad had noticed it but they couldn't understand where his new found talent had come from.

Was the professor really such an influential coach that he could amazingly bring out the best in players beyond an unexpected level?

Of course what the Kingsbarr United players didn't yet realise was that Leon Davis was now a vampire thanks to his lustful moments of passion with Afina, so he had the power and ability to play football just like Andrei, Ringa and Tracaldo. It had also been noted how curious it was at how these three players and the professor seemed to be the only *people* that Davis bothered to show any respect for. He was constantly displaying his usual bad attitude towards the remainder of his team-mates.

"Jody, I have introduced you to Paildo and Catarino Popovic this week in training, and I believe they are ready to sit either side of you in the back three with Tracaldo and Ringa pushing on of course down the flanks."

Paildo, another Brazilian boy and Popovic, a Romanian, were the two latest impressive pupils to emerge from the Fosturnea School of Football Excellence. Professor Prodanescu had been receiving some high praise in the media about his school of excellence where he had been highly commended for rescuing orphan boys from the awful conditions of children's homes in his native Romania, and even saving the *sewer boys* from the slums of Brazil who would otherwise be forced to live in the underground sewers like rats hunting for food. The irony being although he has given these boys shelter and a very comfortable life, albeit a life of belonging to the world of the undead, Prodanescu had still turned these boys into hunters anyway just as if they had been left to fend for themselves in the sewers of Brazil. But the media, the fans and indeed the British nation as a whole only recognised the one possibility that presented itself to them—that these once unfortunate, but now extremely fortunate young boys, had been given the chance of a lifetime to play football under the kind guidance and mentorship of an amazing professor.

But Jody Roper was beginning to have his silent doubts about the "too good to be true" Professor Prodanescu and his products from the Fosturnea School of Football Excellence. He hadn't discussed it with the others, but since his own personal ordeal in Scotland he knew only too well that vampires existed.

And Jody was beginning to put two and two together very quickly. He had noticed that these fantastic footballers were at their most fantastic only after the sun goes down.

He realised that the power and skill portrayed by all of them, but in particular by Andrei Botezatu paralleled that of something that could not be human. The big striker requested Black Sabbath far too often for his liking also.

Shocked into realising their very existence, Jody had begun to educate himself on the world of vampirism by trawling through the internet and painstakingly deciphering any gothic literature he could find. He was vastly becoming quite an expert. He queried, and wondered why nobody else seemed to ask the question, if all these individuals associated with the Fosturnea School of Football Excellence are from the sun drenched shores of Brazil and Romania, then why are they so extremely pale in their complexion?

And then there was the question of Romania itself?

Indeed he had realised only too vividly himself how vampires need not necessarily come from Romania, but his research had confirmed to him how the most prolific colonies of vampires in the world had strong origins in Transylvania, Romania.

The more he researched his findings and then subsequently studied the professor, the more he was convinced that his team manager must surely be a member of the living dead.

But for now he had no proof so he would have to say nothing, and he knew that while he didn't say anything his life didn't appear to be in danger.

For it seemed that while the team did not realise that the professor and his *boys* were vampires they were allowed to live and breathe amongst the Prodanescu clan unharmed. For no matter what Jody did or did not believe, one thing he was sure of was that Professor Prodanescu had a genuine passion for football and a desire to bring success to Kingsbarr United, and for now at least the likes of himself and players like Johnny Knox were most definitely part of the professor's master plan.

It was true that one by one players like Charlie Cheng, Gerry Spalding and now Giuseppe Rossi were losing their places to the products of Fosturnea, but at least that was all they were losing. Their lives certainly did not seem to be in danger.

Not yet anyhow.

Another man becoming wise to the amazing turn in fortune of Kingsbarr United was number one fan Gene Macgoree. As he nestled into his seat for tonight's game he began to reflect on his beloved teams one hundred percent record since the takeover of the team by the professor. Gene was recently beginning to struggle with his conscience. He too had noticed that the Fosturnea players played even better after dark, but he was trying very hard to continually give them the benefit of the doubt and not recognise them as vampires.

He had even unscrambled the letters of Fosturnea to create the word Nosferatu, but still he did not want to believe that the changing fortune of Kingsbarr United could possibly be down to the introduction of a nest of vampires to the club.

Gene Macgoree understood that his first duty in life was to cleanse the world of the undead; he had been a successful vampire slayer for many years now with a slaying record that was as impressive and Andrei Botezatu's strike on goal ratio. But how could he kill the very heart of the resurgence in his team? How could he drive a stake through the heart of the greatest striker he has seen for many years in a Kingsbarr United shirt? How could he bring himself to decapitate the manager who had rejuvenated the football club of Kingsbarr United?

Deep within him he knew the answers.

If he knew for sure that Cezar Prodanescu and his products of the Fosturnea School of Football Excellence were indeed vampires he would indeed have to slay them. But for now he wasn't going to rush himself into a quest to research the new members of the club in any great detail. He was instead going to enjoy the success at his beloved Kingsbarr United. Yet he knew if a performance was to show tonight that far surpassed even anything that he had already witnessed from the stand since Cezar's leadership came into place, he would understand only too well the reason why.

For tonight was Halloween, and the vampires in the team would get more inspiration and channels of energy then any other night of the year.

For Gene Macgoree knew that Halloween was the one night that vampires, ghosts or anything else from the world of the supernatural were allowed to walk the Earth, by right, unchallenged and prominent on this their own special night.

Gene looked across to his left and saw a young boy take his seat. They exchanged acknowledgements by the nod of the head and uncannily seemed to find a mutual respect for one another instantly.

Unlike Gene, this youth had no doubt whatsoever in his mind about the origins of the Fosturnea School of Football Excellence or their leader Professor Cezar Prodanescu. He had no conscience to wrestle with at all.

This young man was on a mission of vengeance, for he had already attacked the Fosturnea *nest* on a previous occasion when it had been based in Romania. Unknown to Gene this young man was a fellow vampire slayer who had had the best teacher a slayer could have ever wished for. An old gypsy man of the mountains named Bogdan.

And it was the death of Bogdan that had compelled him to come all the way to England to claim his revenge.

Back in the Kingsbarr dressing room, Professor Cezar Prodanescu was continuing his team talk.

"Okay, boys this is another moment of change for tonight's game. The kit."

"Well we knew that boss," said Johnny Knox. We knew that we would be wearing our black kit tonight as Wanderers wear gold in their shirts."

"Johnny as much as I like the black kit myself, believe me I think black is a wonderful colour in many ways, now we are in the Championship the sad reality is a black kit clashes with what the referee wears."

"Yeah you remember the song guys, who's the wanker in the black."

"Yes thank you Vinnie for your usual eloquent input into matters."

"So is it the all white kit then?" enquired Johnny.

"No, Johnny we now have a fourth kit, financed and designed by yours truly. As you will have noticed on your pegs, you each have a clothes carrier hanging upon them. Unzip it and the contents shall be revealed to you." And with saying that the players proceeded to obediently follow Cezar's instructions, curious to what they would find.

The clothes carrier that shielded the kit was itself impressive, black in colour with the Kingsbarr United crest of three crowns elegantly placed to the left of the zipper in gold embroidery.

As one by one the kit revealed itself from within the individual carriers it was Johnny who spoke first. "Hey, red I like it," said Johnny. "It's an unusual shade actually."

"Indeed it is Johnny. I like to refer to it as *blood red*."

The only sound that could be heard in the midst of the awkward silence that fell was Andrei's laughing.

And the knocking of Jody's knees.

The atmosphere was electric as the teams entered the field of play at Wanderers' ground on this very cold Halloween night. Both sets of fans were in fine singing voice, with the home team welcoming the exciting prospect of an ex-premiership outfit to their stadium, and Kingsbarr's loyal band of travelling supporters keen to watch another exciting display of football since the leadership of Professor Cezar Prodanescu had taken place. Indeed, their beloved team had won all six previous games under the guidance of the mysterious Romanian, without conceding a single goal and scoring a hatful themselves.

This form had moved Kingsbarr United into seventh place just outside the play-off positions, and with Wanderers in an automatic promotion spot sitting at second in the league, tonight's game was being billed as a mouth-watering clash between two of the most exciting promotion hopefuls of the Championship.

Confidence had grown within the Kingsbarr United circle of players, how could it not with the previous six high scoring wins under their belts? But as the game kicked-off one of their players was not feeling completely at ease. Jody Roper couldn't get the thought out of his head that he was most likely playing football alongside at least five of his team-mates who were quite possibly vampires (he did not yet know about Leon Davis's crossover) on Halloween of all nights. How surreal could his world become?

Wanderers had started the game quite brightly, keen to view Kingsbarr as a worthy scalp to take, and had contained reasonable possession of the ball since their kick-off.

Johnny Knox and Vinnie "Bruiser" Bradshaw had been holding the play in midfield quite strongly though and a Wanderers player decided that his best option was to bypass the tough-tackling duo by playing a long ball from deep into the direction of the Kingsbarr goal in the hope that a Wanderers striker could run onto it.

The Wanderers striker read the situation well and was moving towards the ball with only Jody Roper in a position to intercept the pass on Kingsbarr United's behalf. Jody still with his mind in a state of turmoil lost concentration and jumped too early in an attempt to head the ball back up field. Embarrassingly the eighties loving defender totally missed any sign of a connection with the ball and the Wanderers striker was well placed to capitalise on Jody's mistake and run with the ball towards the oncoming Alvin Braxton in the Kingsbarr United goal.

Braxton's good positioning was in vain as the Wanderers striker released an impressively accurate and hard driven shot low to Braxton's left hand side, and the keeper watched helplessly as the ball nestled into the bottom corner of the net to put Wanderers 1-0 ahead.

Jody put his head into his hands realising his error had gifted Wanderers their goal and an angry Andrei Botezatu was soon standing beside him.

"If you make a mistake like that again you fool I will rip your throat out and feed it to the dogs at Fosturnea."

Then one of the new boys Paildo uttered his dissatisfaction towards Jody, "and I'll drink every last drop of your blood after Andrei has finished removing your windpipe."

Andrei's and Paildo's chilling words were enough to convince Jody once and for all that his new found *team-mates* were indeed vampires.

Then a more familiar and welcoming voice spoke to Jody. "Come on Jody keep your chin up. We were bound to concede a goal sooner or later; it's the law of averages that's all. Just put it behind you and concentrate on the rest of the game."

Johnny's words of encouragement strangely seemed to have as an influential effect on him as had the words of the vampires, albeit in a different way, and he looked deep within himself and realised that he had to pull himself together and concentrate on the game at hand. He made a promise to himself that for the remainder of the game he would play more akin to his characteristically high standards. He prided himself on always being keen to play well for the fans and the team and decided that nothing should ever stand in the way of that; he would hate to let the fans and players down. In his darkest reflections of the moment though, Jody was also keen not to put his life in danger. He wasn't about to make the same mistake twice for either consequence, in particular the latter.

Jody shuddered as he recalled Bill Shankly's famous quote when manager of Liverpool and now heard his words in a far more chilling new light: "Some people believe football is a matter of life and death . . . It is much, much more important than that."

The egos of all the Kingsbarr United players had been bruised at the scoring of the Wanderers goal, the first they had conceded in this their seventh game under the guidance of Professor Cezar Prodanescu.

The vampire members of the team were particularly agitated that their favourite night of the year had begun in such an undignified manner. They would not allow it to stay that way for long and soon after Wanderers had taken the lead they began to control the game to suit their desires, and fortunately for Jody he had a hand in readdressing the balance.

Andrei Botezatu had shown yet again evidence of his lightning pace and skill and had forced the Wanderers goalkeeper to pull off a wonderful save to concede a corner-kick to Kingsbarr United.

The familiar chants of "Knox, Knox get in the box" had been shouted from the Kingsbarr United supporters, but it was a relieved Jody Roper who had got his head onto the in-swinging corner from Ringa to level the score. Naturally pleased with scoring his first goal of the season, Jody was even more pleased however, to realise that Andrei and the other vampires had forgiven him for his earlier mistake, portrayed by what appeared to be a genuine smile and wink of approval from the blood-sucking striker himself.

Jody Roper felt the weight of the world fly from his shoulders like a dedicated angel of relief.

Andrei himself then scored moments later to put Kingsbarr United into the lead for the first time of the night and to show Wanderers that any plans of celebration they may have had was going to be a well and truly short lived affair.

Jody needn't have worried for the rest of the game about making another mistake as Kingsbarr United began to well and truly boss the game, and the ball rarely ever returned to the Kingsbarr United defending players. Even his new counterparts in defence Paildo and Catarino Popovic were forced to have a quiet game. This was largely due to the explosive manner of play from the other more attacking-minded footballing vampires of Andrei Botezatu, Ringa and Tracaldo. At the half-time interval they had each grabbed a goal to make the score 5-1 to Kingsbarr United.

The occasion of Halloween was now easily delivering a literally extraordinary display of football from the vampires of Kingsbarr United. Not only were they free to roam the Earth on this special night; they were free to express their footballing talents to an incomparable level ever witnessed on any field of football.

The second half was barely underway when Andrei Botezatu had grabbed his hat-trick to put the score at 6-1 and any hopes of a dignified Wanderers result firmly settled without a hope in hells chance.

The electric form of the Fosturnea players had further fuelled Jody's observations of their increased ability to play better in the dark. It came as no surprise to him that they further excelled their ability tonight in the knowledge that it was Halloween. If they couldn't have raised their game tonight his suspicions of them being Vampires would have seriously been misplaced. Jody looked up to the bright light of the moon in all its full glory and understood perfectly what was taking place on the pitch before him.

Gene Macgoree's suspicions were also becoming more and more likely as he witnessed the marvellous spectacle of the Fosturnea players before him. He too realised that the occasion of Halloween was inspiring the players to amazing feats of energy and ability.

The remainder of tonight's captivated audience and the general public, who were learning about Kingsbarr United's talented football team from a detached position, were simply left in amazement at the abilities of the Fosturnea players, not suspecting a thing as to why their abilities to play football were so magical.

Obviously the remarkable methods and dedication that Professor Cezar Prodanescu has put into place to groom these young boys into tremendous footballers were the key to the Fosturnea school's and now Kingsbarr United's success?

How right they were that it was indeed all thanks to the guidance of the professor, but of course how wrong they were in understanding the true nature of his methods.

Just like Gene Macgoree and Jody Roper there was another person in the football ground who was witnessing the display in front of him and realising that it was of an unnatural nature.

Tonight's extraordinary game of football had helped the pupil of Bogdan to identify the true vampires within the camp that were on the football pitch tonight as he glanced at the shirt numbers on the back of the blood-red football strips and cross-referenced them with the names on the player listings of the match day magazine. Botezatu, Tracaldo, Ringa, Paildo, Popovic and . . . Davis.

Yes, Davis. Jody Roper and Gene Macgoree had both noticed the remarkable change in ability in the young and cocky Kingsbarr United player, obviously *not* a product of the original Fosturnea School of Football Excellence, and they each feared the worst for the once mediocre footballer with an appalling attitude. Whatever Leon Davis's misgivings were they would never have wished him to become a victim and subsequent member of the vampire world, in spite of the footballing skills he was now bringing to the Kingsbarr United team. In this second half alone Leon Davis had impressively matched Andrei Botezatu's hat-trick to make the score 9-1 with 10 minutes of the match left to play.

The Kingsbarr United supporters were inspired to innocently chant for their team to reach double figures. So often in the past teams had gone in at half-time 3 goals or more to the good and them simply shut up shop and played out a dull second half, happy to protect their lead in order to win the game.

This was not how a team under the leadership of Professor Cezar Prodanescu approached the game and within minutes the Kingsbarr United supporters had their request answered as Leon Davis incredibly scored his fourth goal of the night and Kingsbarrs tenth!

The Kingsbarr supporters went berserk, even Gene Macgoree was celebrating realising with every minute why his beloved team were indeed so good in their ability, but how could he not applaud and revel in his beloved football club reaching double figures in a single match?

He glanced over to the young man and found it strange how there was no sign of emotion from him. Perhaps he was a Wanderers fan, but even the majority of their fans had began to applaud the amazing display of the visiting team to their stadium, resigned to their own team's dreadful fate on the night but astute enough to understand what they were witnessing was a truly magical display of football that would be talked about for many years to come.

Gene's celebrations slowed as he looked at the youngster's eyes and recognised a familiarity in their expression, as if he had met the young man before. But he couldn't picture where.

As the final seconds of the game were dawning the referee was checking his watch ready to put a legalised stop to the onslaught of the Wanderers team, but there would be time for one more Kingsbarr United attack and as Johnny Knox sprayed the ball out to Tracaldo, who was nestled in a perfect position on the wing, the familiar chant echoed around the ground once more. "Knox, Knox get in the box."

Johnny obliged with a run towards the Wanderers goal as Tracaldo made yet another impressive run down the flank, easily gliding past the oncoming tackles of the deflated opposing defenders.

Tracaldo had bought himself enough time to comfortably look up before delivering the ball to its destination and he spotted Johnny indeed getting into the box as requested by the Kingsbarr United faithful. Tracaldo delivered an inch perfect cross for Johnny to amazingly head Kingsbarr's eleventh goal of the game.

The travelling supporters were euphoric, and the referee also realising that he had just remarkably marshalled a game of a lifetime blew his final whistle amongst the Kingsbarr United celebrations to finally put an end to the Wanderers' misery.

However it was all four sides of the ground that were standing to attention applauding the marvellous spectacle that they had just witnessed, Kingsbarr United and Wanderers fans standing together recognising the amazing display of football that Professor Cezar Prodanescu had undoubtedly brought to the English game.

Still even amongst all this euphoria, Gene Macgoree noticed that the young man was sitting down and not joining in the celebrations, and then became further puzzled to watch the youngster simply get up and leave the stadium.

How strange? Gene thought.

Tonight even the most hardened Wanderers fans were applauding the undeniable expression of football talent to grace the world of football since the game began, so even if this churlish faced young man was a neutral supporter, not belonging to either team, why was he not joining in with the admirations?

It was a thought that would nag away at Gene Macgoree's active mind for the rest of the night. *Why bother to come to the game if you couldn't even enjoy that marvellous spectacle?*

As the Kingsbarr United players eventually left the field after receiving a most wonderful and deserved moment of adulation from the spectators, Johnny noticed a spindly looking man waiting at the tunnel. His hair was greased back with a kind of lotion that seemed to belie modern times, and his hunched stance suggested that he wasn't someone from the playing world of football. The man's beady eyes were unmistakably fixed upon Johnny as he headed towards the players tunnel.

"Can I help you mate? enquired Johnny.

The man remained stony faced, obviously someone else who had somehow failed to enjoy the night's entertainment. He spoke with a ridiculous sounding Oxbridge accent.

"I need you to come with me, Mr. Knox."

"Is everything alright Johnny?"

"Err fine thanks Andrei?" replied Johnny to his Romanian team-mate ahead of the stranger, slightly taken aback by the usually aloof Botezatu's display of allegiance.

It was the stranger who spoke next.

"Mr. Botezatu, I need you to accompany myself and Mr. Knox as well."

Chapter 38

"How undignified I find this to be Johnny, we are ordered to piss in a bottle before we've even had a chance to get showered and changed."

It turned out that the sinister looking stranger who had asked Johnny and Andrei to accompany him to a private room was a "dope-tester" representing the Football Association simply to obtain a random sample of urine in order to check that the footballers hadn't been abusing themselves, or the laws of the game, with any performance enhancing drugs or any other illegal substance for that matter.

On realisation of the situation Johnny had understood totally the need for Andrei to be tested in light of the tremendous talent and energy that he had been displaying since joining the club, although he thought better of it than to share his opinion with the surly Romanian.

Johnny did however find himself agreeing with Andrei that the request to be tested was indeed an undignified inconvenience, but he took some pleasure from his own inclusion for having to provide a sample as being perhaps a veiled compliment. Perhaps it had been recognised by the FA that his own form had been of such a high standard of late that they had concluded it a necessity to test him also. This did raise questions for Johnny though as to why the brilliantly capable Tracaldo and Ringa had been excluded from the indignity.

"Hey, skinny man. What if I refuse to piss in your little bottle?"

"Do you have something to hide Mr. Botezatu?" enquired Oxbridge with a more than sarcastic tone. "And you should address me as Mr. Bellamy."

Johnny felt that Mr. Bellamy's mockery of the big Romanian was an unwise tactic and indeed the evil stare that followed from Andrei into the FA representative's beady eyes suggested to the perpetrator that it might be best to alter his attitude.

"Of course Mr. Botezatu, you are not compelled or obliged to supply a sample, heaven forbid I am totally unable to force you into such matters, but I must inform you that I would have to report your refusal to the FA and a full investigation would be forthcoming." An uncomfortable smile appeared on the now un-nerved face of Mr. Bellamy.

"Come on Andrei, let's just piss in the bottle and be done with it. We have got nothing to hide after all. The quicker we are done the quicker we can get out and celebrate our victory tonight. I aim to buy you a drink after your goal-scoring spree anyway. As your honorary skipper it would be a privilege. We are allowed to drink alcohol tonight are we not Mr. Bellamy?"

Mr. Bellamy looked relieved at Johnny's intent to "play ball" and appreciated his support with the situation at hand. "Oh, but of course Mr. Knox. We are not totally unreasonable at the FA you know, and indeed Mr. Botezatu I think you have earned the right to a swift half at least after your fine display."

"Okay. I'll piss in your little bottle if it means I can get on with tonight's celebrations. It is Halloween after all."

Both Johnny and Mr. Bellamy were curious at Andrei's reference to Halloween but both chose to leave it at that.

Johnny and Andrei provided their samples, gave them to Mr. Bellamy and all three men continued with their very different plans for the evening.

Chapter 39

"Are you comfortable?" enquired Cezar.

"Yes, thank you" answered Audrey Chillingsworth.

"Then I shall begin."

Audrey Chillingsworth was lying spread-eagled on a hospital-style bed in the basement room that Professor Cezar Prodanescu had converted into his laboratory at his Staffordshire home.

Cezar had first met Audrey some sixty years earlier when he had briefly been a footballer for the Romanian Club Steaua Bucharest and the team had travelled to England as part of a European tour.

Audrey, herself an English master vampire, conceived by her parents performing the necessary required ritual on 7th July, Adrien Connor's birth date, had held a torch for Cezar ever since.

Cezar and Audrey had been attracted to one another all those years ago and had indeed been lovers, but for Cezar only in a very casual sense, the kind of love that carried no emotional ties that was purely based on the vampire sexual desires of lust and aggressive love-making.

Audrey, however, had fell in love with Cezar from the off and had always wanted a more meaningful relationship. They had remained in touch from a distance after Cezar had returned to Romania, but for Cezar it was a requirement to keep the vampire network alive than for any romantic feelings he harboured towards Audrey.

Cezar had concerns in contacting Audrey again on his recent return to England, knowing how she felt for him and her tendency to be a bit "bunny-boilerish," but he realised that Audrey would do anything for him, and more importantly she would do anything to serve the vampire community. Cezar therefore soon concluded that Audrey Chillingsworth was a sound choice of vessel to carry the foetus of Adrien Connor.

So Audrey Chillingsworth, lying spread-eagled on a hospital-style bed, was a willing participant in the plans of Professor Cezar Prodanescu.

Cezar, dressed in a white coat looked every inch the mad professor at this moment in time as he held up a test tube and smiled inanely at the submissive Ms. Chillingsworth.

"You see Audrey; it's quite a simple process when you know how."

"It's truly remarkable Cezar. I am so glad that you were able to extract the DNA from Adrien Connor's bones. I feared that the bones may have been too old and decomposed for you to successfully work with."

"We were lucky Audrey, but destiny has clearly guided me to return to England and find some living DNA of Adrien Connor."

"It could have been the powerful guidance of Satan."

"Perhaps."

"Will the procedure hurt me Cezar? Not that it matters for what will be accomplished."

"There will be no pain Audrey. All I need to do is place the egg into your womb and the rest will take care of itself over the next nine months. You see, all that needs to be done to create a clone of anyone is to take an egg, remove the nucleus out of the egg and then replace that nucleus with a cell of the chosen DNA to produce the perfect identical specimen of who you are cloning. On this occasion I will be able to bring Adrien Connor, our one true original master vampire back to life."

"And I will be able to give birth to Adrien Connor and then nurse and mother him into adulthood. It seems so surreal."

"You had better believe it Audrey. Do you understand how privileged you are to have this opportunity."

"I understand fully Cezar. It will perhaps make up for the fact that we never had a child together."

"Don't start that shit Audrey," snapped Cezar. "I can always find someone else to carry and raise the child. There would be no shortage of volunteers."

"Cezar, you know that you will find no-one more loyal than me to make this act of greatness a reality."

"I know Audrey," said Cezar mellowing slightly. "You have always been a good-serving vampire."

"I am always willing to serve you Cezar. And as I'm sitting here with my legs wide open in front of you it seems such a waste for you not to enter me again. I've yearned for your touch again for so many years; surely Adrien Connor can wait a few more minutes before his journey of recreation begins."

To be honest Audrey did look a tempting proposition as her raven hair fell behind her and Cezar could obviously view the inviting genitallia of his ex-lover.

But he knew that he could not be unfaithful.

The temptation was not so strong that he could betray his beautiful Lily and it some how did not feel right to soil the vessel that was soon to harbour the foetus of the original master vampire Adrien Connor.

Instead Cezar placed his mouth between Audrey's legs and gave her womanhood a quick kiss, which caused her to groan and shudder at his touch before he carefully inserted the fertilised egg complete with Adrien Connor's DNA into its rightful resting place for the next nine months.

Chapter 40

Jody Roper was lounging in front of his 50-inch flat screen TV with a half-drunken bottle of lager perched loosely in his right hand, when the phone rang to interrupt his viewing of one of his most treasured DVDs—the 80's vampire movie *The Lost Boys*. It had always been one of his favourite films from his favourite decade, but recently his reasons for watching the movie were largely for educational purposes than for any distinct pleasure as he increasingly considered and analysed his current suspicions of sharing the football field, and perhaps more worryingly the dressing room, alongside a cluster of vampires!

"Hello," he said as he hit the pause button on the DVD remote control, which succeeded in producing a motionless and distorted image of a young Kiefer Sutherland sporting an inane fang-filled smile. Jody failed to notice the irony.

"Hi Jody, its Trudy."

"Oh hi Sis, so what did you find out?"

Miss. Trudy Roper, younger sister of Jody by four years, was a veterinary surgeon serving both the rural and domestic community of England's Southern Staffordshire district. She was responsible for treating a varying degree of animals from town and country alike. A typical day of duties for Trudy could consist of venturing into the farmland of the English countryside to help a distressed mother deliver its baby calf or lamb into the world, followed by the need to treat a sick cat or similar family pet from any of the homes of the surrounding villages. Though never a tedious profession for Trudy, her expertise had been stretched on this particular occasion by her brother following Jody's curious task of asking his sister to run some tests on the urine sample of Andrei Botezatu!

It was at the end of the Wanderers match on Halloween that Jody had hatched his plan. Whilst Andrei and Johnny wondered helplessly as to who the stranger could be who was about to greet them at the players tunnel, unlike his team-mates Jody had already realised exactly who he was. He had spotted Bellamy's old-fashioned black leather doctors-type bag at his feet and it had reminded him instantly of the theory that Jack the Ripper had been none other than the personal medic of Queen Victoria herself. Never one to trust figures of authority Jody realised that Bellamy was a dope-tester.

Ceasing his chance, Jody had very graciously offered to carry Bellamy's bag for him, but soon after he had *clumsily* dropped the holdall spilling its contents across the floor of the player's tunnel. With the swiftness of an alley cat Jody had managed to sneak a couple of clean sample bottles about his person as an influx of willing helpers dressed in muddy football kits retrieved the contents from the tunnel surface and placed them back into their rightful place for Mr. Bellamy.

Mr. Bellamy didn't appear particularly amused, but his announcement of "No harm done," had signalled to Jody that so far his plan was on course to succeed.

Jody knew for sure that Andrei's urine would test okay with the FA, for it was infact Jody's that they would unknowingly be testing instead.

Whilst Johnny and Andrei were with Bellamy providing their urine samples, Jody was providing his own sample in the dressing room toilets.

Following the game Jody had made an excuse to his team-mates of having a headache and having to reluctantly avoid the celebrations following their emphatic win, but instead he tailed the FA doctor to his home address, which fortunately was less than a forty-five minutes drive away from the Wanderers stadium and not much further from Jody's own residence. Fortunately Jody had chosen to drive himself to the

Wanderers ground on Halloween as the game with Wanderers had been a local derby match and Cezar had agreed for a handful of the players to travel independently to the team bus if it was considered more convenient for them to do so. Of course all of the Fosturnea vampires had chosen to travel together.

Amazing himself as to what he was becoming capable of, Jody crept around the back of Bellamy's house, which fortunately was fairly open-planned with very little security features, and proceeded to put the window through with a brick. As a shocked Bellamy rushed to the rear of his house to investigate the assault on his home, Jody had bought himself enough time to switch urine samples by picking the lock of Bellamy's front door, a skill he had become accustomed to whilst growing up on a deprived housing estate as a youth.

Fortunately the unsuspecting Bellamy had left the black holdall just a few feet into his hallway and Jody was able to quickly find the sample marked with Andrei Botezatu's name. He tipped Andrei's urine into the empty bottle and then tipped his own urine into the Botezatu bottle.

Brilliant!

The puzzled Mr. Bellamy finally returned to his house none the wiser, annoyed by having his window broken but simply putting the episode down to local kids mucking around, whilst Jody had cunningly managed to get hold of Andrei's urine sample in order for his sister to run a test on its content.

It had indeed proved to be a triumphant yet dangerous plan and so far Jody was delighted with the outcome, now he just needed to know what Trudy had discovered from the sample to truly see if his risk-taking had all been in vain.

"Well Jody, I don't know why you decided to set me this little test but I do have an answer for you."

Jody hadn't informed his little sister what urine he was giving to her. As close as they were, he felt it difficult to explain that he suspected his team-mate was most likely to be a vampire!

"So what do you think?"

"Well the aroma is very pungent for a start."

"Strange. I thought how void of odour the urine actually was."

"Ah, yes, at first this urine is odourless but over a period of time the smell can become quite strong and overpowering. What puzzles me is how you managed to get such a huge sample from such a small mammal. Is it taken from more than one animal?"

"Err, no Sis, just a single err, specimen."

"Wow, it must be a large bat that's all I can say?"

"A bat, I knew it!" said Jody forgetting himself as he punched the air. Although he had been proved correct to suspect Andrei Botezatu as being a vampire, he quickly realised that things would possibly be a whole lot better if his suspicions had actually have had no foundation to them. It was no great comfort to finally realise once and for all that he was indeed keeping regular company in the presence of at least one vampire.

"Well of course you knew it, you provided the specimen for me to test." Trudy was very puzzled by her brother's apparent fascination with bat urine.

"Oh yes, Trudy. Of course I knew what it was," said Jody recomposing himself and playing along. "Were there any other signs that gave the game away for you?"

"Indeed there is. Bat urine crystallizes at room temperature and that is exactly what is happening to this sample right now. Strange how you came about this urine though Jody, I tested the proteins and various other aspects of the urine and it points towards a largely carnivorous diet. I would like to sample some excrement if at all possible?"

Jody shuddered at the thought of collecting such a sample of Andrei Botezatu's excrement. "Err, I might be a bit weak-stomached to get hold of some bat crap, Sis."

"I understand. So how have you come about this creature? Have you been exploring old bell towers or something? I always thought that you had an uncanny resemblance to Quasimodo."

"Very funny. Well actually, err, some bats have decided to settle in the roof area of the kit room at Beacon Park," Jody wasn't convinced that his explanation actually sounded plausible to the normally astute Trudy.

"Well just be careful, if the club want to get rid of the bats from the premises they need to go through the proper authorities as the creatures are protected by all sorts of legislation."

"No worries Sis, I don't actually think that the club will want to get rid of this particular, err, creature."

"I have to say Jody that this bat's diet is very strange. British species such as the Barbastelle, Noctule and the whiskered bat will all eat insects, but certainly nothing on a larger or more demanding scale. Perhaps somebody has brought a vampire bat to the UK from Latin America and then let it escape. I can't think of any other explanation."

Vampire bat, it was Trudy who had described it as just that. Not him.

"A vampire bat you say. Fancy!"

"Like I say Jody, it doesn't usually live in the British Isles but someone could have introduced the colony to our shores. Thousands of various animals and birds are smuggled into the country every year. Exotic snakes, alligators, parrots, turtles to name only four, you would be surprised what gets in. And I have to say that a football ground in Birmingham certainly seems an unlikely habitat for vampire bats."

If only you really knew Sis!

Chapter 41

"That was a lovely meal Cezar, thank you for surprising me."

"I like treating you Lily; you know how special you are to me."

"You certainly do treat me well Cezar. Sometimes I feel like I've died and gone to heaven."

Cezar shuddered at Lily's choice of phrase as he kept his eyes on the dark road ahead before speaking again.

"How was the king scallops in white wine?"

"Oh, they were simply divine, Cezar. It had a wonderful flavour of garlic too."

Cezar shuddered again.

"Rather you than me darling. You know I can't abide garlic myself."

"I hope it won't stop you kissing me Cezar."

"Kissing you with a smell of garlic on your breath is not the same as swallowing the vile food myself. There are very few things that could stop me kissing you Lily."

"You are such a smoothie. You should try garlic though; you may like it, or at least try something different next time we eat out. Don't you get bored of having steak every time? And I don't know how you can always have it served so rare with all that blood oozing out. Yuck."

Cezar just smiled.

"I'll tell you something else as well Cezar, seafood with garlic and a drop of wine really works wonders as an aphrodisiac."

"Is that right," smiled the professor mischievously.

"Oh yeah, especially when in the company of such a handsome fellow like yourself." Lily playfully squeezed Cezar's thigh as she spoke.

The temptation radiating from his beautiful girlfriend was too much for Cezar as he smiled and pulled into a lay-by that fortuitously presented itself on what was already a fairly deserted road sweeping through the unlit countryside of Staffordshire's Cannock Chase.

"So what do you have in mind now kind sir?" said Lily seductively.

"Well as it is such a beautiful night I thought that we might get out of the car and take a little stroll."

"That sounds good to me."

Cezar and Lily both stepped out of the car into the slight chill of the night and met at the bonnet of the vehicle.

"I think this is far enough, don't you?"

Lily didn't bother answering her lover; instead she thrust her body against him and began to kiss him passionately.

Cezar manoeuvred Lily down onto the bonnet of the car and began to kiss her neck, resisting as always the temptation to sink his teeth into it her. Suddenly the moment was compromised as Lily gave out a yelp and brought her hand to her mouth.

"What's the matter?"

"I caught my hand on the wiper and now it's bleeding."

"Please allow me."

Cezar had at last found a way to accomplish what he had been aching to do for so long.

He began to taste Lily's blood.

To Lily's surprise she enjoyed this invasion of her most vulnerable state and her moaning signalled to Cezar to continue what he was doing.

Cezar's tongue pushed in and out of her wound, lapping at her blood, swallowing it, allowing it to trickle down his throat, then with dramatic swiftness Cezar proceeded to make love to her. Lily couldn't care less that she was so openly exposed on the bonnet of the car in the collective surroundings of the night. If any one were to drive or walk past they would surely see what Cezar was doing to her.

She didn't care.

Against all her previous inhibitions and morals, the thought of being a potential spectacle of live sex actually excited her.

Lost in her state of lust and ecstasy Lily managed to open one eye and could see that the only witness to this fantastic moment of rapture was a full moon peering down at her from the sky.

It looked beautiful.

It looked perfect for this moment.

It seemed approving and non-judgemental in some way. Nothing could be more natural than making love under the light of a full moon in Mother Nature's back garden. She felt as if she was actually celebrating her womanhood by allowing this to happen.

As for Cezar all his Christmas's had come at once. He was able to enjoy the taste of his beloved Lily's blood without having to harm a single hair on her head. And he found it even more gratifying that he was giving his lover so much obvious pleasure by the very nature of his unorthodox sexual act towards her.

Eventually it was over.

Lily climaxed the most wonderful climax and Cezar left no trace of blood from around his lips. It was safe to say that both lovers had been left totally satisfied.

Back in the car Lily spoke as they drove away from Cannock Chase and onto the main road.

"I can't believe you did that, I didn't think any man would want to do that."

"Well I love you more that any man could Lily. You did enjoy it didn't you?"

"You bet I did."

"That's okay then."

"I just can't understand why you would enjoy it; didn't the blood put you off?"

"Lily, your blood is sweeter than wine. Believe me I enjoyed it more than you could ever understand."

"You really do love me don't you?" Lily placed her hand on Cezar's inner thigh as he drove. It was a habit that she had become accustomed to in a playful bid to get her own way with things or simply to show affection without any particular motive. On this occasion she wanted something. "Can we go back to your place tonight Cezar?"

"I prefer to go to your place Lily. It is more private; Andrei or one of the other boys could disturb us at my house."

"But your house is huge. There are enough rooms for us to get lost in away from the other boys. I'm sure it wouldn't be a problem."

"No," answered Cezar firmly. "I want to go to your place Lily. It gives me a sense of escapism. Remember my home is also the base for my work too. I need a break from there sometimes."

"So is that all that I am to you? A convenient plaything to indulge yourself with when you feel the need to get away from your work? When you're tired of playing with me and ready to go back home you can simply discard me until the next time you want a bit of escapism."

"Lily, you know that's not true. Stop behaving like a child."

"But we always go to my place."

"Yes and I want to go there tonight."

"Well I don't. I want to go to your place." Cezar was sure Lily would be stamping her feet if she were standing upright and not sitting down in his car. "And whatsmore I don't only want to go to your house tonight, I want to move in with you."

"Oh, Lily not that old chestnut again. Lily we've been through this."

"Well it is a little hard for me to understand. You tell me you love me but you won't live with me. How am I meant to feel? I'm not just someone you can have on tap when you feel like it. We are either in a relationship or not."

With all the arguing Lily hadn't being concentrating on the journey and soon realised that they were actually already back outside her block of flats.

"Oh I see," she said. "So it does look like my place after all then doesn't it? Well what if I don't ask you in tonight."

"Fine. I'll drop you off and see you tomorrow."

"Oh you will, will you. You take a lot of things for granted don't you Cezar. I let you suck my blood while you fuck me, I give myself to you in my most vulnerable state, in the open for all and fucking sundry to see but you don't want us to live together. Well I tell you what Cezar Prodanescu I am not going to invite you in tonight or any other night; just go home back to your precious football team. For all I know they have an army of whores waiting for you at that house. How the hell do I know what goes on there. That's probably the real reason why we never go back to your place. You're having the best of both worlds."

"Stop speaking with such vulgarity Lily, it doesn't become you." There was anger in Cezar's tone, but he seemed to be speaking to Lily like he was chastising a naughty schoolgirl.

"Well what do you expect you patronising old prick? Can I come and live with you or not."

"NO!" Cezar's anger in this single-word reply was a lot more venomous.

Taken aback Lily waited several seconds before speaking again. "Why?"

"It's complicated," snapped the professor appalled at the way Lily dared to challenge him. He was after all not only a vampire who could kill her in an instant if he so wished, but he was a master vampire, the pinnacle of his kind. But he soon realised that he was also of a humbled disposition these days and it was solely because of the love that he had found with this young girl who was ranting and raving at him this very moment in time. The same girl who only minutes earlier had supplied him with the sweetest taste of her blood, but he couldn't be challenged on his position over their living arrangements. To protect his secret and to protect Lily she must stay away from the home that he shared with the products of the Fosturnea School of Football Excellence, which just happened to be incognito as a cover for the nest of his most personal colony of vampires.

"Then Cezar it seems that only one of us is committed to this relationship and it certainly isn't you."

"Fine if that's how you feel. I do love you Lily but I am not ready to have you live with me and that is my final word on the subject." Cezar was clearly still angry but a lot more composed.

Lily opened the car door and stepped outside. "Fine then," she shouted with tears streaming down her face. "As far I am concerned then we're over. I'm not just some play-thing you can pick up and then throw away again until you are next ready to play with me. I've got feelings Cezar. I'm a woman with needs. Goodbye Cezar, have a happy life in your house of footballers."

She slammed the car door, turned her back on the car and Cezar and headed towards her flat.

Her heart sank as she heard Cezar's car pull away at high speed. He wasn't coming after her.

How could a night that was once so wonderful turn into a night of such anguish and distress?

She looked up at the full moon peering down at her once again. Was he laughing this time?

The full moon had suddenly lost the tranquillity and purpose that Lily had been able to fully aspire to earlier in the evening, and it now appeared a whole lot more eerie and in line with the conventional belief of a full moon signalling terror as portrayed in horror films and books.

Lily shuddered as tears of pain rolled down her cheeks.

"Thanks for nothing," she said softly looking into the moon's sunken eyes.

Chapter 42

Christmas Eve, a hotel in Warwickshire

"Well I truly never thought that I'd ever see the day. The great love god himself Giuseppe Rossi getting hitched. I seem to recollect that you always stated that you couldn't commit to one woman."

"Johnny, my dear friend, even I can be mistaken and now of course I realise that I was when I used to make such statements. I only *thought* that I could never commit to one woman, but that was simply because I hadn't met the right one."

"And Cathy is the right one?"

"Oh without doubt, I will never look at another woman again."

"Bollocks," stated Vincent Bradshaw. "A leopard never changes his spots, there is no way that you can resist the fairer sex, you're fucking addicted to women."

"I tell you honestly Vincent from now on I am only addicted to one woman, my Irish Princess Cathy."

"So having her knocked up has no bearing on the situation at all then?"

"Well, I must admit Vincent that the pregnancy has forced our arm slightly to bring the wedding arrangements ahead, it is best not to have a child out of wedlock when you each belong to a family of such strict Catholic principles. But I tell you what better time of the year is there to get married for a Catholic than at Christmas. For me and Cathy this is just perfect."

"And the fact that Cathy's brothers are both the size of brick shithouses never had a bearing on the decision either? joked Johnny.

"He wouldn't worry about those two bozo's would he Johnny? I bet London to a brick, *soft southern bastards,* that Giuseppe has got connections with the Mafia, *The fucking Godfather, Marlon Brando, Al fucking Pacino.* If her numskull brothers were to mess with Giuseppe they would find a horse's head in their fucking bed."

"You both watch too many movies. For your information her brothers are great guys and there is no other reason why I have married Cathy except for the fact that I love her."

"Well Giuseppe if you and Cathy can be half as happy as me and Sheena have been over the years, you'll not go far wrong."

"Cheers mate," said Giuseppe as he offered his glass towards Johnny's to clink "cheers."

"You pair of soft twats."

"Fuck off Vinnie," said Johnny and Giuseppe in unison.

The three friends laughed together.

At that moment Johnny glanced over to Sheena who was talking to Cathy and after all these years he still felt the luckiest man on Earth to have her as his wife. She was laughing and he was pleased that Cathy and his own soul mate had hit it off so well together. He smiled as he admired the way she tossed her thick shiny hair when she laughed. He had always loved the way she did that and the way her lips did a little double-take when she drank from a glass, like a little twitch that could hardly be noticed, but it was unique to Sheena and therefore to Johnny it was something special. He watched her as she sipped her glass of merlot and pictured in his mind what delights Christmas Eve had in store for him following the wedding reception. Like most of the guests Johnny and Sheena had booked a room for the night at the hotel and Johnny had been delighted that their room included a four-poster bed for them to play upon.

For Johnny's vision of ecstasy to bloom into reality he accepted that he may have to sacrifice drinking into the early hours of the morning with his buddies, as much as he would like to do that also, for he and Sheena planned to have an early breakfast in the morning. They wanted to see Radu at the hospital on Christmas Day morning and the couple were eager to be with their newly adoptive son on his first Christmas with them. Sheena was determined that the little boy would have a whale of a time opening his presents with them in spite of him having to do so from a hospital bed.

The Rossi's wedding itself had been a lovely affair earlier in the day at St Margaret Mary's Catholic Church in Cathy's adopted village in rural Warwickshire since moving to England from County Kerry in Ireland. Plenty of well-wishers had attend the ceremony from both the groom's and bride's repertoire of family and friends, however, Giuseppe had voiced his disappointment of the fact that none of the Fosturnea camp had bothered to make an appearance at the church. Not even the manager Cezar Prodanescu had attended. Johnny, although inwardly disappointed himself that his manager had chosen not to attend the church had tried to make light of the absence for Giuseppe and Cathy's sake stating that maybe it was too short notice, it was after all a quickly arranged wedding. But Giuseppe could only conclude that the absence of the Fosturnea players and the manager was simply a snub to him and his new bride. Just why they would choose to snub the Rossi wedding was a mystery, which had privately been a talking point in little clusters of the guests throughout the day away from the eyes and ears of the newlywed couple.

But as Giuseppe and Johnny both put their drinks to their lips after clinking their glasses together perhaps the mystery was about to be answered. Professor Cezar Prodanescu entered the room with all the charisma and presence of a Hollywood movie star. Andrei Botezatu, Ringa, Tracaldo, Paildo and Catarino Popovic all followed him with a similarly striking existence. For reasons never really understood the products of the Fosturnea School of Football Excellence always had the ability to make heads turn. They were not necessarily the best looking people in the world, but of course mere mortals didn't realise that it was their vampiric sexual magnetism that infectiously spilled out like sexual rays of sunlight lapping at their inner psyche and dormant emotions.

The vampires were accompanied by a handful of attractive looking ladies, who also generated the same magnetic sex appeal.

Another noticeable absentee from the day had also entered the wedding reception with the swarm of vampires. It was the youngster with the very bad attitude and the current occupant of Giuseppe's striking position on the field, Leon Davis. On his arm was another very pretty girl with very striking looks and Johnny felt that he recognised her, though at the moment he couldn't quite recall where from.

On the other side of the room Jody Roper and Gene Macgoree had been deep in conversation when they too noticed the vampires spill into the room.

"I'm convinced Gene I tell you, that lot are definitely blood-sucking vampires. I've done a hell of a lot of research since that experience in Scotland with the *wee flesh-chomping lass* that you saved me from. I'm convinced of it."

"I've certainly had my doubts myself Jody, but while I had no real proof—that is until your marvellous bit of detective work on Botezatu's urine sample, I guess I chose not to dig too deep into things myself. Kingsbarr United have been doing so well since Cezar and the Fosturnea camp's inclusion at the club and I guess subconsciously I just didn't really want to change that. I mean my very presence here tonight is due to my lifelong commitment to the club and the thought of driving a stake through the heart of a Kingsbarr United player doesn't exactly fill my mind with pleasure."

"But Gene, does slaying vampires ever give you pleasure?"

Gene thought for a moment before answering, seriously analysing Jody's question. "If I'm being honest I do find a sense of gratification in ridding the Earth of a parasite that is responsible for taking away innocent lives, otherwise I wouldn't do it, but slaying a vampire is not exactly a pastime you know, it's not something that I find enjoyable like watching Kingsbarr United on a Saturday afternoon. Mind you saying that, watching Kingsbarr United the last few seasons before Cezar took over wasn't altogether enjoyable either."

Jody decided to momentarily change the subject. "Who is the young guy in the corner sitting on his own?"

Gene glanced over and his eyes met the image of a young man, or perhaps even a boy. He couldn't be more than 17 years old at the most. He wore his hair in a pony tail and had handsome chiselled features including a strong jaw line. He seemed to have a toned, athletic build but he was still fairly lean. Although seated Gene could tell that the youngster was not small in height. His long legs were clad in blue denim and his feet were home to a pair of lived in, dark coloured and slightly dog-eared trainers, an odd choice of clothing for a wedding reception.

"I'm not sure; he looks familiar but I can't place where I've seen him before. Perhaps he is related to Giuseppe or Cathy."

"Well why sit on your own? I haven't seen him speak once to Giuseppe or Cathy, or anybody else for that matter. He looks a little troubled if you ask me."

"Hmmm, now you mention it, it does seem strange that he has been sitting there all night on his own. One thing I did notice about him though was the way his eyes lit up when Cezar and the others walked into the room."

"Perhaps he is just a fan who has managed to sneak in."

"As opposed to a fan that has been invited."

"Well you are more than a fan Gene; you are like the club mascot. Not to mention the hard work that you have displayed in creating the club fanzine over the years."

Gene's mind was too preoccupied to value Jody's praise of him. "The look in his eyes wasn't what I would call admiration when he saw Cezar."

"Perhaps he is a crazed fan who is out to get Cezar. Or perhaps he is a vampire slayer like you."

Gene knew that Jody had meant it as a joke, but he recognised that look in the young man's eyes. He recognised it because he often had the same look when faced with a vampire himself.

Could this young boy also be a vampire slayer?

Gene knew he wasn't the only one around.

Gene had also noticed the rucksack perched under the table where the youngster was sitting. Why bring a rucksack to a wedding? And what was the young man carrying in there?

Then Gene noticed Cezar making his way out of the room towards the toilets and the young man stood up and moved in the same direction, picking up his rucksack as he went. The youngster looked very nervous and Gene noticed a bead of sweat run down his slick forehead. His ponytail bobbed slightly as he moved towards the gent's toilet a safe distance behind Cezar.

"I just need to take a leak Jody. I'll be back in a minute."

"Sure thing Gene. Watch out for the vampires."

When Gene entered the toilets he could see Cezar with his back to him who was obviously making full use of the urinal.

Gene allowed his eyes to scan the toilets for the pony-tailed youngster as he was obviously not taking a pee at the obvious utility.

Gene peered down at the gap beneath the cubicles and could see a pair of dark coloured trainers. He was sure it was the young man with the rucksack. There was no sign that the jeans were around his ankles so Gene concluded that he obviously wasn't in the cubicle to take a crap.

Not feeling altogether comfortable Gene made his way to the cubicle occupied by the young man and pushed the door open. As he suspected it wasn't locked.

"Oh, do forgive me I didn't realise this cubicle was taken."

The young man was holding a handgun and he instinctively pointed it at Gene, sweat pouring from his brow.

Gene simply winked through his magnified lens and slowly shook his head, whispering the words "not now. It is not the time." He didn't want Cezar to hear him.

To Gene's relief the young man lowered the gun.

Cezar could be heard washing his hands and then the noise of the hand drier kicked in soon afterwards.

For some unknown reason the young man felt that he needed to take Gene Macgoree's advice and he put his gun away into his rucksack.

He looked at Gene and didn't know if he should thank him or curse him for preventing him from taking the life of the master vampire Cezar Prodanescu. It was his personal mission to kill the parasite and he had travelled a long way to do so. But instinct told him that the small man with the round glasses that magnified his wise eyes was acting as a friend and not an enemy.

The noise of the hand drier died away and footsteps could be heard moving towards the cubicle.

Gene's stomach churned.

A Romanian accent spoke.

"If you two lovebirds want to get together can you please find a room, there are plenty in this hotel I am sure."

"You are mistaken Mr. Prodanescu," said Gene. "I just wandered into the wrong cubicle by mistake."

"We are not gay," spoke the young man in a far more unpleasant tone, which made Gene a little nervous.

Fortunately Cezar was in a good mood and chose not to indulge himself in the situation any longer. He simply smiled and left the Gents toilets without any further incident.

With the coast clear for the imminent future the young man spoke to Gene with some anger in his voice. "You shouldn't have done that, I had good reason to have this gun."

"I trust it was loaded with a silver bullet."

The youngster looked amazed. His tone changed to that of surprise. "How did you know that I had a silver bullet in the gun?"

"Because when using a gun to kill a vampire, only a silver bullet can ever bring success. Regular bullets are totally useless."

"So, you too are a vampire slayer?"

"Indeed I am. The name is Gene Macgoree." Gene offered his hand and the youngster didn't delay in shaking it.

"Then why did you stop me? Don't you believe that Cezar is a vampire or is it that you want his scalp for yourself?"

"It is not until this very moment that I have only just realised that I would perhaps like to slay Cezar myself, but that is not why I stopped you. A murder at the wedding of a KingsBarr United footballer is not the time and the place, and that is exactly what it would have looked like had you killed Cezar just now, a simple murder. I take it you are not a fan of Kingsbarr United."

"Football is not my passion, slaying vampires is."

"Mine too, well both are actually, but why Cezar so badly?"

"He has killed a lot of innocent people in Romania for many generations now. It was also a member of his nest that was responsible for killing my friend. They killed the man who was like a father to me."

"Was that man a slayer too?"

"Yes, his name was Bogdan."

"Bogdan, I haven't heard of him. I take it you and he are Romanian, like Cezar. You have a slight Romanian accent but it is not over strong."

"I am English, or so I am told, but I was raised from a very young age by Bogdan and the gypsies in the mountains of Transylvania."

"Transylvania. My god you really are from vampire country. How did you become to be raised by gypsies in the mountains of Transylvania? It's a long way from home."

"Bogdan found me injured one day at the side of the road. I was in quite a bad way apparently, I don't remember much about it I was only a small boy. I kept shouting out incoherently in English, this is how it was determined what nationality I was."

Suddenly Kingsbarr United's number one fan felt a ping of realisation in his heart. "My god, I think I know who you are? Do you remember your name at all, or did the gypsies have to give you another one."

"I couldn't remember much at all, but I could always remember my name. At least I have always believed that it was my name."

"Is it Callum by any chance? Is your name Callum?"

"Yes it is actually. Are you psychic as well as a slayer?"

Gene placed his hands on Callum's shoulders as he looked in astonishment into the youngsters face to take stock of the situation and to try and digest just who this young boy really was standing in front of him.

But Gene concluded with little doubt.

"This really is a night for surprises isn't it? Now I've got one for you young Callum. Would you like to meet your mom and dad?"

Chapter 43

When Gene and Callum returned to the wedding reception Cezar had rejoined the members of the Fosturnea camp and Jody had made his way over to where Johnny, Vincent and Giuseppe were standing. Also joining them were Gerry Spalding, Alvin Braxton, Charlie Cheng and Matt Floyd.

The laughter that erupted through the latter section of Kingsbarr United players signalled to Gene that Jody must have drank enough alcohol to permit himself to break the news to his team-mates that they were now sharing their dressing room with a bunch of blood-thirsty vampires. He quickly made his way towards them to see if he could salvage the situation on behalf of Jody.

"Is everything okay guys?"

"Gene, will you tell these juveniles that I am not lying. Tell them that the guys from Fosturnea are all vampires."

Alvin was particularly in stitches at Jody's announcement, "Yeah man, enlighten us Gene and tell us that Cezar is the Prince of Darkness too."

The group, except Jody, Gene and Callum roared with laughter.

It was the words of the stranger that brought the laughter to a halt.

"Actually Cezar is a prince of darkness of a sort. And the man with the curly hair is not lying to you. They are all vampires."

"Who are you stranger to tell us this?" enquired Matt.

Gene felt obliged to offer an explanation. "Err; this young man is what's known as a vampire slayer. It may seem difficult to believe but I am a vampire slayer too. It seems that neither he nor Jody are lying to you about the Fosturnea School of Football Excellence either. I believe that it is a breeding ground for vampires and Cezar is the master vampire of what we call the *nest*."

The laughing had stopped but the players still found it a difficult concept to believe. None of them believed in vampires but Jody and Gene seemed so sincere in their revelations, and the fact that a stranger was corroborating their stories seemed to support their statements to be the truth.

"But since they came I've seen them tucking into the garlic bread," stated Gerry. "I thought vampires couldn't eat garlic?"

"Yes, the buffet is of a Mediterranean nature. There is a lot of garlic in the food tonight," added Giuseppe.

"Yes but you invited them in Giuseppe. That means the garlic won't work as a means of a deterrent or even cause harm to a vampire."

"Gene is correct," offered Johnny, amazed at his own desire to analyze the situation. "I saw it in a movie once. If you invite a vampire into your home or place of choice your powers against them are deemed useless."

"Listen guys, do you remember when Johnny and Andrei had a drug test after the Wanderers game?" whispered Jody with the now attentive ears of his team-mates taking him more seriously.

"Which was on Halloween," added Alvin Braxton.

"Yeah, well don't ask me how but I managed to get hold of Andrei's urine sample and I got my sister Trudy to analyze it at the lab."

"And what did she discover?" enquired Matt now genuinely intrigued.

"That Andrei's piss matched that of a vampire bat!"

"Did you test Johnny's?" joked Vinnie.

"Very funny Bruiser," said Johnny. "Listen guys, I'm finding all this stuff about vampires as hard to take in as you all are, but I know that Jody and Gene wouldn't lie to me and you've got to admit that Trudy's findings regarding Botezatu's piss test are a bit alarming."

"Johnny, I have some more news that may alarm you and you may find hard to believe."

"What's that Gene? Don't tell me that Peter Cogshaw is a fucking werewolf."

"It's about this young man here, my fellow vampire slayer."

"Oh really, what about him? Move a bit closer son, so I can take a look at you."

The youngster moved forward and as Johnny looked into his eyes he knew there was no mistake at what he saw before him. The realisation was incredible and emotions of joyfulness erupted from inside the Kingsbarr United midfielder.

Johnny felt a release of sheer joy that had always been bubbling away within him, remaining suppressed but always kept alive by an undying devotion of hope, waiting for this very moment to arrive.

He had searched and searched for his son, year in and year out refusing to give up hope that he was alive.

A single word sounded from his lips.

"Callum."

Chapter 44

While Sheena and Johnny sat in the corner getting to know their son again Gene proceeded to enlighten Matt, Alvin, Charlie, Vincent and Gerry on the subject of vampires and more importantly the suspicions regarding Professor Cezar Prodanescu and his boys from the Fosturnea School of Football Excellence.

"So you are saying that the Fosturnea School of Football Excellence is a breeding ground for vampires?" said the Jamaican international goalkeeper Alvin Braxton. "Man, me used to hear stories of witchcraft and vampires when me were a young boy in Jamaica, it used to scare the shit out of me but as me grew up me just thought they were stories and nuttin more."

"Vampires are in every country the world over Alvin," answered Gene Macgoree. "But they are particularly rife in Romania."

"Yeah and where are our new recruits from?" asked Jody already knowing the answer but keen to get everyone to buy into the notion that their team-mates and manager were vampires.

"Romania," answered Giuseppe. "Hey, Transylvania is in Romania and that's where Dracula was from in that book by Bram Stoker."

"Indeed, Giuseppe you are correct," said Gene. "But where Stoker's book was a story of fiction I can assure you that vampires are very much alive and kicking in our very community every single day. I must tell you also that I was intrigued by the name of Cezar's football school."

"Fosturnea," said Alvin.

"Yes Fosturnea," continued Gene. "It was a word I had never heard of before so I began to wonder if it could be an anagram of some sort and started to mess around with the letters."

"Did you come up with anything?" asked Charlie Cheng.

"Yes I did. If you re-jiggle the letters of *Fosturnea* it spells the word N*osferatu*."

"*Nosferatu*! Hey I've heard of that," said Gerry Spalding.

"It is a word gentlemen that unfortunately means we all stand danger if we decide to act upon what has been revealed tonight."

"Who says we don't stand danger anyway," stated Jody Roper.

"*Nosferatu*, what does it mean then Gene?" enquired Giuseppe.

"*Nosferatu* is the name given for the most powerful ruling class of vampires of Eastern Europe."

"So in vampire terms these boys are Premier League."

"More like Champions League Giuseppe."

"Wow!"

With all the startling revelations about Cezar and the Fosturnea School of Football Excellence it would only be a matter of time before Vincent "Bruiser" Bradshaw fell victim to his Tourette's Syndrome and he unwillingly shouted out a most unfortunate turn of phrase.

"*Cock sucking vampires*."

The team-mates froze as they noticed Professor Cezar Prodanescu turn his head and look in their direction.

Chapter 45

"Shit he must have heard you Vinnie," said Giuseppe as Professor Cezar Prodanescu made his way towards them.

Johnny and Callum had also heard Vinnie's outburst even though they were currently seated a fair distance away, as did Father Anthony McGill the Catholic priest who had earlier married Giuseppe and Cathy. They too began to make their way over to the apprehensive group of footballers.

Cezar got there first.

"What did you say Bradshaw?"

"Who me boss?" answered Vinnie sheepishly.

"Yes, you Bradshaw. You shouted something out about vampires."

Vinnie tried his best to look innocent. "Vampires? I never said vampires boss! Why would I be shouting out stuff about vampires? *Bella Lugosi, Bella Lugosi. Vlad the fucking impaler.*"

Vinnie's anxiety was acutely affecting his Tourette's Syndrome.

Just then Johnny and Callum arrived.

"What was that you shouted over to me Bruiser, something about campfires?"

"Err yes that's right Johnny," said Gene. "I was just telling the boys how you were thinking about enrolling Radu into the Boy Scouts, and Vinnie here got a bit excited as he began to fondly reminisce about his time in the scouts when he himself was a young boy."

"*Great fucking campfires,*" roared Vinnie as sincere as he could muster.

"Err, yes I distinctly heard the word campfires, and I heard the conversation previously about Johnny's young son wanting to start in the Boy Scouts so I came over to explain that the church hall runs a Cub Scout pack every Thursday evening if Johnny was interested in sending the boy along."

This was a plus. The boys hadn't banked on the priest's support with their dilemma.

Cezar stared incongruously into the priest's eyes, and Father McGill was under no illusion that he was staring into the windows of evil itself. In his line of work he had learned to recognise evil and even work against it, for unknown to the general domain Father Anthony McGill was a competent exorcist often used and sanctioned by The Vatican to perform such rituals.

He was also acutely aware of the existence of vampires.

Cezar eventually broke his stare with the priest, not wishing to openly display his contempt for the man and what he stood for any further. Cezar was also keen not to draw any further attention to himself or the boys of Fosturnea. It seemed he had had a moment of paranoia when Bradshaw shouted out and he was keen to keep their secret safe.

Yes they were vampires of a very powerful status who indulged in orgies of blood drinking and debauchery, but in Cezar's mind he was happy to keep this world as separate as he could whilst he built up his empire at Kingsbarr United Football Club. He felt that his intentions for the football club were noble and genuine and he truly enjoyed this new line of work as a football manager.

And he was proving to be good at it.

The fact that half his team were vampires and had an unfair advantage over the opposition due to their increased fitness levels once darkness fell was neither here nor there.

In a bid to gloss over the altercation the geneticist and football manager turned his attention to the bridegroom, "Giuseppe, congratulations on your marriage to Catherine. I wish you every happiness."

Giuseppe hoped that his hesitancy to shake Cezar's hand hadn't been noticed by the professor, but Giuseppe certainly noticed how cold the touch of his manager's hand felt.

"Thanks boss."

"It's unfortunate that you can't have much of a honeymoon with the game being on Boxing Day, but I have a present for you and Catherine. For the entire month of July I have arranged a Mediterranean cruise for you both, which includes valuable time in your native Italy and some time in my home country of Romania."

"Cheers boss, that's really kind of you. The baby's not due until late August so that should be okay."

"My pleasure Giuseppe, and if the baby is a boy just remember that Cezar is a fine name. Now excuse me gents, but I had better return to Andrei, I need to make sure that he doesn't drink too much red wine."

"Okay, cheers boss."

"See you later boss."

As Cezar made his way back to the Fosturnea crowd the vampire debate hotted up.

"Now do you believe me, he is a definite vampire."

"I think you are right Jody, his hand felt so cold when I shook it I would swear I was shaking the hand of a dead man."

"And do you remember the way that he described the new kit? The kit he had personally designed I hasten to add."

"Yes, I do Jody. Blood red."

"Exactly Johnny, a bit of a coincidence don't you think? And have you noticed how Andrei and the others from Fosturnea seem to have super fitness levels during night games, especially the game on Halloween."

"Come to mention it Jody, you're speaking a true word there. I mean me hardly ever have cause to make a save these days."

"Let me explain further Alvin, boys," interjected Gene Macgoree. "Vampires have supreme fitness levels during the hours of darkness; they are largely nocturnal by nature."

"Just like a bat."

"That's right Charlie, so they are going to be able to display almost super human strength during times of darkness, err except they are not super human."

"No they are fucking vampires, err sorry Father, I didn't mean to curse in front of you."

"Do not apologise Mr. Spalding, it is easy to display an act of such a nature when faced with such unusual and challenging circumstances."

"Tell me Father, I am a Catholic and it is hard for me to make any sense of this. Do vampires really exist?"

"Giuseppe my son, you know that evil exists in this world don't you?"

"Yes, sadly I do Father."

"Well evil can manifest in many different forms, and vampires are just one of those forms."

"So it is true then, are we all agreed?"

Everyone agreed with Giuseppe. The evidence and testimonies at hand were too overwhelming to ignore.

"Then we must do something about this situation," said Gerry Spalding.

"Too right man," agreed Alvin Braxton. "We gonna have to get used to not winning ten-nil every game."

"I think you could use my help too," offered Father McGill.

"Thanks Father, it's good to have you on board. We will wait until the new year, and then we will create a strategy," said Gene. "Remember Callum and myself have done this thing before so I urge you to take our lead. Sadly Callum also knows from bitter experience just what a mammoth task we have ahead of us if we are to defeat the Fosturnea School of Football Excellence."

"Cezar Prodanescu and his nest have been responsible for thousands of deaths and carnage in the area where I grew up in Romania. They killed Bogdan a great slayer himself who treated me like his own son," the youngster turned towards his biological father, "now that I have found my real dad I'm not going to let Fosturnea take any one else from me again."

"It's settled then. In the new year we rid Kingsbarr United and the Heart of England of the Fosturnea School of Football Excellence"

Everyone agreed with Gene Macgoree.

Johnny glanced over to the Fosturnea crowd and unlike Cezar it wasn't red wine that concerned him regarding Andrei Botezatu. The Romanian Striker seemed to be very friendly, too friendly for Johnny's liking, with his daughter Saffron.

"Come on Callum, it's time to reunite you with your twin sister."

Chapter 46

"Excuse me Andrei, I need a quiet word with my daughter."

"Is it really necessary Johnny? We are having such a wonderful time here."

"Yes, it's necessary. She's my daughter and I wish to have a word with her." Johnny's tone was becoming increasingly more assertive and less patient.

"Hey, we are not on the playing field now Skipper. You can't tell me what to do."

"I can when it concerns my daughter, especially as she is barely 16 years old."

Saffron visibly reddened. "Dad, you are embarrassing me. We are only talking"

"Saffron, don't make a scene, I just want you to come away for a moment. I have some truly amazing news for you."

"It seems to me you are the one making a scene, Knox. You don't even trust your own daughter to speak with me. Why not go all the way and put a leash on her."

"Watch your mouth Botezatu."

"Come on Knox, you said yourself she is 16. That makes her legal in my book."

Johnny finally lost patience with the churlish Romanian and the disrespect that he was showing both him and his daughter provoked Johnny to angrily grab Andrei by the lapels of his suit.

"Back off Botezatu. I'm warning you."

Before Botezatu had time to react Cezar had entered the frame and proceeded to calmly intervene.

"What is wrong with you two infants? This is your team-mates wedding and you are spoiling for a fight."

Johnny reluctantly released Andrei but continued to stare at the Romanian hard. His eyes never left Andrei while he spoke to Cezar.

"Sorry boss, I don't mean to cause a scene but your fellow countryman here wasn't showing enough respect to either me or my family."

"On the contrary, I was showing Johnny's daughter plenty of respect. You ask her if she was enjoying my company."

Saffron giggled.

"I'll fucking kill y—"

Cezar quickly placed himself between his two star players in a brave attempt to defuse Johnny's imminent attack on Andrei.

"Okay, okay perhaps we have all had too much to drink and things may have gotten out of hand. Now Johnny and Andrei I want you to shake hands and put this incident behind you. And Andrei if it pleases Johnny then stay away from his daughter."

Andrei smiled and put a hand out to Johnny. "Sure boss. Johnny if I have offended you then I truly apologise." Andrei's words were carefully articulated but offered little sincerity.

Johnny turned to Cezar and the professor nodded his head as an instruction to shake Andrei's hand.

Reluctantly Johnny took the hand of his "team-mate" and indeed they shook hands.

Johnny was alarmed at not only the strength of the Romanian's grip, but also the icy coldness of his skin.

"That's much better boys. Now please, let's enjoy the rest of the party."

With the disagreement seemingly resolved, just as Johnny turned his back on Andrei to get on with his business, Callum decided to speak up.

"You heard my dad grease-ball, stay away from my sister."

"Sister!" said a startled Saffron turning to the young man who had accompanied her father. But once she looked squarely into his eyes Saffron realised everything. "Callum, it really is you isn't it. I knew you were alive, I could always sense it."

Saffron hugged her brother, emotions of joy and relief overwhelming her.

"Well we are twins. That's how you knew Sis."

"I hate to break up the happy party, but I don't like being called a grease-ball."

"Leave it alone Andrei," ordered Cezar with a distinct sharpness in his voice. "It is clear that emotions are running a little high this evening."

Andrei obediently stood down.

As he looked at the reunited twins getting to know one another again Andrei couldn't help but think that he had seen the boy called Callum before. He looked very much like someone who had been part of an ambush one particular night when Fosturnea had been originally based in the hills of Transylvania.

He looked very familiar indeed.

But logic told Andrei the boy could not have been at Fosturnea that night. How could an English boy, the son of Johnny Knox no less have been part of the ambush on the Fosturnea School of Football Excellence?

It didn't make sense.

Callum simply looked like someone else. Someone who just happened to be from the vampire slaying gypsy community of Transylvania.

Meanwhile Johnny had noticed the intriguingly conspicuous girl standing next to Andrei who appeared to share the same pale complexion as the Romanian striker. Though close to Andrei at present, no doubt enticed to see what all the commotion had been about, she seemed to be very friendly with Leon Davis. With her raven coloured hair and contrasting skin colour she was without doubt a stunningly attractive young person. Johnny knew that he had seen her before.

The nagging question was *where?*

"Why are you staring at me Mr. Knox?" she said. She had the same and now increasingly familiar Romanian accent as Andrei and Cezar.

"I'm sorry, I, err didn't realise I was. Please forgive me I didn't mean to make you feel uncomfortable. It's just that you look kind of familiar to me."

"Oh really," the girl did not seem to be offended. "Well my name is Afina. I'm very pleased to meet you."

"No, the pleasure is all mine, Afina."

Afina. Even the name was familiar to Johnny.

Then the memory hit him like a football catching him in the pit of his stomach, momentarily pushing all the air and breath out of him.

Johnny needed a moment to gather himself so he could adjust to the shock of his recollection.

He realised that it was on the beach in Romania that he had first seen Afina.

He had noticed her beauty that day as she elegantly walked along the tide, her pale skin and raven coloured hair perfectly complementing the blue sky above her.

And he remembered thinking that he had seen her photograph in the newspaper that he had been reading only moments before her presence had radiated itself across the burning sand. The accompanying article had explained how a young woman had been found dead in Bucharest, but she had then mysteriously disappeared from the autopsy room.

The article had said that the dead girls name had been Afina.

Johnny had been convinced then and he was convinced now.

The girl that he had seen on the beach was the same girl who had supposedly been killed by two puncture marks to her neck and then subsequently vanished off the face of the Earth under a cloud of unexplained mystery.

Except she hasn't vanished off the face of the Earth at all.

She is very much alive and kicking, for she was standing here as large as life in front of Johnny once again.

And Johnny knew something else about Afina now.

Just like Andrei, Cezar, Ringa, Paildo, Tracaldo, Catarino Popovovic (and most likely Leon Davis too) Afina was a blood-sucking vampire.

Chapter 47

Johnny Knox killed the engine of his Audi as he finalised the parking of his vehicle at the hospital car park.

"So I'm going to meet my little brother?" came a voice from the passenger seat.

"That's right Callum," beamed Johnny, delighted to have his natural born son back in his life once again. "Don't feel that you have missed out on too much time with him though, he hasn't been in the family for too long anyway."

"Its crazy to think that you adopted him from Romania considering what happened to me there."

Callum hadn't intended to use the irony as a weapon towards his dad, merely as an observation of the quirky fate that can be served up in life, but his words reminded Johnny of the pain that he had felt during the missing years that he had experienced apart from his son.

"I never gave up on you Callum. I returned to Romania every year asking questions, searching for you. I never gave up hope. Not me or your mom."

"Its good to know Dad, I just wish that I hadn't lost my memory after the car accident that we had all those years ago. We would have all been reunited a whole lot sooner. But I can assure you that Bogdan and the gypsies really did take good care of me, Dad. You have no need to worry on that score."

"I can see that they did right by you son. Look at you, a fine young man you've turned into. I'm so proud, and now you are back with us, it's like a dream come true. What better Christmas present could me and your mom possibly ask for?"

"Me too, Dad. I'm looking forward to Christmas dinner at home with the family later. I think I can actually remember how good Mom's cooking used to be. It's a shame Radu can't join us."

"We never adopted Radu to replace you Callum. Please don't ever think that. He just seemed to be in a lot of trouble and needed our help. We could offer him a stable home."

"I know you didn't adopt Radu to replace me, Dad. It's good to know I have a little brother. It's also good to be with my twin sister again too."

Johnny hugged his son. "Come on let's go and see Radu. You can help him unwrap his presents unless he has already done so."

Johnny rang the bell to the hospital ward, causing Minnie Harvey to smile as she recognised the image of Radu's father on CCTV. She released the door by pressing the appropriate button to momentarily disable the security system.

Callum followed Johnny onto the ward.

"Happy Christmas, Mr. Knox. Who is the fine young man accompanying you today?"

"This Minnie is my other son Callum."

"Happy Christmas Callum, I'm very pleased to meet you."

"Pleased to meet you too Minnie, happy Christmas."

Callum noticed the genuine kindness in Minnie's eyes. It was hard to place an age on her; she could have been anything from between 28 to 45. She was of mixed race, a little overweight with a very gentle face.

"How is Radu today? Has he opened all of his presents yet?"

"Well I checked on him about an hour ago and he was still sleeping bless him. I didn't want to disturb him, he looked so content all snuggled up under the sheets, like a sleeping little angel, so I felt it best to leave him be. I knew that you would be coming in to the hospital soon enough and I thought it would be nice if he could open his presents while you were with him."

"Thanks Minnie, it would be great to watch him open his presents. Is there any news yet on the latest test results?"

"You should really wait for Dr. Charnwood to inform you of that Mr. Knox. I don't want to speak out of turn and I'm not really that medically qualified."

"Listen Minnie, its Christmas Day and I'm sure that my path will not be crossing Dr. Charnwood's today. I'm sure he is busy admiring his new set of golf clubs that he has undoubtedly acquired in his Christmas stocking. I'd really like to have some news to give to Sheena later."

Minnie smiled; Johnny always seemed to have a nice way of putting things. If he wasn't such an obviously happily married man she could easily make a play for such a charming individual herself. "Okay, I do know a little about Radu's progress, but please you must not repeat that you have heard anything from me."

"Our lips are sealed," reassured Callum.

"Okay, well the good news is that all the ongoing tests for leukaemia are still coming back negative."

"That's good news," said Callum again. "Is there any bad news?"

"Well only that Radu's condition is still largely a mystery. Everything points to a rare form of haemophilia, but its not just the deterioration of blood cells not clotting sufficiently, the physical symptoms that accompany Radu are very worrying."

"How do you mean?" pressed Callum.

"Well we know from tests that have been carried out on Radu's mental state that he is of perfectly sound mind, but he seems to, how shall I say, hallucinate when his body is in need of a blood transfusion."

"Hallucinate?" asked Johnny, knowing himself that he and Sheena had witnessed such behaviour by Radu first hand.

"Well he starts to become incoherent and nothing can be done to console the poor little mite. He starts saying that he craves blood, that he needs blood so bad that he wants to drink it or take it into his body as quickly as possible. It can be most distressing to watch. Then when he has his blood transfusion and he comes out of sedation he is the happy, lovely little boy that we all know and love."

"He couldn't be schizophrenic?" asked Callum, more for elimination purposes as alarm bells started to ring in his head.

"No, as I say all his tests for any mental health problems have unearthed absolutely nothing. He would be very young to show signs of schizophrenia or any type of multiple personality disorder anyway. It's almost unheard of in a boy of his age."

Johnny, as always was concerned and mystified at his younger son's state of health but denial can always work as an effective coping strategy.

"Oh well, Radu is in the safest hands that he could possibly be in right now here at the hospital. Come on Minnie I want to go and help him open his presents."

Minnie smiled and led the way to Radu's private room, which was only about twenty paces or so on the left hand side of the corridor.

Minnie opened the door to Radu's room and spoke simultaneously, "Radu, your dad is here and he has another surprise for you for Christm—" Minnie was alarmed when her eyes finally fell on to Radu's bed. "Oh, I'm sorry Mr. Knox; Radu doesn't seem to be in his room."

"Could he have gone to the toilet?" enquired Johnny, realising as soon as he spoken the words that it was highly unlikely as the door to the en-suite bathroom was wide open exposing the fact that nobody was inside.

Minnie began to frantically run around the room, checking behind the curtains and furniture, then even dropping to her knees to look under the bed but Radu clearly wasn't anywhere to be seen.

"Has anybody unusual come onto the ward today Minnie?" enquired Johnny, beginning to fear that his son could have fell victim to an abduction. Being in the public eye of course carried many advantages for people like Johnny, but what came with that was always the threat of some twisted nut waiting to pounce and conflict some harm or extortion to the famous person in question or their family.

"No, Mr. Knox, I've been on duty all morning and I haven't seen anyone come onto the ward today except for the parents and family members of the kids in here. I make it my duty to keep very vigilant at all times."

"I know you do Minnie; don't worry no-one's blaming you."

"The window is open," stated Callum.

Minnie raced to the window and looked outside. Her initial panic subsided when she could see that the concrete floor below revealed no indication of a young boy's body having fallen out of the window.

"He must have gone out the window," continued Callum. "There is no other explanation."

"No, that's impossible. He would never survive the fall and there is no evidence to suggest that he has gone out of the window."

But Callum knew that if his suspicions were correct about his little brother, then Radu would have been more than capable of leaving the room via the window, as vampires are able to shape-shift into the form of a bat. Therefore Radu could simply have flown away.

"Okay, there is no point standing here all day debating how he has gone from the room, let's concentrate our efforts on finding him." And with that Callum raced away from the ward.

"I'll call security," offered a helpless Minnie.

"Okay, I'll follow Callum's lead and go and search around the hospital too."

"I'm sure he will be okay Mr. Knox." But Minnie was inwardly deeply concerned at the disappearance of the little boy who had been placed under her supervision. She was mystified how Radu could have sneaked past her at the front desk. Okay she wasn't there permanently, she had to go to the toilet once in a while or grab a cup of coffee, but even so she was convinced that there had never been enough time for Radu to sneak out without her knowing.

Callum Knox knew exactly where he was heading to as he raced along the hospital corridors, noting the directional signs on the walls as he ran.

Bingo! Haematology unit this way.

Callum was oblivious to the startled looks he was receiving as he dashed onward with his mission to find Radu.

Moments later he arrived at his destination.

As it was Christmas Day the haematology unit was practically deserted. There was no schedule for outpatients and any hospital activity was of course only being maintained at a necessary minimum.

He distinctly changed his pace of approach now that he had reached the unit and with all the skill of a lioness stalking its prey in the long grass of the African plains, Callum crept through the transparent plastic swing doors and along the corridor, until finally he arrived at the exact location he was targeting—the hospital blood bank.

Callum found no satisfaction in proving himself right. He would have loved to have been wrong about his little brother, but the evidence was just too overwhelming as the child's face looked up at him—covered in blood.

Radu was sitting on the floor, surrounded by discarded bags of blood that had been ripped open and drained of their contents.

At this present moment in time Radu was holding a frozen block of blood and was licking it just as any other child would be enjoying a fruit flavoured ice-lolly.

"Hi Radu, my name's Callum and believe it or not I am your older brother."

Radu just snarled like a wild animal.

"Oh, don't worry buddy, I'm not exactly thrilled to meet you either—I mean I didn't bank on getting a low-life blood sucking little shit like you when I hooked back up with the family. The ironic thing is I usually spend most of my time destroying vermin like you, but I'll have to work something out for the time being otherwise Mom and Dad are gonna freak. So consider this your lucky day."

Although Radu's appetite was reasonably satisfied for another twenty-four hours, the small vampire couldn't resist this opportunity to have a go at some fresh human blood direct from the vein and he suddenly leaped towards Callum.

However, Radu soon retreated and dropped to the floor like a stone as Callum pulled something from his pocket at equally lightning speed as the tiny vampire's flight had been.

"What's wrong? Don't you approve of my crucifix little brother? I never leave home with out it."

Radu just cowered as Callum now moved towards him, still holding the crucifix at arms length.

"Why don't you kiss the cross in my hand Radu?"

Radu winced, as any child of his age normally would when absolutely terrified of something.

"Sorry to tease you little lad, but that's my job as a big brother you see. Okay, I'll stop and this can be our little secret—for now. Let's get you back to your room; Dad has come to see you so behave yourself."

Callum reached down and picked up his little brother, keeping the crucifix in his hand so that it rested into the spine of the young vampire as he carried him. Radu tried to move but it was useless, he was paralysed by the power of the crucifix, no limb could be moved no matter how much he tried.

"While I hold this crucifix to your spine little brother you can't move. You will be paralysed until I move it from you. Now I'm going to carry you back to your room, but make no mistake Radu. If you try any of your vampire shit when we get there I'll have no hesitation. I will put your lights out permanently. Do you understand me?"

"Yes, I understand is Dad waiting for me?"

"Yes, he is and I know how much he loves you."

"Believe me big brother I love him too. I love him very much. Although I drink blood I would never harm Dad or Mom."

Callum's heart softened ever so slightly as he looked down at the seemingly innocent face of his new little brother. "Okay I believe you. I've got to work out a way to cure you. It will be a challenge; I usually just wipe your sort off the face of the Earth, but as you're family now I'll just have to sort it." Callum was able to hold his little brother with one arm temporarily, still securing the crucifix against his spine, as he grabbed a cloth and wiped the blood from Radu's face. "There, now you look more presentable."

"Thank you Callum. I like having a big brother, even if he does enjoy killing vampires."

Johnny was the first to return to the room.

"It's no good Minnie, I can't find him."

"Security have had no luck so far either."

"It's okay I've got him," said Callum's voice from behind them. He was carrying Radu in his arms, unbeknown to anyone else that a crucifix was strategically placed at his back to keep the tiny vampire temporarily paralysed. Callum eased it away slowly; he figured that Radu would behave himself now that he had a bellyful of blood.

The relief whizzed out of Johnny. "Radu, you are okay. Well done Callum, where did you find him?"

"That's not important Dad, the main thing is that he is safe. Now come on lets open his Christmas presents with him."

And the male members of the Knox family did just that.

Chapter 48

Saffron Knox was helping her mother prepare Christmas dinner in the kitchen while her father and twin brother were sitting patiently in the dining room of the Knox residence.

"Typical men those two, sitting on their lazy backsides while the women do all the hard work."

"You're not wrong Saffron, but to be honest I wouldn't let your father anywhere near the Christmas dinner after his all too vivid history of cooking disasters. He struggles to even poach an egg and do you remember the breakfast-in-bed fiasco he concocted for my birthday last year. Oh, he meant well bless him, but the cold, burnt toast with a carpet of butter unimaginably accompanied by two-tone coloured sausages and a cold fried egg—with the snotty element still remaining may I add, was less than appetising. He doesn't seem to grab the concept of cooking things on both sides, so can you imagine what the Christmas dinner would have turned out like if we'd have let him loose in here."

"Yeah, you do have a point, Mom. One thing I hate is uncooked potatoes and I bet Callum is more likely to have inherited Dad's culinary genes rather than yours." Saffron replaced the saucepan lid after stirring the sprouts and turned the heat down slightly on the cooker to create more of a simmer than a boiling effect. "Mom what's wrong, are you crying?"

"Only tears of joy, Saffron," answered Sheena as she quickly wiped a tear from her eye with the back of her hand, freeing herself momentarily from chopping the fresh sage that she was soon to add to her homemade soup. "It's like a dream come true that your brother is back with us again and particularly at this time of year too. We couldn't have asked for a better Christmas present."

"I know. I find it slightly surreal to be honest. It's great to have my twin back again though, there's so much I need to ask him about Romania and everything."

"Don't rush him Saffron, he will tell us things when he feels he wants to. It must feel a bit strange for him at the moment. He may need some time to readjust."

"It's a shame Radu isn't here with us too, then the family would be complete on Christmas Day."

"Well unfortunately hospital is where he needs to be today. Your dad says he is still quite unwell." Sheena returned to chopping the sage as she spoke in a harsher and blunter tone, leaving Saffron puzzled at the markedly different expression in her mother's voice when she spoke about her two sons. The affection she showed for Callum was clearly not evident when she spoke of Radu. She was saying all the right words but they lacked the emotional conviction that a mother should have for her sick child. Saffron decided to leave the matter alone and she returned to attending to the bubbling saucepans.

"I'm really concerned about your little brother, Callum. He has had problems with his platelets, he seems anaemic, he only responds to treatment periodically. Will he ever be fully cured of whatever he has?"

"Oh there is a cure Dad."

"How can you be so sure Callum?"

Callum wasn't quite sure how to answer his father. His plan had been to keep his thoughts about Radu away from his parents to protect their feelings, but he also knew that the clock was ticking and it was not in Callum's nature to leave a vampire lurking in society who was at some point destined to prey on human blood, even if that vampire happened to be your little brother.

"Just leave it Dad."

"Callum, how can you be so sure there is a cure? Tell me."

"No. Anyway it's not exactly a cure like you are thinking."

"I don't understand Callum. You are frustrating me now, son."

"Dad, it's you who is being frustrating. Can't you work it out for yourself, you have about the others."

"What do you mean the others?"

"Don't be so naïve Dad. You are in denial just because he is your son."

"Denial about what?"

"Jesus Christ Dad, do I have to spell it out for you?"

"Don't worry Callum; I'll inform your father."

"Mom, sorry I didn't think you could hear us."

"Johnny, what Callum is trying to tell you is that Radu, our son is a vampire."

"Quiet, Sheena. Saffron will hear you."

"She would have heard *you* Johnny, the way you were enticing Callum to raise his voice out of frustration. I've left her blending the soup and I've closed both doors so if we are quick she won't know what we are discussing."

"Dad, look at the evidence will you. You know that Cezar, Andrei and the others from Fosturnea are vampires don't you?"

"What? Cezar and Andrei are vampires!" said Sheena, who like the other wives and girlfriends of the team had so far been exempt from the knowledge. "Of course, they are from Romania too."

"That's no proof that Radu is a vampire, have you heard yourself?" answered an incredulous Johnny. "Not everyone from Romania are vampires you know."

"No they are not, but vampire activity is rife in Romania, in particular in the Transylvanian region, and how do you explain Radu's thirst for blood?"

"Don't be so melodramatic Callum. It's not a thirst for blood he has; it's a need for blood like a haemophiliac needs blood."

"Okay Dad I didn't want to tell you this but you have left me very little choice. When Radu went missing I found him in the hospital blood bank. He had been devouring bags of blood, drinking them dry and he was even using a frozen block of blood like a fucking ice-lolly when I found him."

"Don't curse in front of your mother Callum."

"Sorry Mom."

"Don't apologise Callum, your father's lack of acceptance of the facts is enough to make a saint swear."

Johnny took a moment to gather his thoughts while Sheena and Callum waited anxiously for the penny to drop. Incredible as it was Johnny indeed believed that Cezar and the Fosturnea boys were vampires, and he had even worked out by his own accord that Leon Davis and Afina were most likely vampires as well, so in his own mind, as illogical as it seemed, he understood that vampires could exist.

Johnny's mind churned in an attempt to rationalise the facts but his trail of thought was broken momentarily when the phone began to ring.

"Leave it," said Sheena, keen for her husband to get on with facing up to the truth about their adoptive son. "Saffron will pick it up on the kitchen phone."

Johnny thought back to the time he first found Radu, indeed when he rescued him from those men who had been chasing him.

But why had they been chasing him, and with a pitchfork in their possession too?

They had wanted to kill Radu.

He had never really understood why. Until now that was.

Johnny reached into his pocket and felt the warm edges of a precious metal in his pocket.

He pulled the object out and stared at the silver crucifix that Dr. Lazar had given to him.

Sheena and Callum looked at one another; it seemed that reality was finally setting into Johnny's thinking.

Johnny continued to stare at the crucifix.

Dr. Lazar had given it to him as a means of protection.

Dr. Lazar had warned him that he may need the crucifix one day. Now he finally understood why.

The men who had been chasing Radu on that day had warned Johnny about the small child.

He finally understood everything about his adoptive son.

Radu was also a vampire.

Just then Saffron entered the room.

"Mom, Dad. Can one of you come to the phone? It's Minnie from the hospital. Radu has gone missing again."

Chapter 49

Lily was a little unsettled as she pulled up at the gates of the Fosturnea School of Football Excellence. Snarling at her through the gates were the two most ferocious looking Rottweiler dogs that she had ever seen.

Still, she decided that the gates were protection enough as she pressed the button on her dashboard to enable the car window to come down, exposing the cold air and the few drops of snow that were falling, and then a couple of seconds later, still with the dogs barking manically, she was able to press the intercom and announce who she was and why she had come.

Lily was a little puzzled at the necessity of the intercom and Rottweiler dogs, Cezar hadn't mentioned to her that such security measures were in place at Fosturnea, but she quickly concluded that perhaps it was a necessary precaution in light of both Cezar's and the team's advancing publicity and recognition on the football stage.

What she didn't realise of course was that any residence that harbours a master vampire are protected by what are known as the "Hounds of Hell".

An accent not unlike Cezar's came through the speaker of the intercom.

"Can I help you?"

"Err, is Cezar home please?"

"Who wants to know?"

"Its Lily, his err, girlfriend." *I think.*

"Okay Lily, I will let the gates open and you can enter."

"What about the dogs?"

"Do not worry, once they know the gates are being opened they will stop barking and leave you alone. They will understand that this is a signal that a friend has entered Fosturnea."

"Okay thanks. Is Cezar ho—?"

But before Lily received an answer to her unfinished question, the intercom fell silent and the gates began to open. Whoever she had been talking too had been true to his word because the dogs, against her initial belief, fell silent and sat down obediently as the gates opened. In fact once Lily had commenced onto the drive, they accompanied her car as she drove through the crisp snow covered driveway to the house, walking slowly next to the car as if they were now protecting her.

Lily got out of the car, half-expecting the dogs to turn again and rip her limbs off, but instead they now chose to walk beside her as she went to the door.

She didn't need to ring the doorbell as a tall young man answered the door. "Lily, how nice of you to come to Fosturnea. Allow me to introduce myself, my name is Andrei Botezatu."

"Oh, I know who you are, I've began to follow the adventures of Kingsbarr United now that I have shall we say a vested interest."

"Please, will you come in? Lily, such a lovely name and perfectly belonging to such a pretty girl. I'm sorry to say that Cezar hasn't spoken that much about you."

"Oh, really," said a disappointed Lily, her heart sinking.

"Oh, don't read into anything I've just said Lily, Cezar is simply a very private man. Why should he tell us young, hot-blooded delinquents anything about what is going on in his life outside of football? I know if I had such a pretty girlfriend I'd certainly want to keep the relationship valued and protected."

Lily began to blush. Though flattered she was unsure if Andrei was making a move on her or was simply being welcoming. She felt that an explanation as to why she was here would set the correct tone for the conversation to unfold. "Actually, I've come to see Cezar to apologise and make things up with him. We had a bit of a falling out the other day, and well to be honest, today being Christmas Day I'm having a pretty miserable time on my own so I thought that I'd try and patch things up with him."

"Oh, well he isn't here right now but I'm sure that he won't be too long, perhaps you would like to wait for him?"

"Well, I don't have much else to do so I might as well."

"Come on, I think *A Sound of Music* is about to begin, I'll open a bottle of red wine and we can sing along to the Von Trapps while we wait for Cezar. I do a mean rendition of *Edelweiss.*"

"That sounds wonderful Andrei, let's do that."

Lily was surprised at how quickly her head had begun to spin. "Wow, what wine is that Andrei, it seems very powerful."

"Romanian of course."

"I'm not that familiar with Romanian wine, is it stronger than most wines? I'm just feeling very woozy that's all. I'm just going to go to the toilet if that is okay."

"Of course, there is one downstairs actually, second door on the left past the kitchen area. But don't be too long you don't want to miss out on the film."

"Oh, I've seen it a thousand times already. If you had grown up in England you would know what I mean. I'll be back soon." Lily was surprised to find herself stagger as she got up from the comfy sofa that she had been sharing with Andrei, but she managed to compose herself and make her way to the bathroom.

As she walked down the hall she peeked into the kitchen and saw a young boy sitting at the table drinking a glass of milk.

"Hello, I'm Lily what's your name?"

"My name is Radu."

"Radu, that's a nice name, are you a nephew of Andrei? You too seem to have the same Romanian handsome features." Lily suspiciously began to wonder if Radu was more likely to be a son, or even possibly a grandson of Cezar.

"No Andrei is just a friend of mine."

"Oh, that's nice. Is Cezar your friend too?"

"Yes he is."

"Just a friend?"

"Yes, just a friend."

"Do you have any family Radu?"

"Yes, I do. My father is Johnny Knox."

"Oh I know him, I mean I know who he is, and your dad is also a Kingsbarr United footballer. I've started taking an interest since I err, have met Cezar."

"That's nice." Lily was a little confused because Radu had a Romanian name and spoke with the same accent as Cezar and Andrei, yet she understood that Johnny had played international football for England. She wasn't aware of the Knox's adoption of Radu as the Knox's had miraculously been able to largely keep it out of the spotlight of the sensationalist media except for maybe the die-hard football fan who would have a valid interest. She also found it strange that if Radu was indeed the son of Johnny Knox why was he not at home with his father, especially on Christmas Day of all days.

"Is your dad here Radu? I'd like to meet him."

"No he isn't here."

"Oh, okay. Well I'm just on my way to powder my nose. It was nice meeting you Radu."

"You too Lily."

As Lily moved away from the kitchen she was startled to almost crash into another person whom she had not heard approach at all and gave out an involuntary shriek.

"Please forgive me, I never sensed you nearby."

The woman remained stony faced and didn't offer a reply. She was beautiful in a sadistic sort of way, with piercing and intriguing eyes and a mane of raven hair with just the odd wisp of silver showing through.

Lily couldn't pitch an age of the woman but felt her appearance to possibly belie her state of pregnancy.

"Excuse me; I need to go to the bathroom."

The woman still remained stony faced and seemed intent on blocking Lily's path.

"Excuse me please."

The woman finally spoke. "You should be more careful where you are walking. You wouldn't want to bump into a lady in my condition now would you? Especially when the baby I am expecting is such a special one."

Lily found this an odd thing to say and couldn't resist a slight retaliation. "I'm sure all pregnant ladies feel that their baby is special."

This caused the raven headed lady to burst into howls of eerie laughter. "You have no idea do you?"

"Look can I please just go to the toilet?"

"Who are you anyway?"

"I'm Lily, Cezar's girlfriend."

The woman laughed again. "Girlfriend. Impossible. Don't be so ridiculous. He would never fall for a simple lower-class citizen like you."

"I don't know why you are being so rude to me. Do you fancy Cezar or something? Perhaps it would be more appropriate if I should ask who you are?"

"My name is Audrey, and I don't fancy Cezar. I'm in love with him."

Just then Andrei appeared from behind Lily.

"Come along Audrey, you and Cezar haven't been lovers for many years. Allow our guest to pass and go to the toilet."

"Wait," said Lily. "You and Cezar were lovers. If you are no longer lovers then why are you in this house? And more importantly whose baby are you carrying?"

"Well I suppose you could say that Cezar is responsible for impregnating Audrey," said Andrei churlishly, Lily sensing he was no longer the ally she had initially believed him to be. Both Andrei and Audrey burst into fits of laughter at Andrei's words.

"I tell you what I'm leaving; I don't want to spend another moment in this house. I don't know what sort of weird set up you have got here but I don't want to experience it any longer."

Andrei just smirked as Lily made her way to the front door, still feeling woozy from the effects of the wine she felt it unwise to drive but felt she presently had little option.

When she opened the front door she realised why Andrei had allowed her to leave with such ease, for there barking ferociously were the two Rottweiler dogs from earlier clearly waiting to tear her apart if she were to set a single footstep outside of the house.

As Lily retreated backwards into the house, not daring to take her eyes off the two hounds of hell she felt two sharp prangs enter her neck.

Once Lily was paralysed with fear Andrei paused momentarily to advise her not to fight against his vampire mission, and as his teeth sank back into her again she could feel her blood draining from her neck. Then curiously an eventual pleasant feeling of exquisite ecstasy came over Lily as her world fell into darkness.

Chapter 50

New Year's Eve, Knox residence, Toppmost Avenue

"Thanks for throwing the party Johnny; I wasn't sure what to do tonight. It's always a nightmare trying to get home from pubs and clubs at this time of year with the ritual fights in the street for taxis."

"You are most welcome Jody, I'm glad you can make it. Besides Sheena and I thought it would be a good idea to host a party in light of celebrating Callum's return to us. I think it's important he knows how much he means to us, especially as he has now discovered that he has an adopted little brother that he never knew about."

What Johnny had failed to tell Jody and the others was that his adopted son was also most likely to be a vampire and was currently missing. He had managed to convince them that Radu was still in hospital and had miraculously managed to keep Radu's disappearance out of the media, informing *concerned* journalists and the hospital staff that Radu was recovering in his own bed at home with the help of a private medical team and thanked them for respecting the family's privacy.

Johnny and Sheena had taken the agonising decision not to involve the police in Radu's disappearance in light of their son being a vampire and possibly putting him in more danger and controversy than was necessary. Instead Johnny had hired a discreet private detective, choosing not to inform him of the vampire connection, which may actually account for his lack of being able to locate Radu so far.

Incredibly the Knox family were now faced with the irony that now Callum was home again with them their newest son was once again missing without a trace. They had thought about not having the party tonight but Sheena had stated to Johnny how important it was to maintain normality, plus she was beginning to show a sense of detachment from her adopted son now she fully believed the little boy was actually a vampire and was therefore at risk of putting her family in danger. Saffron was still being protected from the truth.

"Does Callum talk much about his time in Romania?" enquired Jody.

"Not a great deal. Luckily he doesn't seem too mixed up by it all, but you know these things can dwell in the subconscious mind for years and then horribly manifest into some sort of chaotic release one day. He reckons the old guy Bogdan and the rest of the gypsy community really looked after him though. I'm just pissed off that they never had the decency to try and track down his rightful family."

"It's a different mind-set altogether Johnny, I'm sure they done what they thought was right, although I totally understand your feelings. Well I'm sure of one thing mate; next year can't be any weirder than this year has been."

"Tell me about it. First of all our manager disappears without a trace after the team gets relegated and starts off piss poorly in the Championship, then a mysterious new messiah and his side-kicks arrive out of nowhere and their influence results in an unbelievable turn of fortune for us where we soon shoot to the top of the league, winning every game by a cricket score. Then putting football aside for a second we discover that vampires really do exist and the mysterious messiah and his side-kicks that have brought such good fortune actually turn out to be vampires themselves. Then without any prior intention I adopt a little Romanian orphan boy soon to be followed by the glorious reuniting with my long lost son whom many had presumed dead, and just to enhance the 'vampires really do exist' theory I find out that in his missing years he has been groomed to operate as a vampire slayer! I tell you what Jody, if we were stood here last New Year's Eve trading New Year predictions and we had ever come up with any of that lot we would have concluded that we had hit the beer in far too much abundance."

"Yeah, it's a bit unbelievable really isn't it? Not even stuff that films are made of."

"Its fucking surreal Jody, that's what it is my friend."

"And where is Saffron? She's not the type to miss out on a party."

"Oh, don't worry Jody. She's partying alright. She's persuaded me and Sheena to let her go up to Birmingham city centre to do a bit of celebrating. We've categorically told her we want her back here to see the New Year in with us and her brother though. She's 16 going on 25 that one. She'll be the death of me."

"Oh, we all hit the rebel teenage years Johnny. She may be a bit wild but she's a good kid really."

"Yeah I guess so, mind you after what Gene and Callum have exposed her to the last few nights I'm not surprised that she wants to get out for a bit. It can't be much fun having your bedroom stink of garlic."

"What?"

"Yeah, because Botezatu had been sniffing around her at Giuseppe's reception Gene and Callum thought we should play safe and protect her at night by encircling her bed with cloves of garlic."

"So have you told Saffron about the vampires?"

"No, we've managed to keep it from her for now. Callum convinced her that in Romania the gypsies would put garlic around their bed to fill the air with special gases that purify your skin. What she doesn't know is that we have also placed a crucifix under her mattress."

"Well better safe than sorry I suppose Johnny. These are certainly crazy times though my friend. Anyway, talking of Gene here he is."

The little bespectacled figure of Gene Macgoree approached Johnny and Callum with an air of excitement that looked like he was fit to burst.

"Hi boys, it all fits. I've made some enquiries and I've managed to piece together my existing knowledge of vampire history with what I've unearthed over the past few days. Where are the rest of the boys?"

"They are in the conservatory?"

"Are they with the women and are any of the Fosturnea lot here?"

"The boys are on their own watching some football mishaps DVD that Vinnie had for Christmas. The women didn't fancy watching that, I can't think why? And I didn't invite any fucking vampires."

"Okay perfect, let's go into the conservatory and I'll update you all. At last I can reveal why Cezar Prodanescu has come to Kingsbarr United."

Chapter 51

"Hello boys are you sitting comfortably its time for a history lesson."

"Fuck me Gene, I was about to watch Rossi miss an open goal on the DVD. He's the only representative from Kingsbarr United."

"Fuck you Bradshaw, when did you last score a goal."

"Not my job mate. I'm there to terrorise the opponents."

"And you succeed only because of your ugly face."

Johnny hit the remote to kill the plasma screen of his TV amidst the laughter that had been generated by Giuseppe's remark regarding Vinnie.

"Listen up guys, Gene has some new information on the Fosturnea freaks."

"I'm all ears, *Dumbo, flying fucking elephant.*"

"Thanks Vinnie. If I can have your entire attention please Gentlemen. I have some very interesting and enlightening news. Callum, you may want to help me out every now and then if you see fit. I know you have your own particular knowledge regarding the Fosturnea School of Football Excellence."

Callum simply nodded.

"Okay, I'll begin. Now some of the information I tell you may seem pretty mind blowing but please keep your mind open. After all you are now all too sadly aware that vampires really do exist so please believe what I am about to tell you. Now for starters does anyone recognise the man in this photograph?"

Gene held up an old black and white photo that had been blown up to A4 size exploiting the modern technology that was available today that wouldn't have been around when the photograph was originally taken. It was a picture of a footballer taken from a very different era.

"I don't recognise the kit, it has no crest?" offered Gerry Spalding. "I know it's a black and white photo but a badge usually depicts the club."

"This photo was taken in 1947, the year that Steaua Bucharest was founded. They didn't have a crest until 1948 and that was to be an image of a star when it did arrive."

"They still have a star now, but it's on a background of red and blue stripes. It's a bit more like a coat of arms these days."

"That is correct Johnny."

"Fucking hell, I know who the player is. Look at the eyes boys. It's Cezar Prodanescu. But he doesn't look much younger than he is today; he just had a dodgier haircut back then."

"Who are you to criticize dodgy haircuts 80's perm boy?"

Everyone laughed at Jody's expense.

"Go and fuck yourself Vinnie."

Gene continued with his enlightening revelations too engrossed in his quest to acknowledge the banter around him. "Remember that Cezar is a master vampire Jody, and master vampires age very slowly. Cezar is already a few hundred years old at the time this photo was taken."

"Fuck me. Things get crazier by the second these days. So Cezar was a footballer, was he any good?"

"Well he was a midfielder like you Johnny. Very much like you actually, a ball winner with a great engine who could get from box to box in an instant and chip in with plenty of goals. What you need to remember about Cezar's time of football is that there were no night games, so unlike Andrei, Ringa, Paildo, Popovic and any other vampire footballers in our camp he never had the luxury of enhancing his game when darkness fell. He was a naturally excellent footballer, strong and quick but not given the opportunity to utilise his skills beneath the floodlights. Interestingly after three years of playing for Steaua Bucharest he decided to disappear from the game altogether, until now it seems becoming involved with Kingsbarr United. It was rumoured that he was unhappy with the Romanian Army's involvement with Steaua Bucharest; he could see no reason for the worlds of football and military to fuse together so he disappeared without a trace. Or rather Cezar Stancu did."

"He used a different name?" asked Charlie Cheng.

"That's right; this is why today's press have been unable to trace Cezar's background. A master vampire needs to protect the knowledge of his immortality and his slow ageing process. The press would have been startled to see Cezar in his present form today looking pretty much like he did in 1947!"

"Is Cezar Prodanescu his real name?"

"Yes it is Johnny, as I'm sure Callum can also confirm. I did wonder about this myself. Why hasn't Cezar used a false name again now he is so firmly in the limelight? I believe that Cezar is undertaking such a mission that he feels that he doesn't need to concern himself with concealing his own identity. Not that I expect him to shout 'I'm a vampire' from the rooftops of course, but you see in his eyes he is soon to bring to Earth someone far more superior than himself or any other vampire that has ever lived for that matter. I believe that Cezar has in his mind a master plan, which if it were to materialise would result in the human race becoming a minority to address the current imbalance of vampires in this world."

"How will he do that?" enquired Matt Floyd who had always been included in the social functions of Kingsbarr United since his ill-fated move from Marseille.

"Well we know that Professor Cezar Prodanescu is a professor in football, and lets be honest, what he has achieved at Kingsbarr United along with his playing credentials that were once recognised at Steaua Bucharest, few could argue against his expertise in the sport. So we must assume that his credentials in his other field of work are equally as impressive.

Cezar is also a professor in the field of chemistry and genetics. Which quickly translated makes him an expert in DNA. Now do any of you remember Dolly the sheep?"

"Yeah, that's the sheep that was cloned from another sheep."

"That is correct Johnny. By using a sheep's DNA scientists were able to create an exact replica and Dolly indeed became that exact replica of the original sheep right down to the last fluffy piece of wool of her cute woolly fleece."

"So what do you think Cezar's got planned with the miracles of DNA then, Gene? enquired Johnny.

"Well it all seems to fall into place now. I asked myself why Professor Cezar Prodanescu would choose a North Birmingham football club in England as his quest to return to football from out of the wilderness. He obviously has a love of football but why not join an established Premiership club, typically one based in London? And the answer is Sutton Park."

"Sutton Park? Our training ground is there but primarily it's just a park for kids to play in and for people to walk their dogs?"

"That's right Charlie, but believe me Sutton Park holds the key to this whole mystery. I knew that there had to be a reason for Cezar and his Fosturnea camp to come to the Midlands and this morning I was able to confirm my theory. I decided to take a stroll around Sutton Park, not far from the training ground as it happens and I could see that a mound of earth had been disturbed recently, quite unremarkable to the average mind ignorant to vampirism, but to me I knew that it must be the disturbed grave of Adrien Connor."

"Who the fuck is Adrien Connor?" asked Vinnie on behalf of everyone.

"The first ever vampire.

Now just as Christians have the Holy Bible, the Muslims the Koran and so-forth, vampires and other evil creatures, Devil worshippers and the like have their own book of faith to follow namely the *Live Tome*. The name of the book was purposely chosen as *Live* is simply *Evil* spelt backwards and *Tome* meaning a written work also had the attractive quality of being similar to the word *tomb*. Now amongst the vampire slaying network, as Callum I'm sure can validate, there has always been a rumour of a lost gospel from *Live Tome* penned by Adrien's son Bourne who actually fled to Romania, Cezar's homeland, from Sutton Coldfield would you believe. This lost gospel is thought to identify Adrien Connor's resting place after he was killed by the villagers of Sutton Coldfield. Initially it seemed logic to me that the evil Connor's resting place may have been somewhere around Cannock Chase as Fosturnea has set up its home there, but Sutton Park makes so much more sense now. I believe that the lost gospel of *Live Tome* must be in Cezar's possession. That is why he knew he had to come to Sutton Park to find the body of Adrien Connor, the first ever vampire. I believe that as with Dolly the Sheep, Cezar hopes to find enough DNA from Adrien Connor in order to clone the first vampire to allow him to walk this Earth once more. As I said if his credentials at football management mirror his credentials as a geneticist, I'm sure that you will agree this quest is well within Cezar's capabilities."

At this point none of the boys were able to speak as they attempted to digest this amazing information that they were hearing. Gene continued.

"Now gentleman take yourself back to the fifteen hundreds, can any of you tell me what dominated these decades?"

"King Henry VIII and his Reformation I guess."

"Yes Giuseppe, I expect your knowledge of Catholicism armed you with the answer, but nevertheless shame on you Englishmen in this room that an Italian gentleman was able to answer a question relating to your own national history before you could."

"Just get on with it Mr. Fucking History Teacher. *Corduroy jacket, leather fucking elbow patches, flask of tea that's really fucking whisky.*"

"Sorry Vincent, now King Henry VIII had actually given the town of Sutton Coldfield its royal status, you may have heard of it referred to as Royal Sutton Coldfield before now. Henry actually liked to roam the land now known these days as Sutton Park and he used it to hunt deer and other animals, something that annoyed the local villagers who had seen the once prosperous town fall into new depths of poverty caused largely by the effect of the War of the Roses, so when big fat Henry came to the park literally throwing his weight around and stealing *their* food they were understandably aggrieved. Furthermore many locals were of the Catholic faith and were unhappy at the destruction of the monasteries and slaying of Catholic priests at the orders of Henry. Many even became disillusioned with the whole concept of religion and the ridiculous conflict that it generated, so instead it made sense to them to retreat to the world of Witchcraft. And this Gentlemen is how vampires came to enter this world.

Two such local villagers were the Connors who were a particularly evil couple and would often *pray* if that's the right word to their leader, who was namely Satan of course. They were always outcasts to the rest of the population of Sutton Coldfield, people had suspected them of all sorts of atrocities but at times without evidence, and generally it seemed wise to just keep a wide berth from them, something that also suited the Connors who hated the sight of everyone around them except each other. In a similar way I suppose that Myra Hindley had been attracted to Ian Brady and vice versa, Josiah and Alison Connor had been attracted to one another by a quirk of evil fate and they plunged willingly into their world of darkness. It was they who actually wrote the *Live Tome* so that Satanists, devil worshippers, vampires and the like would have a reference to work to in the generations to come. In their mind, and I stress *their* mind, why should the ridiculous Catholics and Protestants share a *Bible* when they believed in the same god anyway and were yet at war. It all seemed so pointless to them, a war for a god that is meant to be good?

And when they would hear people refer to it as a holy war, surely war and holy were a contradiction in terms? So in light of their disillusionment at conventional religion they wrote the *Live Tome.*

And then one night roughly nine months before the 7th July 1530, a date that I will refer to in greater detail soon my friends, they conjured up the work of the devil himself. They drank blood, stripped naked and had sex chanting a spell that they had carefully orchestrated paying homage to Satan and he blessed them with a child, but not an ordinary child, he blessed the womb of Alison Connor with the foetus of a master vampire, soon to be born as Adrien Connor. This was their reward for being such loyal servants to Satan and for giving him the *Live Tome* when his enemies had had the Bible for over 1000 years.

Adrien Connor was born on the 7th July 1530, since then on the anniversary of Adrien Connor's birth Devil worshippers the world over follow the ritual as outlined in the *Live Tome*, drink blood, have sex and thus conceive and give birth to master vampires, starting dynasty after dynasty of blood-sucking parasites. Professor Cezar Prodanescu is such a master vampire who would have been created on a 7th July ritual, or maybe the only other possible date—Halloween, this being most likely the night that the evil child Adrien Connor was conceived."

"Sorry to interrupt Gene but there is a further royal connection that starts to appear in addition to King Henry VIII."

"Yes that is correct Callum, I was going to speak of this later, and perhaps you would like to explain so I can give my excitable tongue a rest."

Now all eyes in the room became fixed on the younger vampire slayer in anticipation.

"Well, as Gene has stated Adrien Connor was born on 7th July 1530 to begin the vampire race. Just over 3 years later on 7th September 1533 Henry had a daughter."

"Elizabeth I" piped in Johnny.

"Yes Dad, Elizabeth I, herself rumoured to be a vampire."

"What!"

"It makes sense I suppose", stated Jody. "After all she always has such a pale complexion in those old paintings you see of her."

"Indeed Jody and the rumour further goes that she used to ask for the blood that spilled out from all of the beheadings that she ordered. So she could drink it."

"That also makes sense as well I guess," continued Jody trying to focus on some logic.

"So young Callum, you will also know who one of the first vampire slayers was then I trust?

"Oh yes I do Gene, Mary Queen of Scots of course."

"Bloody hell no wonder Liz had her killed."

"Yes Jody and further more Elizabeth had Mary Queen of Scots imprisoned less than forty miles from here in Wingfield Manor in the county of Derbyshire. Her full imprisonment was 1568 to 1587 until the time of her execution."

"Bloody hell," said Jody again, not realising his double pun. "Tell us more guys this is fascinating stuff."

"You say that Adrien Connor was born on the 7th of July, the seventh month of the seventh month. Is there any significance in that?" enquired Charlie Cheng.

"Seven is a lucky number isn't it; I always use it in the lottery."

"And have you ever won the lottery Vinnie?"

"No Johnny I haven't"

"It's not that lucky then is it."

"It's a good point to raise Charlie. The seventh day of the seventh month is indeed significant," continued Gene Macgoree picking up the story once again. "Seven is a very spiritual number and is considered to be lucky because of its link to goodness. The Bible tells us that there are seven days of creation, there are seven gifts of the Holy Ghost, Christ spoke seven times on the cross and the Catholic Church has seven sacraments."

"There are other wonderful things connected to the number seven if you think about it. The rainbow has seven colours and there are Seven Wonders of the World. So why plan to give birth to a child who represents evil with the number seven so predominantly in the date?"

"Easy Jody, mockery."

"Mockery?"

"Yes. I told you how the Connors found it laughable that the Catholic Church were in conflict with the Protestants and how this cemented their complete disillusion with conventional religion. Well, in the Bible there are also seven virtues of course—faith, hope, charity, fortitude, justice, prudence and temperance. Now if you were putting all your faith into the Antichrist what better way than to use the number seven as a vehicle to mock this religion of Christianity, which according to the Connors, was actually not exercising any of these virtues whilst Christians were killing and being killed in the name of the church.

Now it is my guess that on the night that Adrien Connor was conceived the Connors acted out a very passionate ritual in accordance to the number seven, not only as mockery to those who worshipped the Lord, but also as a recognised more evil interpretation of the number seven."

"The seven deadly sins"

"Yes Johnny, the seven deadly sins. The Connors worshipped the Antichrist, the complete opposite to Lord Jesus Christ and the seven deadly sins are a complete opposite to the seven virtues."

"Complete opposites of course. A sign of Satanists is often an inverted cross."

"Yes, Jody. So this is why vampires are unable to look at a cross, they stand for everything evil in a complete opposite function to good. Vampires are servants of the Antichrist."

"Fuck me, its mind blowing"

"Well getting back to how the Connor's tale unfolded, as I said earlier, the villagers knew that the Connors were well weird but could never pin anything on them though it was suspected whenever a lamb went missing from the flock of sheep that scattered on the common land it was thought that the Connors were responsible for its disappearance. It was thought that they would sacrifice the lamb and drink its blood, but people didn't really want to believe it too much for obvious reasons.

But when the child was born, Adrien, things just got too weird to be ignored. By his tenth birthday the lambs were being found with puncture marks in their necks mysteriously drained of all their blood. All suspicion pointed at the Connors. Then one day, or should I say one night, Connor junior was caught in the act, not killing a lamb mind, something much sinister. Adrien Connor was discovered sinking his teeth into the neck of a young lass and a chase from an angry mob of villagers ensued. Now, Adrien Connor escapes into the nearby woods and the mob can't find him for love or money, so the villagers see that their only form of retribution is to catch the next best thing, his parents. The Connors are subsequently bound, flogged and burned at the stake right in the middle of the town's square while Catholics and Protestants unite to quote damnations at them from the Bible as the evil couple burn to death.

Adrien Connor lived in those woods right up until his fortieth birthday. Now remember he was the first vampire so true to legend he could only come out at night, something else that used to freak the local folk out."

"So how come Cezar and Botezatu can come out at daytime? The daylight doesn't seem to hurt them."

"That is a very good point Charlie. Cezar and the rest of the Fosturnea group are simply a product of evolution. We humans were once covered in hair, but as we adapted to our surroundings and wore clothes we simply shed our body hair. Another example of being able to adapt to its surroundings is that of the snow leopard. Its nasal cavity has enlarged over time in order to warm freezing cold air before it enters the lungs of the snow leopard, and its oversized paws helps it to walk on snow like some natural form of snow shoe and its small ears minimises heat loss. A master vampire has always been immortal unless it receives a stake through the heart, is set on fire, takes a silver bullet or is beheaded. The species will always age slower once it reaches adulthood this is why Cezar doesn't look hundreds of years old. However, the vampire evolved to stand sunlight, yet will naturally always be stronger in darkness."

"Like when we play night matches."

"Yes Johnny, like when Kingsbarr United play night matches."

"You said Adrien lived in the woods until his fortieth birthday. What happened then?" enquired Jody.

Gene continued "They finally caught him and killed him. The villagers killed Adrien Connor by driving a stake right through his heart, but they were so fearful of the curse of the vampire that they buried him in a secret place swearing never to tell anyone in order to protect their town. There had been a history of girls being killed in the night by Adrien Connor who would come down into the town and kill young girls by sucking their blood. Now what they didn't bank on was Bourne Connor."

"Who the fuck was Bourne Connor?" asked Vinnie in his usual eloquent style.

"Bourne Connor was Adrien's son. While he lived in the woods, taking his pickings of the humans that fell prey to him, he had actually taken captive a local girl. Everyone had assumed that she had simply fell victim to Adrien and been killed but he had actually imprisoned her and treated her as a sex slave, a simple toy to amuse himself while he hid out in the woods. He would only partly drink her blood to cruelly keep her between life and death and to never turn her into a vampire completely. She bore him a child, namely Bourne. He was 17 when he saw them capture his father and drive a stake through his heart. He watched from the bushes as they buried him in the grounds of Sutton Park. But anger got the better of him, he ran towards them demanding they leave his father rest in peace now that they had killed him and buried him, and promised that one day he would avenge his father's slaying. Realising that the vampire curse wasn't over when they had killed Adrien, the villagers quickly turned on Bourne.

Like his father before him they chased Bourne through the woods, but they stopped when they stumbled across a log cabin where they found a broken woman screaming for help begging to be let go. This was Adrien's sex slave and Bourne's mother, but more importantly she was still alive.

Soon word got around that Bourne had fled to Europe and had made his settlement in the Transylvanian region of Romania. Stories reached England about many mysterious killings in Romania and this cemented the belief that Bourne had indeed reached there. Keen to move the vampire stigma away from England and in particular away from Sutton Coldfield the propaganda began and as you will undoubtedly have heard in the legendary stories of vampires everyone usually accepts that vampirism actually began in Romania, in particular Transylvania due to the activity rumoured to occur there.

Bourne went on to write the lost gospel of *Live Tome* to document what had truly happened to his father. This lost gospel I believe is in Cezar's possession and has helped him to locate the resting place of the first ever master vampire Adrien Connor, in order to dissect his DNA and to resurrect this evil entity into our world once again.

So now you know everything boys and I think the jigsaw is now beginning to make sense."

The room fell silent as they all digested the information, some shook their heads, some simply had open jaws unable to comment sufficiently at the story they had been told.

The silence was broken by the beeps of a text message coming through.

Callum retrieved his mobile phone from his pocket and stared down at the screen as he read the message.

"It's Saffron, Dad. I think she may be in danger. She's with a fucking vampire."

Chapter 52

Hi Cal tell Mom Dad not 2 worry. Met Andrei on Broad St going on to Fosturnea. Happy New Year X

Saffron watched the cartoon image of the tiny envelope on the screen of her mobile phone disappear with the accompanying words of "message sent" to assure her that her text message was destined to reach the mobile phone of her twin brother.

Content that she could continue to party into the night with a clear conscience Saffron placed her phone back into her handbag and smiled at Andrei who was sitting next to her on the back seat of the taxi. Beside Andrei was Catarino Popovic whilst the front passenger seat was occupied by Saffron's best friend Dionne.

"This party at your place had better be worth it Andrei, it's not easy to walk away from Broad Street on New Year's Eve."

"I promise you that you will not be disappointed, Saffron. We Romanian's know how to show a girl a good time." Andrei was playing with Saffron's hair as he answered her. She didn't seem to mind.

By now the taxi had left the bright city lights of Birmingham and was travelling along the A5 towards Cannock. Originally constructed by the Roman's the A5 was characteristically a very straight road, much to the relief of Dionne who had opted to sit in the front seat as she didn't generally travel well. A journey of twists and turns could have disastrous consequences for her susceptibility to travel sickness, although at present in spite of the straight road, the varied blend of cocktails that she had indulged in courtesy of Catarino and Andrei over the past two and a half hours or so were threatening to make an appearance from the rumblings of her stomach. The result was a temporary and uncharacteristic sobriety of quietness being demonstrated by the normally bubbly Dionne. She had however managed to apologise to Catarino and promised to make it up to him in her own insatiable style once they arrived at the Fosturnea house.

The conversation had also diminished in the rear of the taxi too although for very different reasons. Andrei and Saffron, who were undoubtedly attracted to one another, had proceeded to neck passionately much to the delight of the taxi driver who would occasionally view the entertainment courtesy of his rear view mirror. The driver named Rashid was forced to halt his voyeurism however once he caught a glimpse of Catarino Popovic who gave him a single look that translated into a thousand words of evil, signalling the immediate abandonment of his joyous letching.

As Saffron kissed Andrei and allowed his wandering hands to explore her clothed buttocks and naked legs, she couldn't help but think how she would be the envy of many a young girl in England. Since his rise to stardom at Kingsbarr United, Andrei had become quite a pin up with the female population appearing in girls magazines, securing the occasional clothing contract and even promoting his own brand of aftershave. It was a development of his career that Cezar Prodanescu had not welcomed with open arms believing that it could hinder the Romanian striker's outlook on football and attitude, but in stark contrast chairman Peter Cogshaw had naturally been pleased with the extra revenue and publicity which Andrei's high profile had brought to the club.

In truth Andrei was slowly becoming a victim of his own success, losing sight of the principles in which the disciplarian Prodanescu had instilled in his prodigy, no better demonstrated perhaps by Andrei than his daring to kill Lily, the girlfriend of his master. This despicable act by Andrei signalled how in his mind that as his status in the world of football was changing then so too was his status in the rank of vampire. Cezar was still to learn of the tragedy which sadly ensured that the painful efforts he himself had undertaken to protect his precious Lily from entering the world of vampirism had now all been in vain, and worse still at the hands of the man he had treated as a son.

The action that was taking place on the rear seat of the Mercedes, accompanied by the effect that alcohol can disproportionately have on the passing of time, enabled the journey to the Fosturnea house to be a quick one as far as Saffron was concerned.

Incidentally, and somewhat miraculously, Dionne had also managed to survive the journey with her stomach contents intact.

The two girls had reached the front door of the house ahead of their two chaperones for the evening, as the footballers had asked the girls to carry on in front while they paid the taxi driver.

The walk up the long drive had at least gone some way to having a sobering effect on the two friends as the cold night air lapped at their bare legs whilst two sets of Rottweiler dogs flanked them either side of the pathway as they walked. Andrei had assured them that the dogs wouldn't attack after his initial command. This had proved to be a correct declaration by the young Romanian but had established little diminishment of terror for the girls as the dogs escorted them with attentive eyes.

The two girls daren't knock the door until Andrei and Catarino appeared and it wasn't long before they were thankfully in sight. Dionne thought she noticed Catarino wipe his mouth; quickly surmising that perhaps he had needed to throw up after the taxi journey instead of her. She thought it best not to mention it in fear of embarrassing the poor lad.

It was Andrei who enabled the foursome to enter the house courtesy of his key turning in the lock. Saffron noticed how unconventional the key was appearing roughly four inches in length and jet black in colour with a largish key head. Very different indeed to the conventional key to her home that fitted snugly in her small handbag with her mobile phone, lipstick, purse and very little else. She realised that the key head needed to be the size it was in order to fit into the large key hole of the very old door. She quickly concluded that when this old oak door was made, most likely at the same time the house was built therefore making this the original door, there would not have been any contemporary type locks around. As the door creaked open she decided not to waste her time thinking about the lock and key any further. This was New Year's Eve and she was looking forward to a continued night of partying and much frivolity.

Once the door was closed behind her what Saffron actually witnessed was complete debauchery. Whereas her own display of having a good time had been fairly respectable on the back seat of the Mercedes she was astonished to see oceans of semi-naked bodies cavorting and twisting putting on displays of sexual athletics that she had never even dreamed of at her innocent stage of life.

Even the relatively liberal Dionne was standing mouth a gape at what was on show, quickly likening the situation to that of Roman orgies that she had read about during her educational studies.

There were bodies on the stairs, across sideboards and other antique furniture, falling into doorways and basically all over the house. Hoards of candles lit the darkness casting shadows of rigorous and erotic movements. It was only occasionally that Saffron and Dionne witnessed sex taking place on a one to one basis, as groups of individuals indulged in universal acts of pleasure.

For the first time tonight Saffron grew a little concerned.

"Andrei, I hope you haven't got anything like this in mind for Dionne and me."

"Speak for yourself girlfriend," answered Dionne as she grabbed Catarino by his tie, dragged him towards her and proceeded to put her tongue into his mouth. For a moment she thought she could taste an unfamiliar metallic flavour from his saliva. It didn't detract her though as her free hand reached down to his crotch and Dionne gave it a playful squeeze.

Andrei simply smiled and then said "Don't worry Saffron; we can all go somewhere a little quieter. This house has plenty of rooms."

Thanks a lot Dionne, thought Saffron. *Thanks a fucking lot!*

Chapter 53

"Come on Johnny lets go and kill those fucking blood-sucking pricks."

"Vinnie, thanks for your support but this isn't your fight. I can't drag you boys into this."

"The fuck you can't," interjected Giuseppe Rossi. "Look we've all had our heads buried in the sand for too long, Vinnie's right. Let's go and rescue Saffron and put an end to those vampires once and for all."

Johnny looked at Gene.

"I think we have little choice Johnny. If Saffron's in danger then we must rescue her. It was inevitable that at some stage Callum and I were going to have to attack this nest. I had discussed matters with Father McGill but he had requested that we respect the Christmas period before any blood was to be shed. However, with this recent escalation of events the fact that we can attack them now when they're least expecting it, with the power of all of you behind us will give us a greater strength to succeed. I'm sure that Father McGill will understand."

"Gene is right Dad. We must rescue Saffron and it is also time for me to avenge Bogdan's death."

Johnny looked around for confirmation that everyone was in agreement. In turn each footballer nodded.

"Come on then guys lets go and sort out those vampire bastards and rescue my daughter."

"Hold on a moment Johnny, we just can't steam in there like it's the Wild West. These are vampires we are fighting; there are specific ways to defeat them."

"Gene's right Dad. Have you got any balloons that haven't been blown up yet?"

"Yes, I bought a load for the New Year thinking Radu would like them. But how will balloons help us son?"

"Stay with me, Dad. Right who isn't too pissed so that they can drive? After all we are going to have to get to Fosturnea somehow."

"We are all pretty pissed, but under the circumstances I'll take my chances and drive."

"Thanks Vinnie but I've got a better idea," said Johnny. "I invited Frankie along tonight, I always feel sorry for him that he has no family and I hate to think of him tucked up alone at home on New Year's Eve. He declined my offer saying that he has a stomach problem and is currently taking anti-biotics. We can give him a call and he can pick us up in the team coach."

"Okay brilliant Dad, and if he is taking anti-biotics the chances are he hasn't had a drink. Now phone Father McGill to tell him Frankie the team coach driver will pick him up en-route. Right, has Radu got any water pistols around the house?"

"Callum, where are you going with this son?" asked Johnny looking slightly bemused.

"I know exactly what you are thinking Callum."

"Of course you do Gene; you are also a vampire slayer after all."

"So enlighten the rest of us *you four eyed little twerp*, sorry."

"It's simple Vinnie. What do priests do to water?"

"Turn it into holy water."

"That's right Jody. If we fill the water pistols and balloons with water. We can ask Father McGill to bless the water then we have revolvers and bombs specifically designed to harm a nest of vampires."

"Fucking hell that's brilliant."

"Glad you approve Vinnie, now I want you all to get out into the garden. I want you all to start finding branches, timber or whatever is useful around the place so that we can make crucifixes and wooden stakes. We are not going to wish those vampires a Happy New Year!"

Chapter 54

As the team coach headed through the country lanes of Staffordshire towards the Fosturnea house, the footballers turned vampire hunters discussed their strategy of how to attack the dwelling of the Prodanescu vampire nest and compared their weapons of choice.

Father McGill had indeed blessed the water inside the water pistols and balloons, which now served as bombs fuelled with holy water, and Johnny had been able to locate a collection of Saffron's silver jewellery, (Sheena only ever wore gold), which his daughter had luckily chosen not to wear this evening, and had managed to melt the precious metal down and reshape it into a collection of silver bullets. Fortunately Johnny's grandfather had been a gun maker in the Second World War and his bullet mould and gun had been stored for sentimental value in Johnny's loft. Little did he know that one day he would be using his old grandad's memorabilia to hunt down vampires!

Gene and Callum of course already possessed a capable array of artillery from deadly crossbows to wooden stakes, and their weaponry had been considerably augmented by the inclusion of an ad-hoc collection of wooden stakes and homemade crucifixes crafted in record-quick time courtesy of the natural elements of the Knox family garden.

Charlie Cheng, a Kung-Fu expert as well as being a quality footballer, had brought along his nunchacku. Not exactly a traditional means of combating the threats of a vampire but in the slick hands of Charlie the nunchaku was definitely a savage and effective weapon.

The boys were indeed well prepared to face their enemy.

As prepared as they could be anyhow.

Jody Roper had brought Frankie up to date en-route to the Fosturnea house as to why his services were so unusually and drastically required on New Year's Eve, and it had crossed the stunned driver's mind to turn the coach around and find his way to the nearest police station to turn this bunch of lunatics in!

But as he began to digest the incredible information that Jody was feeding him and no matter how unbelievable it seemed, Frankie had known most of these boys for a number of years now and he had never had any cause to question their judgement or behaviour before. Frankie realised that it is of course possible for one person to turn mad, but he had more than half the team sitting here on his bus plus the local priest, so he concluded that the probabilities of them all turning mad collectively at the same time were pretty slim, and no matter how unbelievable he found the facts to be they must indeed nevertheless be the facts.

They were heading towards a vampire nest in order to slay a colony of vampires!

It was as simple as that!

This is why he never hesitated to carry out Johnny's instruction once they arrived at the gates of the Fosturnea School of Football Excellence to drive full throttle at them and rip them from their hinges.

As the coach crashed through the gates patterns of sparks danced in the darkness as the electrics that were used to remotely open them short circuited and blew all of their associated fuses.

Fortunately the electrical system for the gates was on a separate circuit to any of the other electrical requirements of the house, so the failing of the gate's electrics had no impact on any of the appliances being used and so didn't alert the occupants to the team's unexpected arrival. Fortunately the party was in such full swing coupled with the noise being generated from talking; music and general humping it also prevented the activity at the foot of the driveway from being noticed.

The left-sided gate took the most impact and it hooked on to the front of the coach in a tangled and mangled mass of metal and was carried forthwith as the coach made its ascent towards the property.

Not long after striking the gate Frankie felt the coach come into contact with something else on a far lesser scale.

"I think I've just ran something over, possibly deer they are quite common around these parts, they've probably wandered in to the grounds from Cannock Chase. Bloody shame I love deer, they are such a magnificent creature."

"Don't worry Frank your conscience is clear," said Gene Macgoree. "It wasn't deer it was dogs."

"Dogs, that's even worse. I love dogs even more."

"Not these dogs you wouldn't. They are known as the 'Hounds of Hell'. They protect the nest of the master vampire so if you have killed them believe me my friend you have done us all a big favour."

"Okay Frankie this is far enough, park the coach here but then turn it around and wait for us to come back after we have finished our mission."

"Okay Johnny, good luck."

"We may need it my friend."

Catarino Popovic was about to sink his teeth into the unsuspecting neck of Dionne Coleman when he heard a thunderous bang on the door. As he and Dionne were the nearest *couple* to the door following her insistence to fool around as soon as they had entered the establishment, the Romanian footballer reluctantly pulled away from his companion and headed to let what he thought to be the latest batch of party goers into the house. Furthermore he suspected that Professor Cezar Prodanescu was not at home tonight and if it was he at the door he wouldn't take too kindly to being left waiting in the cold while his prodigies indulged in acts of debauchery at his expense.

When he opened the door he was greeted by a silver bullet burrowed into his forehead killing him instantly.

The room fell silent, all except that was for the manic screams that were coming from Dionne Coleman as she failed to comprehend why her best friend's father had just shot her new found boyfriend in the head at point blank range.

All eyes fell on Johnny Knox as he stood there with his smoking gun. There was no immediate advance towards him as it was obvious that by the instant demise of Catarino Popovic the gun harboured silver bullets. Furthermore Johnny was accompanied either side by two strikingly different images in the shape of Callum Knox and Gene Macgoree, but who both seemed to be armed with identical lethal pieces of kit which they realised must be tailored specifically to hurt the vampire race. The crossbows were pointing straight ahead and the glistening from the arrows suggested that these too were most likely to be made from silver.

The male vampires began to withdraw their penises from their women and both genders began to get dressed and group together and move slowly in a pack, hissing and showing their teeth like a pack of wild animals who stalked their prey not quite showing when the exact moment for attack would be.

Johnny, Callum and Gene also moved forward slowly, and the vampires could now see that more enemies were within the house. Jody Roper and Vincent Bradshaw were standing behind Callum and Gene respectively, so the advancement took the shape of a pyramid with Johnny leading at the front, his gun with five remaining silver bullets pointing straight ahead. Fortunately the light was so dim the vampires couldn't notice the sweat racing down his forehead.

The pyramid was also harbouring another figure, and the creatures turned away as they saw it was a priest, the epitome of all enemies and he was holding aloft a crucifix which hurt their eyes.

All the while Dionne was standing in her bra and knickers screaming hysterically and Callum felt there was only one thing to do. He promptly freed a hand from the grasp of the crossbow and struck his sister's best friend on the chin causing her to fall unconscious and silence her with immediate effect.

"What did you do that for Callum; I wanted to find out where Saffron is?"

"You could hear her Dad, she was hysterical. She'll be okay but she was just too much of a distraction."

But ironically Callum's actions and the subsequent exchange of words with his father allowed enough time for the vampires to begin an attempt at avenging the slaying of Catarino Popovic.

Chapter 55

Frankie had managed to turn the coach around and was waiting anxiously for the others to return. He hoped that it would be sooner rather than later and he was worried about what casualties the people he considered to be friends would encounter. If that house really was full of vampires then how were the footballers of Kingsbarr United, mere mortal humans, going to compete? This wasn't a cup tie or a league match they were involved in, it was a war against the living dead! He shuddered as his mind raced.

Just then he remembered that just before he crashed through the gates of the house he had had to manoeuvre past a parked car, which he thought looked like a Mercedes. He hadn't given it much thought in the heat of the moment, but he now began to wonder why the car had been parked there at all. If it was a car that belonged to one of the vampires, then surely they would have come through the gates, up the drive and parked somewhere in the grounds of the Fosturnea School of Football Excellence.

His curiosity was soon to be answered in the most graphic of ways.

From nowhere his window got punched in and in a flash he was dragged from his cabin with the strength of someone he couldn't compete with. As he lay cowering on the ground he saw the figure of what appeared to be an Asian man looking down at him.

"Hello, my name is Rashid. I drive a cab and you drive a bus. How amusing. Hold on a second, let me re-phrase that. I drive a cab and you *no longer* drive a bus." And with a look of insanity in the taxi driver's eyes the newly recruited vampire began to savage Frankie's neck with an almighty amount of venom and ferocity.

It was not long before Frankie's world fell into darkness.

Johnny had managed to shoot dead another two vampires with the power of his silver bullets as they moved towards him, but he was well aware that he now only had three bullets left in his revolver and finding time to re-load did not appear to be on the cards in the foreseeable future.

Callum and Gene were slaying the vampires with their cross-bows as competently as expected considering their line of business, and Jody Roper had thrown aloft a couple of water bombs that splattered over a number of vampires, though the impact of splashes in the main would disfigure or maim a vampire at best rather than destroy them completely.

Vincent "Bruiser" Bradshaw had typically chosen to stand and trade punches with a couple of vampires, who had proved to be his most challenging opponents to date, but he was keeping them at bay and he and the others had been briefed by Gene that as long as they could avoid being bitten the team always had a fighting chance of survival.

Vincent was able to pleasingly discover that a head butt still had the desired effect of spreading a nose across a vampire's face as much as it did a human's. But he also discovered that their strength was generally superior to that of a human, and he was after all only human, so he realised that there was an almighty battle ahead for him and the others tonight. The strength of his opponents helped him realise why his vampire team-mates were so effective when the sun began to go down in the football matches that they played.

At the risk of Johnny, Vincent, Gene, Callum, Jody and Father McGill being outnumbered the odds evened up when the rest of the guys began to ambush the vampires from the rear. They had strategically broken down the back door in order to surprise the creatures and an almighty battle commenced between the footballers and the vampires.

Gerry Spalding and Matt Floyd took a similar approach to Vincent Bradshaw and waded in like a couple of heavy weight boxers, but they also soon sensed the strength and resilience of the vampires.

It was not long before they were dipping into their supply of wooden stakes from their converted boot bags that straddled their backs and forcing them into the chests of the vampires killing them instantly.

Charlie Cheng was fighting the vampires off with his lightning fists and feet, his small frame and demeanour ensuring an uncanny resemblance to Bruce Lee or Jackie Chan. When the mood took him he cracked their skulls with his nunchaku.

Stakes were being driven into the hearts of the vampires at a furious rate. The footballers improvised their weaponry using anything at hand and when tables and chairs were smashed across the backs and heads of the vampires the dismantled table legs and chair legs also became useful stakes to drive through the evil hearts of their opponents.

Giuseppe Rossi had been using Radu's water pistol armed with holy water to good effect but augmented his armoury by improvising the use of a broken snooker cue as a lethal weapon to drive through the hearts of the vampires.

At one poignant moment of the battle Jody Roper had experienced mixed feelings as he drove a chair leg through the heart of his defensive colleague Tracaldo. Jody reflected on the amount of times they had stood side by side in the defensive line together and how he had marvelled at the young Brazilian's ability. Now the Brazilian vampire's eyes looked into Jody's shifting from a source of evil to one of desperation, as they become entwined together for what seemed an eternity but what could only have been seconds. Eventually with a heavy heart Jody allowed his former team-mate to fall to the floor for the left-back to finally meet his death, but it had been a clear case of self-defence. Tracaldo had approached Jody with the intent of doing the 80's loving defender some real harm, so Jody had had no choice but to drive that piece of wood straight through his former team-mate's heart as he pictured the slogan from one of his favourite T-shirts—"CHOOSE LIFE" and that is precisely what Jody did.

Charlie, still striking down vampires with his martial arts skills was then able to spot a useful piece of decor on the oak-panelled wall that he could use to his advantage.

A Samurai sword.

He could not have been more fortunate.

He fought his way through the bodies and pulled the sword from the wall. As Charlie held the black handle of the Sword the blade glistened sending a signal of approval as if it was Charlie's destiny to hold the sword in the same way King Arthur was meant to have had Excalibur.

As he marvelled at the impressive piece of armoury an ugly looking vampire moved towards him. Without hesitation Charlie pushed the sword into the vampire's chest and withdrew it again with the greatest of ease. It was like putting a knife through butter the blade was so slick.

Another vampire foolishly attempted the same quest to attack Charlie and this time after driving the blade into the vampire's heart Charlie left him for a few seconds impaled on the blade and supported only by Charlie's will to hold the blade aloft. Terror filled the eyes of the vampire and blood began to curdle from his mouth. Charlie sniggered as he enjoyed teasing the evil being before finally withdrawing the blade and relieving the vampire from his suffering as he collapsed on the floor as dead as a dodo.

Charlie began to get lost in a little world of his own performing swipes in the air with the sword like someone from an Indiana Jones movie and began posing as he practised mock swipes and stabbings.

But then Charlie spotted Alvin Braxton, the team goalkeeper in a spot of difficulty from the corner of his eye.

Alvin was using all his strength to try and keep a vampire from biting his neck and Charlie called out to him.

Alvin spotted the sword and understood what Charlie had in mind. Taking a leaf out of Vincent's book Alvin dropped the nut as hard as he could on the vampire's nose, followed up by a swift knee to the balls. Alvin was pleased to see that this had the same effect on a vampire as it did on the next man! Alvin earned himself enough time to end the wrestling match and free his hands.

Charlie tossed the sword through the air and with all the goalkeeping skills he could muster Alvin made the greatest catch of his life as he wrapped his fingers around the black handle. If he had caught the sword at the blade he would have surely sliced his hand in two!

Alvin took a swiping action with his sword ironically aiming at the neck of the vampire and again the effectiveness of the blade was evident as it slickly sliced through the flesh and spinal cord and sent the vampire's head spinning through the air.

The head was spinning its way towards Charlie and with the instinct and great skill of a footballer of his calibre Charlie rose in the air to meet the head as if it was a football and volleyed it across the room.

It was a great display of footballing technique and a great shot too! The head cannoned off another vampire and the power in the volley made him stagger allowing Johnny Knox enough time to drive a splintered chair leg through the heart of the stunned beast.

Charlie realised that he had momentarily at least lost the sword to Alvin Braxton who was slaying vampires left, right and centre with a broad smile on his face amidst zealous cries of a Jamaican accent saying things like "yeah man", "yahoo" and "take that you blood-sucking scum". Charlie had to consider his next means of attack.

When Johnny spotted Charlie momentarily free of slaying duty his quick mind, usually reserved for magical decisions on the football field, had to think in double-quick time to assess the situation. He realised that amongst all of these warring bodies two prominent figures were blatantly missing—Andrei Botezatu and his daughter Saffron. He forced himself to quickly blot out the fear that suddenly rushed through him regarding his daughter and what could have happened to her at the hands of the evil striker.

Johnny realised that Charlie was the best fighter amongst them with his Kung Fu expertise and realised he was currently best positioned on the edge of the battle to enter further into the house to explore its rooms. Just as he would on the football field Johnny called out instructions to his Chinese team-mate.

"GO AND FIND SAFFRON."

Charlie saluted his skipper and ran down the hallway blinding a vampire on his way by poking his fingers into his eyes. Alvin put that particular staggering vampire out of his misery by promptly decapitating him.

Up to now the valiant footballers had impressively not suffered any casualties but as Vincent "Bruiser" Bradshaw was punching hell out of the face of a vampire he had already slayed, one of the females jumped onto his back and sank her teeth into the midfielder.

Vincent screamed with pain and hurled abuse at the female vampire such as "get off me you fucking bitch!" but she held onto Vincent's huge frame wrapping her arms around his neck.

Vincent spun around giving the vampire an unexpected piggy back as she screamed like a banshee and he finally managed to pull her off and slam her body on the floor. He followed this up by promptly driving a stake through her heart.

Vincent felt his neck and felt the warm trickle of blood on his hand. He realised that the bitch had succeeded in biting him which meant one thing for sure. At some point he was to become a vampire himself.

This predicament that Vincent found himself in was an indication of how difficult this battle was proving to be. The footballers seemed hopelessly outnumbered despite all of their slayings and Johnny ordered his team to make a retreat down the hallway.

His team-mates obeyed his instructions just as they would on the football pitch and they managed to group together and retreat forming an effective impregnable shape. A stand-off ensued as the Kingsbarr footballers walked steadily backwards with Johnny at the fore pointing his gun, still holding three silver bullets and Callum and Gene pointing their crossbows at the cautious vampires.

Father McGill, shaken at the volume of violence that he had been forced to witness, opened the first door that he could find and the room happened to be the kitchen. Father McGill found some comfort that God must have guided him to this room as he realised that once the Kingsbarr team had barricaded the door, saucepans of water could be filled and he would be able to bless them to transform them into vessels of holy water. There would also be knives and the like to enhance the footballer's weaponry.

As the footballers retreated into the kitchen a vampire broke loose from the crowd. Johnny was about to pull the trigger to release one of his remaining silver bullets when he realised that the manic face grinning at him was Leon Davis.

Johnny couldn't bring himself to shoot the youngster.

Callum instead warned Leon to back off and made it clear in no uncertain terms that he would be wearing an arrow if he didn't.

With a hiss and a display of his fangs Leon heeded the warning.

Then Johnny began to notice other familiar faces in the crowd.

There was Afina, Leon's girlfriend, the girl who he had seen on the beach all those months ago in Romania.

Then he couldn't believe his eyes as he got an even bigger surprise. He saw a face that he recognised only too well.

It was Daryl Weir!

Leon, Afina and now Daryl. They were all vampires.

Johnny felt an air of sadness in his belly as he thought about the three familiar vampires.

By now he was the last person to enter the kitchen. Before he could get in and lock the door he was forced to fire a bullet into the skull of an unknown vampire who had broke from the crowd wanting to be a vampire hero. This managed to silence the vampires for a second long enough for Johnny to enter the kitchen and lock the door.

But now of course he only had two bullets remaining.

Charlie Cheng had estimated that the most likely place that Andrei could have taken Saffron was to one of the bedrooms of the old mansion. Fortunately he had made his way up the old oak stairs unchallenged as the remainder of the vampires had chosen to pursue the Kingsbarr footballers into the kitchen. When Charlie reached the dark landing, lighted only by candles along the wooden panelled walls he was met with the daunting task of what seemed like scores of closed doors. He knew that Saffron and Andrei were behind one of them but which one was anybody's guess. He just hoped he wasn't too late for Saffron's sake.

"Can we go back downstairs now please Andrei? I want to see how Dionne is?" asked a nervous Saffron Knox not really understanding how she had managed to get herself to be in this vulnerable position in what was obviously Andrei Botezatu's bedroom. She couldn't deny that she found Andrei mysteriously attractive, he possessed a certain magnetism that was difficult to resist, but unlike Dionne she realised the seriousness of being alone with a slightly older man in a strange environment. She knew that her dad wouldn't be too pleased if he knew where she was that's for sure. The bottom line was she had drank a little too much with it being New Year's Eve and had allowed herself to end up in this vulnerable position that she currently found herself to be in.

"Relax baby. Dionne is busy enjoying herself with Catarino, I suggest that you and I follow suit." There seemed a little impatience in Andrei's voice; Saffron sensed that he had very definite plans for how exactly they should celebrate the New Year.

She allowed him to kiss her. She had wanted to kiss him all night but did this man understand that she wanted to take things slow? She wasn't the sort of girl who automatically made herself wholly available on the first night. In spite of her enjoyment at kissing Andrei she momentarily broke away from him.

"What's the matter Saffron, you are one crazy bitch do you know that? What is with this blowing hot and cold bollocks?"

"Andrei don't speak to me like that please. I like you but I'm not like Dionne, I don't want to go much further than a nice kiss, don't you respect that?"

"You've been giving me signs all night like you wanted a good seeing to, acting like you are a real woman but you're just a fucking kid aren't you?" Andrei was becoming increasingly more threatening.

"Actually Andrei I would say that my feelings to not go any further with you are a sign of maturity. Perhaps you should try it some time, now I would like to go downstairs. Come on don't spoil what has been a lovely evening."

"You are going nowhere until I say so little girl. And it will not be a lovely evening until I'm inside your knickers."

Saffron couldn't believe what she did next. The lack of respect that Andrei was showing her was just too unjust and she slapped him as hard as she could across his face. She put her hand to her mouth, surprised at her own actions and instantly in fear for her safety.

Andrei just smiled as his head was still turned away from the power of Saffron's smack, his cheek increasingly reddening. But when he faced her once more she saw that his face had slightly changed. He hissed like a wild animal and his eyes seemed to take on a demonic force that she had never seen in her entire life. He also showed her his teeth and they seemed sharper than before and she was convinced that she actually saw a set of fangs in the mouth that she had not long been kissing.

Andrei threw her on the bed and she was surprised at his strength. He then grabbed her around the throat and with his free hand he reached up her skirt and tore off her knickers.

Oh God she thought. *He is going to rape me.*

Andrei stepped back then crudely sniffed the knickers, tossed them aside and began to undo his belt. All the time he had the same sharp toothy grin on his face and the demonic look in his eyes that was scaring Saffron rigid.

Suddenly Andrei was stopped in his tracks as he felt something strike him hard on the head almost making him lose consciousness.

He turned around as the blow had come from behind him; it had not come from Saffron in a bid to defend herself. She instead had simply closed her eyes literally scared stiff of the encounter she was about to suffer at the hands of what she finally realised was a vampire!

To Andrei's surprise he was faced with his Chinese team-mate Charlie Cheng who was displaying a remarkable display of martial arts trickery with his wooden devices married by a small chain. It was then that Andrei realised that Charlie had struck him with a nunchaku.

In spite of his dazed state the anger in Andrei enabled him to run full pelt at Charlie and he wrestled him to the ground with some ease. He began to move his mouth towards Charlie's neck as he lay on top of him with his full weight and Charlie knew that his intention was to tear a chunk out of his throat.

Fortunately Charlie's legs were free and he was able to drive his knee into Andrei's groin with such force the Romanian fell to the side writhing in agony. Charlie sprang up with an athletic back flip and whilst he was now on his feet and Andrei was lying crumpled on the floor he kicked Andrei as hard as he could in the vampire's ribcage. Saffron winced as she heard her potential rapist's bones crack.

Charlie then jumped up in the air so that his foot would come down with as much force as he could muster on the head wound that he had already inflicted on Andrei from his nunchaku. Charlie knew that in combat if the same injury was attacked over and over again it greatly weakens the opponent as the enemy has the natural instinct to protect what is hurting which in turn hinders their ability to fight.

Leaving the vampire dazed on the floor Charlie went over to Saffron and helped her off the bed. Saffron hugged him relieved that she had been saved from the evil footballer who only hours earlier she had admired so much. Now all her admiration was for Charlie who had been her hero. She wept into his chest realising what could have been if Charlie had not shown up when he did.

"Thanks Charlie," she sobbed.

"You're safe now Saffron, come on let's go and find your dad."

They left the room leaving Andrei Botezatu grunting in pain. As they left Saffron stamped her stiletto heel onto his head wound for good measure. That made Charlie Cheng chuckle.

Chapter 56

Professor Cezar Prodanescu entered the country lane with a heavy heart. The snow covered branches of the trees that peppered the landscape and surrounding fields were a beautiful sight but they were wasted on the professor.

He had taken a drive over to Lily's house in an attempt to patch things up following their quarrel before Christmas. He had missed her more than he could have ever possibly imagined and his emotions confused him. He was a master vampire, a supposed killing machine, devoid of any real loving emotions. He had been born to hunt and his genetics had been developed to always dictate that the primary importance in his life was to ensure that the vampire race prospered.

Yet he had to admit to himself that he loved this girl dearly, and furthermore the empty feeling that he was experiencing since their break up was hurting him badly.

He ached for her.

Uncharacteristically he was finding it very hard to function and to concentrate on the duties that he had always been destined to carry out.

He was feeling like a lovesick teenager.

There was no doubt about it he needed *his* Lily.

For the first time in his extensive life he realised what the humans had meant when they had spoken of their soul mate, of their undying love for one another and how they could never carry on if they were to lose the partner that they had committed to sharing their life with.

And now that he had further discovered that Lily was not at home when he called, that she had not been there to greet him with open arms and to accept his apology and peace offering of the bouquet of roses, complemented of course by a cluster of Lilies, his mood was at an all time low. He had planned to tell her that he had found his soul mate in her, that he wanted to share the rest of his life with her and if need be he would move away from Fosturnea to live with her.

He didn't have to live there with the other boys; he could just frequent it as the overseer of the School of Football Excellence and he could leave Andrei in charge as a resident for the times he was away.

He was still unsure however if he could tell her the secret he had been hiding for fear of losing her. Could he really inform Lily that her lover was a master vampire? If he were to explain to her that she could never be in danger and it was indeed his love for her that had spared her life until now would she understand?

But maybe once he had explained the situation to her she would have chosen herself to become a vampire so that they could share a life of immortality together. But Cezar was also afraid that Lily, the sweet natured girl that she was, would never understand the necessity to kill human beings and to drink their blood. He was afraid that she would freak out if she ever discovered the reality of Cezar's existence and would never want to be a part of his world and more importantly his life.

Deep down Cezar didn't want her to be a part of the vampire world. Yes, he loved the idea of sharing immortality with her but he loved her the way she was, so pure, so sweet and so innocent. He didn't want her to be tainted by his world of blood drinking and lustful killing.

But he struggled with the concept of whether she had a right to know who he really was.

Would he have told her everything if she had been home?

As Lily had not been at home when he called unfortunately he would never really know.

As he reached the foot of the driveway to the Fosturnea house Cezar was astonished to see the state of the gate structure, or rather lack of it. The gates had been completely torn from their hinges.

He proceeded to guide his car up the driveway and it was not long before he realised what had caused the demolition of the gates.

He saw the team coach facing him and his heart sank even further. Always a man of astute perception Cezar quickly realised that the presence of the team coach, in addition to the violent assault on the gates, could only equate to one thing and that one thing was the realisation of his worst fears.

The human footballers of *his* team had discovered the truth. That he and the products of the Fosturnea School of Football Excellence were vampires.

When Charlie and Saffron reached the foot of the stairs Saffron was exposed to an array of bodies on the floor, and she spotted that her best friend Dionne was one of them. Now that moments before she had been forced to accept that vampires existed she feared the worst for her best friend, but fortunately Dionne began to stir as she woke from her unconsciousness.

"Saffron, go and sit with your friend this is the safest place for you. It appears that the battle has moved further into the house. I will go and assist your father and I promise you that we shall return and all leave together. Please do not be afraid."

Saffron simply nodded to Charlie and moved across to her friend where they began to discuss the impossibility of the night's events.

"Halt who goes there?" chuckled Rashid as he sat on the steps to the team coach, Frankie's blood dribbling from his mouth.

Cezar looked at the former taxi driver and beyond him could see the coach driver with half his neck missing.

"Andrei you fool, I've always taught you not to do this on our own doorstep."

Rashid frowned at the professor's words.

"You just sit there whoever you are I don't want you following me into the house do you understand?" Cezar's tone was very firm.

"Oh, you are the main man. Okay I'll sit here like a good little vampire. Hee hee," tittered Rashid. "That is what I am isn't it? A vampire? Hee hee hee."

Cezar just rolled his eyes before walking towards the house, knowing that he would always curse Andrei for recruiting such an annoying little shit into the nest.

Andrei had almost reached the bottom of the stairs as he stared at the terrified girls sitting on the sofa amongst the remains of the carnage that had resulted from the night's conflict. He was purposely taking his time to ensure that the girls felt a maximum amount of fear; he was playing with them, toying with them, amusing himself. But soon he would pitch his moment to attack and go in for the kill—and he would enjoy it.

"Hello girls, my night is about to get a whole lot better."

"No it isn't."

Andrei, Saffron and Dionne all looked at the image that had spoken. It was Cezar Prodanescu.

"What are you talking about master, we are fucking vampires it's what we do?"

Cezar was angry at his fellow countryman's words. How could he be so arrogant, so stupid?

"Since when was it on the agenda to recruit the daughter of a team-mate, a highly respected team-mate at that? Have I never taught you to live the vampire life with honour and dignity?"

"Fuck Johnny Knox, he is a muppet, the guy is just a fucking has-been. He will be out of this club before long anyway; we at Fosturnea will soon make up the whole starting eleven."

"That was never my intention and you know it. And for the record Johnny Knox will always have a place in my team."

"You need to work out whose side you are on boss."

Cezar was becoming increasingly incensed but his wrath was halted when a young girl broke away from the crowd who were intent on entering the kitchen to get to the humans.

Cezar was amazed yet disturbed to see who it was.

"Lily, you look different what has happened to you?"

Lily just smiled showing her newly formed fangs and tragically displaying her loss of innocence that Cezar had so fell in love with.

"Lily, oh no, I never wanted this for you."

Lily even began to talk differently, more sultry and out of character.

"Well hey Cezar baby where have you been? You've been missing out on the party. Do you not like the new me, now I'm a vampire too?"

Cezar's head dropped in the realisation of what had happened to Lily. He felt his eyes well with tears.

"No I don't like it; I loved you as you were Lily, my sweet innocent Lily."

Then Cezar turned his intentions to Andrei, "you have done this to her haven't you? You had no right."

"Relax Cezar, what is this anyway? Feelings for humans, going soft on a human girl, it seems to me that it is time for you to move over old man."

Cezar felt his anger rage.

"How dare you be so insolent boy, I treated you like a son, taught you everything I know."

"That was your mistake Cezar, you taught me too well."

"I will kill you, Andrei."

As the words left Cezar's mouth Andrei was already in full flight from the stairs gaining the advantage over his mentor as he landed on him.

He began to punch the professor hard in the face several times, but just as Charlie Cheng had done so only minutes earlier Cezar raised his knee into Andrei's groin to get him off of him.

With his vast years of combating experience behind him Cezar was soon on his feet and landing blows left, right and centre into his young treacherous understudy. In between each blow from a punch or a kick Cezar would utter words of anger such as "after all I've done for you boy" and "you are a disgrace to the vampire world."

But Andrei was young and strong and despite absorbing some horrific pain he managed to get to his feet to face his mentor. Cezar welcomed the challenge that lay ahead and smiled as he signalled at Andrei to give him his best shot.

The mob of vampires was starting to eventually loosen the door to the kitchen and it would only be a matter of seconds before the footballers were destined to fight them again. As the door finally swung open, Gene and Callum timed their holy water assault to perfection to take out the initial few vampires as they entered the arena. Father McGill had been busy blessing saucepans of water to make them holy and he had by now even blessed the forceit itself as water was being sprayed over the unsuspecting vampires by Vincent Bradshaw strategically placing his thumb to create a spray of lethal holy water.

Although he laughed manically at the plight of the vampires as he sprayed them, Vincent hadn't yet informed his colleagues that he had been bitten by a vampire in an earlier confrontation and he wondered at what stage he himself would turn into one of the bloodsucking scum. He noticed that the holy water was starting to burn his thumb and he knew that the reaction signalled that he couldn't be too far away from changing.

One vampire approached him as he momentarily broke free from the forceit to give his thumb a moment of respite.

"Why do they call you bruiser?" the vampire enquired.

Promptly *dropping the nut* onto the vampires nose Vinnie simply answered, "I guess that's why."

Once all of the saucepans of water had been thrown at the vampires, the footballers went on the attack to force the fight back out into the hallway. Armed with kitchen knives and other various utensils they had augmented their weaponry and on pure survival instinct had once again managed to gain the upper hand on the vampires and reduced them to a much lesser amount of opponents.

In saying that Johnny at one point found himself pinned to the ground by what he considered was the ugliest of all the vampires he had seen tonight. As the vampire used his full weight to pin the midfielder down Johnny got a whiff of his rank breath as his jaws moved closer towards his throat.

Fearing for his life Johnny was unable to reach the gun from his left pocket. Desperately he was just about able to free his right hand enough to reach inside his right pocket and he quickly felt the hard edges of a small metallic object.

All at once he realised why Dr. Lazar had given him the silver crucifix that night he smuggled Radu out of Romania. He had been given it as a form of protection against vampires.

The ugly vampire's fangs were now just millimetres from Johnny's throat but he was able to pull the crucifix from his pocket and make contact with the face of the vampire. The vampire screamed in pain as his skin burnt into the shape of a cross giving the impression he had had a religious tattoo imprinted on his left cheek.

The vampire's agonizing dilemma was enough for him to loosen his hold on Johnny who now used the crucifix like a mini dagger thrusting the bluntness of it with such force that one of the blows speared the vampire's skull right between his eyes killing him instantly.

The cross was still smoking as Johnny retrieved it from the dead vampire's bone and tissue. He gave it a wipe on his trouser leg, and not usually the most religious of men proceeded to give the crucifix a kiss in appreciation of it saving his life before recommencing battle with the remainder of the vampires.

By this time Charlie had been able to attack some vampires from the rear taking them by surprise and his Kung Fu expertise continued to impressively diminish the vampire assault.

But then the battle seemed to stop as the opponents from either side were amazed to see a different brawl that spilled into the thick of the action, for the two bodies fighting and wrestling on the ground were none other than Professor Cezar Prodanescu and Andrei Botezatu!

As everyone stopped to watch the battle it was Johnny who eventually acted first as his anger found the better of him and he dragged Andrei from the fight and punched him himself.

"Where is my fucking daughter you scumbag?"

Taken by surprise at Johnny's sudden inclusion in the fight Andrei chose to adopt a wrestling strategy by grabbing Johnny knowing that if he could inhibit the movement of his arms he had a better chance of success than trading punches with the wild and furious human football captain. As the two images wrestled Johnny's gun spilled to the ground and Cezar picked it up.

But before Cezar had a chance to use it, if indeed that was what he was going to do, Callum placed a loaded cross-bow to the head of the master vampire. "Don't move Cezar, I've waited a long time for this moment. Now listen to my words you piece of blood-sucking shit and listen well," and with that Callum began to reel off a sermon rather than an ad-hoc piece of dialogue, not unlike a movie actor with a very well rehearsed part of a script. *"Anyone who eats blood – I will set my face against them and will cut him off from his community."*

Then Cezar picked up the sermon in a mocking tone, not moving his head but darting his eyes temporarily at Father McGill. *'For the life of the body is in the blood, and I have given it to you on the altar to make atonement for your souls; for it is the blood of the life that allows atonement.* You make me laugh you holy people, you are such hypocrites pretending to drink the blood of Christ then casting aspersions on vampires for being more honest. Tell me why drink the pretend blood of Christ and then gladly consume the blood of an animal at Sunday lunchtime or during a meal out at a fancy restaurant with the family? Okay so you disguise the flesh by cooking it first before eating it but you all crave the taste of blood just in a more hypocritical fashion than we do. The only difference is you choose the blood of animals over human's blood."

Father McGill's only answer was to cross himself. Although Cezar was technically quoting from the Hebrew Bible, his words struck an uncomfortable chord with the Catholic priest.

Gene Macgoree and Callum then continued the passage in perfect unison ignoring the professor's mockery as Callum prodded the cross-bow into Cezar's temple re-enforcing the threat that it carried and silencing the master vampire. *'Therefore I said to them, 'No person or alien among you may eat blood'. So when any man or aliens who gather among them, when hunting catches a beast or fowl to eat, he shall pour out its blood and cover it with dust. For its blood is identified with its life. Therefore I said to them, 'You are not to eat the blood of any flesh, for the life of flesh is its blood; whoever eats it shall be cut off from his people.'"*

Gene supplied the identification of the passage whilst Callum continued to aggressively poke Cezar's temple. "Leviticus 17, verses 10 to 14."

Vampires and footballers alike were stunned to see Professor Cezar Prodanescu in such a vulnerable position and were now more intrigued as to the outcome of this stalemate as opposed to fighting one another. After all every single one of their destinies now hung in the balance with whatever would happen next.

Even Andrei and Johnny had momentarily stopped but they eyed each other with equal hatred and they both held one another's clothing neither one wishing to concede the upper hand.

Cezar spoke carefully realising he was risking his life. Callum was itching to fire the cross-bow into the professor's skull.

"Gentlemen you recited that passage so comprehensively but your quoting may be slightly premature. Johnny, I presume this gun that I now possess holds silver bullets?"

"That is correct and there are two bullets remaining."

"Two bullets huh, well that just happens to be perfect. Paildo, Ringa grab hold of Andrei. The boy is a traitor."

"You are the traitor Cezar, you fell in love with a human girl after you wanted to make Kingsbarr United a team of vampires and now you have lost your mind. Even now as we sit amongst this carnage you want these humans to live. My name is Botezatu, meaning someone who wants his religion. I am the true master vampire."

"You disillusioned fool, you need to be born a master vampire such as I. Ringa and Paildo grab him now." The two young vampires, though confused, didn't hesitate any longer and they grabbed hold of Andrei at the request of their master. Unlike Andrei they knew that Cezar was the man to obey, it had simply always been that way.

"Now Johnny, if I give you the gun you can fire a bullet into Andrei and no doubt kill him. And if you do that I will allow you to use the second bullet for me. But first I would like the opportunity to do some explaining."

"How do I know I can trust you?"

"You have my word."

Johnny took a moment to consider the words of his manager and didn't doubt their sincerity in spite of everything. The Kingsbarr United skipper offered his hand so that Cezar could pass him the gun.

But before Cezar could place the gun in the hand of his team captain Andrei desperately reacted.

"There is no way I am standing for this," and with those words Andrei used all his strength to pull away from his two usual allies and headed straight for Johnny Knox. The frantic vampire was only millimetres from his teeth sinking into Johnny's neck when Andrei Botezatu was floored by a gunshot to the head.

"Oh dear, that leaves one bullet now doesn't it," said Cezar calmly holding the smoking gun, and with the turn of great speed he was soon pointing it at Callum. The master vampire and vampire slayer were now locked in a stalemate of cross-bow against gun.

"Now allow me to say my piece and I assure you Johnny, you will be victorious in your plight."

"Okay speak, but I should warn you that Callum is a trained vampire slayer and he is my son. So even if you do manage to kill him first, which I doubt very much, I swear to God Cezar I will kill you." Callum pushed the butt of the cross-bow into Cezar's head once more to reinforce the threat.

Just as Cezar was about to speak a distressed Saffron ran into the room with Dionne not far behind her. She was clutching a wooden stake with blood dripping from it. "Dad, I've had to kill someone. It was self-defence honestly."

"Don't worry baby, I've killed plenty of these scumbags tonight," answered Johnny relieved to finally see that his daughter was safe and seemingly well.

Then Cezar spoke in a solemn resigned voice, already sensing the answer to his own question.

"Saffron my dear was the person you killed the young girl I was speaking to before Andrei and myself commenced battle?"

"Yes, Sir. I'm very sorry but she attacked me and Dionne, she tried to bite us. If she was a vampire, whom I think she was, then I know from watching films and reading teenage science fiction that you have to drive a stake through their heart to stop them. I swear I had no choice but to do this."

Cezar smiled. "Do not worry Saffron; you may never understand exactly what you have done for Lily, that was her name you see, Lily. She should never have become a vampire. And Andrei was right when he said I loved her."

Paildo and Ringa frowned at one another. Cezar continued. "And you have actually made my plight more the easier dear Saffron. May I apologise for the ordeal that Andrei has put you through this evening, but as you can see he will not be bothering you ever again."

Saffron gasped at Andrei's lifeless body.

"Okay Cezar, say what you want to say." The whole audience waited with bated breath.

"Thank you Johnny. Dear Johnny whom I truly respect and admire. I trust you do know that, as I respected and admired all of the Kingsbarr United football team. I am a professor in football and to be a professor in a subject, to have that desire and dedication one must also have a passion, and football is indeed a big passion of mine. This is why I chose to manage Kingsbarr United. Oh, the setting of Kingsbarr was very fortuitous as buried at Sutton Park was Adrien Connor the world's original vampire. As another passion of mine is genetics I was able to develop the ability to clone Adrien to allow the vampire race to have its true leader restored again on this Earth. I have been able to *kill two birds with one stone* as you English say. I have been in a very privileged position to work on my mission of reintroducing the sole originator of the vampire race into the world whilst managing Kingsbarr United Football Club, which in its former state of underachievement was also a very perfect club to blood, if you will pardon the pun, the products of the Fosturnea School of Football Excellence into the game."

"You are mad Cezar. You are just a mad professor."

"Am I Johnny?" said Cezar angered by his captain's words. "Tell me are you and the team not in a much healthier position since I have taken over? Are the team not in a better position now that Fosturnea have injected some enhanced talent?"

"Of course Cezar in spite all of this madness a part of me has to be grateful for what you have done for the club, to get us back to winning ways has felt good. But half the team are fucking vampires and that is simply wrong. And furthermore you got rid of Daryl Weir and made him one of you, as you have done with Leon Davis the poor bastard. What was your ultimate intention Cezar to turn us all into fucking vampires?"

"At first maybe some of you it's true, but never you Johnny, your ability on the pitch was of raw natural talent, I never wanted to mess with that. I never wanted to mess with your values of honesty and integrity. I certainly never wanted you to find out about us, about me and now my heart is truly heavy. But instead of you thanking me for what I have done for Kingsbarr United I wish to thank you. I have been impressed by the human world since coming to Kingsbarr. I hoped we could all live side by side, vampires and humans together for the good of the football club and you would never learn of our secret. But now that you do know I am not a fool. Something has to give."

Paildo and Ringa couldn't believe what they were hearing. Humans and vampires living side by side! The professor had indeed gone mad. They nodded to one another and they both connected telepathically.

As they moved forward to attack their one time mentor, the master vampire who they looked up to, whom they had hung on his every word, Cezar pointed the gun just below his own chin.

Johnny couldn't believe his own voice—he shouted "No!" he didn't want to see Cezar dead. He truly believed that in spite of his unconventional methods Cezar had indeed always had the best intentions for Kingsbarr United. Okay he was a vampire but he was certainly not a threat to any of them.

As Ringa and Paildo moved closer Callum had enough time to point the cross-bow at Ringa and fire an arrow straight into his heart killing him instantly.

"That's for Bogdan you piece of shit"

Then Cezar spoke uttering his final words before taking his own life with the final remaining silver bullet. "Lily we will have immortality, I will see you on the other side."

As Cezar dropped to the floor it was all over.

The entire audience was stunned and it was left to Gene to break the silence.

"I don't believe it, the ultimate sacrifice."

"What do you mean?" asked Johnny.

"Look around you, the vampires are no longer vampires. If a master vampire is killed, and in particular by his own fair hand then the remainder of the nest are cured, they are no longer vampires and they will have no recollection of ever being one. Look at Daryl and Leon, they are human beings again."

"And what of the ones we have killed?"

"Too late I'm afraid Dad. That's why I wanted Ringa to pay for what he did to Bogdan. And that's why Cezar wanted Andrei dead before turning the gun on himself. Sadly he also knew that thanks to Saffron his precious Lily was also never to walk this Earth again."

"Well I hope that they do meet again somewhere, but I doubt it will be in heaven in Cezar's case," said Gene. "He and Lily were obviously in love and they could never have made it work on this Earth—a human and a vampire? It was doomed from the start. Prodan means 'abandoned child', I guess that's what Cezar was in the end, an abandoned and lost child caught between two worlds."

"Hey guys," shouted over Vincent "Bruiser" Bradshaw. "You know I had been bit and I was nearly a fucking vampire, *blood sucking bastards. Close fucking shave, close fucking shave.*"

"Vincent," shouted back Johnny. "When were you thinking of telling us then? Then again you have always been a bit of a monster anyway."

Everyone laughed.

Just then a little boy ran up to Johnny, a little boy full of the innocence and delight that little boys should be.

"Can you still be my daddy?"

Johnny stroked the little boy's hair and kissed his forehead. "Of course I will Radu, would you like to come home."

"I've always wanted a little brother," said Callum with a smile. Radu hugged his big brother.

Just then Johnny's mobile phone rang to the tune of "Nessun Dorma."

"Hi honey!"

"Johnny, where the fuck are you all? You missed seeing the New Year in with us."

"Oh, sorry Sheena, we have seen the New Year in with a bang don't worry. Err, we got a call from Saffron, she had a little party lined up for us. We will be back soon. By the way I have found Radu, he is totally cured, he was err how can I put it, actually being cared for somewhere else. He is totally okay. I'll explain later."

"Okay that's great news about Radu, just get your arses back over here Cathy Rossi's going apeshit for one. She wanted to see her first married New Year in with her husband and who can blame her. Keegan seems to have welcomed the New Year in anyway. The dumb cat is back to his old loving ways. He is fussing round my legs like he hasn't done for months. He is very affectionate indeed."

"Okay honey, just reflect a second. We've got a new son, we have found our missing son, and we have a lovely daughter and the greatest of family pets. This is going to be a great year."

"Yeah we are lucky Mr Knox aren't we? We should count our blessings. And I've even got you you great lummox!"

"Yeah and I've got you. I'm the luckiest man alive. See you soon."

As he hung up the phone his smile diminished when he noticed a fire raging from the hallway.

"Fucking hell," said Gene. "The candles must have spilt over in the fight, quick let's get out the back way.

Everyone followed Gene Macgoree and safely escaped the fire into the snow before the old house and all its ancient timber burnt to the ground in minutes with the dead corpses, including those of Professor Cezar Prodanescu and Andrei Botezatu, soon to be gone forever.

Chapter 57

"It doesn't get any better than this boss," said an excited Jody Roper straightening his gold tie and massaging the hallowed turf of Wembley Stadium with his loafer shoe. Even on cup final day, with Kingsbarr United kitted out in commissioned blue suits and gold ties direct from Saville Row the defender had to have a part of eighties clothing about him. He was even wearing white socks, another eighties mark of fashion, but fortunately the cut of the blue trousers rarely revealed these to the outside world.

"It sure doesn't get any better than this," agreed Johnny as he looked around the red coloured seating which he knew would be fully occupied within the next two hours by a sea of gold and blue created by Kingsbarr United supporters wearing their team colours through the likes of football scarves and replica shirts.

Johnny took in a sharp breath as if to physically inhale the sheer presence of the marvellous stadium which at this moment he was fully able to appreciate as it lay empty in unaccustomed silence.

Even though Johnny had graced Wembley Stadium before he was always in awe of the tremendous arena and he knew that this was what every English player dreamed of, to play in an FA Cup Final at Wembley Stadium. It was the things dreams were made of for every small English boy who pretended to be their heroes as they kicked a ball down the local park, scoring goals through make shift goalposts of coats or other unnecessary clothing strategically placed on the ground.

Johnny Knox had never been any different as a child himself when he regularly fantasised about being one of his Kingsbarr United heroes every time he capably dribbled the ball around his dumb-struck mates and hit the back of the net with a glorious shot, except the goal net was only in his mind as the ball would in reality travel for a great many yards and the poor lad who had drawn the short straw to play in goal would have to get his exercise by running after the ball and retrieving it for the cycle to happen all over again. An accepted punishment for not being able to prevent the goal from being scored.

"Come on Jody lets go and get changed, we've got a cup to win."

"You bet boss."

Jody had taken to calling Johnny Knox boss, as opposed to the previous endearment of skipper, as since the fire at Fosturnea at New Year, and the death of Professor Cezar Prodanescu, chairman Peter Cogshaw had seen it fit to appoint Johnny as player-manager of Kingsbarr United. It was Jody himself who now owned the accolade of club captain.

Kingsbarr had secured a return to the Premier League by clinching the second available automatic promotion spot, avoiding the play-offs by their record breaking superior goal difference over the team below them. It had to be acknowledged that the goal feast had come under Cezar's reign with those huge victories that unfolded beneath the floodlights of Beacon Park, chiefly led by the prolific goal scoring ability of the now also deceased Andrei Botezatu.

With the entire footballers from the Fosturnea School, except Paildo, being killed at New Year, Johnny had been faced with the daunting task of regrouping a much depleted squad under extreme media scrutiny for obvious reasons.

Of course Paildo, now less his vampire powers and thankfully his memory of his life as a vampire, had returned to being a very good footballer but obviously not as good as he had been in the reign of Cezar when he could possess super human powers when darkness fell. Likewise, the surviving and now human again Leon Davis had returned to his usual average footballing ability and to being the cocky, mouthy little shit who had always just about annoyed anybody he ever met!

Under the successful and unique reign of Cezar Prodanescu, Leon Davis had convinced the world that he was a fine footballer, but of course the unsuspecting admirers failed to realise that his turn in ability had been due to his vampire powers, and now that he was no longer a vampire his footballing ability was never going to rekindle its momentary flame.

This is where Johnny Knox as player-manager pulled a master stroke in the January transfer window. He sold both Leon Davis and Paildo to a Premiership club for a very impressive sum of money. A Premiership club incidentally that Kingsbarr United would now be replacing in the Premier League next season as City had become relegated. The attraction of a young up and coming starlet and a Brazilian footballer was very tempting for many clubs and the bidding grew and grew until City got their players. Too bad that Davis and Paildo had never shown the form of their Kingsbarr days.

The huge amount of money generated from the Davis and Paildo sale had enabled Johnny to build a new squad by complementing the spine of the team made up of his faithful buddies with some new players. There had even been enough money left over to keep Peter Cogshaw happy.

Besides Johnny had needed to take action to bring in new faces as squad numbers were automatically low due to the loss of the Fosturnea products.

Cogshaw, never missing a chance to capitalise on an opportunity, even if it came from an accepted tragedy (amazingly he never knew of the vampire connection), had also generated vast amounts of money by establishing a line of merchandise and exclusive media coverage about Cezar and the Fosturnea School of Football Excellence. Johnny had worked hard to ensure that Cogshaw fed it back into the club and not wholly into his own pocket, and additionally secured the avenue for the money to be well invested by setting up a charity and announcing on live television that "Peter Cogshaw had agreed to pay considerable amounts of money generated from merchandise to the charity in the name of the Cezar Prodanescu Memorial Fund, which funded orphanages and helped to get deprived kids a start in life," something despite everything that had happened Cezar seemed to be a catalyst for so it proved a very fitting tribute.

Johnny struggled with the concept that he had shared his life with a breed of spine-chilling vampires, bluntly intent on taking human life for their own gain, but he also couldn't ignore the positive impact they had had on the football club that he had loved since a child. Therefore he also ensured that a memorial statue of Cezar was placed outside the north entrance to Beacon Park complemented by a gold placard detailing the names of the Fosturnea School of footballers who had lost their lives in the fire on New Year's Eve. Fortunately the truth of them being vampires had never got out and the unsuspecting world, as backed by a heartfelt press release from Johnny and his team-mates, were informed of how the house of Fosturnea was a *3 minute building*, known to always be at risk of burning down within three minutes. The world believed that the New Year party tragically got out of hand and a spillage of candles burnt the house down taking the lives of the footballers with it. No more, no less. Any surviving vampires, like Leon and Paildo typically lost their memory about ever being a vampire when they returned to being human at the death of their master vampire, and head of their particular nest Professor Cezar Prodanescu.

Another vampire now cum human who remembered nothing about being a vampire was Daryl Weir. He had turned his back on football management and was carving out a successful career as a television footballing pundit. In fact he would be in the studio later today to comment and analyse the cup final.

Johnny Knox and the footballing world recognised the achievements of Cezar Prodanescu and the upturn in fortune he had left the club in at his point of death, but player-manager Johnny still had half a season remaining to steer the squad to try and achieve promotion to the Premier League. The fact that he had succeeded in his first shot at football management was very commendable.

However, reaching the cup final pleased him even more because he knew it had been solely achieved by *his* team and *his* team alone. The FA Cup started in January for Kingsbarr United, following the deaths at New Year and the Fosturnea products of Cezar Prodanescu had never kicked a ball in the English FA Cup competition. Johnny, even in the face of such recent tragedy, had managed to achieve a successful cup campaign to ultimately reach the FA Cup Final.

Now all he had to do to put the icing on the cake was guide his team to win it.

His team.

As Johnny lined up in the tunnel ready to lead *his* team out on to the field of play he reflected on the last twelve months and how amazing it had all been: the poor start to the season under the guidance of Daryl Weir, the injection of a mysterious foreign manager and his school of excellence footballers, the dramatic turn in fortune with the inclusion of record-breaking score lines, the realisation that the squad were sharing daily interaction with a set of vampires, the loss of several star players and despite everything a wonderful football manager and now under Johnny's own guidance the season had crescendoed for Kingsbarr United into reaching an FA Cup Final. Johnny knew that no matter what had occurred over the past twelve months it was simply all history and today was what was now important.

Winning the FA Cup Final.

It was time to focus on the task at hand.

Johnny listened to the sound of the crowd which sent tingles of excitement up his spine and in his stomach as he stood proudly in front of his players, who were all fired up following Jody's usual eighties musical warm-up in the dressing room. In spite of the monumental occasion and fine voice coming from the supporters Johnny could still hear George Michael singing the infectious melodies of a string of Wham! songs in his head, a Wham! medley had seemed the ideal feel good factor to set the team up for the occasion.

With the sale of Davis and Paildo Johnny had partly used the money to buy a centre-back to partner Jody Roper, and this centre-back was a good footballer with quick feet in addition to being a sound defender. He was capable of taking the ball from the edge of his own area and at just 20 years of age still have the confidence to run with the ball, dribbling past players and even scoring the odd goal getting on the end of set-pieces where his presence was always feared by his opponents. His name was Victor Yates and he had progressed to become an England under 21 international since joining Kingsbarr. His youth complemented by Jody's experience made a good partnership in the heart of United's defence.

Johnny also needed to find two full-backs. He realised he could never re-invent the pace of the Fosturnea full-backs of Ringa and Tracaldo so instead he decided to purchase full-backs with a no-nonsense attitude, who could attack and press forward when required but who were mentally strong and could defend the flanks. He would instead leave the majority of attacking play down the wings to his two exciting wingers namely Charlie Cheng and a USA international winger whose style of play was a carbon copy of Charlie Cheng but whose skills were artistically displayed down the left hand side of the field as opposed to the right hand side which was more than competently occupied by Charlie. His name was Toby Storm and he lived up to his name as he would powerfully *storm* down the by-line, terrorising the opposition and sending in killer-balls for the likes of Giuseppe Rossi and Gerry Spalding to get on the end of. The two full-backs incidentally were both German internationals, and both brothers, Ludwig and Klauss Kircherr.

Johnny had also signed a young up and coming goalkeeper from the lower leagues to keep Alvin Braxton on his toes, namely Kyle Starkey, a local lad who like Johnny had been a Kingsbarr United fan all his life.

So Johnny had adopted a very successful 4-4-2 formation to reach the cup final, reverting from Cezar's 3-5-2 and he stood proudly ahead of his team ready to lead them onto Wembley's hallowed turf. The team sheet for the match read like this: Goalkeeper: Braxton, Defence: L. Kircherr, Roper (Captain), Yates, K. Kircherr. Midfield: Cheng, Knox (Player-Manager), Bradshaw, Storm. Attack: Rossi, Spalding. Amongst the substitutes was Matt Floyd who had been plagued by injuries since joining Kingsbarr but who was now making a good return to match fitness. If things were going well Johnny had promised him a part to play in this cup final. Matt had been as supportive as anyone when the battle had commenced against Fosturnea and he remained loyal to his footballing buddies. They had all shared a unique experience and the experience had made them a very united and inseparable force. For them the word *United* held far more significance than merely a name of a football club.

Following the opening ceremony and meet and greet with a member of the Royal family it was Kingsbarr who kicked off the FA Cup Final and immediately went on the attack trying to feed the ball as much as possible to Charlie Cheng and Toby Storm for them to work their magic and get as many crosses into dangerous areas as possible for Gerry Spalding or Giuseppe Rossi to get on the end of.

It was recognised by the Kingsbarr players that they were not playing a team of push-overs today though against City (not the same City who had signed Paildo and Davis), who were both reigning Premiership champions and European champions. Kingsbarr, though a very capable outfit under Johnny's guidance, no longer had the unrivalled energy and ability of the vampire players and by contrast City had a glittering amount of world-class top international stars in their team. The contest was proving to be a remarkable spectacle with both sets of supporters rising to the occasion in fine voice and encouragement for their team as the game unfolded.

In spite being perceived as the underdog for the cup final, for the first 25 minutes of the game Kingsbarr had done most of the attacking and Toby Storm had already seen one of his blistering left foot shots hit the post. Johnny had his team extremely well-organised and very methodical in its approach and City, in spite of the natural ability in their side were finding it difficult to penetrate the Kingsbarr defence.

But then disaster happened.

In spite of their organisation, Kingsbarr momentarily became a little too complacent due to the amount of ball possession they were enjoying and both Jody Roper and Victor Yates had pushed too far up the pitch.

Within a split second the City keeper had pulled-off a fantastic save from Giuseppe Rossi but the rebound had fell to a City defender who sprayed the ball up field to a loitering City striker who skilfully caught the ball on the volley with the heel of his boot, taking it over Jody's head and into the Kingsbarr half where he was able to reclaim the ball and run towards Alvin Braxton's goal unchallenged.

Klauss Kircherr made a valiant attempt to reach the City attacker but he was always making up too much ground.

With no means of Kingsbarr defence to protect him Alvin Braxton had little option but to run from his goal to try and make some sort of challenge himself, which he did on the edge of his 18 yard box.

It was a freak goal!

Alvin had challenged the City player bravely and the ball had hit Alvin, proving to be initially a very good save, but the rebound had hit the City striker straight on his knee and the ball pinged into the net.

1-0 City!

To make matters worse for Kingsbarr Alvin Braxton would play no more part in the game, his bravery had caused him to take a nasty knock on both his hand and his knee and he was writhing in agony whilst the City players mobbed their goal-scorer and their supporters cheered with elation.

Kyle Starkey couldn't believe his luck! He was genuinely concerned for the plight of his mentor, Alvin had been good to him since he joined the club coaching him and giving him tips to improve his game. But the fact remained that he was going to make his Kingsbarr United debut, the team that he had supported since a child, at Wembley Stadium in an FA Cup Final!

He couldn't get out of his tracksuit quick enough.

As he proceeded to enter the pitch he paused a moment to speak to Alvin Braxton who was being stretchered off.

"Are you gonna be okay big fella?"

Despite his pain Alvin smiled at his young understudy and spoke in his deep Jamaican drawl.

"Go and make this your cup final boy. Me gonna have a nice rest and enjoy the game from the comfort of a seat, watching you carry out all the tings me taught ya mon. And me be watching to make sure you been paying attention to old Alvin Braxton."

The two goalkeepers gave each other a high-five and Kyle entered the pitch.

To everybody's astonishment the young goalkeeper immediately began to play a blinder.

For sure he had butterflies but pure adrenalin enabled him to reach shots and make saves like he had never done before. The young goalkeeper was putting on a display as if he was on a mission to protect the Kingsbarr goal as if it had been his life's destiny.

City attacked more and more as their natural skills and ability began to control the game.

Kingsbarr responded by working as hard as they could in an attempt to stifle City's increasing grip on the game, and were even succeeding in getting in some fine strong challenges. The commitment and desire of the Kingsbarr players could not be questioned, but the confidence of the European and Premiership champions had grown since the scoring of their goal and their superior class was starting to shine through.

Johnny realised that half-time was approaching and if Kingsbarr could ride the storm for now going in to the dressing room at the break 1-0 down would not be considered too much of a disaster, after all he knew that Kingsbarr were perceived to be the underdog and the media had been saying as much since the FA Cup Final was destined to be between Kingsbarr and City. He felt confident that he could use the half-time break as a chance to re-group his players and inspire them to cancel out the 1 goal deficit in the second half of the game.

But unfortunately Johnny's hopes of keeping the score at 1-0 were compromised when just on the stroke of half-time City were awarded a penalty.

From where Johnny had been standing it certainly didn't look like a penalty to him and his protest against the referee articulating his beliefs earned him a yellow card.

To add insult to injury Ludwig Kircherr had also been booked for the challenge which was to most viewers, and as proven by subsequent video replays which of course the referee was unable to benefit from at the time, was a clear dive by the city striker, an unfortunate trend that was increasingly spoiling the "*beautiful game*". It was one of those moments when video evidence (if allowed to influence the decision) would have seen justice prevail and it would have been the City striker who would have actually received the booking for cheating.

Disgracefully pleased with his contribution at *earning* his team a penalty the same striker stepped up to take the spot-kick with an evil grin on his face.

All eyes were now on the young Birmingham born goalkeeper to see if it was possible for him to make a name for himself in the FA Cup Final.

Unfortunately on this occasion it wasn't to be.

With literally the last kick of the half the City player hit the roof of the net with a very well placed shot to make it 2-0 at half-time.

A dejected Kyle Starkey was told not to worry by his boss Johnny Knox as they left the field, praising the young keeper that he had read the shot as well as he could and had even managed to get a hand on the penalty-kick.

The half-time talk was undoubtedly Johnny's biggest test to date as player-manager. As the players sank onto the dressing room benches, heads dropping down to their chests, Johnny looked around at their deflated faces and quickly analysed in his mind what they had actually gone through these past few months. It was in truth quite unbelievable. The things that they had experienced certainly went bigger than football itself but nevertheless this was the FA Cup Final, the competition they had all dreamed about as little boys and they were only 45 minutes from winning it! Okay so they needed to overcome a two goal deficit but at this moment, knowing what he knew, Johnny was convinced that these boys deserved to win this cup more than anybody else. It was simply their right following the experiences that they had gone through. Furthermore if they can outwit a nest of blood-thirsty vampires then recovering from a two goal deficit should be a walk in the park!

"Okay boys," began an inspired Johnny. "I'm really proud of the way you have committed yourselves out on the field today. We have been playing really well out there but we can do even better. We know we have been cheated by the penalty decision but we still have another 45 minutes to put things right. Dig down deep inside your soul and find the strength I know you all have. We have been through a lot worse than this together and you know what I mean."

"Yeah, if we can defeat an army of blood-sucking vampires then we can beat City even if they do have a two goal lead," barked out an emotional Vincent Bradshaw as subtle as ever.

The new recruits to Kingsbarr United frowned at one another curiously. *Vampires did he really say vampires!*

"I like your passion Vincent, it can never be faulted. We all need to take Vincent's approach, he is correct we have overcome bigger milestones than this before now." Johnny realised that he needed to offer some sense of Vinnie's words to the newer players in order to put his remarks in a lesser state of alarm. "When Vincent means vampires, obviously he is metaphorically speaking for all of the doubters of Kingsbarr United Football Club; they are like vampires sucking away our life supply. Remember twelve months ago the media and the football world doubted and ridiculed us for being relegated. Then at the start of this season they doubted us again as we got off to a bad start. Now that we have tragically lost the players from the New Year's fire they doubt us again and believe we can't be successful in today's game against the mighty City, and probably ever again for that matter, sympathising with us yes, but never believing that we can overcome such a tragedy. Bruiser's right all these doubters are fucking vampires. Well are we going to let them drain away the blood from Kingsbarr United? Are we?"

"No boss," came the enthused reply in unison.

"That's right we are not going to lose this game boys. This FA Cup is ours, we fucking deserve it. We are vampire slayers of the highest order, now go out there and slay all those fucking doubting vampires. Show them that this tragedy has simply had one effect only on Kingsbarr United, and that is to make Kingsbarr fucking UNITED."

Within a minute of the restart Kingsbarr United had pulled a goal back. The Kingsbarr United supporters had hardly had time to shout out their well-rehearsed chant of "KNOX, KNOX GET IN THE BOX!" when the player-manager did just that and got onto the end of a move that he had originally initiated. Leading by example Johnny became a catalyst for his half-time team-talk scoring with a magnificent diving header, getting between two City defenders, and driving the ball powerfully into the bottom left hand corner of the goal following a sensational cross from Charlie Cheng.

City 2 Kingsbarr United 1. Game on!

As the second half unfolded, inspired by their manager's words, the vocal support of their supporters and their own self-belief the players of Kingsbarr United increasingly began to dominate the game. Both Giuseppe Rossi and Gerry Spalding had come close to grabbing the equaliser only to see their efforts bounce back off the wood-work. The City fans were extremely nervous as Kingsbarr pressed and pressed for the equaliser but the Kingsbarr fans were equally as nervous realising that in light of their team's good play as yet they simply hadn't scored again which therefore meant that they were not currently in a position to win the FA Cup. Until that ball ended up in the back of the net for Kingsbarr United the reality was that City would be the team to win the FA Cup.

Many a game had gone by in the history of football where a losing team had had the better of the game but for some unknown reason were never graced with the blessing of scoring that vital goal no matter how intense the onslaught on their opponents had been. Justice never seemed to prevail in football as the ball would get cleared off the line by a last ditch defensive clearance, the opposing goalkeeper would play the game of his life, the wood-work would keep the ball from entering the net, the referee would give incorrect offside decisions and so on and so forth. The list was endless and the Kingsbarr supporters were concerned that as the clock ticked by their team would also fall into this category of being cursed with not being able to score in spite of their domination.

But as countless fingernails were being bitten down to the skin finally Kingsbarr United did manage to score again to even the score-line.

With just 15 minutes of the game remaining and as a result of a complete second half display of supremacy Kingsbarr United got their rewards from a classic piece of Italian skill by Giuseppe Rossi. It was not so long ago that Giuseppe had had his own critics as part of the team that had been relegated just over twelve months earlier, often accused as being a "show-boater" and not playing with a committed sense of dedication and purpose. However, the Italian's fine form of late, now signified by this excellent FA Cup Final goal would certainly go a long way to silencing whatever of his critics remained.

The position that Giuseppe found himself in when he collected the ball suggested that he looked unlikely to score as he had his back to the City goal. Showing a fantastic presence of mind and natural skill, the Italian striker simply flicked the ball up and kicked it over both his and the City defender's head, spun round at lightning speed and collected the ball at the rear of the shell-shocked defender who completely taken by surprise had not had the inclination to turn in time to get a decent challenge in. There wasn't anything that the City defender could do but panic and he grabbed hold of the Italian's shirt, but to Giuseppe's credit he didn't go down. He remained strong and his perseverance and single-mindedness enabled him to break away from the defender, with the referee fortunately showing enough initiative to play an advantage. It would have simply been a catastrophe to put a stop to the genius that was unfolding. It is fair to say that other players the world over, like the City striker who got the penalty in the first half, and maybe even a Giuseppe Rossi of old, would have collapsed like a "sack of potatoes" at the slightest intervention near to an opponent's goal, but Giuseppe's pure determination and genius now rewarded him with a clear goal-scoring opportunity. After crafting such an opportunity there was only going to be one outcome for Giuseppe Rossi and he drove the ball high into the net giving the City keeper no chance of stopping it.

Kingsbarr United had dramatically pulled the game back level from being two goals adrift. It was a courageous and phenomenal display. Giuseppe was mobbed by his team-mates, who like the Kingsbarr fans were ecstatic. The celebrations were so euphoric that the referee eventually had to break up the merriment so that the game could proceed, but he could never know what it meant to this particular team of footballers who now stood together on the verge of a real possibility of gaining an FA Cup triumph. This unique group of footballers had fought together to slay a herd of vampires and had literally faced both evil and their own deaths in the face. No-one could ever know or understand the journey that these boys had been through.

After the eventual restart following their intense celebrations Kingsbarr quickly dispossessed the ball from City again and continued to control the game. With the momentum clearly with an inspired Kingsbarr United, City were at a loss on a way to get back into the football match following the surrendering of their two goal lead. In stark contrast Kingsbarr were now pressing for the winner.

Giuseppe Rossi had ran his socks off during the match and ten minutes after his goal which had brought Kingsbarr level in the game Johnny decided to replace him with Matt Floyd. This decision served four purposes.

Johnny realised that Giuseppe would receive a standing ovation from the Kingsbarr United supporters as he left the field, something that the Italian thoroughly deserved following his contribution to the game, signified mainly through his selfless work rate and excellent goal. The Italian himself applauded the fans as he left the field of play cementing the mutual relationship of respect that he and the fans held for each other.

Secondly Giuseppe simply needed the rest, true there was only five minutes of the match remaining but this cup final was likely to run into extra-time and Johnny believed that although Giuseppe would have gladly served his club for as long as he was allowed, Johnny felt that the fatigue generated from Giuseppe's impressive commitment to the game would at some point hinder his performance.

Johnny had always wanted Matt Floyd to play some part in this game. It was likely to be his last season at playing football and being a local Kingsbarr United fan Johnny understood what it would mean to him to play in the FA Cup Final for his boyhood team. Johnny of course understood exactly what this meant as he was also living the dream.

The astute manager also realised that a pair of fresh legs coming in to the football arena at a time when most legs on the field were weary could bolster his attack. Johnny wanted to win this game and he believed that Matt Floyd had the capability to help achieve that aim. Johnny's shrewd decision appeared to be confirmed when Matt Floyd's initial contribution to the game was to hit the bar with a powerful header courtesy of a Toby Storm corner. Victor Yates then too went on to suffer an almost identical piece of bad fortune as his powerful header also cannoned off the bar following a Toby Storm corner.

In spite of all their possession Kingsbarr just couldn't seem to convert that elusive winning goal and in a rare moment of control City ironically found themselves with a chance to win the game.

The European Champions had put together a good move, hitting Kingsbarr with a classic counter-attack as Kingsbarr peppered their goal with chance after chance. City had managed to work the ball up the field and into the Kingsbarr United goal-mouth. With undoubting ability in their team a City striker had showed a piece of footballing wizardry to wrong-foot Klauss Kircherr who like his brother had succeeded to give away a penalty, though on this occasion it was a legitimate claim. A committed professional Klauss was extremely disappointed with himself but the skill of the City striker would have ensured that the same result would have occurred with most defenders in the game, after all the City team had enough skill and ability to win both the Premiership title and the Champions League.

Johnny looked into the eyes of his young goalkeeper and he could see an element of fear. The young lad had suffered a rollercoaster of an afternoon, coming on to make his debut for the club that he loved, initially letting in a penalty but going on to make a very exceptional display of goalkeeping. Johnny felt for him, at what he had been thrown into, with only minutes, if not seconds left of the game the responsibility that now weighed on the youngsters shoulders was a big one to have to deal with.

But then Johnny thought about how this young man had a golden opportunity to end up being a hero.

What if he saved the penalty?

Alvin Braxton for one, who was now dressed and sitting in the stands, believed that his young understudy could do it. He was indeed a very capable young goalkeeper. After all wasn't that why Johnny had purchased him? The young man had pulled off some miraculous saves earlier in the game so perhaps this could be a moment of glory for him.

But Johnny, Alvin and everyone on the pitch and in the stands knew when it came to penalty-kicks it was very difficult for the goalkeeper to come out on top no matter how good they were.

The City player placed the ball on the penalty-spot. With a display of arrogance he looked straight into Kyle's eyes and gave a smirk as if to say "this is going in the back of the net and there is nothing you can do about it."

There was pressure on the City player to score too, but this same City player had previously converted the penalty that had clinched the Champions League Final in much more hostile surroundings than Wembley Stadium.

Kyle didn't react to the City player's mocking except for to momentarily close his eyes to focus.

Like some meditating guru he shut out the noise of the crowd, he shut out the nerves, and he didn't dwell on the earlier penalty.

The referee's whistle sounded and Kyle took it as the one and only signal to open his eyes focussing on nothing but the black and white football before him.

Johnny at once noticed that the fear had gone from the young goalkeeper's eyes and he just knew that in the next second that followed everything was going to be okay.

The City striker hit the ball well enough but Kyle didn't guess which way to dive as so many goalkeepers do, he followed the ball with his eyes and stretched with his body as far as he could reach to the far right of his goal to touch the ball and turn the shot onto the post. The ball then rolled back towards Kyle and safely into his hands.

Kyle Starkey was indeed a hero, he had saved a penalty in the FA Cup Final.

The Kingsbarr supporters went wild and it was also a natural reaction for the Kingsbarr players to congratulate their young hero. Vincent "Bruiser" Bradshaw playfully rubbed the young man's well-groomed hair whilst other players physically grabbed and kissed him amazed at the wonderful save that he had performed.

Johnny too wanted nothing more than to run over to his young goalkeeper and shower him in adoration and praise, but always thinking one step ahead he knew that he was going to save that penalty when he looked into his eyes on that second occasion.

It was a miracle that Kyle heard his player-manager shout his name through all the mayhem but almost in a similar display of telepathy that the vampires used to share when they pulled on the Kingsbarr United football strip Kyle knew exactly what his player-manager wanted him to do.

While the Kingsbarr players were still celebrating the wonderful save and while the City players were totally unfocused and dejected at their failure to win the game Kyle threw the ball out to Johnny who was waiting on the edge of the area and he ran the next fifteen yards totally unchallenged.

As the City players began to realise what was happening two of their defenders began to make their way across the pitch to challenge Johnny.

As the seconds of such a gruelling game ticked by Johnny wasn't convinced that he had enough strength left in his legs to run all the way to the City goal and successfully be able to avoid the challenges of the City defenders who were in a much better position running across the field to make the ground up.

The City goalkeeper stood clearly out of position having come out of his goal to view what he considered to be the winning goal for his team only to then bury his head in his hands realising that the penalty-kick had been missed.

As he moved back towards his goal he, like everyone else in the stadium did not guess what was coming next.

Johnny was still in his own half when he amazingly decided to shoot from that usually unrealistic position but the accuracy of his long range shot was executed to perfection as the ball looped high and far into the air finally dipping under the crossbar and into the City goal beyond the reach of the retreating City goalkeeper.

What an amazing moment in time this had been for Kingsbarr United. Having initially been faced with exiting the FA Cup, thanks to the fabulous save by their young goalkeeper and subsequent fantastic goal by their player-manager they had now surely won the FA Cup themselves.

And when the referee blew the whistle to signify that the game was over only seconds after City kicked-off again, the world of football had to take note of this Kingsbarr United team.

They had won the FA Cup following an initial two goal deficit beating the Premiership and European Champions 3 goals to 2 in extraordinary fashion.

Jody Roper had never felt so proud as he lifted the FA Cup with its blue and gold ribbons blowing gently in the

English summer breeze. The Kingsbarr United supporters were still going wild at the achievement of their team and the City supporters to their credit had applauded the Birmingham team with dignity and admiration at the way they had achieved their success.

For years to come people would speak of this cup final. Of how a young goalkeeper had been thrown into the lion's den and had yet gone on to show a fine display of protecting his goal-posts culminating with a last minute penalty-save.

Of how a team from the Championship had defeated the reigning Premiership and European Champions against all the supposed odds.

And how a player-manager named Johnny Knox had courageously led his team to that victory despite the tragedy only months earlier where the previous manager and team-mates had been killed in a tragic fire. Leading by example in the face of adversity Johnny Knox had scored a quite remarkable winning goal in the dying seconds of the game struck from his own half, joining an elite club of very few players who had achieved scoring a goal in this way. But to do it in the final seconds of an FA Cup Final was something very special indeed.

Daryl Weir shed a tear as he spoke passionately of the achievement by his former team as he commentated on the spectacular event that had just unfolded. He would always be proud that he was once connected with this famous Birmingham club and he would always be proud of how Johnny Knox, once a young player with an inquisitive mind and strong work ethic, who had served him well during his time at Kingsbarr United, had now steered that club to such remarkable achievements.

And although characteristically modest Johnny Knox was quite rightly proud of himself as well.

But Johnny was even more proud of his squad of players.

He was proud that his team had gained promotion from the Championship at the first attempt of trying.

He was proud that they had defeated an army of vampires but amazingly still had the state of mind to be able to overcome such unique circumstances to become a successful football team.

And more importantly he was proud to be associated with such a great bunch of blokes in spite of everything that had been thrown at them.

And he was proud that they had won the FA Cup without a single ball being kicked by a product of the Fosturnea School of Football Excellence.

Epilogue Part I

In a rare moment of serenity Johnny Knox began to reflect on the events that had affected his life over the past few months.

He realised that everyone else who had been connected with the unbelievable events could also never forget what they had experienced.

His original family of Sheena, Callum and Saffron would certainly never forget. They had adjusted themselves accordingly and had to accept that supernatural entities walked amongst them.

Johnny had surprised Saffron with a Jack Russell puppy named Beckham, not only as a companion for Keegan the cat, but also as an attempt to occupy the mind of his only daughter who had undoubtedly been affected the worst by her own personal experience of the Fosturnea saga. Saffron was often found staring into space replaying the events of that particular New Year's Eve over and over again in her mind, shivering at how close she came to being a victim of a vampire.

Johnny was still unsure if Radu would ever learn the truth of what he once was.

At this moment in time and since the destruction of the Fosturnea vampire nest he was simply a lovely little boy, charming, delightful, mischievous and above all as normal as any boy of his age should be. He was a welcome addition to the household loved dearly by Sheena and Johnny in equal measure and a wonderful little brother for his twin siblings.

The players cum vampire slayers of Kingsbarr United—Alvin Braxton, Vincent Bradshaw, Giuseppe Rossi,

Matt Floyd, Jody Roper, Gerry Spalding and Charlie Cheng would also never forget.

As Johnny habitually stroked the cross given to him by Dr. Lazar, that now hung around his neck since using it to dramatic effect in the battle with the Fosturnea nest of vampires, he realised that the experiences that this collection of footballers had shared together would give them a unique bond for as long as they lived, and possibly even beyond that.

As he sat on his rear patio, taking a sip from his bottle of lager whilst listening to the sound of the songbirds in his leafy garden, Johnny wondered just how they would remain entwined once their footballing careers were ultimately over. He sensed that somehow, someway they would always be close to one another and find a way to remain in close proximity.

With their unique sharing of unbelievable experiences and gained knowledge of vampires how could they not?

As Johnny reflected fondly of his comrades he began to focus on the forthcoming months and how some of his Kingsbarr United allies would actually be competing against him!

Johnny's fantastic form for Kingsbarr United had not gone unnoticed by the England international manager and he had named Johnny in his squad for the forthcoming World Cup commencing in June. Johnny would be the first ever player-manager to represent his country at the World Cup Finals. Could Johnny really also bring back a World Cup winners medal to cap such a fantastic year of footballing achievement?

One thing Johnny had learned from the past twelve months was that anything was possible.

He also knew that Alvin Braxton and Charlie Cheng would be sharing the same thoughts as they represented Jamaica and China respectively.

Giuseppe Rossi had never been in the frame to make the richly talented Italian squad, however he had been given a distinct and hopeful message from the Italian manager that if Rossi produced the same form in the English Premiership next season then he may be considered for a recall to the squad, albeit any representation for his country would fall outside of the forthcoming World Cup Finals.

The Kircherr brothers were also to feature in the German squad though were unlikely to feature in the starting 11, their manager also preferring to field top-flight footballers.

Toby Storm would represent the USA and with his electrifying pace and as yet fairly undiscovered ability would undoubtedly make a name for himself in the World Cup Finals.

Johnny's trail of thought was then delicately interrupted when he noticed a grey squirrel dart across the top of his rear fence and leap onto a branch of a pine tree.

The small creature reminded him of Gene Macgoree the loyal Kingsbarr United football supporter who had also been on the amazing journey along with the players of Kingsbarr United.

He smiled as he thought of the little man and how he had assisted in the slaying of the Fosturnea nest and educated them all on the history and existence of vampires.

Gene Macgoree's reward was to be named as a director on the board of his favourite football club.

Peter Cogshaw had needed little persuading when Johnny had suggested it to him, realising it would be a great way to relate to the fans to actually have such a prominent supporter working behind the scenes. Typically he also understood the marketing value of a story of a "super fan" being allowed into the machinery of a football club. Cogshaw also realised the fact that a devoted supporter such as Gene would never demand a huge pay packet.

Putting the World Cup aside, Johnny wondered what other plans the little vampire slayer had for the summer ahead.

Epilogue Part II

The cry of the baby sounded innocent enough but as Gene Macgoree snaked through the long grass on his belly he knew that the sound belied the evil that it truly represented.

He knew that the cry was from the recently born clone of Adrien Connor.

Gene had realised that a master vampire such as Professor Cezar Prodanescu would have been keeping a record of his vocation and by deliberately seeking it out had been fortunate enough to discover Cezar's journal that New Year's Eve, and subsequently protected it from the fire that burnt down the old house and eradicated the lifeless corpses of the Fosturnea nest of vampires. Gene had gone looking for the journal knowing that it could provide him with even further understanding of vampire activity in his quest to fight them at every possible opportunity.

The journal detailed the late professor's astonishing work and gave a valuable insight into his cloning activity. Incredibly the latter words of the journal began to hint at Cezar's regret of his genius actions to clone DNA, due to his love for Lily and the respect he held for the human footballers of his team. The master vampire had begun to question his original desire for vampires to rule the Earth in dominance over humans.

The journal was not the only thing to survive the fire that night, Audrey Chillingsworth had managed to flee to the mountains of Transylvania and give birth to the reincarnation of purest evil, Adrien Connor.

The heat was blistering from the summer sun as Gene got nearer to the remote refuge where Audrey and Adrien hid away from the unsuspecting world.

No doubt Audrey was biding her time, she would rear "Adrien" in the security of the Transylvanian mountains until he was strong enough to spread his evil across the world once again with the distinct aim to ensure that it was the human race that became a minority in its own world and the vampires would rule the planet as the hierarchical race. Unaware of Cezar's doubts towards the end of his life Audrey's focus remained clear.

Well Gene Macgoree was here to spoil the party.

Gene was poised just below the window of the cottage now and as he crouched he slowly raised his head until he could actually peer into the cottage.

He could see that Audrey Chillingsworth was placing the baby back into its crib after settling it back to sleep.

She left the baby as it slept soundly and moved out of the room.

Gene realised that it was only a small cottage and quickly snuck around the back of the dwelling.

Just as he suspected Audrey had moved into the modest kitchen of the house, he could hear the running of the tap and he was now poised at the outlet pipe that fed the running water into a simple and basic drain.

Gene suspected Audrey was running water to make a drink or perhaps to fill a saucepan to warm the baby's milk. The reason for the running water was irrelevant as Gene's ploy was simply to get inside the cottage.

Being a seasoned slayer he chose the timing of his entry well taking Audrey by complete surprise who had never stood a chance.

She turned around just as Gene kicked open the rear door but she barely had time to scream as Gene Macgoree drove a stake into her heart not displaying an ounce of emotion.

Like a high quality assassin Gene Macgoree left his initial victim on the floor and moved into the room where the baby slept.

Gene looked into the crib and hesitated as he observed the face of the baby. It seemed so peaceful, so innocent as it slept but with a shake of his head Gene was forced to remind himself that the innocent features of the infant belied the pure evil that it represented and the potential it held for spreading pure evil across the world. That was after all why it had been created. The baby was a vessel for pure destruction.

Gene pulled a stake from his holster and lifted it high above his head ready to drive it into the chest of the sleeping baby.

He hesitated once again.

It seemed so wrong.

Then he realised it was right.

But his hesitation had earned the baby a few more seconds longer of life as Gene was prevented from driving the stake into the child as he felt a presence behind him.

He turned to see the largest, ugliest vampire that he had ever seen, and he had certainly seen many in his days of slaying. Gene had made a grave mistake. He should have realised that Audrey Chillingsworth wouldn't be alone in the residence.

This dwelling was after all harbouring the clone of the original vampire Adrien Connor. It could never have been left to Audrey alone to protect it.

The grotesque vampire spoke in a Romanian accent as he pushed Gene to the floor with ease.

Translated his words had said "leave the master alone."

The giant of a vampire was now standing over Gene as Gene quickly estimated that he must have been at least 7 feet tall, some 2 feet taller than himself.

He placed a foot on the vampire slayers chest and proceeded to press harder and harder, gradually engaging his massive weight onto Gene's rib cage.

Gene felt his ribs snap and eventually puncture his lung as the gross weight of the giant vampire became too intense for his little rib cage to cope.

With the sound of snapping bones the giant vampire gave a deep and booming laugh.

Gene was not going to go down without a fight and with the stake still in his hand he decided that he could still hurt this horrible beast. Gene drove the stake upwards with as much strength as he could muster and felt it connect with the rubbery tissue of the vampire's genitalia and thrust it deep into his lower body from a complete and perfect vertical angle.

The vampire fell to the floor screaming in agony which in turn woke the infant.

Gene knew that he was dying, his chest had been crushed to an excessive state and he realised that his breath was destined to shortly run out. He also realised that the vampire would soon die too. The stake that he had planned to use on baby "Adrien" had been tipped with a silver cap for maximum effect. It would not be long before the poisoned blood of the vampire would ultimately kill it.

Fighting for his breath Gene managed to pull his mobile phone from his pocket and he searched through his stored numbers and quickly came across the entry for "Callum". He hit the single digit to ring his friend.

"Is that your phone Callum?" said the pretty dark haired girl who was lying on her belly reading her book, sweat perspiring from her naked back.

"Yeah, who wants me at this moment in time for fucks sake?"

The girl named Afina, who had grown tired of Leon Davis's ego, chuckled as her latest boyfriend seemed annoyed having his moment of pleasure halted.

"You can still sunbathe you know even if you are on the phone."

"Yeah, yeah it's just the fucking effort of it all." Callum retrieved his phone from the sand and answered it. His annoyance changed instantly when he heard the desperation in Gene's voice.

"Gene, what's wrong buddy you sound terrible."

Through the screams of the giant vampire and the cries of the baby Gene proceeded to enlighten his fellow slayer of his fatal predicament.

"Listen to me Callum I don't have much time."

"What are you talking about you don't have much time."

Afina stopped reading as she saw the concern on her lover's face.

"I'm dying Callum so listen. I've found Adrien Connor or at least the clone, incarnation or whatever you want to call the little freak."

"Where is he . . . it?"

"Where else but the hills of fucking Transylvania."

"You went alone, why didn't you tell me?"

"I'm telling you now."

Gene felt some contentment as he saw the giant vampire's head hit the floor having reached the end of his painful and undignified death before Gene had!"

"Where in the hills Gene, where? Afina and I are holidaying in Mamaia we can be there soon. Hold on buddy we are coming to get you."

"When you get here friend I'll be dead. But make sure you get here and kill this fucking little freak."

"I will mate I will, hang on in there, please Gene, please buddy."

"Goodbye friend."

"Gene, Gene," screamed a distraught Callum down the handset.

But Callum quickly realised that his friend was dead.

But he could hear something at the end of the phone line.

The cooing of a baby.

Lightning Source UK Ltd.
Milton Keynes UK
UKOW052110250112

186038UK00001B/2/P